COME DANCING

COME DANCING

A NOVEL

Leslie Wells

The author gratefully acknowledges permission from Robert Laffont/Seghers Publishing Company to reprint lines from "Des Yeux D'Elsa" by Louis Aragon, Copyright © 1942.

The author gratefully acknowledges permission to reprint the translation of lines from "Des Yeux D'Elsa" by Louis Aragon, translated by William Jay Smith, Copyright © 1947.

Dedicated to the memory of my sister, Jennifer.

I miss you every single day.

"It's rather curious, you know, this sort of life!

I wonder what can have happened to me!"

— *Alice in Wonderland*

BY LEWIS CARROLL

CONTENTS

1: One Way or Another

13

2: Brass in Pocket

19

3: Wrong Idea

33

4: Stormy Monday

39

5: One Bourbon, One Scotch, and One Beer

45

6: Lively Up Yourself

57

7: Welcome to the Working Week

75

8: The Girl Can't Help It

85

9: Career Opportunities

103

10: Could You Be Loved

113

11: Walking on the Moon

135

12: Love is the Drug
143

13: Bottle It Up and Go
165

14: Big Apple Dreamin'
173

15: Nite Klub
189

16: Crosseyed and Painless
205

17: Slippery People
211

18: Just Lust
221

19: The Harder They Come
229

20: Talk of the Town
237

21: Should I Stay or Should I Go
249

22: Don't Get Me Wrong
257

23: Sugar on My Tongue
265

24: Boom Boom
273

25: Fame

291

26: Highlife

309

27: Stranger in the House

317

28: Love Bites

321

29: The Bed's Too Big Without You

329

30: Scary Monsters (and Super Creeps)

335

31: Making Flippy Floppy

343

32: Three Little Birds

353

33: Reconsider, Baby

359

34: White Rabbit

365

35: 'Deed I Do

373

Acknowledgments

377

About the Author

380

ONE WAY OR ANOTHER

)⊃⊂(

"Are you ever getting out of there?" my friend Vicky complained.

I crooked the receiver in my shoulder, scrabbling papers together. "I'm heading out now. Harvey dumped a bunch of stuff on me right before he took off." My boss, the publisher, liked to clear his desk at the end of the week—which meant I got to stay late every Friday night.

"About time. I'll see you at your place in an hour."

"We're going to stick together tonight, right? Avoid the meat market?" I loved dancing off my pent-up energy from long hours sitting at my desk. Vicky saw it more as a smorgasbord of men, served up buffet-style.

"Depends what's on the menu. See you in a few."

The minute she hung up, my line rang again. "Is this Julia?" a familiar voice screeched.

"Hi, Louise. How's it going in Seattle?" Our high-strung author was on a twelve-city tour for her new thriller, and the campaign had been plagued with problems. A celebrated Texas crime reporter, she had braved drug dealers' bullets but couldn't cope with delayed flights and lumpy hotel pillows. Harvey had stopped taking her calls a week ago, and ever since she'd been haranguing me.

"The escort hasn't shown up yet. Why can't these people be prompt?" Louise fretted.

I held back from pointing out that it was over three hours until her event. "Let me see if anyone's left in publicity; maybe they can locate her."

I scurried around the corner to the desolate PR department. The lights in Erin's cubicle were still on, which gave me hope. A few doors down, I found her on her knees in front of the copy machine. Erin looked up at me and smiled. "Got it!" she exclaimed, extracting an inky wad.

"Could you come deal with Louise? She's all pumped up for her signing, but the escort has gone awol." I rolled my eyes.

"God forbid she should ask the front desk to call her a cab," Erin grumbled as she followed me down the hall. "She's stared down gun-toting Mafiosi, but on the road she turns into a quivering mass of jelly."

"Typical of her," I said. Most of our authors were great, but a few were real doozies. "Do you want to come out with me and Vicky later? We're going to hit the Palladium around eleven."

"I have to finish a press release for that astrology guide. Another glam night in the big city."

"Okay, be that way. Call me if you change your mind." I ducked into my office and switched Louise over to Erin, covered my typewriter, then crammed my weekend reading into my backpack.

I sprinted down the deserted hall past shelves overflowing with manuscripts, a few framed awards gathering dust. Our titles ranged from literary to pure fluff; with the economy still in the pits, we were hawking anything from pop psychology to diet fads. This had been a shock when I'd arrived as a starry-eyed editorial assistant after a brief stint in grad school, thinking I'd be spending my weekends holed up with hot talent from *The New Yorker*. But now I was seasoned enough to plow through the B-list celebrity memoirs and breastfeeding manuals, while relishing any good novels that came my way.

I caught the elevator with a jittery messenger who bounced his bike tire, making the floor shimmy. I waved to the security guard and headed down lower Park Avenue in the balmy air. Usually I walked home to save money on subway tokens; I figured I had time tonight since my best friend was probably still primping.

Vicky had left the company a few months ago to join the publicity department of a larger midtown publisher. I missed her at the office, and I was also envious of her escape from assistantdom. But we still got together on weekends, and now I couldn't wait to go to our favorite club. We liked the Palladium for its edgy mix of punks, rockers, and regular people like us.

I wove through some guys hissing "Sens, sensimilla!" in Washington Square and stopped at a street vendor selling earrings. A pair with long strands of beads and feathers caught my eye. I fingered them for a minute, calculating. *Seven bucks for drinks; three for a cab home tonight . . .* Reluctantly I put them back.

Halfway down MacDougal, I came to a screeching halt. An absolutely perfect small table was sitting right in the middle of the sidewalk. I stepped close for a better look. Gold leaf curlicues adorned its surface, and ornate lion heads were carved into its corners. I gave it a shake to see if the legs were loose, but it didn't even wobble. I couldn't believe someone had thrown out something this nice—it wasn't even large garbage night! At last I could get rid of the stacked milk crates I ate on.

Now I just had to get it home. My place on Broome Street was eight blocks away, and the table was about three feet square. Maybe if I swung my backpack around to the front and hoisted the table on my back . . .

As I stood there considering, a guy in a dirty tee-shirt approached, holding a can of beer. "You need some help with that?" he asked, swaying a little.

"I think I can get it. Thanks anyway."

The man leaned against the brick wall of the apartment building to watch. Turning around, I backed up to the table. I tried to reach behind and grasp its sides, but I couldn't bend back far enough—why I'd always stunk at the limbo-la. Maybe if I bent lower . . . I crouched down, the backpack wedged against my belly like an unwanted pregnancy, and strained to get a grip on its legs.

Suddenly a woman ran screeching out of the building. "Stop that! What are you doing with my table?"

I stared at her. "This is yours? I thought somebody was throwing it away."

"Are you kidding? This is an antique! You couldn't have thought it was being thrown out." The woman glared at me, hand on her hip.

Oh my god, how embarrassing. "I didn't realize—I mean, it was sitting here all by itself with no note on it or anything. I thought it was meant for the garbage."

"The garbage!" the woman shrieked. "I paid six hundred dollars for that! I was waiting for my husband to bring it upstairs! You should keep your paws off things that aren't yours," she huffed as she flounced back inside.

The man in the tee-shirt smiled and took a gulp of beer. "Baby, you just took a bite of the B-i-i-g Apple."

"Actually, I think it just bit me."

Chapter 2

BRASS IN POCKET

My cheeks burning, I continued across Houston toward my loft. I had rented it a year ago from the building's owner, an old Italian man that I paid in cash. $330 a month wasn't bad, now that SoHo no longer consisted of vacant warehouses. Some art galleries and clothing shops had sprouted up recently, along with a few sushi bars and espresso cafes. It seemed safer to walk the streets at night, but I hoped Mr. Iaccone wouldn't catch on and raise the rent.

Cutting over on Prince, I averted my eyes from a diner where I'd spent many Sunday mornings with my ex-boyfriend, Arthur Klein. It was awful to break up with someone who lived nearby; there were constant reminders unless you detoured around entire blocks. An NYU professor recently separated from his wife, Art's sandy brown curls and racquetball-toned body were admired by all the female English Lit majors. I felt unbelievably lucky when he asked me to have coffee one afternoon after class. From our first conversation about Virginia Woolf, I was head over heels. Ten months later, he told me he was going back to his wife.

For weeks I was a total wreck, sniffling in token lines and sobbing through double features. Then, thinking something purely physical might cheer me up, I brought a guy named Eric home with me from a party. But when he stumbled out the next morning and never called, I felt even more miserable.

Every time I experienced the sting of rejection, it dredged up feelings about my father. We had been so close when I was growing up—or so I'd thought. Dad was an inspector in a factory in our small Pennsylvania town. When he got home from his shift, he'd roll up his sleeves, crack open a beer and turn on the rabbit-eared radio in our linoleum kitchen. If a good dance tune came on, he'd scoop me up in his wiry arms and swing me around, dipping me dramatically and making me giggle as I gazed into his boyishly grinning face.

Sometimes after he'd had a big argument with my mother, he would play the mournful country music he loved—Hank Williams, Patsy Cline—on the little plastic record player he'd given me. He also loved the blues, and by the time I was six, I could distinguish the way Albert King strummed his guitar, from T-Bone Walker or John Lee Hooker.

Things started to fall apart when I was eight, after my mother, Dorothea—"Dot" to her friends—began moonlighting as a cocktail waitress on weekends. I liked having Dad all to myself; he let me stay up past my bedtime, dancing to Motown 45s. My mother would come in much later than one a.m., when the bar stopped serving. She claimed to be helping the owner close out the register, but my father suspected otherwise. The next morning, their shouting made me retreat to my room with a pile of library books.

Eventually she quit that job, but the damage was done. Then, the September when I was fourteen, he discovered that she was having an affair with her manager at the hardware store. When Dot and I came back from running errands the following Saturday, his side of their closet was empty. My mother shut the closet door, lit a cigarette, got out her checkbook and sat staring dry-eyed at it on the kitchen table. I went to my room and lay shaking on the bed, terrified of what would happen to us. My father simply vanished into thin air that day, leaving Dot with the bills, and me feeling abandoned.

I came out of my memory-induced daze just in time to avoid stepping on a broken crack vial lying on the sidewalk. My mind skittered back to the present. I wondered whether Art ever thought about me, now that he was reunited with his wife. I had gone out with one or two guys in the past eight months, but nothing much had come of it. After my lousy one-night stand, I'd decided that I should sleep with someone only if there was the *possibility* of a relationship. Which meant I'd had a long dry spell, with no relief in sight.

In the summer heat, the city smelled like a rotting overripe fruit. I turned onto Broome, glad to see that Vicky wasn't cooling her heels on the sidewalk. After climbing three flights and unlocking the double deadbolts, I pushed up my screenless windows to catch a breeze. I removed the scarf covering a wooden crate of my favorite albums, chose a B.B. King and lowered the needle.

Hmm, what to wear . . . I held a cold beer against my cheek and stared at the things hanging from nails in the wall, since my loft didn't come with a closet.

The selection was sparse, to put it mildly. I'd snagged my second-hand leather skirt for eight bucks because the lining was torn. *Maybe it'll hold up for one more night's dancing . . .* I grabbed my stapler and fixed the trailing hemline. From my three-legged dresser—a legit curbside salvage—I drew a ripped top from Screaming Mimi's and black elbow-length gloves that I'd cut the fingers out of. The finishing touch was ten rubber bracelets on each arm. Now for a few safety pins to add a punk edge. I attached a couple to my sleeve. *Nice one, Julia. Looks like a failed home ec project*, I thought, unclipping them. No matter how hard I tried to seem "downtown", I felt like I still looked fresh-off-the-farm. I ran a brush through my chestnut layers and licked my finger to smooth an eyebrow. Sometimes people commented on the blue of my eyes, but I usually pictured myself in the Coke-bottle lenses I'd worn until college, when I finally got contacts.

"That's as good as it's gonna get," I told the girl frowning at me in the mirror. I gave up and went to put on another record.

A familiar voice was calling from the street. "Get your *Post* here! Hot off the press: Julia Nash Leaves Office before Midnight—Publishing Industry Collapses in Ruins."

I leaned out the window to see Vicky grinning up at me. Her cropped blond hair and pert nose made her look like a mischievous pixie. "Just a sec." I got my key and threw it down to her, stuffing it inside a sock so it was easier to catch. She unlocked the door and stomped up the stairs in a flirty short skirt and heels; she could afford better clothes since her new company paid well.

"Nice hem job there." Her green eyes danced as she gave me the once-over. She plopped down on the couch and I handed her a beer. "Could we listen to something a little less dour? Sheesh. You and your blues."

"Sure, if you insist. Too bad you don't appreciate the higher art forms." I removed Howlin' Wolf and put on The Pretenders, whipping my hips to the pounding bass.

"Is this the haircut album?" Vicky asked with a smirk. The other weekend before we went out, I'd propped the record cover against my mirror and tried to trim my hair like Chrissie Hynde's.

"Those of us who are still assistants can't afford salons. I thought I did a pretty good job; maybe if this publishing thing doesn't work out, I'll try beauty school."

"Lucky thing it wasn't Bow Wow Wow you were in the mood for that day."

"Yeah, a huge purple mohawk would go over really well at the office." I sat at the other end of the couch. "How are things with Emily?" Her new boss was demanding, but at least she was fair.

"She liked the press release I wrote today. It's for a pop psych book on how to keep a man interested. I can condense the whole thing into two words: Act *un*interested. Speaking of work, is the old letch still trying to get into your pants?" Although he was married, Harvey had a sleazy history of putting the moves on junior women.

"He keeps asking me out for a drink. That measly five-hundred-dollar raise isn't going to get him over. Not that I'd go out with him for a million." So far I'd been able to fend Harvey off, but it made working for him a real drag.

Vicky propped her skinny legs on a wooden crate. "We have to find you a new job. I asked Emily to let me know if she heard of any openings, if the hiring freeze ever gets lifted. Wouldn't it be great to work together again?"

"Yes, I miss being able to grab lunch anytime. At least *your* career is launched; I'm just treading water. If I don't make editor at some point… I have this nightmare I'll still be typing Harvey's letters when I'm thirty, in a moth-eaten cardigan with specs hanging from a chain around my neck."

Vicky laughed. "Try not to obsess over it. You've only been there a little over a year."

Which was about how long she'd been there when Emily rescued her. I went to grab another beer and cranked up "Stop Your Sobbing," snarling the words along with Chrissie.

"Did that guy from the party ever call you?" Vicky asked.

"Nope. By the time I got back from the bathroom, a redhead in fishnets had him cornered."

"You have to be more assertive. You let other girls move in who aren't nearly as hot as you are." She took a sip of beer and continued. "You can't just sit back and let the guy do all the work. You aren't in Pikesville, Pa. anymore." Vicky often had advice about my love life, or lack thereof. From what she'd told me about growing up on Long Island, she hadn't gone two weeks without a date since she was fourteen.

"Message of Love" came on, and Vicky hopped up to dance. I joined her, pogoing to the beat. She raised her arms and did an exaggerated grind against my hip.

"We should moonlight as erotic dancers," I said, laughing and pushing her away. "Then I could afford a decent haircut."

"If we made those moves at the Palladium, we'd have every dude in the place salivating."

I collapsed on my sagging couch. "I don't think I want them salivating on me."

"Why not? You'd have the pick of the litter." Vicky flopped down beside me.

I peeled the label off my sweating bottle and smoothed it on my thigh. "All I want is one good guy who'll appreciate what I have to offer. Once I figure out what that is."

"I don't get why you're so particular. Sometimes it's nice just to have a warm body next to you. Wards off the lonelies on a Saturday night." She downed the last drop of beer.

"You have a point. But it would be good if it could be a little more meaningful."

"It *is* meaningful. It means you got boinked."

I laughed. "I'll keep that in mind, Victoria."

At eleven, we walked the twenty blocks north to the Palladium. The club had a cavernous ballroom on the main floor and an upstairs VIP lounge for private parties. The line to get in snaked around the block.

Vicky went right up front, ignoring glares from some over-dressed women and their dates. "Hi Barry," she said to the bouncer.

"Vicky. And Julia." Barry grinned and moved aside. "Come on in, girls."

"Hey, we've been here half an hour!" a guy in a suit complained.

"Go back to Wall Street," Vicky muttered as I followed her through the entrance.

We shoved our way into the crowd, the music so loud it was useless to try to talk. I could feel the bass throbbing in my throat. The concrete floor was already sticky with spilt beer, the smell of sweat mingling with the cloying scent of clove cigarettes. We found a spot next to a man with a chain running from nostril to ear, his blond foot-high spikes glowing in the black lights. Vicky blissfully swayed her slim hips, and I shut my eyes and lost myself in the rhythm.

The video guy came around, aiming his shoulder-mounted camera at us. We kept dancing normally in the spotlight's glare, unlike a lot of people who put on a show for him. It was distracting because our images were projected larger-than-life against the huge back wall, so everyone could see. Finally he moved on to some girls in tight rubber dresses who shook their booties at the camera.

As a Clash tune played I noticed a man standing near me, holding a drink. He touched my arm and started to say something, seeming to point at the ceiling.

"What?" I shouted.

"A friend of mine wants to meet you gals. We're up there," he said with some kind of Southern accent.

I wondered why this guy had to run interference, but Vicky was interested. "What's going on in the lounge?" she asked.

"Just a little party." He grinned and took a sip of his drink.

Vicky smiled her assent, and he started toward the stairs.

"I heard some rock and rollers might be here tonight; there's a private party or something," Vicky said as we followed him, weaving through slam-dancing bodies.

I wasn't dressed to impress in my ragged leather skirt, but at least we might score a free drink. We went up to the dark lounge where a bouncer was sitting on a stool with a check-list. I wondered why they needed a door-minder, but once we got inside, the crowd was pretty upscale. Slick-looking SoHo types struck blasé poses, while the women circulating the room looked like models.

The Southerner turned to us, and the light from the window overlooking the dance floor shone on his face. "Name your poison. I'm Sammy, by the way."

With a shock it hit me who he was; I hadn't recognized him in the dark, with his soul patch and shorter hair. All of a sudden I was really nervous. I'd been a huge fan of the British group Four to the Floor since I was a teenager, like everyone else I knew. Vicky, as usual, kept her cool. "Good to meet you; I'm Vicky. I'll have a tequila sunrise. Julia?"

"Vodka and tonic, please."

"One party water and a Ta-kill-ya, comin' right up." Sammy went over to the bar, tended by a girl in a black leather bikini.

"Can you believe it? That's Sammy Parnell," Vicky said. "I wonder if the others are here." She scanned the crowd. "Who do you think his friend is? He said someone wanted to meet us."

"No telling. I can't believe it's him either." Whoever this friend was, he was probably interested in Vicky. She tended to attract across-the-room attention with her waifish blonde hair and endless legs. I hoped I had enough for a cab ride if she wound up going home with him; I had planned on splitting the fare.

Sammy returned with our drinks. "My buddy Jack's over there. Why don't you go say hello?" He jerked his head toward a dark corner where some women were standing before a low sofa. Could he mean Jack Kipling, the guitarist of the group?

The vivacious clump of girls directed their enthusiasm toward whoever was sitting on the couch.

"Why don't you introduce us?" Vicky said, smiling her Cheshire-cat smile that slanted her green eyes.

"Tell you what, I'll just let him know you're here." Sammy went over and squeezed in between two twiggy blondes. A dark head of hair was briefly visible when the women parted. I glanced away, not wanting to seem star-struck, but Vicky continued to gaze in their direction.

"Oh my god! He's looking our way now."

"Stop staring. They must get that all the time." I sipped my drink, which had twice the usual amount of vodka in it.

Sammy sauntered back. "Jack said to come say hi."

Vicky had experience dealing with celebrities in her publicist role; I couldn't imagine what I'd say to someone that famous. Nor was I in the mood to kiss up to some arrogant, obnoxious rock star who expected women to roll over and beg—even if I was a huge fan. "Go ahead. Maybe you can get an autograph."

Vicky followed him to the sofa and exchanged a few words with Jack, who was still seated and mostly blocked from view. Then she laughed with Sammy for a few minutes and scribbled on a piece of paper. I polished off my drink as she came over smiling.

"Well, that was a thrill. Now I can tell my grandchildren that I met Jack Kipling. And Sammy Parnell. I gave Sammy my number."

"Maybe they'll both call you. Can we go downstairs and dance some more?" I didn't want to blow her chances with Jack if he got unglued from his groupies, but I felt out of place in this fancy crowd.

"Let's stay a few more minutes. Aren't you going to say hi to Jack?" she asked, combing her fingers through her hair. "Is my lipstick smeared?"

"Lick your front tooth. There, it's gone."

"Listen, Jules, I think it's you he wants to meet."

I laughed. "Sure. He probably came here tonight hoping to run into me. I'm near the top of his list, just below Starlet Number One and Starlet Number Two."

"I'm not kidding. He asked me where my friend was."

I tried to take another sip of vodka before remembering it was all gone. So maybe it *wasn't* Vicky that Jack had singled out when the video guy threw our images on the wall. He was standing now; I could just make out his bored expression as he faced his entourage. A girl grasped his arm, clinging tightly until he detached himself.

"Sammy's coming back," Vicky said. "Look who's with him."

My pulse bolted; Jack was heading our way. Wild dark hair shot up in all directions, an earring glinting through the tangle. His long legs were encased in skintight jeans, frayed at the cuffs over python boots. He had a few days' stubble and dark circles under his eyes, as if he hadn't slept recently. When he stood next to me, I almost passed out. Even this disheveled, he was as rakishly good-looking as on his album covers.

"You made me lose my spot on the couch," Jack said, his Cockney accent stronger than I would have expected.

"I'm sure they'll let you have it back." I forced myself to tear my eyes away from him. Projected on the outer wall, two girls in death-mask makeup were thrashing about.

"D'you come here often?" Jack said, moving closer.

I tried to remember to breathe. "Fairly often. The music's more danceable than some other places."

"I noticed you dancing down there." He gestured at the main floor with his drink. "Verrry nice."

My cheeks flushed. "I was just trying to avoid a head-on with those slam-dancers."

Jack laughed. "Why don't we give you girls a ride home? I'm ready to split."

I was so surprised, I didn't know what to say.

"Jack's car is right outside," Sammy added.

"Fantastic," Vicky said.

My heart pounded as we followed them to the stairs, Jack putting on sunglasses before he hit the first floor. The men hurried out to the street where a big black car was waiting at the curb. The driver opened the back door and Jack dove in, followed by Sammy. Vicky slipped inside and I got in by the window. The interior smelled of new leather, and had drink holders with various bottles and little lights along the sides. *I think I'm in someone else's movie,* I told myself.

The driver turned to look at us through the open partition.

"Where to?" Sammy asked.

"If you could drop us at Mott and Hester, that would be great." I'd walk the few blocks home from Vicky's.

"Mott and Hester, Rick."

The driver maneuvered expertly through swerving cabs as we flew downtown.

"Do you two go dancin' a lot?" Sammy drawled.

I glanced over; Jack was leaning forward, looking at me. I felt my face get hot.

Vicky smiled. "When I manage to drag Julia away from work."

"Where do you do your woork?" Jack asked, drawing out the word.

"She's an editor at a publishing house," Vicky said.

"An assistant editor. Vicky's in publishing too," I added.

"Publicity. Not the brainy stuff," Vicky said.

"So you're a brainy gal," Jack said to me.

"Only on days that end in 'y'." I managed to smile at him despite my butterflies. The driver stopped at Mott and I got out. The door on the other side opened and Jack emerged, trailed by Sammy.

"Thanks so much for the ride." I waited for Vicky on the sidewalk.

"Hold on a tick," Jack said in a low voice. He ambled over to me, stepping into the light from a storefront. His shirt was untucked and unbuttoned halfway to his waist, revealing a thin chain with a slash of lightning dangling from it. He ran his hand through his hair, making it stick out even more. "Why don't I see you home? Make sure you get in safely." He cocked his eyebrow and gave me a wolfish grin.

"Um, that's okay. I'll be fine." I was way too nervous to bring Jack Kipling home with me, no matter how sexy he was.

Jack's face took on a puzzled look. "But . . . "

If I waited any longer, I'd be tempted to take him up on it. "Thanks again!" I said brightly. I grabbed Vicky's arm and drew her along, leaving them staring after us.

"Are you insane?" she asked as we rounded the corner. "You could be ripping off his clothes as we speak. And Sammy and I could be getting to know each other. In the Biblical sense."

"If we'd gone for the wham-bam-thank-you-ma'am, do you think we'd have ever heard from them again?" I said as she groped in a pocket for her key. "We'd be just another notch on their guitar necks. Plus I haven't shaved my legs in over a week."

"So what? I hope you haven't blown it." She pushed the door open. "Talk to you tomorrow."

I hurried down the block, swerving to avoid a man rummaging through a tipped-over garbage can. How bizarre to go out for a typical Friday night, and then meet not one but *two* members of the Floor. The four of them—Patrick, lead singer and bass player; Jack, guitarist and back-up vocals; Mark on drums; and Sammy, the lone American of the group, on keyboard—had started in Britain, and then exploded in the States. I'd pored over their album liner notes so many times, I knew them by heart. And it was amazing to have met Jack, who'd always been my favorite.

But that was in terms of their music. I'd read about the band's excesses, particularly Jack's; he was the epitome of the bad boy rock and roller. Even though at this very minute I could have been wrapping my fingers in that wild mane of hair, I knew I would have felt awful the morning after. Aside from my fling with Eric, I'd seen my mother mope around lots of times after sleeping with a guy and then never hearing from him again. Let's just say I'd learned from her example.

Maybe I'm not really missing Art after all this time, I thought as I clumped upstairs. I was probably just lonesome from the solitary weekends spent editing. But I wasn't about to have a one-night stand with a rock star, no matter how much I liked his music. That would be the dumbest thing I could do.

Chapter 3

WRONG IDEA

)·==·(

"I just read in the paper about that rich New York bachelor who's in real estate," my mother announced when I picked up the phone the next morning. "Why couldn't you go out with someone like that? He's with a different girl every week." Hearing the strike of a match, I pictured Dot, her hair dyed a brassy shade, lit cigarette in the ashtray at the Pennsylvania plumbing supply store where she worked.

"I don't think he'd be interested in me, Mom. His taste runs to blonde bombshells." I started to tell her I'd run into Jack Kipling, but I was too tired to answer a zillion questions about someone I'd never see again.

"Well, you have to get out more. You won't meet anyone stuck in your apartment. Time goes by really quickly, believe me. When I was your age, I was married to your father, and you were three."

I pictured myself walking into the office, dragging a scream-ing toddler attached to my leg. "I'm focusing on my career right now. Anyway, it's hard to meet people here. Publishing isn't exactly a hotbed of romance."

"I don't see how it can be that hard. New York is overrun with men. You're going to be twenty-five next year, Julia. Around here there's something wrong if you aren't engaged by then."

I twisted the phone cord around my finger. "It's different in New York, Mom. Not everyone's biggest goal in life is to get married."

"You were dying to move up there, but I don't see that it's doing you much good. You could be spending weekends alone back here in Pikesville."

"I'm not spending all weekend alone. I went to a club with Vicky last night," I retorted.

"I still don't get why you dance with girls. I think it sends the wrong signal."

Our erotic grind would've given her heart failure. "It's not like that here. I can dance with whoever I want. People aren't hung up over it like they are back home." I heard cooing, and waved my hand to shoo a pigeon off my open windowsill.

"You're not . . . *attracted* to Vicky, are you?"

I couldn't resist. "Well . . . she *is* pretty cute. Those long legs of hers are kind of a turn-on."

For a moment Dot was silent. "I was worried something like this would happen. I guess up there, anything goes. Now I'll never have grandchildren," she said glumly.

"But just think, you'll never have to put up with a son-in-law who leaves his shavings in the sink."

"What am I going to tell Paulette and Joan?" she wailed.

"Mom. I'm kidding. I still like guys. You don't have to tell your friends anything." I waved my arm again, and the pigeon flapped off.

"Well, that's a relief. I mean, I'm pals with a bartender at Buck's who swings the other way, but…"

"You can relax. No one of either gender has been beating down my door lately."

"I'm going to have to pay you a visit soon," she said, exhaling smoke. "Get you out of your rut."

This proposed trip came up often, but I had mixed feelings about it. I knew she'd turn up her nose at my cramped living quarters, not to mention the way she tended to make loud comments about passersby.

"I'm really busy with work right now, but maybe later in the fall. My place is tiny, though; I don't think you'd be comfortable," I said.

"Oh, you know me. I can curl up and fall asleep anywhere."

I certainly did. "What are you reading this week?" She kept up a steady stream of novels that she swapped with her friends.

"I just finished one of Joyce Sutter's. This sea captain meets a young girl whose father owns a sheep farm. He doesn't want her seeing the captain, but one day she goes for a ride on his big stallion …"

My mind wandered as she described the plot.

"… then in the end they get married on the poop deck," she concluded. "I'll have to loan it to Paulette; her husband was in the Marines."

"That sounds like a good one. Have you had any interesting customers lately?" My eye fell on the piles of paper spread across my futon, awaiting my marking pen.

"There's a guy who's doing the plumbing for a mall in Uniontown. Turns out he was an engineer at Bethlehem Steel before he got laid off . . ."

My mother could strike up a conversation with anyone, and lack of knowledge about a topic never held her back. She was the least self-conscious person I'd ever met, which had mortified me as a teenager. I often thought I must have inherited my entire persona from my father. But when I tried to recall specifics, his memory seemed to fade faster the harder I tried to hold onto it.

"I bet you sold him more stuff than he even needed. Well, I guess I'd better get back to this manuscript."

"All right, Julia. Talk to you tomorrow."

I tried to call my mother several times a week since I knew she got lonely at night. She wasn't drinking as much as she used to, but she still tended to have a few too many. She liked to sit on a stool nursing her rum, chatting up anyone within earshot. Buck's Bar & Grill had been her hangout ever since my Dad moved out when I was in ninth grade.

As a teenager I'd saved what I could from my after-school job bagging groceries; my only splurge was those contact lenses right before I left for college. To my relief, I got a scholarship to a small in-state school and a job in the campus cafeteria. It was a delicious freedom to live where no one knew my mother, or that I'd been a four-eyed bookworm who never had a date in high school. I made good friends in my dorm and picked up some culture from my French professor, who took me under her wing and taught me which fork to use. I also managed to lose my virginity to a sweet guy who worked with me in the cafeteria. By that point I was just relieved to get it over with, even though no bells had gone off. I'd been so put off by Dot's flopping around with various and sundry, I'd come to dread the whole process.

Then in my senior year, at the urging of my English advisor, I applied to grad school and got a full ride at NYU. The month before moving to Manhattan sight-unseen, in my anxiety I ran so many miles I got shin splints. I mused over out-of-date issues of the one NYC magazine our tiny library carried, absorbing the ads and articles. I didn't understand half of it, but I couldn't wait to start my brand new life.

I took a Greyhound to the city in August, my belongings crammed into a used duffel from the Army-Navy store. Seeing the sooty skyline across the Hudson for the first time, I'd had a moment of panic. I didn't know a soul in this intimidating place—what was I doing here?

Wide-eyed, I got out at Port Authority and took the wrong express train, winding up at 125th Street. A sympathetic woman walked me over to the downtown side. After asking six strangers for directions, I finally found my dorm and collapsed on the single bed. Once I'd caught my breath, I waded into the moving-in chaos to meet my hall mates.

I had thought I'd go for a Ph.D., but when I learned about publishing, my plans changed. I knew the entry level was low-paying, but working with novelists and Pulitzer winners seemed much more exciting than academia.

My mother didn't understand why I wanted to live in one of the most dangerous cities in the world. She'd thought I was going to teach English in our local high school after college. At times, when it hit me how slim my chances were for moving up at work, I worried about winding up back there. I was terrified of proving her right by flunking out of my budding career; New York could rip you open like a wind-blasted flower.

But anything would be better than moving back to Pikesville. That seemed like being buried alive. The thought of returning with my tail between my legs sent ice water through my veins. Back home, I would have been teaching participles to bored high school seniors who'd rather be scoring touchdowns, or pot. Braving the cockroaches and graffitied subways won, hands-down.

Chapter 4
STORMY MONDAY

Vicky called me Sunday afternoon. I was standing in front of my open fridge, trying to get some relief from the sweltering heat. "I still can't believe you didn't let Jack come home with you," she said. "Just think, right now you could be licking whipped cream off every inch of his body."

I laughed. "Right now I could be wondering if I caught VD. And wishing he'd stayed in bed at least fifteen minutes before he dashed out to his next conquest."

"But Jules, you have to admit, he's the coolest... I mean, what a sexy guy. And you're so into their music . . . Anyway, you're going to be a little mad at me."

"Why, did you give them my number? That's fine with me." I waved the fridge door back and forth, rattling an empty catsup container.

"No, but I might have mentioned your address. And Sammy has my number."

"I imagine they've already forgotten about us. So I wouldn't hold your breath waiting for Sammy-boy to call." I gave up and shut the door, unwilling to melt my one stick of butter.

"Well guess what, he just did. He asked me out for a drink with him next week. He said you could come too, so maybe Jack will show up. Oh, and by the way, Sammy said you're the first woman who's ever—he emphasized *ever*—turned Jack down. So maybe you really did make an impression on him. All this is great timing; I've been in a slump lately."

For Vicky, a slump was six days without a date. "Don't worry, I won't barge in on your big night out. I do think it kind of intrigued them that we didn't fall all over them."

"You could be right. Why don't you come with me, though? Maybe Jack will be there."

"That's okay." It would be humiliating to tag along hoping Jack would show, and then sit around like a third wheel while Vicky and Sammy flirted.

"All right. But let me know if you change your mind."

After we hung up, I thought of what Sammy said. It would be amazing if Jack got in touch—but what were the chances of that? I plopped down on the couch and peeled up my tank top to wipe my sweating face. Maybe I should have let him come home with me. But if he'd accompanied me to my lumpy futon, wouldn't there be a horrible letdown when I never saw him again?

With an effort, I forced myself to stop thinking about Jack Kipling and focus on the manuscript I'd brought home. This one was by Timothy Collins, a novelist Harvey had signed up. I hoped that if I worked on enough of my boss's projects, he'd eventually let me acquire some books and I'd get what I dreamed of: being an editor instead of an assistant, and having my own stable of bestselling authors.

Harvey's mood fluctuated in an inverse relationship to how many calls he got from his wife. Monday morning she left four messages, and he was an ogre. I'd been told she worked at her rich father's investment firm, but she seemed to spend most of her time monitoring Harvey. After he got back from his two-martini lunch, I gathered my notepad along with the project I hoped to bring up and went into the editorial meeting.

I took a spot at the table next to my friend Meredith, our managing editor. She always supported my attempts to pursue a book, although in the past I'd gotten shot down every time. We were joined by Edgar, who handled arts and crafts. Kate and Charlie took the seats opposite. Harvey bustled in, scowling.

"What's on the bestseller list? What's hot?" He fired his opening salvo.

"Diet, sex, and woo-woo," Charlie said, running a hand through his thinning hair. In his late twenties, he'd risen through the ranks by specializing in pop culture.

"We need more of the first two categories and less New Age. At Esiness we usually had several blockbusters in the works." Harvey always managed to bring up his glory days at the more commercial house, where he'd been fired for grabbing one too many young assistants. "Kate, what's up?"

"I have in a debut novel; it's sex-and-shopping, but not badly written. Maybe Julia could give it a read," Kate said. The stylish editor had been hired away from Hawtey Press, supposedly to bring in bestsellers.

Harvey frowned. "What we need is another brand name. The only one in our lineup right now is Freeman Fyfe. You people have to work the phones more; come up with your own book ideas. Find out what the agents are hatching before they send it out to everyone else. At Esiness, I was always hounding people to give me a first look."

Meredith leaned toward me. "He was hounding them for a first look inside their knickers," she muttered.

"Was that something you wanted to share with the group?" Harvey asked.

"Not at all," Meredith replied blandly, polishing her half-rims.

Anxiously I cleared my throat. "I have a project. It's a proposal on how polluted the ocean is becoming."

"Who sent you that?" Harvey demanded.

"I found it in the slush pile, but it's really well-written. It's shocking the way these factories are dumping their chemical wastes. The author has some credentials; he's written for *Science Times*—"

"But who'd buy a book about that?" Kate cut in.

"And who reads *Science Times* anyway?" Harvey said.

This was sinking faster than the Titanic. I decided to give it one more whirl. "I think people worry about the contaminants in fish."

"Some of these environmental books can do well if the writing is lively," Meredith said.

I scribbled THANKS!! on my notepad.

Harvey shook his head. "Too much of a downer. Pass-ola!" *Pollution project—ixnay.*

"Okay gang, I'm not hearing anything that's rocking my world," Harvey said. "You need to get some fire in your bellies if we're going to put ourselves on the map. Oh, did anyone see that novel about the Italian monastery that went so high in auction last week? Something with 'rose' in the title."

The editors all shook their heads.

"I can't imagine it'll sell in the provinces." Harvey gathered his memos, the paper shivering in his stubby hands. "All right, class dismissed."

Sighing, I went back to my cubbyhole and resumed typing an endless pile of rejection letters.

Chapter 5

ONE BOURBON, ONE SCOTCH, AND ONE BEER

The following Friday night as I headed home from work, I noticed something sticking out of my doorway. At first I thought someone had left their boots there, but then I saw they were attached to a ripped-up pair of jeans. A squarish bottle sat between the toes. Sure enough, the black car was idling further down the block. As a rill of anticipation ran through me, I told myself not to blow my cover.

"Been a while since I sat on a girl's stoop," Jack said, gazing up at me. He wasn't as rumpled as he'd been at the club; he had shaved, and his thick, dark hair was clean. In fact, he looked incredibly good. I had to remind myself not to stare at him.

"If Mr. Iaccone was around, he'd make you move on. He doesn't put up with people hanging out."

"Who's Mr. Iaccone?" His eyes were an extraordinarily deep brown.

I smiled. "My eighty-year-old landlord. He likes to takes a broom to loiterers."

"I came by," Jack said, rubbing his hand through his hair and making it stand on end, "to ask why you won't come out with me. You aren't even giving me a chance." He pushed his lanky body up from the steps and smiled down at me, creating sexy creases on either side of his mouth. His maroon shirt was missing a few buttons; over it he wore a crinkled suede jacket that looked like a puppy had used it for a chew toy.

Sammy had called Vicky to postpone their drink date, so I'd thought the whole thing was a non-starter. But I wasn't about to let on that I was thrilled to my threadbare socks. "I have a manuscript in this bag that I've been trying to make headway on."

"Can I take a look? I've never seen a book manuscript." His London inflexions would make a grocery list sound fascinating. When I hesitated, he said, "C'mon, enlighten me."

I unzipped my backpack and pulled out Timothy Collins's doorstop, marked up in red ink.

"Looks like you've done a lot of work on it already," Jack said, taking it from my hands.

"It needs it. I'll be lucky to finish by July."

I watched as he rifled through the pages with his long fingers, still hardly believing that he was standing there. "What would be the most important part? This bit in the middle?" he asked.

"All of it, really. I have to go through it and make suggestions. Half of which he'll probably ignore."

"How about this?" He pulled the last forty pages out of the rubber band.

"Yes, the ending's pretty important. Leaving it out would be kind of like… when the radio cuts to a commercial before they play the last verse."

"Good. Then I'll take this," he said, folding the pages and stuffing them down his shirt.

"Hey, I need that!" I reached out my hand. We only had one copy; Harvey would have my head if I lost a section.

"You'll get it back, don't worry," Jack said with a grin. He wrapped his arms around his chest. "I'll give it to you tonight when you meet me for a drink. Where should we go, Fanelli's?" He cocked a dark eyebrow mischievously.

"You really aren't going to give it to me?" I said, trying not to smile.

"Sure I will, after we have our drink."

"Okay, Fanelli's at eight. Does Vicky know?"

"I'll tell Sammy to make sure she comes. Do you always need an escort, or is it just me?"

Taking the rest of my manuscript from his hands, I considered my answer as I unlocked the door.

"It's just you."

I called Vicky as soon as I got in. She didn't know Jack was going to be waiting for me, but Sammy had mentioned they had a plan to get me to come out tonight. I told her I'd meet her at Fanelli's, said goodbye, and tried to calm down. I kept picturing the way Jack's eyes seemed to light up when he first saw me. To squelch my mounting excitement, I told myself that probably happened with any girl who caught his attention momentarily.

I put on Billie Holiday and sang along to "Summertime" as I tried to figure out what to wear. I was so antsy, I mechanically tried on each of my four skirts while gulping a beer. What would I talk to Jack about—and why would he be interested in me? Was it that I presented a challenge, as Sammy said; a girl who didn't bring him home right off the bat? *Try to maintain your cool,* I told myself. *You'll turn him off if he catches you drooling.*

Finally I gave up and put on jeans and a blue shirt with pearl buttons from Alice Underground, my favorite second-hand store. I fixed up my eyeliner and mascara, smeared on a little lip gloss, and then quit fiddling. Grabbing my backpack, I hiked up Mercer toward the familiar red neon "Café".

I opened the frosted glass door and waved at Hal. Squeezing past a raucous crowd, I continued to the end of the bar, where I spotted Vicky on a stool talking to Sammy. Someone in a large floppy hat was seated with his back to me. Vicky was so into the conversation, she didn't notice me until I stood next to her.

"I was starting to think I'd have to come get you," she said.

Beneath the big hat Jack wore a dark green jacket, not chewed-up like the one earlier. He pulled an open stool over to him. "She wouldn't stand us up. I have something that belongs to her."

"Yes, you do. Is it still in your shirt?" I sat and hooked my ankles around the rungs in case I started feeling faint. Even in the droopy hat he was sexy, his thighs taut in tight faded jeans, obviously *sans* underwear.

"Your papers are safe in the car, right outside. I didn't want to spill anything on them."

Hal came down the bar and made eyes at me as if to say, *You're moving in fancy circles tonight.* "Usual draft?" I nodded.

"You look like you could use a shot." Sammy indicated the line of glasses.

"No, I'm okay." If I had any Wild Turkey, I might really pass out.

"We were just saying how packed it is in here tonight," Vicky said in an Earth-to-Julia tone of voice. "They usually avoid public places on weekends."

Jack seemed intent on topping off their shot glasses with whiskey; after that, he drank right from the bottle. Vicky and Sammy murmured to each other as I cast about for something to say.

"Did you get some editing done?" Jack asked, his face partially hidden by the hat.

"I'll get a lot done tomorrow. Mr. Collins likes to use three adjectives where one will do; every time I think I've weeded them out, several more crop up. They're twined around his words like kudzu."

Jack laughed, then pushed back the brim and gazed at me. "I'm not used to beautiful girls being so smart."

To my horror, a slow burn started in my chest and spread to my cheeks. I took a gulp from my frosty mug.

"Well, would you look at that," Jack said. "It's been fifteen years since I saw anyone blush like that. Like watching the sun rise in your face."

"It's just this humidity." I fanned myself with a bar napkin.

He started to reply when two heavily made-up women barged over.

"It *is* you," the first one said breathlessly. "I told you so," she added to her friend, who was staring at Jack as if afraid he'd disappear. "Can you sign something for us?" She batted her prickly eyelashes.

"Sure." He fumbled in his pockets as Sammy produced a pen. Jack plucked a cardboard coaster from the bar and scratched his name. "Oh thank you," she gushed. "Wanna come party with us? We're huuuge fans of yours."

"Ladies, we were just havin' a conversation with our friends here," Sammy said. "Maybe some other time."

"Can you sign too?" the woman asked, and Sammy obliged.

"Here's our numbers," the second one said, thrusting a piece of paper at Jack. "Call us. We'll show you a really good time." Scowling at me and Vicky, the two flounced away.

"Sorry 'bout that," Sammy said. "Sometimes the out-of-towners ain't cool. Speaking of which, another contingent's headed our way . . . tattoos and really big hair. Wanna split?"

"See you outside," Jack said, and bolted for the back door.

"Let's boogie on out of here." Sammy threw down some bills, took hold of our arms and hustled us along. We rushed into the warm night air toward the black car waiting at the curb. There was a commotion behind me as the bunch from the bar exploded out the door.

"Where are we going?" I asked.

"Get in, we'll discuss it on the way," Sammy said, drawing Vicky with him. I jumped inside just as a meaty fist pounded on the window. I looked back when we pulled away, and one of the girls gave me the finger.

"Come over to my place," Jack said, leaning across the others to hand me the loose pages. "I kept my end of the deal, but we haven't had our drink yet."

Vicky smiled. "Sure. We always keep our promises, don't we, Julia?"

We're going to Jack Kipling's apartment, was all I could think. I tried to quell my jitters as the men gave Rick a hard time about his getaway driving.

Five minutes later we pulled up in front of a big gray building. Jack and Sammy spoke to the doormen as we crossed a slick-looking lobby. The elevator whooshed up to the penthouse and Jack pushed through the front door. When it opened onto a vast loft, I realized he must own the entire floor. Running along the wall was the biggest collection of albums I'd ever seen. Reels of tape spilled off the ends of shelves, and guitars were scattered throughout on stands, on chairs, and propped against furniture.

Sammy swept his arm toward a couch and chairs grouped around a long glass-topped coffee table covered with empty bottles, shot glasses, newspapers, and overflowing ashtrays. "You gals make yourselves comfortable and tell me what you want to drink." He grabbed a couple of ashtrays and dumped them into a wastebasket.

"I'll switch to white wine if you have it," Vicky said.

"A beer would be great." Nervous and not ready to sit yet, I walked over to the shelves. "Wow, look at all your records." Jack stood nearby as I scanned the stacks of albums, some of which looked very old.

"Pick out something," he said.

Carefully I withdrew a 45 in a faded wrapper; "Long

Distance Moan." I'd only ever heard two of Blind Lemon Jefferson's songs. "Could we play this?"

"You dig Jefferson?" Jack asked, seeming surprised.

"I like just about any blues. Especially from the twenties and thirties."

"I'll put it on. This one really takes me back."

Enormous speakers were placed strategically around the room, enveloping us in sound. The record was crackly, but that only enhanced the effect. I sat in one of the armchairs and let the mournful cadences wash over me. Sammy handed me a beer and sat next to Vicky on the couch. Jack sank into a chair cattycorner to mine, long legs extended, one boot keeping time. The song ended on a single plaintive note.

"D'you know Gatemouth?" Jack asked, going over to the turntable. "I bet you'd like him. Or I could play some Charlie Patton."

"Sure, if it's not too much trouble. I love this stuff, but my friends are more into The Voidoids. Or Throbbing Gristle."

"No trouble at all," he replied with a hint of a smile. He put the music on, then grabbed an empty paper cup and went to the window, where a moth was frantically fluttering. He deftly clapped the cup over it and slid his hand between the pane and lip. "We'll let him go later," he said, covering it loosely with a lid.

Jack sprawled back in his chair. I risked a peek at him; hair splayed around his shoulders, eyelashes dark above sculpted cheekbones. *He's even better-looking in person than in photographs*, I thought. Halfway through the record, he turned the volume down.

"How did you get into the blues?" he asked. "Most girls your age would be just weaning themselves off of disco."

I laughed. "I admit I got down to 'Last Dance' a few times in college. But my dad played blues and country for me from the time I was small. The blues make every other kind of music seem a little . . . tepid, don't you think?"

"Yeah. Definitely tepid." He took a swig of whiskey.

"How did you first get into it?" I ventured to ask. The Floor had done their bluesiest album a number of years ago; it was my favorite, but I wasn't going to mention that. I didn't want to come across like those slobbering groupies at the bar.

"I hung out with some older kids in secondary school, and they collected American records. The first time I heard Robert Johnson, I was gobsmacked. That's what got me started down this long, twisted road. You know the saying, 'The blues are the easiest music to learn, but the hardest to play.'"

Jack got a distracted look on his face and went silent for a minute. The phone rang; a hang-up, but then it rang again. He went to have a long mumbled conversation in the other part of the loft. Already I was developing a colossal crush on him—probably the emotional equivalent of having a "Kick Me" sign taped to my back.

"I forgot about this thing I was supposed be at an hour ago," Jack said when he returned.

I jumped up, hoping I hadn't overstayed my welcome. "I was just heading out."

"I think we're going to stay here a few more minutes, and then maybe go somewhere else." Vicky gave me a wide grin to let me know she was taking Sammy to her place.

"I'll catch up with you tomorrow," I said.

Jack grabbed the cup with the moth, pressed the elevator button and got in with me. He reached over and fingered a button at the base of my neck. "I like this shirt of yours with the pearl buttons. Where did you get it?" His hand just whispered on my bare skin before he moved it away.

I swallowed. "I get a lot of my stuff from Alice Underground. It's this below-street-level shop on the Upper West Side. They have second-hand and nicer vintage things too."

"I could use some new threads. You'll have to take me there sometime."

"Okay," I said, wondering if he really meant it. The elevator opened and we went across the lobby. The doorman held the door as we stepped out into the street. "Thanks for playing those records."

"Anytime." Jack took the lid off the cup. "Go on back to your old lady," he said as the moth spiraled up into the night sky. "I was really into insects when I was a kid. I'd catch a jar of fireflies and bring them to my room at night. I liked to watch them flickering on and off while I fell asleep."

He ran his hand through his hair and gazed down the block. "What are you up to Sunday night?" he finally said. "I'll be in the studio all day; we're finishing the tracks for a new album. You can come over here and listen to some more music."

I suppressed the urge to shout "Yes!" and took a breath. "Sunday's great."

Jack smiled, the breeze ruffling his hair. "Vicky can come, too. I love turning people on to these old blues. I'll pick you up around seven since you have to work Monday."

"Don't remind me. I need to be there by 8:30 to take notes in a meeting for my boss, Harvey. He's the publisher."

Jack rolled his eyes. "I can't remember the last time I was up that early. Unless I'd just never gone to bed."

"We working stiffs have to rise and shine."

"My motto is, 'All work and no play make Jack a dull boy.'" He raised his eyebrow at me, and I almost dissolved into the litter-strewn sidewalk. "How about giving me your number?"

"Sure." I got a scrap of paper from my backpack, so flustered I had to think for a minute before writing it down. He took the pen from my hand, scribbled on the bottom and tore it off. "Here's mine."

I poked it deep into my jeans pocket. "Well . . . thanks again! Goodnight."

I crossed Houston in a blissed-out fog. *So here's what happened today: I typed letters. I answered phones. I came home to find Jack Kipling sitting on my stoop.* And now his number was in my pocket. I felt for the curl of paper to make sure it was really there.

It was impossible to get to sleep. I wondered if Vicky was already rolling around in bed with Sammy. I pictured Jack's face as he listened to the music, eyes closed, his lithe body stretched out in the chair. I couldn't wait to see him again Sunday night. My breakup with Art was starting to seem light years away.

Chapter 6

LIVELY UP YOURSELF

The next morning as I sat on my futon having coffee, my eyes fell on the notebook resting on my bedside table. I put down the mug and opened the marbled cover. Written in block letters were the titles of the first books I'd ever read: *The Cat in the Hat, Harold and the Purple Crayon.* I flipped through more pages, coming to fifth grade when my mother still had the night job: *Little Women*, Anne Frank. Ninth: *To the Lighthouse, Madame Bovary.* The emptiness of the house without my dad.

After he left, Dot struggled to make ends meet. We moved several times, each rental smaller than the one before. She began going to Buck's every night and lost a string of jobs because of calling in sick—i.e., hung over.

Sometimes she brought a man home with her from the bar. Scuffed work boots on the doormat; muffled noises behind her bedroom walls. A stranger in the bathroom when I was trying to get ready for school. She got a reputation for being loose, which was a shocking thing in our little town where everybody knew everyone's business.

Just as I was heading out to the bus stop one morning, I heard a man leaving her room. Quickly I ducked into the kitchen. Dot followed him down the hall to the front door, asking him not once but twice, *Don't you want me to fix you some breakfast?* The guy didn't even answer in his rush to get out to his pickup. The motor gunned and the truck screeched away. I stayed put until Dot returned to her room. On my way out, I heard sobbing behind her closed door.

Her rejection clouded my thoughts as I bagged an endless line of groceries after school. Why couldn't she see what was so obvious to me; that hopping into bed with those men wasn't going to make any of them fall in love with her? In fact, just the opposite.

I turned to another page. After Dad left, my notebook became one of the few ties I had to my past. I didn't keep a diary because I knew Dot would pry—and I didn't need one. I could recall what I was doing at any point in time, just by what I'd been reading.

I was deep into editing that night when the phone rang. I could hear music and people talking in the background. "What page are you on?" came an accented voice.

"Two hundred forty-eight, no thanks to you." I was smiling so hard my face hurt.

"What d'you mean, no thanks to me? You got home before eleven," Jack said. "What did you do today?"

I tried to slow my hammering heart. "You might need to sit down. I got up at six and went for a run on the West Side Highway, then I started marking up Mr. Collins. I've been at it ever since, except for an intermission to hear some Billie Holiday."

"I played several good records after you left. Do you know Leadbelly? He laid down some nice stuff back in the twenties. Hang on—"

A woman's voice asked something, and he mumbled a reply.

"I'll put that on for you tomorrow." He came back on the line. I heard the woman laughing.

"That would be great."

"All right then, I'll let you get back to work."

I heard a click, and hung up. *Jack Kipling just called me. On the phone.* I went to get their latest record and put it on, staring at his picture on the cover. Suddenly I was really anxious. *What will we talk about tomorrow? Maybe I can ask about their new album—then again, maybe he can't discuss it yet. I wonder if anything will happen at his place. But maybe he just wants to play some more blues for me, like he said.*

Vicky hadn't gotten in touch on Saturday, and I wanted to give her some breathing room. The next morning I called her.

"Boy, my limbs feel like jello," she said.

"You're just trying to make me jealous. Had fun, hmm?"

"It's true about those Southern guys; they really do aim to please. Guess what, Sammy said Jack likes that you're smart. His last few ladies were total airheads. And he was amazed that you're into the blues."

I told myself to take this with a grain of salt; "last few ladies" indicated his short attention span.

"So be nice to him tonight, okay?" Vicky continued. "You resisted him once, but now you should go for it."

"I don't know. I'd feel awful if we slept together and then he never called me again." I went over to the window and gazed down at Broome Street. "I'd feel like I was following in Dot's footsteps."

"This has nothing to do with Dot. It sounds like she didn't have a shred of self-respect. You're the one in control—you can sleep with whoever you want. Although you may have the right idea about not seeming too easy, since he wants to see you again."

"Maybe he's tired of women fawning over him. He looked bored out of his mind at that party." A man shook out a blanket on the sidewalk and began spreading his wares.

"Then again, you don't want to put him off. Why don't you gussy up a bit? I'll bet he stops by your place first, so you can be alone in the car before he picks up me and Sammy."

"I almost wondered if Sammy lived there, he seemed so comfortable."

"I think they're best friends, or whatever that is for men. Sammy said he spends a lot of time at Jack's place."

"What was up with that glass coffee table?" I asked.

"The better to chop up the coke, my dear."

"Ohh… I didn't get that."

"Yeah, you'd better watch out. Jack's a Big Bad Wolf."

I didn't gussy up; I didn't want to seem like I was trying too hard. I put on jeans and a sleeveless top that I'd scored for three bucks at Trash and Vaudeville. I was so twitchy, I had to redo my eyeliner twice. Gazing at my reflection, I wished I looked more sophisticated. It would help if I could afford better clothes. But there was nothing to be done about that, unless I wanted to start freelancing on Tenth Avenue.

At eight I heard someone banging on the downstairs door. I peered out my window and saw Jack gazing up at me.

"This building needs a buzzer," he called. "How do people come up to see you?"

"I throw down my key if someone's coming up. I'll be right there." If he saw my scruffy apartment he might feel sorry for me, as opposed to feeling attracted.

I grabbed my backpack and went downstairs. Jack was leaning against the brick wall, looking sultry in a rose-colored shirt with the top four buttons undone and low-slung suede hip-huggers. He looked so handsome smiling at me that it made me even more on-edge.

"How do you get your supplies up three flights?" he asked as we went to the car. His British accent gave everything he said a polite air.

"Sometimes I make two trips," I replied. "Builds character. And calf muscles."

"I noticed you had a set of those." Rick opened the back door for us, and Jack's gaze lingered on my legs as I climbed in. "How many miles a day you running?"

"About five. I go for an hour."

"Sounds disgustingly healthy." He slid over toward the middle, next to me.

"It's stress relief. I got into the habit in college; I used to take a study break at night and go for a jog with friends from my dorm."

"Hmm. So you girls would come back in all sweaty and what, shower together?" he asked, raising an eyebrow.

"We'd shower, but not together. Sorry to ruin your visual there." I smiled at his expression.

"That's all right, I've been told I have an overactive imagination. How long have you had your place here?"

"A year in May. I rented it when I got out of NYU."

Our shoulders bumped as Rick swerved to avoid a scarecrow draped in tattered garbage bags, waving on traffic.

"I thought you went to college in Pennsylvania."

"NYU was grad school."

Jack considered me. "So you really are brainy."

"I only went for a year, to get my Master's. The ivory tower didn't prepare me for much in terms of real life. Like knowing how many quarters to run a cycle at the laundromat. Or which express to take so you don't wind up in Flatbush."

Jack laughed. "Yeah, I guess only the real deal can prepare you for that. How'd your day go?"

"I did more editing and ran a few errands. What about you?" I had no idea how someone like him spent his time.

"This and that. I got up about noon—I know, I'm a lazy bugger—and messed around with a few riffs. Then I put some things on tape at the studio, overdubs and such for the new album."

Rick caught a stoplight. "Vicky's over on Mott," I said.

"Yeah, I remember. The night of 'No, I don't want you to walk me home,'" Jack said wryly.

I gave a little shrug. Vicky was waiting outside, wearing a short denim skirt that made her legs look miles long. Her blonde hair was spiked up pertly, silver hoops in her ears.

"Hello," she said to Jack. "Sammy said to pick him up at his place."

"I hope he didn't drink up all your liquor."

Vicky actually stammered. "N-no, he brought some over."

Sammy was smoking a joint on the sidewalk. He got in and pulled Vicky to him for a bong kiss. She blew smoke out her nose. "Way to greet a girl."

"Happy to oblige," Sammy said. "Did you get your press release written? Can you imagine, she kicked me out this afternoon so she could work."

"It's for a book by a shrink," Vicky explained. "Pop psychology's a hot topic these days; Julia deals with a lot of it too. This one's about being in touch with your inner self."

"*I* like touching your inner self," Sammy said. "'Specially with my—"

"You really do have a one-track mind," Vicky said.

"Julia, she's insulting my fine, upstanding character." Sammy took one last suck of the roach and stubbed it out in the ashtray.

When we got to the building, they each took a guitar out of the trunk. "Tom, Stan, this is Julia," Jack said to the doormen as we waited for the elevator. "And her friend Vicky." The men looked us over and nodded politely.

Jack opened his door without a key, as he'd done the other night.

"You don't lock your door?" Vicky asked him.

"I can't keep track of keys. Tom and Stan know who to let up."

The loft was much cleaner this time; nodding sunflowers on the glass table and no overflowing ashtrays. They went to put the guitars in their stands, and I heard cracking ice from a tray in the kitchen. Vicky put her arm around my neck. "I have a feeling tonight's the night."

"Shh," I whispered.

Sammy came back carrying a bucket of beers, and Jack cradled a bottle of whiskey. Jack pointed to the shelves. "You pick something."

I pulled out a Pinetop Smith in a worn cover and Jack put it on the turntable. Sammy drew a bulging joint from his pocket, lit it, took a big hit and passed it to Vicky, who puffed and handed it across the glass-topped table. Jack drew an extended inhale and held it out to me.

"No, thanks." I didn't want to be out of it tonight—and pot really made me feel out of it.

Jack handed it to Vicky and blew a long stream of smoke. "You're a pure gal, huh?" He gave me an appraising glance.

Vicky spluttered. "Depends on your definition of pure."

I made a face at her. "Speak for yourself, Victoria. I'm really boring when I smoke pot," I said to Jack. "I just giggle for an hour and then fall asleep."

Sammy smiled. "Now, that doesn't sound bad a'tall."

"Leave her alone," Jack said. "More for the degenerates."

"She's a lightweight," Vicky said, passing the joint to Sammy. "But I mean that only in the finest sense."

"How long have you two known each other?" Jack asked.

Vicky thought for a minute. "Almost a year, right? My first day of work, Julia grilled me on what books I liked. I was so grateful to have a friend, even if I hadn't read half the intellectual stuff she had, like the Proust she's so obsessed with. She introduced me around and told me which department heads to watch out for."

"Then you cut out for greener pastures, leaving me to the wolves."

"Yeah, the wolf named Harvey," Vicky said, then caught herself. "I mean, and all the others," she added lamely.

"Julia's boss," Jack said.

"He knows?" Vicky asked.

I shook my head at her and decided this would be a good time to use the bathroom at the far end of the loft. Peering into the spacious shower as I zipped my pants, I pictured Jack in there, water streaming down his face, plastering his hair to his bare shoulders . . . Shaking the image, I went out and tried not to look at his big, messy bed beyond an open door. There was another sitting area with what appeared to be a working fireplace. Guitar stands, a keyboard, drum kit, and amps were grouped around it; I wondered if the downstairs neighbors ever complained.

"Anyone up for going out for a drink?" Sammy asked after conferring with Vicky.

Jack looked at me. "Why don't we stay here and listen to some more records," he said softly. I felt a funny flutter in my stomach. I didn't want to leave yet, and I knew from the mob at Fanelli's that it might be difficult for him to go to a bar. But I was almost afraid to say yes.

I took a breath. "I can stay to hear the Leadbelly."

Jack smiled, creating those sexy creases on either side of his face. "I picked out some things today. I'd forgotten half the stuff I had on my shelves."

"Copacetic. We'll see you all later," Sammy said. They exited in a rush just as the album ended, and the apartment rang with the sudden silence.

"What's in that backpack you're always carrying around?" Jack asked.

"Just a book and my keys."

"You planned on doing some reading over here?" He looked at me quizzically.

"In case I got bored…Just kidding. I always bring one along for when I get stuck on the subway, or in line at the drugstore. It's Flannery O'Connor; *Wise Blood*. She writes about these really dark, twisted characters."

"Dark and twisted, sounds good. Want to read some of it to me?"

I was taken aback. "Sure…I mean, or you could borrow it. I've read it so many times, I almost have it memorized."

"I'd rather hear you read it, if you don't mind." He kicked off his boots and stretched out lengthwise on the couch. *God, he looks enticing in that position.*

I got the book and perched on the edge of my chair. "Guess I'll start at the beginning." I finished a page and glanced at Jack, who was lying there watching me. He made a "keep it rolling" gesture, so I continued to the end of the chapter.

Jack sat up, crossing his bare feet at the ankles. "That's powerful stuff. You have a good voice but I can't place your accent. Where'd you grow up?"

"A small town in western Pennsylvania. It has a couple factories, some scenic farmland. You're from London, right?" I was pretty sure I'd read that about him.

"Forty minutes away in Hounslow, a dirty industrial burg. The sky always had this greenish cast like it was about to puke. Everyone worked in the factories there too, after they finished whatever schooling they'd suffered through. Most of the kids talked about going to London eventually, but hardly anyone ever did. I was lucky to get away."

"And your first group was with one of your roommates?"

"Yeah, after the bands I had in school. I was in a group with a flatmate of mine who was a drummer. We got a few gigs, and one night Patrick saw us play in this little fifteen-seat hole. He asked me to come see his band, and the next day we decided to get together and ditch the others. And that," he said, making a strumming motion, "was all she wrote. What about you, how'd you get out of western Pennsylvania?"

"I couldn't wait to get out. I scraped my summer job money together and got a scholarship to a small state college."

"Your parents couldn't help you?"

"They broke up when I was fourteen, and I haven't seen my dad since," I said, feeling a familiar ache. "My mother tended to bounce around from job to job."

"Mine split when I was nine. I had no idea what was going on; one day I came home from school and he'd moved out. I thought it was my fault because I'd done something bad the day before, tracked in a lot of mud or something." Jack frowned. "I still saw my father on weekends but I started getting into scrapes, got known as a troublemaker. So I've had to live up to that reputation." He raised an eyebrow as I laughed.

"Let me show you these records I found," Jack said, untangling his legs. He scooped a pile of albums from the shelf and brought them over to the table. "You said you liked Billie, so here are a few of hers. And these are some early Robert Johnsons. Matter of fact, they're kind of rare."

"How about one of the Robert Johnsons?"

Jack put the record on. "I was messing around with some of

those riffs this afternoon. Want to hear them?"

"I'd love to." *Shoot me now—he's going to play the guitar only for me!*

Jack glanced around the room. "Wonder where Carla's hid me new picks. I thought I left them here." He noticed my inquisitive look. "That's my housekeeper; she deals with my mess. She's got this peach of a little kid who loves our music. Carla and my manager Mary Jo help me keep it together."

He paced around, lifting papers off the front table. "Where the hell are those picks?"

I followed Jack into the kitchen, and he started yanking open various drawers. It looked as if Carla had scooped up every smallish object from the surfaces of the apartment and dumped it in; keys on chains tangled with Zig-Zag rolling papers, pens, loose cigars, nail clippers, corkscrews. One that he opened revealed a cache of condoms mixed in with some salt and pepper packets. He quickly slammed it shut. I could just imagine how many women he'd had up here with him, and how many of those little packages he'd gone through.

"Here they are," he said finally. "Right in with the knives. Unbelievable."

Jack grabbed more beers from the fridge and tore open the bag of picks with his teeth. We sat on the couch, and he began strumming his Fender along with the record. When it stopped he kept going, eyes closed, his lashes a dark fringe over high cheekbones. As he shifted among bluesy chords, I observed the changing moods on his face. The soulful notes dripped from his fingers like melting tallow.

"That was really beautiful," I said when he set aside the guitar. "I've always wondered how people compose songs. Do you stumble on the tune while you're playing random notes?"

Jack thought about it for a second. "It's… kind of like wandering around in a place I've never seen, yet it's familiar. Like going for a walk in the woods and you take a path you haven't been on, but suddenly you know the way. Once in a while something comes to me in the middle of a concert. Did you ever catch one?"

"Sorry, I never did." I couldn't afford the tickets, but I thought it would sound cheap to say that.

"We'll be touring at some point. You should come see a few."

"I'd love to. It must be a thrill to play for a huge audience. Do you ever get stage fright?"

"I did the first time we were in something larger than a club. But then you bust a few strings and realize the show goes on, with or without you." Jack drained his bottle and opened another. "So what does an assistant editor do?"

"Oh, type up letters and contracts; tell Harvey's wife he's in a meeting when he wants to avoid her. Edit his authors, and he takes the credit. He'd have me tying his shoelaces if he could. I need to acquire a book if I'm ever going to get promoted."

"So why do it?"

"Well, because I love books. And authors are a fascinating breed, if a little high-maintenance. Plus occasionally you get to go to a glitzy party or awards dinner." I took a sip of beer. "And I think I have a knack for editing. It's the one talent I possess."

"That's the reason to do it, then. Only thing I was ever good at was playing and singing. Lucky for me, that worked out."

"How did you connect with the other guys after you and

Patrick got together? I've read a bit about it, but ..."

"You can ignore everything you've read about me; they love to exaggerate," he said with a twitch of his eyebrow.

I had a feeling they hadn't exaggerated much. "I'll forget what I've read if you'll tell me yourself."

"Okay, how we got our start. Patrick and I brilliantly realized we needed percussion if we were going to do anything more than strum'n' hum, so we found Mark. Then we required a keyboardist. At first we weren't going to go with Sammy because we thought an American might not blend in with us blokes. But when he drank us all under the table, we knew he'd fit the bill."

"What was he doing in London?" I'd always been curious why the group included one non-British member.

"Getting the hell out of Marietta, Georgia," Jack said. "He'd been kicked out of military school, if you can believe his parents thought that would work out. His mama figured he might pick up some culture if he spent a few months in England." He paused to down a slug of beer. "I've always felt Southerners are akin to the Irish. The best ones are bullshitters, lushes, and underdogs. I've got some Irish in me, so watch out," he added with a grin.

"I'll keep that in mind," I said, smiling back at him. Our eyes met, and I had trouble pulling mine away.

Jack reached for his guitar. "You ever listen to anything other than blues?"

Was he fishing around about his own music? I didn't want to turn him off by sounding like some gushing fan. "I like jazz, although I need to get more educated about it. And rock, of course."

"So you do listen to rock and roll. Who do you like?"

No way was I going to admit I owned every one of their albums, and had played them until the grooves were worn thin. "All the great ones," I said. Jack looked a little disgruntled, but I left it at that.

"You ever played?" he asked, thumbing the strings.

"Only some piano lessons when I was young. After my father left, we didn't have the money for it. Did you take guitar lessons?"

"Nope, never had one in my life. I don't read music. I always figured it was more in the attack than the technical stuff. Here, give it a try." Before I could demur, he laid the guitar in my lap. Reaching for his beer, he took a sip and put the bottle between his thighs.

"I'll show you a one-four-five blues progression. Put your hand on the neck." He leaned in and positioned my fingers. "You have to press hard; that's where it all flows from." He started to place my other hand over the middle.

"Aah, I can't do it backwards." Jack moved closer and put his arm behind me, his left hand covering mine on the guitar neck. He looked over my shoulder. "Put your fingers here," he said, reaching around to position my right hand on the strings.

His chin brushed my shoulder; I felt his warm breath on my cheek. I started to scoot forward a little, but his arms tightened around me. "Now hold these down and strum."

Awkwardly I tried to pluck the strings. If I turned a fraction of an inch, my face would be touching his. He seemed intent on teaching me the chords, when all I could think of was the intoxicating heat of his body.

"All right, that was your A. Sort of. Now we're gonna situate you . . ." He repositioned my left hand, his voice soft in my ear, " . . . so you can play a D."

His chest pressed against my back, his heartbeat like a drum kick through my shirt. My stomach was doing somersaults.

"Just hold those in and then strum. That's your basic D." When I didn't move, he stroked the strings for me. His arms encircling me felt like an embrace. *Why is he showing me these stupid chords when I'm dying for him to kiss me?*

"Next you go to an E." He lifted my pointer and positioned it, then my middle finger, then my fourth. "Don't be afraid of it, Julia," he said in a low timbre, his lips brushing my cheek.

Suddenly my skin prickled with goosebumps, and I gave an involuntary shiver. I couldn't stand the tension any longer. As I turned toward him, the guitar clanked against the bottle between his legs and knocked it sideways.

"Oh my god! I'm so sorry!"

Jack grabbed the frothing bottle and slammed it onto the table. He stood up, his jeans soaked. "Well, that cooled me down. Let me go change."

He went back through the loft to his bedroom. *What a klutz! I can't believe I dumped a whole beer in his lap. He must think I'm an idiot!* I stood and paced around the table. *How moronic! Maybe I'd better go before I make an even bigger fool of myself.* I waited a few more minutes, but when he didn't return, I grabbed my bag and punched the elevator button until it came.

Outside it was pouring rain, so I sloshed over to the subway. I got on the train and stared at the graffitied doors as the crowded car lurched its way downtown. *Only I could blow a night with Jack Kipling. He probably wishes he hadn't invited me over.* The doors slid open and people shoved their way on. A couple with safety-pinned eyebrows sat across from me and started making out. A bedraggled guy came through ranting about rent control and shaking his cup in people's faces. The passengers studiously ignored him, and each other. I got out at my stop and slogged over to Broome, thoroughly disgusted with myself.

The phone was ringing as I turned the second lock. I peeled off my dripping shoes and got ready to settle in for a long call from Dot. "Hi, Mom," I said.

"I've been called a mother before, but not in that sense of the word." Jack sounded amused.

"Oh! Hi. I can't believe I spilled that beer all over you. I hope I didn't ruin your jeans."

"My jeans have survived worse. You vanished on me."

"I'm sorry, I was just so embarrassed. I didn't even thank you for playing the music."

"Glad you liked it. Listen, I have to go to this thing next weekend, this... birthday thing for one of the guys in the band."

I started to get excited, but I didn't want to jump to conclusions. Jack paused for a moment. "Do you want to go?" he said. "All I have to do is show up. Then we could get something to eat. Play some more blues." I felt my pulse thumping. *Did he just ask me out?*

"I'd love to." Suddenly I envisioned a bunch of rich rock stars and their girlfriends at a bash. My raggedy punk stuff probably wouldn't cut it. "What would I wear to something like that?"

"Wear anything you want. So I'll pick you up Saturday after I get out of the studio, and we'll go to this shindig. I'll call you when I'm done, around ten-thirty. Want to give me your office number too?"

Breathlessly I recited it to him.

"Now I can track you down, day or night. All right. See you Saturday."

I hung up and did a little spin on my worn rug. Having his arms wrapped around me had felt incredible. What would it be like to kiss him . . . to touch his chest? It had been months since I'd made love with anyone—not that my sleepover with Eric even fit that description. I had a feeling Jack would be amazing, if we ever got to that point.

I put on my favorite Floor ballad and sat in the open window looking out at the taxi lights coming on further down Broome. I didn't want to get my hopes up too much, but this was the kind of Cinderella story you read about in New York; somebody from nowhere suddenly met someone famous, and all their dreams came true. I just hoped I'd have a chance to really connect with Jack before the pumpkin imploded and all the mice scattered. *Enjoy it while you can,* I told myself. *And whatever happens, don't set yourself up for another heartbreak.*

Chapter 7

WELCOME TO
THE WORKING WEEK

I was so distracted the next day, I made about a zillion typos. As I was redoing a letter for the third time, Harvey came into my cramped office.

"How's the Collins novel coming along?"

"I've been whacking away, but it's slow going."

"Well, keep at it. We can't miss our call-to-print." His gaze dropped to my chest, and I hunched my shoulders to slacken my blouse. "Tell you what. Why don't I take you out for a drink Sunday? A reward for all the extra editing."

Ugh. He'd mentioned several times that his wife took their kids to her father's Park Avenue townhouse for dinner on Sundays. "That's my laundry night," I said.

Harvey's schedule was packed with meetings on Tuesday, so

he had no time to harass me. On his way out to his midday boozathon, he stopped by my desk.

"I'm taking an agent to the Four Seasons," he said, unfolding his sunglasses. "Don't wait up."

I just rolled my eyes. After he left I browsed through the *Post*, my secret vice. I always kept it tucked inside the *New York Times* to avoid comment from my highbrow colleagues. An item on Page Six caught my eye; former sitcom actress Isabel Reed was up for a role in a new big-budget film after several years below the radar. The last line mentioned that she lived in the Chelsea Hotel in Manhattan, and was working on a memoir.

When I was growing up, Isabel Reed starred in my absolute favorite TV show about a schoolteacher who sang the lessons to her kids. I'd never missed an episode, and the theme song was wired into my subconscious. *I wonder who her literary agent is . . . probably her book has already been sold.* Harvey's words echoed in my mind: *Come up with your own ideas . . .* Maybe it was worth spending ten minutes trying to track her down, once I got back from my own lunch date.

Vicky and I always met at a diner halfway between our offices. Today she looked very professional in a conservative gray suit. "I have to get back to the office in an hour. We're having a goodbye toast to Daphne at three," she said as I slid into the booth.

Vicky had introduced me to the editor-in-chief's assistant at her company. "She's leaving?"

"Yes, it's pretty horrible. Bill called her into his office and said that because she hasn't acquired anything, she should start looking for a new job since he can't promote her. But everything's shut up tight as a bad clam with this recession. He's already given her position to the sales director's nephew, or else you could have tried out for it."

My stomach sank. "The minute there's an opening, it always gets filled by someone with inside connections. I've been to three 'informational interviews' in the last six months, but the only information is that they aren't hiring." I tried to flag the waitress, but she ignored me and kept talking to the busboy.

Vicky frowned. "I don't see how they think you can just magically acquire a book if you don't have an expense account to lunch the agents. That's the way to get them to send you projects, right?"

"That's pretty much it. You're supposed to talk yourself up during the meal. I feel so awful for Daphne. What is she going to do?" This was just the kind of fate I dreaded. It was entirely possible to grind away for years and then be told you'd reached a dead-end.

"She's moving back to St. Louis, where she's from. She's going to stay with her parents while she figures things out."

"God, that's depressing. Sometimes it seems like I'll never make it here. It's so hard to get ahead."

"I know. If you stay an assistant for more than two years, you get typecast as just a secretary. And editorial seems worse than the other departments; I guess because there's such a glut of you English majors," Vicky commented.

"If I don't acquire a book soon, Harvey will probably fire me too," I said glumly. I waved at the waitress again.

"That's not going to happen. He'd be lost without you to do all his work." She glanced at the laminated menu. "So I hear you're going to a party with Jack next Saturday."

"I was going to tell you if you hadn't been too busy to return my call."

"I'm in the middle of booking a tour. Every time I think I've got the schedule nailed down, the author changes it."

"I'm just kidding, I know you're busy. Is Sammy taking you to this party? It's for a guy who plays with the band; one of the backup players I guess." She and Sammy had been hot and heavy ever since they'd first gotten together. Vicky was blasé about it, saying she was just going to enjoy the sex, free pot, and booze while it lasted.

"Sammy said he wasn't invited. I think the birthday boy has a beef with him over something. Probably a good thing for you to be alone with Jack."

"I was stunned when he asked me. Especially after what I did." The waitress finally took our orders, and I told Vicky about my beer-spilling episode.

"Geez, Julia. Way to arouse the guy."

"I know. But he was a good sport about it. He seemed to think it was funny."

"Sammy did say Jack likes your sense of humor. And the fact that you don't act too impressed. So maybe you're the woman of the moment," she said as our food arrived.

"He must have women coming out of his ears—or whatever body part they'd be crawling out of. By the way, I'm not mentioning Jack to anyone. Saturday will probably be the last time I ever see him."

She gave me a sarcastic glance. "I promise I won't tell anyone a famous rock musician wants to take you out. I mean, Jesus, how embarrassing is that." She shook the catsup bottle a few times to get it going, and the liquid erupted in a spreading puddle.

"That's a lot of catsup," I observed.

"It's okay, our President says it's a vegetable."

We split the bill and went out onto the white-hot sidewalk. Vicky frowned at my second-hand suit. "You'll need to wear something other than your usual gear. Come over Saturday and pick out one of my party dresses. I have an outfit that'll remind him he wants to do you."

Vicky's story about Daphne made me dread becoming another unemployment statistic. The minute I got back to the office, I called the Chelsea Hotel and asked for Isabel Reed. A sleepy-sounding voice at the front desk told me he'd take a message. I repeated my number twice and spelled out the company's name. Just as I was packing up to leave, the phone rang.

"Julia Nash?"

"Yes, this is Julia."

"I'm Isabel Reed. Did you call me?"

I started to get excited. Her voice sounded vaguely like I remembered from the show.

"Yes! I did. I saw that you were writing a memoir. I wondered if you had a literary agent."

Isabel sighed into the phone. "I barely have an acting agent, much less a literary one. Although maybe that will change if I get this part in the movie."

That was good news; if she had an agent, he'd probably skip over me and send the manuscript straight to Harvey. "I was a huge fan of your show. I'd love to see whatever you've written. I work with the publisher here." I figured I shouldn't start off by saying I was just an assistant.

"Well, there isn't much yet, but I can give you what I've got. I'm out of town next week for the audition, but I'll call you when I get back."

"That would be great! I look forward to meeting you."

I hung up, my mind buzzing. Maybe I'd finally hit upon something that even Harvey couldn't dismiss.

I had a lilt in my step as I walked home, excited about Isabel's call and still pinching myself that I would see Jack on Saturday. He was much easier to talk to than I would have thought. And beneath the cool persona, he struck me as very intelligent. But my god, he was a rock star, and I was, well . . . a glorified typist. Or at least a work-in-progress. I'd puzzled over his interest in me until I gave myself a splitting headache. Surely there was a line of models and starlets waiting their turn—but could he be tired of those types? I guessed I'd just go with it and see where things led.

As I was switching off my lamp, the phone rang. "Were you going to call me this week?" came my mother's two-pack-a-day voice.

"Sorry, I was really busy. Did you just get in?"

"Yeah, I was down at Buck's for a while. When are you coming home? I haven't seen you since Christmas. You can't be—" she coughed— "that busy."

"I'm not sure. I have a lot of deadlines coming up." Immediately I felt guilty; I knew I needed to pay her a visit. "Maybe I can get there in August when it slows down."

"This guy I know from the bar drives a truck up to New Jersey every so often. I told him I might hitch a ride with him and come see you. Lately the weekends have been pretty quiet around here."

"I imagine you've had more going on than me," I said, trying to discourage her. Dot's personality was way too big for my little loft. "What's happening at the store?"

"I finally asked Erwin for a raise, but he's hemming and hawing, the skinflint. This week he's got Marie and me double-checking the inventory. Oh, by the way, her cousin did wind up getting back with that guy."

I couldn't recall which cousin this was; the extended families of her friends tended to coagulate in my mind. "I hope that goes fast for you. I'd better turn in; I'll talk to you soon."

"I'll be at Buck's again tomorrow night, so don't call until after ten." She hung up. I wondered how much my mother was drinking these days. After Dad left, she'd gone on some real benders. I remembered struggling with algebra homework back in high school, forcing myself not to call the bar because it annoyed her. One night I'd picked up the phone at twelve, then cradled it. By two a.m., I'd resolved to call in half an hour if she didn't show. Finally I heard her Dodge Dart roll up the driveway at quarter to three. I ran out into the freezing February darkness, clutching my denim jacket over my gown. My mother was tilting sideways in the front seat, fumbling for something on the floor mat.

"Dropped my smokes," she mumbled. What remained of her lipstick was smeared, and her eye shadow had bled to her cheek. Her shoulder-length shag, an unnatural blonde with coppery highlights, was flattened against her face. I crouched and picked up her cigarettes from the gritty mat. "Come on, let's go in," I said, shivering.

Later as I tried to get to sleep, I wondered if my Dad was going to come back for me. Ever since he'd left in September,

I'd envisioned him pulling up to the house, saying, "I'm sorry, sweetheart, I had to get myself situated. Go pack your things." At first I'd given him a deadline of Christmas, but when the holidays came and went with no phone call, I'd decided he just needed to get set up wherever he'd landed. Now I wondered if he was ever going to show.

I blamed Dot one hundred percent for the destruction of our family. And after all that, her affair with her manager had only lasted six weeks, and then she'd had to quit because it was too awkward to keep working together. To my mind, she almost deserved having to worry so much over paying the bills. And I loathed the way she chased after men. The older I got, the more I picked up on the desperation in her voice when she talked to them on the phone.

That night, I'd turned my face to the wall and watched the shifting shadows from the occasional passing headlights. In the morning, I dragged myself out of bed to call my mother's new boss at the convenience store to tell him that, yet again, she was feeling "fluish" and wouldn't be in today. I knew it was only a matter of weeks before she got fired.

Harvey stopped in my doorway. "I have someone for you to meet," he said. "This is Briar Greene. She's coming from *TownTalk* magazine to join us in editorial."

A smug-looking girl about my age stood beside him, surveying me with a self-assured smile. Wearing a stylish suit that showed a lot of leg, she gave me a dismissive glance. "I majored in Lit at Princeton, so I always wanted to get into books," she said in a boarding school lockjaw.

"Julia's also an assistant editor. She can show you where the bodies are buried," Harvey said. "I expect great things of Briar. She has an incredible rolodex from her year at the magazine."

With that, he led her down the hall toward publicity. I stared at the piles of paper on my desk, shaken by the directly competing hire. With Briar sharing my position, we'd both be vying for the next rung on the ladder. *This is how he repays me after all the grunt work I've done for him?* I thought miserably.

Meredith poked her head in. "Did you meet the new person?"

"I just did. She let me know within the first sixty seconds that she'd gone to Princeton."

Meredith shut the door behind her. "Harvey's always impressed with the fancy schools. I don't see why he needs anyone else; you keep on top of everything."

"He mentioned her amazing rolodex," I said dispiritedly. "I'm really in shock. Is he trying to edge me out?" A chill ran down my spine as I thought of Daphne's firing.

"I suppose he thinks she has some great contacts from being at *TownTalk*." Meredith gave me a motherly pat. "But she doesn't look like the type to work her fingers to the bone, and that's the only way to get ahead. If it doesn't pan out for her here, she can always take her Princeton degree back to magazines, where it's more glamorous."

Chapter 8

THE GIRL CAN'T HELP IT

All Saturday, my nerves were jangling. I had stopped by Vicky's that afternoon, and her clingy black party dress was now hanging from a nail on my wall. Just looking at it made me even more jittery.

By ten I had my makeup on and was bopping around to Little Feat in my jeans. Jack called to say he'd be there soon. There was a lot of noise in the background, so I assumed he was still at the studio and didn't rush to put on the dress. Shortly thereafter I heard someone on the street. I went to the window and stuck my head out. It was Jack, peering up at me from below.

"Rapunzel! Throw down your key."

I laughed. "I'll be there in a second."

" 'Punzel! Toss it down."

Why didn't I finish getting ready? I hope he doesn't think my place is pathetic. I stuffed my key in the sock and threw it to him, then I opened my door and listened to him tromping up the steps.

"Whew, that's some climb," Jack said, handing me the sock. He wore a tawny jacket over a silky peach-colored shirt and tight black pants that accentuated the muscles in his thighs. His shirt was half-unbuttoned, and his dark hair was sticking up all over. *He looks amazing,* I thought as he took off his jacket and laid it on my chair. *I haven't been this nervous since I presented my thesis to a roomful of professors. Come to think of it, that doesn't even compare.*

"How are you, Miss Julia?" Jack said, smiling at me.

"I'm fine. Do you want a beer? I just have to get dressed." I bounced up and down on the balls of my feet to release a little tension.

"Sure, I'll take a beer. It's warm in here; you don't have your AC on?"

"I don't have air conditioning. I get a good cross-breeze from the windows."

I meant for him to sit on my couch, but he followed me to my fridge. "I see you have your books and records." He indicated my wooden crates stacked on top of each other. I handed him a bottle, and he went past me to the back of the room. "These your outfits?" he asked, inspecting my clothes hanging there.

"This place didn't come with a closet, so I just put a few nails in the wall. Maybe not the best decorating move."

He swung over to my futon, which was covered with piles of paper. "What's all this?"

"That's Timothy Collins's book. I'm trying to move things around; it helps to separate the chapters. I don't have a table big enough."

"You pick all that up every night?"

"Once in a while I just sleep on the couch." *Nice one, Julia. You sound like some lonely spinster.*

Jack went to the sofa and pushed down on a cushion. "You've got a few springs poking up."

"I'm used to it. Do you want to sit there and I'll get changed?"

Jack sat and took a gulp of beer. "Hey, did you lose my number?"

"Oh no, I still have it."

"Show me where you wrote it in your little black book."

I fetched my address book and showed him the scrap of paper he'd given me. "See, it's right here in front."

"This could fall out. I'm going to write it in permanent. D'you have a pen?"

Thinking this was a good sign, I handed him one. "I'm going to get my dress on. I'll just be a minute." I went into my cramped bathroom, quickly stripped, and stepped into the beaded sheath. I caught a glimpse in the mirror; my cheeks flushed with excitement, my eyes a deeper blue than usual, the pale curve of my breasts rising and falling above the shimmering dark fabric. My hands were trembling so much, I had trouble doing up the zipper. As I struggled with it, Jack called out, "Who's George?"

So now he was poking around in my addresses. "Friend of mine. Really great guy. Gay."

"Hmm." I heard pages rapidly riffling. "Ted?"

"Friend from college." Quickly I slipped on my heels.

"Jane?"

Laughing, I walked out of the bathroom. "Friend from publishing. You really are kind of nosy, you know."

"You're only just now finding that out?" Jack mused, turning another page. He looked up at me and rose from the sofa with an odd expression on his face.

Oh no, maybe the dress is all wrong. "Is this okay?" I asked.

"Verrry okay," he replied after a moment's pause. "Better than okay." He went to get his jacket and gazed out the window as he put it on. "Nice view." For a minute he stared at the sooty rooftop across the street, then turned and held out the notebook. "Here, I've put my number in ink. Non-erasable."

I laid it on the table. "All right, I guess we're all set. Can you keep my key? My backpack doesn't quite go with the dress."

"Sure, I'll hold onto your key. Anytime."

I followed him downstairs, my knees practically knocking. *I'm going to a party with Jack Kipling of the Floor. I hope he can't tell how jumpy I am—but he must be used to girls going into shock.*

Rick opened the back door of the car. Jack turned, dark eyes sparking, and gestured me in with a flourish.

"Come into my lair," he said, his accent heavy on "lair." "Enter at your own risk." He smiled, and I shivered as I slid across the leather seat.

Jack climbed in beside me and we took off. I was conscious of my bare legs in the short dress, right next to his rangy limbs in the black pants. *Maybe I should have worn hose.* I gave my hem a tug, then realized I'd just exposed a good inch of cleavage. Hastily I yanked up the neckline. I glanced at Jack, who seemed to quickly erase a grin.

He crossed his arms, his shoulder touching mine. "So what did you do last night, more editing?"

"I went to a movie with my friend Erin. This is a big weekend for me; I don't always go out two nights in a row."

Jack gave me an appraising look. "You live kind of a quiet life for someone your age. You're what, twenty-three?"

I wondered how old he was; I assumed in his early thirties. "Twenty-four. Not that quiet really. Maybe compared to you."

"My life isn't that thrilling these days. I've had to mend my ways a bit in recent years; too much burning the wick at both ends. I had a couple of close calls a while back. But when I was twenty-four . . ." He shook his head. "Everything came on so fast, I kind of insulated myself with various chemicals for a while. You seem so well-behaved, though. What do you do to cut loose?"

"Dancing, I guess. Sorry I don't have anything more scintillating to offer."

"Oh, I wouldn't put it that way." He gave my dress-front a quick glance. "You know what, a necklace would go nice with that. Here," he said, reaching for the thin chain with the lightning bolt. He pulled it over his head. "Put this on."

"Oh, no, I might lose it."

But Jack put the chain over my head and then reached around to lift my hair in back. His warm hand brushed the nape of my neck. A wave of heat spread from my chest up to my collarbone.

"There. You won't lose it. It looks good on you." His face was so close to mine, I could see two silky eyelashes twisted together. I was suddenly aware that my lips had parted. Clamping them shut, I swallowed hard.

Rick stopped the car in front of a brick townhouse. "Here we are."

Jack reached over me to open the door. "After you."

"I never asked whose birthday it is," I said as we went inside. Music was booming from an upper floor.

"Patrick's. We'll just make an appearance; we don't have to stay long."

Oh my god, it's Patrick's *party? Maybe I can just blend into the wallpaper.*

I followed Jack up the stairs to a spacious loft packed with people, stereo blasting. Immediately he was surrounded by a group of men and women who seemed ready to pounce on him. He shouted at them over the noise for a minute, and then looked around for me. "What would you like? There's champagne if you want."

I nodded and Jack snagged a couple of flutes from a passing waiter. "Cheers," he said as we touched glasses. I could feel people's eyes on me from all over the room, checking out the new girl Jack had brought with him. It was a weird sensation, like one of those dreams where you're undressed in public. A man in a suit came over, put his arm around Jack's neck and murmured something. "I have to speak to these record company flacks for a minute," Jack said.

He left with the guy, and I decided to find a quiet corner to observe the scenery. I wove through a dancing group of willowy girls who had to be models. The tallest ones seemed to be with short, balding men. I parked myself by a window with a view of the winking downtown skyline. *No one is noticing me now*, I thought with relief. *I can just hang out here and take it all in.*

Two of the model types stopped in front of me.

"You came with Jack, didn't you?" the first one said in an unfriendly tone.

"Yes. I'm Julia." I smiled, but she didn't.

"I see you're wearing his necklace. He never takes that off.

Remember when it broke in the pool and Nicole had to spend a half-hour diving for it?" she asked her friend. They laughed at their little in-joke.

"Sounds like I should take a crash scuba course," I said uneasily.

"Good luck to you," she said, implying I'd need it. They glared at me and continued toward the bar.

Well, that was unpleasant. Hopefully Jack will come find me soon, so I can avoid more confrontations with his bitchy ex-girl-friends. I squeezed past an animated group sitting at a table crosshatched with lines of cocaine, and went to admire an unframed Warhol.

Hearing a British accent, I turned to see Patrick standing nearby. My first impression was that he was a miniature version of himself; he was only about my height, with boyishly narrow hips. His fashionably feathered blond hair and turquoise shirt brought out his blue-green eyes. He and the guy next to him seemed to be scrutinizing me. Patrick gestured with his cigarette and commented, "Jack's new piece." His lips pressed into his signature pout. "He abandon you already?"

I decided to ignore that. "Happy birthday. I'm Julia."

Patrick didn't hold out his hand, so I didn't extend mine. "It's not my birthday yet, but they wanted to throw me a party 'coz I'll be out of the country." He looked around the room, seeming bored.

"Happy party, then."

Patrick took a long pull on his cigarette. "I hear you're a secretary somewhere." He opened his eyes wide. "And you're a big reader, or something," he added, blowing smoke toward me.

"Yes, I like to read."

"Oh really. What kinds of things?" he asked, scanning the room.

"All kinds."

"Like what?" he prodded.

I couldn't imagine why he wanted to know. I threw out "Proust," although I felt like saying "the Sunday comics".

"I never got past the madeleines. *Lis-tu en francais?*" he asked.

"No, I read it in English. My French isn't good enough."

"*Mais tu comprends ce que je dis.*"

"I can speak it, but reading Proust in *la langue* is beyond me."

"Ah, I see." Patrick puffed on his smoke. "Well, enjoy yourself," he said with a little smile before he moved on.

I decided to look for Jack; I'd had enough of this snarky crowd, particularly his world-famous bandmate who felt the need to be rude to a mere publishing assistant. Easing my way through a scrum of laughing women, I spotted Jack at the far side of the room. I touched his elbow as he was about to be enveloped in another group.

"There you are," he said. "I was looking for you. I got stuck with those guys flapping their traps about how they're gonna flog our new album."

"It was fun watching everyone. What a turnout."

It sounded like he said "Bunch of assholes," but I couldn't be sure with the din. The music switched to a reggae tune, and more people started dancing. I shifted my feet to the lilting rhythm.

"Want to dance?" Jack asked. When I nodded, he led me to a less crowded spot.

At first I was a little restrained, but then the song worked its magic. Jack's dark gaze stayed on me as he moved, looking consummately cool with his choppily layered hair and sensuously rocking hips. People kept coming up to talk to him, but his eyes tracked me as he carried on his conversations. Two slinky girls in minis came up on either side of him and wrapped their arms around his waist.

"Patrick's blow just ran out. You've got some, don't you?" the brunette said. She plunged her hand into his front pocket and felt for more than his change.

"I left mine at home," Jack said, smiling at her.

"Sure you did." The second one stuck her tongue in his ear and gave it a big lick. "Share it next time, then we'll all get to play."

They wandered off to accost a bearded guy in a suit. *Of course Jack gets hit up everywhere he goes; just another reason to be careful*, I told myself. When a dreadlocked brother put his arm around Jack's shoulders, I shut my eyes and lost myself in the pulsing drums. The song ended and a slow number began. Jack was smiling at me, holding out his arms.

"Shall we?" he said. I threaded my fingers in his, and he clasped my waist as I rested my hand on his shoulder. My heart was hammering as I met his intense gaze; being held this close in his arms made me dizzy.

"Where'd you learn to move like that?" he asked as we swayed to the song. "You don't dance like a white chick from the sticks."

"Once in a while us white chicks can get our groove on."

Jack nodded and drew me closer. I could hardly breathe for the sensation of his hand on my waist, our chests lightly brushing, his body heat warming me. Every single place he was touching me created sparks. I raised my eyes to his, so turned on I was light-headed.

Suddenly the music stopped and people started clapping. Jack turned to see what was happening; I was so disappointed our slow dance had to end. A gargantuan cake was pushed into the room on a wheeled table. As the crowd started singing happy birthday, a woman and man, each wearing only a g-string, burst through the middle and started licking icing off one another's bodies.

"Time to split," Jack said, taking my elbow. "This is only going to go downhill from here."

It felt good to be out in the soft summer night. A queue of stretch limousines was parked all the way down the block, so we walked until we found Rick.

"Mary Jo made a reservation at Odeon," Jack said, picking up a pair of sunglasses from the seat. "Did you have an okay time? I lost sight of you there for a while."

I didn't want him to think he had to babysit me. "It was interesting. I noticed a high toupee-to-heel ratio."

"What's that?"

"The balder the guy, the taller the girl. Or the more made-up and manicured."

Jack laughed. "You're ruining me for nail polish, you know."

"What do you mean?"

He took my hand and held it up, indicating my unvarnished nails. "I used to like it. But now when I see it on women, it seems kind of fussy."

An image of my mother's many vials of polish came to mind, haphazardly spread around her dressing table, the dried spillage sloppily chipping off the sides. "I never thought it looked good on me."

"You look nice natural." Jack kept my hand in his, resting on his thigh. Slowly he traced my palm with his thumb and smiled at me. So many sensations were darting through my body, I felt faint. *Get a grip*, I told myself. I tried to focus on the back of Rick's head.

Rick pulled up at the restaurant and Jack put on his shades. The maitre d' motioned us to the front of the line—"Good to see you again, Mr. Kipling"—and ushered us to a burgundy banquette. The room had a cozy deco feel, circular hanging lamps dispensing a warm glow. The staff seemed to have it down to a drill; get him in fast before people recognized him.

"Enjoy your dinner," the maitre d' said, handing us menus. Jack didn't even glance at his. "I always get the filet mignon," he said to me.

A waiter approached with a bottle of champagne, and Jack tapped his glass against mine. "To getting out of that place in one piece. Somebody said you were talking to Patrick."

"He came up to me and I wished him happy birthday. Then he informed me that it wasn't really his birthday."

"That's Patrick, always got to be correcting people."

"I think he was trying to trip me up speaking French." I took a few deep gulps of champagne, which was even more nose-tickling than the kind at the party.

"He thinks he's so suave with his languages." Jack looked miffed.

"Well, he speaks it like a prissy schoolgirl."

Jack burst out laughing. "I'm gonna tell the guys."

"Oh no, please don't tell anyone I said that." I could just

imagine if Patrick got wind of it; he'd dislike me even more than he already seemed to.

"Just Sammy, then; he'd get a kick out of it."

I toyed with my butter knife. "Why wasn't Sammy invited tonight?"

"Patrick's got his knickers in a twist about something." Jack drained his glass and poured more for us both. "Where did you learn French? Did you spend time over there?"

"I had a great teacher in college, Proffe Deborah. She was so elegant; she had these chic red glasses, and every day she wore a silk dress with high heels."

"Seems like you were impressed," Jack commented.

"I was infatuated with her. I wanted to *be* her. She was . . . everything my mother wasn't. I was heartbroken when she and her husband moved to Cleveland. Anyway, that's how I learned French."

I took a bite of my flounder as Jack refilled our flutes. The champagne was having a relaxing effect; I'd never known it was such a nice fizzy drink.

"Maybe you can teach me some. Languages always came hard to me." Jack looked at me with lowered lids, his dark eyelashes brushing his cheek. I lost my train of thought for a minute, thinking how nice it would be to trace those lines on either side of his mouth with my finger. Or my tongue.

"In fact, why don't you pay me a compliment in French? It always sounds so sensual." He raised his eyebrow suggestively.

"Okay, but I'm not going to translate it."

"Fine, I just want to hear how it sounds."

Feeling a little tipsy, I gazed at his eyes that I could so easily melt into. A line from one of my favorite poems by Aragon came to me: Your eyes are so deep that leaning down to drink to them, I saw all mirrored suns repair.

"*Tes yeux sont si profonds qu'en me penchant pour boire. J'ai vu tous les soleils y venir se mirer.*"

A slow smile spread across his face. "*Merci beaucoup*," he said. "I'll take that."

"You liar!" My face was burning. "You said you didn't speak French!"

"All I said was, languages don't come easily to me. Hey." He touched my arm. "Don't be embarrassed. I didn't get all of it, just that my eyes look like malted milkballs in a bowlful of milk."

"You tricked me." I picked at my napkin.

"That was one of the nicest things anyone's ever told me. Especially since you didn't think I'd get it."

"All right, I guess." I took a gulp from my flute. "It's a line from a poem I like. Consider it the champagne talking."

"I'll have to give you champagne more often." Jack sat forward, arm on the table. "I know you wouldn't have said it if you thought I understood. Julia," he said, looking me in the eyes, "you have no idea how sick I get of people fawning and flattering; all the parasites wanting a piece of me. A lot of guys'll use you worse than women, even. You think someone's your friend, then it turns out they just wanted something off you—introduce them to the head of a record company, promise to act in the script they're writing, get them in with a model. It barely even bothers me anymore. Most girls would've had me take them shopping before we went out tonight. But you don't want anything, do you?"

Flushing under his gaze, I picked up my glass and watched the bubbles rising to the top. "I like to make my own way. I don't want to be dependent on anyone."

"You're scrappy. Me too; I was always like that. Had to be."

The waiter came and Jack signed for the bill. "They'll send it to Mary Jo," he explained when they took it without a credit card. He left some cash for the server and we rushed past the bar crowd to the car. I tried to decide which of the double back doors I should step into before Jack helped me in.

"Where to?" Rick said.

"Want to sit by the river for a while, get some fresh air?" Jack asked.

"Sure." I hoped it wasn't obvious how sozzled I was.

Rick drove over to the West Side Highway and we found a bench in an area that seemed entirely deserted. A salty funk came off the river, not at all unpleasant. The moon was a golden smattering in the water; I could hear waves lipping the pilings. We sat in silence for a minute, looking at the distant lights of Hoboken. Jack turned to face me, elbow on the back of the bench. The breeze lifted his hair off his forehead, eyes glowing dark beneath his expressive brows. "You've been in New York, what, a year for school and then a year working?"

I wondered why he was asking. "Yes. I plan on staying put."

"You seem like . . . you're not attached. To anyone," Jack said, looking directly at me.

"N-no," I stammered, disconcerted by the intensity of his gaze. "I'm not with anyone right now."

"Who was Art? I saw his name crossed out in your address book. Looked like you stabbed it a few times with your pen."

"Oh, he . . ." I hesitated. "I went out with him last year."

"Serious boyfriend?"

"For a while. He was a professor in the English department. He was separated from his wife, but then they got back together, and that was that." I gazed out over the water. The rippling of the waves created a similar floating sensation in my head. *God, why of all nights did I have to get wasted?*

"Hmm. Nobody else since?"

"No."

"Took you a while to get over him?"

"Yes."

"Over him now?"

My pulse gave a leap. I looked at Jack's thick, tousled hair and the lines at the side of his mouth, and nodded.

"Good enough. Any questions for me?"

Nicole the necklace-diver came to mind . . . *Nah, he's probably been with so many women, he's lost track of 'em all.* "No questions."

"All right then," Jack said. He leaned toward me and touched my hair. My heart started thumping wildly. Then there was the sound of heels tapping unevenly on the sidewalk. Into the light of the streetlamp lurched a figure over six feet tall. She wore a sequined blue evening gown with a ripped shoulder, pendant earrings, and garish eye shadow. Lipstick was smeared sadly across a smudge of stubble on her chin.

"Well hell-o!" she trilled. "Two young lovers out taking the air."

"Hello darlin'," Jack said, removing his arm from the bench.

"I'm Pamela. You know," she said, swaying on her heels, "you remind me of somebody. That guitar player. Anybody ever tell you, you look like him?"

"I know the one. You think I take after that ugly cat?"

"Actually you're muuuch better looking," she slurred. "Well, toodle-oo. I'm meeting someone myself."

"Have a good one," Jack said as she sashayed down the walkway. "I guess this spot is pretty public. Want to go?"

I nodded, then had to hold my head perfectly still to subdue the spinning I'd set off. Instead of waking me up, the night air had the opposite effect; I was even more out of it than before. I stumbled on a pothole going to the car, and Jack took my elbow. We were on my block in minutes. Unsteadily I walked to the door.

"Oh, I have your key." He felt in his pocket and produced it. "Here you go," he said, holding onto my hand for a second. Between the drink and my attraction, his touch made me weak at the knees.

"Thank you for dinner. And the jewelry loan." Woozily I reached for the necklace.

"You're the jumpiest girl I ever saw about wearing somebody's chain. Keep it for a while; it looks nice on you."

In my groggy state I didn't want to risk losing it. I started to pull the chain over my head. It came to a stop, trapped in my hair.

"Hang on." Jack came closer and began undoing the gnarl at my collarbone, his gaze lowered to the knot. I held still, my breath coming fast under his touch. Jack glanced up and his dark eyes locked on mine. The chain dropped to my chest. Warm hands slipped around my waist, and I closed my eyes as he parted my lips. His tongue aroused me so much, I felt like I was melting inside. He kissed me again, our hips pressed together, molding the length of his body to mine. His lips caressed my neck, tingling my skin. "I could do this all night," he murmured into my hair.

I was so turned on. I was so dizzy . . .

God, I was drunk.

"Jack," I gasped as his lips moved on me. "I think . . . I drank way too much champagne."

He pulled away, hands still gripping my waist. "You sure?"

"I'm sorry." My eyes were almost crossing.

"It happens." He raised an eyebrow. "I've been in that condition a time or two myself."

"Can you take your necklace so I don't lose it?"

Jack lifted the chain and put it over his head. "Will you be okay walking up?"

"I'm fine . . . so sorry." I stumbled up the stairs before I could change my mind.

I didn't get out of bed until nine; I'd had a restless night. Every time a truck rumbled by, I awoke remembering Jack's warm hands on me, his seductive tongue, his lips moving down my neck. *I wish I'd brought him upstairs instead of idiotically getting trashed on champagne. Hopefully he'll call me soon, so we can pick up where we left off. I can't wait to kiss him again—and again and again.*

As I popped a slice of bread in my dysfunctional toaster, an unwelcome memory smacked my pounding head. Art and I had been to see an exhibit of Robert Frank films at the Whitney last fall. Snuggling in the cab on the way downtown, he'd whispered the words in my ear. My chest welled up with happiness; I'd been hoping he felt the way I did.

"I love you too," I said, and we kissed.

The very next week, he informed me that he was getting back together with Phoebe. I staggered back to my apartment in a daze. Naively I'd thought that someone wouldn't say they loved you unless they really meant it.

A scorching smell reminded me I'd forgotten to watch my toast. Holding the charred remains, I thought of the girls groping Jack at the party.

I hope I won't get burned this time around.

Chapter 9

CAREER OPPORTUNITIES

>=<

"Where do you go for lunches in this neighborhood?" Briar stood in my doorway, hand on the hip of her chic black dress.

"There's a good diner a couple blocks up. And a pizza place on the corner."

"I don't mean a diner. Where do you take literary agents?" Seeing my surprise, she smirked. "Never mind, I'll ask Kate."

Reeling, I went to see Meredith. She put down her watering can. "What's up?"

I slumped against the doorframe. "Harvey's given Briar an expense account. She just asked where I lunched agents—as if I've ever been allowed to take anyone out."

Meredith frowned. "What is he thinking? She's never edited anything other than her own resume."

"It's tantamount to promoting her. She'll be in, and I'll be out." My voice wobbled.

Meredith sat at her desk. "I'm sure she's good at chatting them up, but that doesn't mean she knows how to cobble together a book."

"I really need to acquire something, fast. There's one project I'm pursuing that has potential, I think. I read that Isabel Reed is writing a memoir. Remember the Singing Schoolteacher? I'm meeting her at the Chelsea Hotel on Thursday to talk about it."

"Julia, that's fantastic! I used to love her show. That's just the kind of thing we need for the list. If you bring it in, Briar won't have a chance of upstaging you. When you get the manuscript let me read it too, so I can help you talk it up."

That calmed me down a little. "Thanks, I really appreciate it. I mentioned it to Harvey the other day, but he didn't seem too intrigued. He said Isabel was passé."

"He may take a little convincing, but we can work on that. I hate to ask, but how's the Timothy Collins novel coming along?"

"I've been plugging away at it, but I haven't gotten as far as I'd wanted."

Something in my tone must have clued her in. "New extra-curricular activity?" she asked with a knowing grin.

I hesitated for a moment. "I met a guy recently that I like a lot, but I'm not sure where it's going."

"Well, I hope it works out. You know, I was married at twenty-two, and then divorced by twenty-six. The whole thing was a mistake; we were just too young. But I have to say, I never dreamed I'd be thirty-five and alone," Meredith said thoughtfully. "Time can really get away from you."

"Was there anyone serious after your marriage?" Meredith always seemed so self-contained; I was flattered that she was opening up to me.

"Oh, I went out with various people, but nobody long-term. Then the dates sort of dried up a few years ago. I see friends and keep busy, but sometimes I wonder if I'll ever be in a relationship again." She took off her half-rims and considered me. "If you think this guy is somebody special, then I wouldn't let it slip away. It's important to focus on your career, but we workaholics have to remember there's another side to life."

"I appreciate that."

"And you have to promise me that if I wind up as one of those publishing women living alone in a smelly apartment with six cats, you'll roust me out once in a while."

"I don't think that's even a remote possibility," I assured her.

I was reliving Jack's kiss yet again Tuesday night when the phone rang. Telling myself *It's not him*, I forced myself to walk over slowly.

"I hope I didn't pull out too much of your hair the other night."

I sat down before my knees buckled. "It's starting to grow back. By next spring it should be all filled in."

Jack laughed. "I didn't think I did that much damage." His accent had to be the sexiest on the planet.

"I was exaggerating; you're good at untangling necklaces. Sorry I was such a party-pooper."

"'s all right. I went back and partied at Patrick's."

I'll bet you did, I thought, picturing all those girls. We both waited for a beat.

"Are you doing anything Friday? I thought I'd stop by your place first, and we could get dinner."

"That would be great! I mean . . . sure. I'm free."

"See you then."

For a few minutes I sat there in a dreamy haze. Then I got a Floor album from my wooden crate and blasted it, singing along and dancing around the room. Only when my downstairs neighbor called did I lower the volume and collapse on the couch. I was going to see him in three days—actually if he came by at seven, that would be two days and . . . 21 ½ hours. Or seventy hours altogether, if you rounded it up.

How was I going to make it through *seventy hours* until I saw him again?

As I was checking the photo captions in a bird-watching guide, Harvey buzzed me on the intercom. I was dismayed to see Briar sitting in his office; I hated interrupting their tête-à-têtes.

"Freeman Fyfe just delivered his next opus. I want it ready for sales conference in November. Can you polish it up by then?" Harvey asked.

"I'm sure I can," I said, excited at the prospect. I had loved working with Freeman on his latest novel, which we were publishing in September. Although he was our biggest author, he was also one of the nicest. Whenever he called, he always took the time to ask how I was doing; he was a real class act. And I assumed editing Harvey's books gave me some points toward my merit badge.

Briar sat forward in her seat. "I'm a huge fan of his. I'd love to have a go at it."

"Great. You two can read it together and compare notes," Harvey said.

Briar gave me a triumphant smile. "I can't wait."

I snatched up the manuscript and took it to my overflowing bookshelf. I'd have to finish plowing through Collins before I could start on Freeman, which would be a treat. And I'd be damned if I was going to share it with that little snot.

Veering around two loudly arguing women in white hot pants and platform heels, I continued down 23rd Street for my appointment with Isabel Reed at the Chelsea. All my dreams of thriving in the city and moving up at work hinged on this one meeting—and whether she'd like me enough to entrust me with her memoir. In the lobby, a man at the front desk said he'd buzz her. He continued his conversation with a heavyset woman in a pink muumuu until I cleared my throat, where-upon he seemed to recall that I was waiting and told me to take the elevator to the fifth floor. Ghoulishly I wondered if that was where Sid murdered Nancy.

I went down the gloomy hallway and found the apartment. A voluptuous woman with bright blue eyes and curly auburn hair opened the door. She wore a low-cut silk blouse and flow-ing slacks in rich earthy hues. If I looked closely, I could see the resemblance to the perky TV teacher of yesteryear.

"Hello, Julia. Come on in. I've got some tea brewing." Inside, two cats immediately wound soft figure eights around my legs. "I hope you're not allergic."

"Oh no, I love cats. What are their names?"

"Dinah and Chess. Don't worry, he growls when he's happy," she said as the larger one gave a guttural rumble.

I sank into the plush sofa and told myself not to dwell on the fact that my entire future was hanging in the balance. As she went into her kitchen, I scratched the chin of the tabby and looked around. The room was bursting with potted plants, framed photographs, faded Persian carpets, and threadbare furniture, the cats having ripped through the upholstery of several chairs. Above the mantel a black and white blowup of the actress in her heyday beamed down at me. It was fascinating to finally see one of the apartments in the fabled Chelsea, a building I'd heard so many lurid tales about. Actually it looked similar to the Upper West Side apartments I'd been to; no used syringes or emaciated dead girlfriends lying about.

Isabel returned with mugs of tea and a pretty plate of little cakes. "I was glad to hear a publisher's interested in my book," she said. "Lately I've had time on my hands to work on it. Before this film role, my agent hadn't sent me a part to read for in months."

I decided not to mention that I wasn't exactly the publisher. "I think your memoir would have a really big audience; so many people were fans of the show. I never missed an episode, and I watched all the reruns too. How did your audition go?"

"I won't know unless I get a callback. I really need this part. My career's been pretty dormant the past few years." She sighed and stirred her tea.

"I'd love to read what you've written so far. Do you have an outline?" I edged forward on the cushy sofa and took a nibble of cake.

"Oh, I don't believe in outlines; I'm far too much of a free spirit. You'll see, once we start working together."

Isabel took a plant mister from a side table, spritzed a fern and then gave her own face a couple of squirts. Droplets drizzling down her cheeks, she gave me a sharp look. "You seem young to be handling my memoir. Have you edited anything else?"

Suddenly I felt very small and inexperienced. "I did just get out of school last year, but I dove right in. I worked on Freeman Fyfe's new book; it's coming out in September." I'd used Freeman as my calling card before with skeptical authors.

"I'm sure that will be a feather in your cap, as will mine," she commented. "Well, you look like you can understand passion. That's what my life story's about—passion, and the places it can take you." She folded her arms. "So you said you were a longtime fan."

Now for the sucking-up. I rotated my plate and took another bite as I concocted my reply. "The show's impact was huge; it inspired people to think more creatively about education," I said, inflating its importance in a way I hoped would flatter her. "And you were the reason it was such a gigantic hit. I used to love it when you turned the spelling lesson into a song. Your voice is so beautiful."

"Thank you. And yes, it was huge," Isabel said with a reminiscent smile. "I got letters from kids all over the world. And some surprisingly graphic ones from a number of daddies. I had lots of adventures leading up to it, too. I grew up in a tough Chicago neighborhood with my father and two brothers. My mother wasn't around." She handed me some loose pages. "I hope you aren't squeamish; I started sleeping with older men when I was fourteen. All that will be in the next section."

"I'll bet the public would enjoy anything you'd like to reveal." If she wanted to bare the seamier side of her life, I figured Harvey would be happy to help with the disrobing.

Isabel gave herself another blast with the mister. "You have to keep hydrated if you don't want to turn into an old hag," she said as beads of water dripped down her face.

"I don't think there's any danger of that. Thanks so much for the tea. I'll read this tonight and call you tomorrow, if that's okay." I unpinned Chess from my lap, and Isabel saw me to the door.

"When would you be planning to publish it? If I get this role, it would be great to have the book out in time for the film."

"First I'll have to present it to our editorial board to get the go-ahead. Then if it's approved, I'll be able to sign it up. But let me read what you've written, and we'll talk."

Walking back to the office, I was thrilled the meeting had gone so well and I had her pages in my hot little hands. I hoped Harvey would come around and see that this had commercial potential.

I sped through the chapter as soon as I got in. The raw material was interesting, but it wasn't in good enough shape to show to anyone. I guessed there was a reason most celebrities used a ghostwriter.

Meredith stopped in my doorway. "How did it go with Isabel?"

"I liked her a lot, and she gave me a chapter. That's the good news. The bad news is, it reads like a ten-year-old wrote it. In my excitement I kind of forgot she might need a ghost."

"Let me see a page." Meredith perused it through her half-rims. "Hmm. I'm afraid you're right."

"Is there any way to hook her up with a writer? I need to get it fixed up before Harvey sees it."

"She'd have to pay for it herself. Would she be willing to do that?"

I pictured Isabel's cat-shredded chairs. "I don't get the sense she's rolling in it. Her furniture was falling apart."

"Why don't you take a stab at it? Half the time you're rewriting anyway."

"That's a great idea. I'll give it a whack."

Invigorated by the need to outshine Briar, I took the pages home with me. It was slow going, but the thought of being passed over for Prickles spurred me on.

Chapter 10

COULD YOU BE LOVED

The next night I walked home, so glad it was Friday, I was levitating two feet above the sidewalk. Jack had said he wanted to come up to my place, and I was more than fine with that. To be honest, I was an ecstatic mix of nerves and excitement. I paced around until I heard him calling my name from the street and threw down the sock. As he clumped up the stairs I waited in my open doorway in jeans, a sheer sleeveless top and bare feet, having put on and rejected my leather skirt and heels. I had started to go braless, but that felt too slutty. *Hopefully my naked toes will remind him there's even more nakedness attached.*

"Hello, Julia," he said, smiling and handing me the key.

He was outrageously handsome in denim that hugged his thighs, worn almost bare in places, and a cowboy shirt with metal buttons. His face had a bit of dark stubble that made me want to rub my cheek against it. Instead, I just said hello and asked if he wanted a drink. "I bought some whiskey."

"I'll have some of that." He followed me to the fridge. "Give me a glass; I don't want to drink so much tonight."

I wonder if that means what I hope it means. I handed him the bottle and let him pour his own.

"You don't get hot in here?" He pinched the front of his shirt and fanned it.

"I'm used to it. Plus I get—"

"I know, you get a cross-breeze. Hey, you've still got that manuscript on your bed." He ambled over to my futon, where several chapters were spread out.

"I've been working on it." Stupidly I'd forgotten to finish clearing them off in my muddle over what to wear. I repressed the urge to leap on the bed and kick them all to the floor.

"So where are your blues records?" he asked, going to my wooden crates.

"In a special place." I sat on the couch, watching him prowling around.

"Where? I want to see what you've got."

"I don't have nearly as many as you." *Please, please don't look in that crate.*

He turned to me, frowning. "That's okay, baby, just show me. I'm in the mood for something good. You got any Muddy?"

Great; now I'm in for it. "In that covered one there. Lift up the scarf."

He draped the scarf over his shoulder and peered into the crate. "Hmm, what have we here . . . you've got all our albums." He thumbed through them and looked at me, eyebrow raised. "You've got our stuff in here with your blues. Is this the place of honor?"

"Um . . . it might be." *Why didn't I realize this might happen?*

"I didn't even know you listened to my music. You sure kept that bit of information to yourself," he said, eyeing me.

Pull yourself together, Julia. "You don't need me to tell you how good you are. You have enough people doing that."

He held up an Albert King. "You think I have a swelled head? Thanks a lot. Here we have Howlin' Wolf; very good. Here's Otis and Billie . . . Wait, what's this?"

He held up an index card I'd taped to the front of the crate. "Please Do Not Touch," he read.

A flush crept up my face. "Sometimes my friends aren't careful with my records. I just didn't want those particular ones to get scratched."

"Well, I'm honored to be in the Please Do Not Touch section," he said with a wicked grin. He sauntered over and sat next to me, putting his glass on the table. "Actually, though . . ."

He slid closer, his dark eyes seeming to glitter in the low light. "I've been really wanting you to touch."

He took my hand, and a swift blue jolt shot up my arm. He pulled me toward him and his lips met mine; whiskers, whiskey, tongues slow. He kissed me again and then again, more urgently as I responded. *God, his lips, his sensual tongue . . .* I wound my fingers in his thick hair, his hands moving on me, flashes of lust darting through me like quicksilver.

"Julia, I've been waiting . . . so long for you," he murmured. He moved his mouth down the nape of my neck, making my skin tingle and my insides melt. "Since your bed's occupied by Mr. Collins," he said, his lips brushing my ear, "let's go to my place." He kissed me once more, sending a pang of desire twanging through me.

"Okay," I whispered. I reached for my sandals under the

table. I could barely fasten them, my hands were shaking so much. I locked the door, and we flew down the stairs and into the waiting car.

"My place," he said to Rick. "Fast as you can."

We sat smashed together, tongues entwined. With a groan he pulled me onto his lap. I could feel him hard beneath me, his fingers stroking my nipples through my blouse, each caress a teasing bee sting. We pulled up at his place and tumbled into the elevator, kissing and grabbing each other as it rose.

Jack tore off his shirt the minute we got inside. I gave a nervous giggle, unable to tear my eyes away from his muscled chest, his hard abdomen, the dark line leading down from his navel.

"You're next," he said, taking my hand and leading me back to his bedroom. He pulled off his jeans, all of him springing out at me. My breath caught as I took in his gorgeous body. He slipped off my clothes, picked me up in his strong arms and lifted me onto his bed; the warmth of his weight, hot skin on skin.

"God, you're beautiful." He tongued my breasts, and my back arched in response. "Do you know how much I've wanted to do this?" The length of his lean body, rock-hard against my slipperiness, his taut arms holding me. The line of his cheek-bone above me, jaw tensed. Then he entered me, making me feel all of him, making me gasp. I splayed my hands on his back, sensing the coil and release of muscle as he glided in long, deep strokes. His breath started to come faster. He gripped me tightly and thrust, building until he exploded, throbbing inside me for a long time. I gazed at his dark eyelashes as he lay next to me, one arm flung across my chest. I could barely believe I was there with him, in his bed.

After a while Jack opened his eyes. He climbed on top of me and lavished my nipples with his tongue, then mouthed his way down to my belly, my inner thigh. When he pressed his face between my legs I propped up on my elbows, a little unsure about this.

"Relax, baby. I'm gonna make you feel great." Jack went back to what he was doing, and I lay back on the pillow and tried to follow instructions. After a while I started to be less tense. A few minutes later, every iota of my being was focused on his lips. *This feels amazing . . . but what if I make a loud noise? Maybe he wants me to . . . Ahh, I don't care what I do . . .*

I did make a lot of noise; it seemed to go on and on. What he did was so intensely pleasurable, I almost couldn't bear it. My whole being was thrumming when he plunged into me again.

"Oh, Julia," he said. "You feel ssooo good."

I wrapped my legs around him and this time we went more slowly, his measured strokes creating ripples of my earlier rapture. He cried out as he filled me, face buried in my neck. The thumping of his chest gradually slowed to a regular beat. He fell asleep before I did, his arm twined around my waist.

In the morning I watched Jack slumber for a while, not wanting to wake him. I was still amazed that I was in his bed—not to mention the way he'd made love to me last night, which was a revelation. Now I got what the magazines and books were talking about; I'd always thought the descriptions were exaggerated, or maybe I was one of those women who didn't get that much out of sex. Now I realized the fault didn't lie with me.

I slipped into the bathroom. When I came out, Jack lay with arms behind his head, his handsome face framed by disheveled hair. His eyes followed my goose-bumped body across the floor. He lifted the sheet and I got in beside him. For a minute we lay smiling at each other on the pillow.

"Well," he said, trailing his thumb down the curve of my hip, "I thought that would never happen."

"Neither did I." I reached up and traced the lines near the corner of his mouth, like I'd wanted to all along.

"I've been grinding away so hard at the album. I decided you were going to be my reward for all the blood and sweat. I'd get home at the end of a long session and lay here all night, imagining what it would be like . . ."

God, he's a good kisser.

"Then I'd get up in the morning and think about it some more," he continued, his growly just-awakened voice sounding even more deeply British. "To tell the truth, it was early afternoon that I got up. Morning sounds more romantic though, doesn't it?"

I laughed. "I guess so." I put my arms around his neck and rubbed my face against the roughness of his cheek. His hands went to my breasts, sending twinges of yearning through me.

"So were you thinking about me?" he asked, pulling back to look at me.

"Maybe once in a while. When I had nothing better to do."

"I'll get it out of you." Jack turned me over so he was behind me, one hand teasing my nipple. His long fingers parted me and dipped inside, then he began to stroke me, dipping again, stroking.

"You feel nice and ready," he whispered in my ear. I was so immersed in the luxurious brimming sensation that I couldn't reply. I heard myself starting to pant like an animal being pursued. My hips were moving in rhythm with his hand; I was mounting, peaking. Suddenly Jack thrust into me, and I burst.

As my cries subsided, he rolled me onto my stomach and began to move faster and harder. He bit my neck, sending a shiver down my spine. Inexplicably he slowed down.

"Don't stop," I gasped.

"You want me?" he asked, holding still.

"Yes," I whispered.

"I didn't hear you."

"Yes!"

"Good, because I really want you." Afterwards, he showed me the indentations of my teeth on his fingers.

We got up eventually and showered, exploring each other's bodies with lips and tongues until the hot water ran cold. The steam was so thick, we went into his room to towel off. The wide-open sex made me feel kind of exposed, but Jack acted like nothing was out of the ordinary. He must be used to women totally losing it in his bed.

"Hmm, I never would have guessed," he said as we sat side-by-side on the edge of his mattress. He licked a drop of water off my shoulder.

"Never guessed what?"

"That you wanted me too." Wet hair fell into his eyes, and he brushed it back.

"Who says I did?" I crossed my arms over my nipples, which were giving me away.

Jack raised his eyebrow. "Baby, you can't tell me that. You were squeezing me like a glove."

I blushed. "Okay, I admit it."

"But you have to tell me when you first did. You were so inscrutable."

I laughed and shook my head.

"See, you've got me using big words now. You're rubbing off on me." He put his hand on my bare thigh and smiled. "I have to confess, when I saw you in that black dress before the party, I felt like a schoolboy with his first wood. I had to put on my jacket to cover it up. I was looking out the window trying to think of something depressing so I wouldn't offend you walking around all stiff."

So that's what he was doing. "I wondered why you suddenly took an interest in the view."

"Well, now you know. Let me go clean up a little before you get whisker burn." Jack went whistling into the bathroom to shave, and I got up to borrow his brush. I stopped short, seeing several long blonde hairs trailing from the bristles. The heat of my passion dissipated. I wondered who'd used the brush, and how long ago. From what he'd just said, I thought maybe he wasn't seeing anyone else; a dumb thing to presume about someone like him. I stared at the tendrils for a minute and then laid the brush down. *I guess I have a lot more to learn about Jack Kipling.*

I looked around the room, so large that even the king-sized bed didn't diminish it. There were two guitars on armchairs, and a big dresser littered with change, rolling papers, and a few pictures of him with groups of people. One photo caught my attention; Jack kneeling next to an adorable little boy with sparkling brown eyes and dark hair standing straight up from his head. *So he must have a son*, I realized with a sinking feeling. *I wonder how involved with the mother he is. Maybe I can ask him about it if we keep seeing each other. Which doesn't seem too likely, given the leftovers in his brush.*

I heard a dryer going for a minute, and then Jack came out of the bathroom. He plucked my discarded blouse from the floor. "I'll give you something to wear. This one's seen better days." He went to his closet, disappeared inside, and emerged with one of his silky shirts.

"That might be a little fancy for Saturday morning," I said. "Unless I was headed over to Tenth Avenue. What else is in there?"

"In here? It's a bit of a mess."

Curious, I went over to the door.

"Go on and take a look. You'll see it sooner or later."

I followed him inside the expansive walk-in closet . . . *Wow.* Clothes were strewn all over the floor, in baskets, on shelves, partially draped over hangers; men's clothes, women's clothes, all in a big jumble. Several of his jackets were thrown over hooks in the back. He picked up a shirt from the floor, sniffed it, then dropped it and picked up another. "I think this one's okay," he said, handing me a ruffled pink blouse.

"I don't want to put on some floozy's clothes," I teased.

"You calling me a floozy?"

"Where did you get that?" I pointed to a frowsy blonde wig tossed on a high shelf.

"I dunno. Once in a while I have to go into deep undercover."

"Which stuff is yours? It's kind of a hodgepodge." I picked through a pile; shirts of all colors, draw-string pants, patched jeans, spangled trousers, scarves, belts, black leather, brown leather . . . "Is it a rule that everyone who comes over has to leave one item of clothing behind?"

"Most of this stuff is mine. It's me look; I wear what I like. I don't care if it's meant for women or guys." I loved the way he slid back and forth between Cockney and American, especially when he used *me* instead of *my.*

"Uh-huh. I don't know that this would fit you." I held up a red bra that had to be a D cup.

"That was one of Sammy's friends'." He grabbed it and threw it into a corner. "You giving me a hard time about my wardrobe?" he asked, putting his hands on his hips. He was still naked, so the effect was intriguing. "I just need to get it organized."

"I like your wardrobe. It's an embarrassment of riches." I picked up one of his cotton shirts and slipped my arms into the sleeves.

"Leave it unbuttoned so I can see the girls while I make breakfast."

"Here you go; if you're cooking, you'll need this." I untangled a lacy maid's apron from a snarl of stockings and tied it around his waist. "Now you look ready for the kitchen." The frothy fabric made quite a contrast with his black stubble and muscled chest.

"This would do wonders for my public image. Let me call for a few supplies." He went to the phone and ordered some groceries. When they came, I answered the door since he was unpresentable.

"What time do you need to go to the studio?" I asked as he unpacked the bag on the counter.

"I dunno, Sammy said he'd call. I'll drop you at your place so you can do some work, then I'll pick you up once I'm done."

He wants to see me again tonight! I didn't bother trying to hide my smile.

Jack poked around in his cabinet and found a cast-iron frying pan. He put a little oil in it and cracked several eggs while I dropped bread slices into his gleaming eight-piece toaster. Then he got the sausages sizzling. "You have some nice equipment here," I said, picking up a copper spatula.

"I noticed you like my equipment." He turned the heat down on the eggs and came over to me. "Don't stop," he whispered.

"Now you're embarrassing me." I looked at the floor.

Jack gave my waist a squeeze. "Don't worry, that made me feel great. Whoops."

He rushed back to the pan and shoveled the eggs onto plates. I poured some juice and we ate our fill, then we loaded the dishwasher that looked like it had rarely been used. Jack put on Billie Holiday at my request. He seemed to have forgotten that he was wearing the apron, which was no longer centered.

"I still can't believe it," he said as we sat on the sofa. "I was starting to think you didn't like me."

"I liked you. I just didn't want trouble."

"But I busted you out, huh? I'm irresistible, aren't I?" he asked with a grin.

"I'm sure you've been told you are."

"Well, I was starting to feel like I was very resistible. You coming over here bringing a book. 'In case I get bored,'" he said in a high-pitched voice. "'I might get bored around you, Jack Kipling, so I'll just bring my Flannery or my what-have-you.

I prefer their company to yours anyway. I'm just here for the records.'"

"That wasn't it," I said, laughing.

Jack leaned back and crossed his arms. "Why didn't you want to come out with me at first? It was like pulling teeth."

His hair was sticking up in all directions, earring askew, dark shadow on his face. His apron had slipped to the side, totally defeating the point. But even in the silly outfit, he was unbelievably sexy. "Now if you'd worn that little number, I would have rushed over right off the bat. Anyway, I thought maybe we were just going to be friends."

"I was afraid if I tried anything, you'd run off and never come back," he said. "You seemed so . . . untouchable. And a little prissy at first, when you didn't want to smoke a joint with me. I wasn't sure if we'd be able to hang out. Besides, it ain't me style to go after women. They usually make the first moves."

"Hmm, I'll bet they do." *I'm sure all you have to do is snap your finger, and the whole pack comes bounding over.*

"I wanted to snatch you up off my couch and take you to bed, but I thought you'd just give me one of your cold looks and say, 'Don't disturb me, I'm listening to Leadbelly' or something." He considered me for a moment. "When did my charms start to work on you?"

"I'm not telling. That's my business." I wasn't about to say it was when he showed up on my stoop.

"Well, I know when I wanted you," he said in a low voice. "I was sitting on this filthy couch in a lounge, surrounded by all these loud, nasty people, drunk, stoned. I look up and out on the wall is this projection of an angel. And she's dancing. She's just so beautiful, I thought somebody'd slipped something into my drink. I watched you move, and you were so sensuous. But it was obvious you were just dancing for yourself; the guy kept trying to film you, and you kept turning away. *That's* when I first wanted you." He kissed me lightly, and then not-lightly. "And you were so very hard to get," he continued. "Sammy kept telling me it was an act; that you were playing hard to get. Then I realized you really *were* hard to get."

Surprised by his comment, I met his eyes. "I'm fine being alone. Sometimes it's just easier."

"I know what you mean. What's even worse is when you're with someone, and you still feel alone."

The phone began ringing insistently, but Jack made no move to answer it. It continued for a few minutes until he went over, lifted the receiver and dropped it. "That's no one I want to talk to." He went to the kitchen for a beer, and on his way back the phone rang once, stopped, and immediately rang again. This time, Jack picked it up.

"Yeah, I can get there by two. Uh-huh. No comment. See you later." He turned to me. "That was Sammy; they're all going to the studio in a while. I'll drop you at your place on the way. You're going to be home all afternoon? Not going for a thirty-mile run?"

I wondered why he was asking. "I'll be there. I can barely walk, much less go running. Thanks to you." I hesitated. "That's a signal of some sort, isn't it?"

Jack had a funny look on his face. "What?"

"The phone, ringing once like that."

"Yeah… it is. I've got too many people calling, wanting stuff from me. I don't even remember who half of them are." *I guess he means women,* I thought. "People I want to talk to know to ring once, then hang up and call right back," he continued. "What else have you noticed?"

"You favor your index finger on your right hand when you strum."

"What else?"

I thought for a second. "You don't order from the menu."

"That's true, I guess."

"You wince a little when you hear a high-pitched tone of voice."

"Do I really? I never knew that. Very observant. Listen, I'm gonna call Mary Jo real quick, there's something I forgot to do." He turned up the volume on the stereo and mumbled into the phone. "Yeah, three. All right. Thanks." He came back over. "I'll give you a little break and then we can pick up where we left off."

I can't wait to do that. "Sure. I need to get Mr. Collins off my bed and start pulling him together this afternoon."

"I don't wanna hear about you pullin' no other man," Jack said in a deep voice. "You get in the sheets with Collins, Ima have to put a hurt on him." He seemed to reconsider. "Actually your assignment is to move that stuff off your futon so we can get into it later. I'm gonna be thinking about that while I'm at the studio. Sex up my playin', if you know what I mean." He gave a little twist of his hips, making me laugh.

He dropped me off at my apartment, and it was nice to be home for a while to gather my wits. I lay back in bed, feeling the echo of his body in the tender places on mine. It was hard to take in the fact that we had now made love together. Many times. Everything had happened so suddenly, it was like a floodgate opening. I thought about the way his tongue felt on my skin; his lips on my breasts. The pleasant ache where he'd been inside me; the lovely length of him. The way I'd cried out when he made me come. I was savoring the whole experience when the phone rang.

"I can't believe you didn't call me," Vicky said.

I smiled. "I just got back a few minutes ago."

"So....?"

"So... yes. I stayed with him."

"And?"

"You know what, it's not that he's so good-looking, or famous. What gets me is that he makes me laugh. You'd think he would just act cool all the time, since he's pretty much the personification of it. But he's so much fun to be with."

"You're leaving out the crucial part."

"Um . . . yeah. Let's just say expectations were exceeded."

"That's all? C'mon. There's not much left to the imagination, the way these guys go bare-assed under their jeans. And that king-of-the-jungle way he prowls around . . . I'll bet he was amazing in bed."

I thought of the chain reaction Jack had set off in me. "All of the above."

"Oh, you're so annoying sometimes! But I can tell from your voice; it has that satisfied ring to it. Sounds like you're head over heels."

"I'm getting there. Much to my chagrin. Don't say anything to Sammy, okay?"

"I promise I'll be discreet."

Just as I was finishing the last pages, I heard a thumping at the door downstairs. Surprised Jack was done already, I went to the window. Two beefy guys were craning their necks up at me. A truck was parked on the curb next to a big box on the sidewalk.

"We got a delivery," one said when I stuck my head out.

"I think you have the wrong address."

"A Mary Jo Callahan called it in for this number on Broome."

I went down to the street to check it out. "We were told to get it here no later than five," the man said.

"What is that?" I asked.

They hefted the box between them, and the first one started backing up the stairs. "Air conditioner," he said. "Man, they didn't say it was three *long* flights."

So that's why he called Mary Jo; how incredibly nice of him. The men installed the unit in my window and I stood in front of it, gratefully letting it blast me and hoping it wouldn't add a lot to my electric bill.

"Ahh, much better," Jack said, coming inside.

"Thank you so much, Jack. This is so generous. You didn't have to do that."

"I wanted to; it must have been ninety in here the other night. Oh, and you've cleared off your bed." He flopped down on my futon. "I'll show you how you can repay me," he said, undoing my shirt as I stood before him. He unhooked my bra and slid down my jeans, tonguing my nipples and belly.

"I wanted to tell you," I breathed as he rubbed his face in my pubic hair, "I'm on the pill."

"Mmmm," he said. "Good."

"How did the recording go?" I asked as we lay back, sipping beers. Jack was sprawled next to me, his chest still heaving. It was strange to have a man in my bed after so many months—even more strange that it was this particular man.

"It went fine, even though my mind wasn't entirely there. Looks like you got your editing done."

"I have to go through it again, but at least I got it in the right order. Lately I'd had trouble concentrating."

"You did? I'm glad to know I wasn't the only one whose concentration was ruined. Mine's been shot ever since I used those guitar chords as an excuse to get my hands on you." He grinned and tipped the bottle toward his crotch. "Want to water it, see if it'll grow?"

I blushed. "That was so embarrassing! I poured a whole beer in your lap."

"I came back in my dry jeans all set to seduce you, but you had packed up and left." He swigged the last drops and reached around to put the empty on the table. "What's this?" He picked up my marbled notebook.

"Oh, that's just how I keep track of things," I said, putting out my hand to take it from him.

"Is this your diary? Man, your writing's even messier than mine." He began leafing through it, ignoring my give-it-to-me gesture.

"If it was, you really should ask before you look at it." *It's kind of cute that he's so nosy.*

Jack ran his finger down one of the lined pages. "Are these book titles?" He squinted at an entry.

"That's my list of all the books I've read. I've kept it since I was six."

"You've written down every one you've ever read?" he asked incredulously.

"Yes, it's sort of . . . It's my connection to my childhood, I guess. My mother threw out a lot of my stuff when we moved from our original house. I feel like if I lost it, I would lose my identity, in a way."

Jack flipped through the pages. "There must be hundreds in here."

"I know it's a little compulsive," I said defensively. "I admit I'm weird."

"I think it's cool that you've kept your list. Do you want to get some dinner? I'm starved."

"I'd love to." I got up and started getting dressed. Jack lay on his stomach and rolled around, rubbing himself against the sheets.

"What are you doing?" I laughed.

"Don't change your covers this week. They'll remind you of me."

He smiled, sat up, and pulled on his jeans. I turned the air off and we went over to a restaurant on Christopher Street. We slipped inside a back door that the maitre d' opened, gesturing us in. He sent us through the kitchen, where the cooking staff barely looked up; I gathered they were used to this routine with their recognizable patrons. We were seated in a dark corner and Jack ordered a bottle of champagne.

"To this weekend," he said after the waiter poured. We touched glasses, and our food came as I was asking Jack how much longer they had left in the studio.

"Maybe another month. We only have a few tracks to go," he said, slicing a bite of steak. "There's this one riff in a blues intro that's been eluding me. What kind of blues did your father like?"

"Mostly prewar stuff. He liked country, too. He was a big Hank Williams fan, Patsy Cline, Maybelle Carter."

"Williams put out some good tunes."

"I'd sit on the porch with Dad, playing 'I'm So Lonesome, I Could Cry' on my little plastic record player. That's the first song that really touched my soul. It reminds me of the good part of my childhood, before I was left alone with my mother."

I put my fork down and took a gulp of champagne. "Your face really changes when you talk about her," Jack observed.

"We had a rocky relationship. I just wanted a regular mom, wearing an apron and making cookies. Instead she was coming in soused after hitting the bar; sometimes she had a guy with her. I would have been a late bloomer anyway, but that definitely left me without much interest in boys for a while."

"She still get around?"

"Not anymore. I think she'd like to find someone, but she's a little past her use-by date."

Two guys were weaving their way through the tables. Jack looked up and frowned.

"Hey, man, how are you doing?" the first one said. "Where were you last night?" He glanced at me.

"Busy," Jack said.

"Nicole's been asking for you. Where've you been?"

"We've been recording. I'll call you."

Jack downed his glass as they returned to their table. Of course he was seeing a million women all at once, if not a few regular girlfriends too. He must be involved with this Nicole, since it was the second time her name had come up. The way he'd acted this weekend—so warm, so into me—was just a slick routine he had down. I was a fool to hope it was more than just a roll in the sack.

"Your fish all right?" he asked.

"It's delicious." I managed to choke down one more bite. Jack pushed his plate aside and signaled for the check. We walked through the kitchen and into the waiting car.

"Thanks for dinner." I forced myself to smile. "I'm going to head home." Sleeping with him was a mistake, after all. I didn't want to be just another mark on his scratching post.

Jack looked surprised. "Aren't you coming back with me?"

"My laundry's piling up. If I don't get some things clean, I'll have to wear tie-dye to the office."

"I've always thought tie-dye was under-rated." He slid his arm around me and pulled me closer. I was mad at myself for being so tempted.

"I'd better not. I haven't gotten anything done this weekend."

"You were doing me this weekend." He smiled. Suddenly he leaned in and kissed me. I couldn't stop myself from responding to his tongue, his fingers caressing my breast. Maybe one more time... I could be facing another long, dry spell after this. If only I could be detached, like Vicky.

"I guess I can come for a little while."

Jack squeezed my thigh. "Good. Hang a left, Rick."

"So ... there's this one woman I was seeing before," Jack said when we got inside. "We only went out for a couple of months, and I was seeing a few other girls too. I broke it off with her several weeks ago."

I was glad to hear this, but I doubted he'd stopped seeing her that long ago. Maybe he just never cleaned his brush.

"As you probably gathered, her name's Nicole. I'd heard she had a few slates loose, but she kept coming after me. At a certain point I figured, why not. Sammy warned me about her though. He had a sense."

I waited, not knowing what to say.

"Compared to you, her brain's the size of a pea."

I smiled faintly. "So mine must be . . . a soybean?"

"Listen, here's why I'm telling you this. She's the one who keeps calling and calling. She's saying . . ." He paused, looking annoyed. "I know this isn't true. But she is saying she's pregnant."

My spirits sank. I ducked my head so he wouldn't see I was upset. If someone was having his baby now, I knew I couldn't have anything to do with him.

"Hey, I know she's not. I used a wrapper every time, and I was very careful. She's just trying to get money from me. I've sent her some, only to get her to go away." He sighed. "She was scheduled to go to a doctor with Mary Jo for a pregnancy test so I could prove it, but she blew it off. She'll leave me alone as soon as she gloms onto someone else."

I recalled the picture of the boy on his dresser. Was he having children left and right with various women? "You're pretty sure she isn't?"

"Absolutely."

"Well, thanks for mentioning it." He seemed sincere, unless he was an extremely gifted liar. But this Nicole situation meant there was no telling what else was going on with him.

"Don't give it another thought." Jack reached for me and undid my blouse. He took my bra clasp in his teeth and bit it open. "I kept picturing what you'd look like under those second-hand clothes," he said, glancing up at me. "For once, even my imagination didn't do it justice."

Chapter 11

WALKING ON THE MOON

Heading in to work Monday I was a little achy—but in a good way. At ten, Erin stopped by. "I tried you several times Saturday to see if you wanted to go to the Pyramid Club. Were you sick?"

"I spent most of it in bed." At least it wasn't a lie.

"All right, back to the grind. Let's catch lunch one day."

Late in the afternoon, the receptionist called to say I had something in the lobby. To my surprise, a huge bouquet was standing on the front desk. I took it back to my room and tore off the tissue paper. The zig-zag handwriting on the note thrilled me: "I had a good time—Jack." Gigantic purple globes on thick green stalks emerged from the wrapping; they looked like something that had grown on the moon.

Edgar stuck his head in as I tucked the note into my bag. "Someone has a creative mind."

"Do you know what they are?"

"They're alliums, my dear. A member of the onion family. So much more interesting than the usual run-of-the-mill nosegays."

"Thanks, I think so too." I shut my door and dialed Jack's number.

"Oh . . . hello." He seemed surprised to hear from me. I heard a voice in the background.

"These flowers are amazing. I've never seen anything like them before."

"I figured they were more original than roses. No, in the other drawer," he said to someone there. I couldn't make out her reply.

"Well . . . thanks again." I hung up, wishing I hadn't called. Who was that at his apartment? Obviously another woman. Already this was tearing me up inside.

Several people came by, either asking what the occasion was or trying to find out who'd sent the bouquet. I was a little embarrassed by the attention, but also proud that I had someone who liked me. At least for two nights in a row. Now I was wondering how I rated compared to the girl he'd had with him today.

At nine I tottered out of the building and headed down Park Avenue in the humid midsummer air. My thoughts simmered over to Jack. All day I'd felt as if the entire weekend was a figment of my imagination. But then I'd look at the moonflowers, proof that we'd really been together. I wondered if he'd thought about me at all. Every time I took my head out of the typewriter, I saw an image of his dark eyes, his unruly mane of hair, the feel of sinews jumping in his back. My belly twisted when I remembered his hands roving all over my body; his seeming hunger for me. Maybe that was Nicole over there today; maybe he was lying about her not being pregnant. Or maybe it was an entirely different girl—like the one who'd copped a feel at Patrick's party.

"The check was mailed last Friday," I told the agent the next morning, neglecting to say that I was the one who sent out the checks. I took some jacket copy in for Harvey to sign off on. He hung up the phone, wove his stubby fingers together and gazed at me with his icy blue eyes.

"I mentioned to Briar that you're going after Isabel Reed, and she's come up with her own celebrity idea. Pryce Rayner may be getting ready to spill the beans. She got to know his manager when she was at *TownTalk*."

Rayner was an actor who specialized in cheesy sheriff car chases, and who'd recently been involved in a messy fourth divorce. I thought he was a little past his prime, but apparently Harvey didn't. "I don't think he's any more current than Isabel," I said. "He hasn't had a hit movie in several years."

"Oh, he still has a huge fan base, especially now that he's joined the ranks of the religious right. He's had quite the spiritual conversion since he dried out, which always makes for good reading. Briar was telling me all about it over drinks last night."

What a sleaze. He isn't hot for Pryce Rayner; he's hot for Briar. "I think Isabel's book would be a bigger draw. Don't women's memoirs usually do better than men's?" I knew this was true from following the bestseller list.

He waved off my comment. "Depends on who the author is. But maybe you can convince me if we discuss it after hours.

I find it hard to concentrate with the phones ringing off the hook. And you know, Julia . . ." He paused and gave me a cold little smile. "I only have room to promote one of you. So I guess you'll have to do your best to win me over."

At home, I drank two beers in a row to calm my rattled nerves. All day I couldn't focus on anything but Briar's unfair advantage. If only I'd been allowed to acquire one of the projects I'd pitched before she was hired. If only Isabel had a complete manuscript, instead of a paltry handful of badly written pages about her childhood.

I picked at the beer label and tried to think. If Briar got promoted, Harvey would have no need for a second junior editor. With the industry-wide recessionary hold on hiring, my foray into publishing would be over. And there was no other reason for me to be in New York, as tough as it was to get by here. The thought of losing my hard-won toehold in the city—and like Vicky's friend Daphne, having to move back home—was utterly depressing. I pictured myself living with Dot again in Pennsylvania, and doing what? Teaching, I guessed, until I could save up enough money to move somewhere else. Everyone would know I'd tried to make it in the city, and failed. It was the bleakest future I could imagine.

To make matters worse, I hadn't heard from Jack. I had the sinking feeling that our weekend fling was just that. The flowers must have been his way of thanking me for the sex. Their faint odor made my stomach churn, so I'd moved them to the top of my bookshelf. He was probably already into his new conquest—most likely a model who'd be much more erotically experienced, and therefore more pleasing to him.

I'd been so stupid; the naïve small-town girl who thought she could hold the interest of a jaded guy like Jack for more than one weekend. I'd tried so hard to avoid this situation, but here I was, bolting for the phone and crushed every time it wasn't him—like I was channeling Dot. I hadn't had a free minute to do my laundry, and the traces of his scent on my one set of sheets made me even more miserable.

When the phone rang Wednesday night, I ran to it, thinking it might be Jack. Instead, a voice from the past sounded in my ear.

"Julia. It's Art. How have you been?"

I leaned against the fridge for support. "I'm fine."

"I've been trying your number for a while. Have you been away?"

"I work late most nights." Chills ran up and down my arms. *What does he want with me after all this time?*

"How's your job going?" he asked.

"It's going well. How about you?" I squeaked out.

"The teaching's pretty routine. I'm trying to finish a paper that's due to be published in the spring." Art cleared his throat. "Phoebe and I wound up not staying together. We just never clicked again after the separation."

I could barely think, my mind was spinning so fast. He hadn't gotten back with his wife after all? "How long have you been . . . apart from her?"

"About a month. This time we're filing for divorce."

"Are you okay with that?"

"Definitely. It's over. So . . . are you seeing anyone?"

This gave me pause. "I've just started seeing someone," I said noncommittally.

"I'd like to get together anyway, to catch up. You've been on my mind. Could we meet for coffee?"

It took me months to get over him. Do I really want to start all that up again? "I'm pretty backed up with editing. Maybe in a few weeks?"

"All right, Julia. I'll call you in a while."

I kept my hand on the receiver for a moment, feeling unstrung. After everything Art had put me through, he hadn't even stayed with his wife. All this time we could have been together; all my pain and insecurity could have been avoided. I wouldn't have even met Jack—which would have been a good thing, now that he'd dropped me like a hot potato.

The following night I realized dismally that I'd have to try to forget I'd ever known Jack. I changed into my cutoffs, and jumped to grab the phone.

"Sorry, it's not who you're hoping."

"Hi, Vicky." I sank onto the couch.

"So he still hasn't called. Let's go out Saturday. You can't sit around moping all weekend."

"Who says I can't?" I wasn't in the mood to go out. I didn't care if I never met anyone else again. What was deeply meaningful to me had meant nothing to him. It was just as awful as when Art had broken up with me.

"Julia. You have to get over this bad habit of feeling attached to someone just because you've had sex," Vicky admonished me. "Think of it purely as entertainment—you had a good time, and so did he. End of story. Now you can meet another guy who'll rock your socks off. And maybe the next one will stick around for more than a weekend, unlike this asshole."

She muttered the last part under her breath.

"Thanks for the advice. I wish I was better at taking it." I glanced at the window unit; yet another painful reminder.

"Listen, I know you fell hard for Jack. Who could blame you—he's one of the sexiest men in the universe. And let's not forget that he really led you on. It's kind of unfair the way he waited to put the move on you, like it was a marriage proposal or something."

"Actually I think that makes me feel even worse."

"I'm sorry. I'm just venting. I'm really pissed off about this. I don't like my best girlfriend to get hurt. Don't think it's just you; Sammy rarely calls me either. He mostly shows up whenever he wants to score. Should I say something to him about Jack?"

"Oh, no! Promise me you won't." I didn't want to join the ranks of clingy, whiny, needy predecessors like Nicole.

"You're right; no sense in letting the bastard know you're pining for him. I'll come over Saturday and if you aren't up for going out, we'll drink our troubles away at your place. I'll even let you play some of your blues, so we can feel even more fucked-up and depressed."

I smiled for the first time in days. "Thanks. I appreciate it."

"Don't worry. If I ever get my heart broken, you can return the favor."

Late Friday afternoon I was staring at the pile of paper in my inbox when the phone rang. There was so much noise in the background, I could hardly hear.

"—crazy week," Jack was saying.

"Sorry, I didn't catch that." Nervously I doinged the cord.

"I've been stuck in the studio 'til all hours," he said more loudly. "Are you around tonight? Mark and Suzanne want to go to a gallery opening together, and then grab dinner."

All this week I've been miserable, just because he couldn't take two minutes to call me? It was so unfair—but I was so excited. "Yes!" I exhaled and tried to calm down. "I'm around."

"Hang on . . . What? I'm coming," he said to someone there. "Pick you up at eight."

"Wait, me or—?" The line was dead.

I hung up in a daze. *So he does want to see me again, after all!* I paced my tiny office, wanting to scream and jump up and down. Momentarily I wondered if I should go home after dinner instead of going back to his place—maybe I shouldn't be too sexually available. But I knew I didn't have enough self-control for that; I couldn't wait to feel his hands on me, his lips on me . . . I shut my eyes, picturing how our bodies would fit together.

On the way home I stopped by the Strand, my favorite used bookstore. Since Jack had seemed to like *Wise Blood* so much, I thought I'd get him a copy of his own. Just as I had put the package on my table and was locking the deadbolts, the phone rang.

"I have some news," Dot announced.

"Erwin gave you the raise?"

"I'm finally coming to the Big Apple."

She went on to say that her trucker friend Darrell had to make a trip to New Jersey the following Thursday. She was going to ride with him, take the bus to 42nd Street and stay until Saturday. I told her I'd pick her up at the terminal, and we said goodbye. I was so elated about seeing Jack that even my mother's visit couldn't puncture my mood.

Chapter 12

LOVE IS THE DRUG

I stood staring at my wall of outfits. My leather skirt was too tattered for a fancy gallery opening, and my work clothes were too sedate. I decided to wear my favorite long-sleeved purple shirt and black pants from Alice Underground, along with the lavender suede heels I'd found on the street one night, disbelieving someone had discarded such nice footwear. They were two sizes too big, but I stuffed them with tissues so they just about fit. I added more padding in each toe and tried to work off my excess energy by shimmying around to the Floor's next-to-last album, which had some fantastic dance tunes. It was unreal to hear Jack's voice chiming in on the choruses, knowing that I would see him tonight.

Finally I decided to wait on the street rather than wear out my frayed rug. The black car turned onto my block; I felt a flicker of anticipation. The door opened and Jack's long legs swung out. God, he looked gorgeous with his snapping dark eyes and tousled hair, a big smile on his face as he came toward me in a half-undone white shirt and red dinner jacket.

"Hello sweetheart, d'you need a ride somewhere?" He leaned in to kiss me; I put my arms around his neck and kissed him back. *It'll be pretty much impossible not to go to bed with him tonight,* I realized. Breathlessly I pulled away. "We'd better get in before you stop traffic."

I said hi to Rick, and then Jack's hands were on me as he slid his lips down my neck. "I almost came by on the way home late last night," he murmured. "But I figured you had to wake up early."

So he'd thought about me at least once—if not enough to bother calling. "That would have been okay. I'd better not get too rumpled now, though, before we meet your friends." I was sufficiently anxious about meeting another bandmate and his wife without looking like I'd been mauled.

"All right, but later I'm gonna be on you like white on rice. Hey, I like these purple shoes," he said, reaching down to lift my calf.

"They were a great find. They're not the perfect size, but I just stuff them with tissue."

"Why'd you buy them so big?" He released my leg.

"I found them on the street. On garbage night." Jack gave me a blank look.

"That's when everybody puts big items out for pickup, and anything else they don't want anymore. I got all my furniture that way. Except the futon," I said, laughing at his concerned expression. "I did buy that new."

"Good to know." He rolled his eyes. "I got bedbugs once in

Madrid, and I'd rather not repeat the experience. How'd work go this week?"

"Kind of a mix. Harvey's hired this assistant editor that he's grooming for promotion, so I really need to buy a book fast. The good thing is, I got in touch with an actress who's doing her memoir; Isabel Reed."

"That's great, Julia. But what's this about a new person?"

"I'm just hoping she won't replace me in the lineup. Anyway, those flowers you sent were the bright spot in my week. Practically everyone in the company made an excuse to stop by. I think my friend Edgar told people to come take a look."

"Who's Edgar?"

"A lovely editor in his fifties. He explained a lot about book production to me when I first started, like what a signature is."

"And what's a signature?" Jack asked. "Not . . .?" he made a scribbling gesture as if autographing something.

"A hardcover is glued into batches of sixteen pages called a signature. So it could have 208 pages, or 256. The last page *number* might be 202, but with the front matter, the page count always comes out to a multiple of sixteen."

"Cool, you're teaching me all kinds of things. I like all this book stuff. Come to think of it, I . . ." He took my hand and placed it over his bulging zipper. ". . . know some things I'd like to teach you. But I can't do it in the car." He raised his eyebrow lasciviously, making my belly flip.

"Here we are." We had stopped at Mary Boone on West Broadway. I'd been there before, and to Castelli and the other SoHo galleries, but never to an actual opening. Several people with large cameras were staked out in front.

"Looks like the buggers are here." Jack unfolded his sunglasses and put them on. He took the droopy hat from the door's side pocket. "You can wear that if you want. There, incognito," he said, putting it on my head.

I held back as the cameramen started aiming our way. "Just keep moving." He took my arm and drew me along with him.

"Jack! Jack!" voices on all sides cried out. "You a friend of the artist? Who's the girl?"

I pulled down the outer edge of the hat, half-blinded by the flashes. One of the men stuck his camera right in Jack's eyes and fired it.

"Out of my way," Jack said, making a fist.

"Watch out, he hits!" another man shouted.

Jack shoved past and I followed him inside the gallery, thankful we'd avoided a tussle. He lifted the hat off my head, rolled it up and stuck it in his back pocket, then removed his shades. People were milling around holding plastic wineglasses and talking loudly over one another. Several noticed Jack right away, creating a sizzle of excitement that popped around the crowded room.

"One of the artists is a friend of Suzanne's," Jack said. "Oh, there they are."

He wove through chattering groups of people, ignoring the gasps and eyeballing. Up ahead I recognized Mark, standing with an extremely thin redhead who topped him by several inches. Given the way Patrick had behaved, I dreaded meeting another member of his group, but hopefully their drummer wouldn't be quite as obnoxious. Mark was shorter and slighter than he looked in pictures, and his nose was more prominent. His straggly shoulder-length hair was streaked blond with purple and green highlights, the front sticking up in a roost-erish fashion. His expression turned gleeful when he saw us. "Hello, luv. I'm Mark."

"Julia. It's good to meet you."

"This is my wife, Suzanne."

Suzanne smiled, showing upper gum that made her look appealingly childlike. "Nice to meet you, Julia."

So she was also British. "Jack said you're friends with one of the artists?" I asked her. Mark said something in Jack's ear, and Jack nodded, grinning.

"Yes, that's Ariel. She did these big ones." Suzanne indicated the abstracts. "We share a studio; I do paintings too."

"She uses feathers with the paint," Mark said. "Our house was starting to look like a chicken shack; I couldn't breathe without getting them down my throat. So now she's got a studio to keep the fluff out of our place."

"Do you want something?" Jack asked me. "I'm gonna get a glass of this gallery swill."

"White wine would be great."

Jack went toward a second room. Before he'd gotten half-way there, three women swarmed him. He seemed to respond to what they were saying, but kept moving despite being surrounded. He was probably so used to being the center of attention that it seemed like no big deal.

"And what do you do, Julia?" Suzanne asked. "I know you have a job; I got that much out of Jack."

"Yes, I work in book publishing. For about a year now." *Although maybe not for much longer.*

Jack returned holding two glasses up high so the crowd wouldn't jostle them. He handed one to me. "Those women were telling me we should go in the back where there's a happening. Some chick's having people cover her in goo." He cocked an eyebrow. "Might be interesting."

"Now, don't you start," Suzanne said. "That's Ariel's friend Fricka. She's an action artist."

"Then let's go check out the action," Mark said.

We squeezed through the crowd to the next room. On a raised dais sprawled a stocky woman, entirely naked except for a pair of combat boots. People were taking spackling tools from a bucket and dipping them into a barrel of sticky gray material, then spreading it on the artist's body. Globs of it were daubed into the bushy hair below each armpit and between her legs.

Suzanne read a plaque on the wall. "It's a protest about the treatment of women," she said, taking a sip of her wine. "The spackling represents the way we've been held back by a false coat of femininity."

"I agree," Mark said, lifting his drink. "Free the women!" He took Suzanne's hand and went to get a spreader.

Jack grinned at me. "I'm tempted to do a little spackling myself. I see a few spots they've missed." He took a gulp of wine. "Actually I'm not tempted in the least. Have you ever seen anything so ridiculous?"

"It does seem kind of silly. Ariel's paintings looked interesting though. Suzanne said she shares a studio with her."

"'Share' is open to interpretation," Jack said as we watched Suzanne gingerly spread a gray blob on the artist's knee. Mark went right for the woman's sizeable breasts, where he gave a few more deliberate swipes than necessary. He winked at Jack, then went back for another scoop. "Suzanne and Mark made a deal where they pay the rent in exchange for Ariel supposedly helping her break into the art world. So far nothing's happened, but at least they've got the feathers out of their place."

"Mark said she puts them on canvas."

"Whatever it is, it isn't art, in my opinion," Jack commented. "But it keeps her happy. Here they come; they're done with their feminist protest." They approached us, Mark with a smear of gray across his cheek. "Looks like you really got into it," Jack said, licking his finger and wiping off the smudge.

"I think it's great," Suzanne said. "Very brave of Fricka to do this."

"Nothing wrong with her that a good shower and a shave couldn't fix," Jack said. "I could loan her my razor, clean her right up."

Suzanne tsk'ed and suggested we get dinner. We darted past the flashing cameras and into the car. "Puffy's," Jack said, and Rick drove west. I was happy we were going somewhere low-key. As the others talked about mutual acquaintances, I sat back and relaxed.

For a change, no one turned their heads as we entered the tavern. I had come here with friends a few times myself; it was a great place with a mix of bikers, artists, and other downtown types too jaded to gawk at a couple of musicians. We pushed two small tables together and ordered a couple of pizzas, Suzanne requesting a salad since she was on something called "macrobiotic."

"I thought the new track went well today," Mark said.

"It would go even better if Patrick didn't keep interrupting the flow," Jack commented. "Always got to be the brightest boy in the room."

"Patrick said he wants you to go to therapy with him." Mark took a sip of his vodka.

"I know. He wants to go to a *couples* therapist," Jack said with a smirk. "He keeps harping on our issues."

"I went with him once." Mark gazed down into his drink. "It was kind of interesting to be psychoanalyzed."

"I know I'm psycho; I don't need to be analyzed. That's just another one of his thick ideas," Jack said in a disgusted tone.

"You have to admit, you two do have some issues," Suzanne said, putting her hand on his arm.

"I don't have any issues with him. I just want to play music. Anyway, we aren't a couple."

"But you argue like an old married couple."

"Well, too bad. I ain't gonna be anyone's bitch."

"Isn't it nice that he's such a sensitive type?" Suzanne said to me.

"Sometimes sensitive is overrated," I said, making Jack smile. "I liked Ariel's paintings. Do you have a show coming up?" I asked Suzanne.

"I think I might be in a group show this fall." She flicked her lighter at a cigarette. "I'm waiting to hear back from a couple of places."

"She'll definitely be showing in the fall," Mark said. "Whatever it takes."

"I don't want you to set it up for me. Then it isn't real. I want to get into a gallery all by myself." Suzanne exhaled a stream of smoke. Obviously this was ground they'd covered before.

"I'd like to see your work sometime. How did you get into that medium?" I asked.

"I've always had a thing for birds. For a while I was designing clothes, and I used feathers on the fabric. So when I started doing canvases, it was a natural outgrowth."

"What she means is, she had so many bags of feathers left over from the designin' that she needed to use them for something," Mark said. "There's that art dealer in L.A. who liked your stuff," he said to Suzanne. "We should go see him while we're there mixing the tracks."

I wondered when they were going. We dug into the pizzas and Mark paid the bill. "So nice to meet you, Julia," Suzanne said, touching my arm. "I hope we'll see you again soon." She kissed Jack on the cheek and they went toward a limo; their driver must have followed us from the gallery.

Jack and I got into his car, and Rick peeled out.

"I like Puffy's," I said. "It's nice they don't make such a fuss about you."

"You mean it's good for my ego to be treated like nothing special once in a while," Jack said with a grin.

"Probably is. Do you ever feel like it's a hassle not being able to go out to dinner without having to hide in the back?"

Jack gave me a contemplative look. "It's been so long since I could, I don't really remember what it was like." He thought for a second. "When we first caught on, it got a bit rough before we figured out we needed protection from the fans. The record company would set up an appearance and we'd think we'd just be answering questions, you know, but it would turn into a free-for-all. Patrick almost got lynched a time or two. Finally we realized we'd better keep out of grabbing range."

"It sounds exhausting."

"I can't complain. The gods have been good to me."

"Suzanne seems to think you ought to go into therapy with Patrick." I'd been intrigued by that part of the conversation.

"Not a chance in hell. Mark did it just to yank his chain. Patrick's always having these blonde moments, hiring advisors and gurus and going off on some screwball tangent. Then he fires them a few months later when he realizes they're just taking his money or using him. It's an insecurity or something. Not to sound like one of your authors."

"Believe me, my authors sound nothing like you. Some of them can't even carry a tune."

Jack raised an eyebrow. "I bet none of them fuck like me."

I crossed my arms. "I wouldn't know. I don't dip my pen in the company ink."

"But some of them have tried." He seemed to expect a response.

I thought of Harvey, but I didn't want to get into that. "Not really. You seem close to Sammy and Mark," I said, changing the subject.

"Oh yeah, we've been through thick and thin. Equipment shorting out on stage, being pole-axed by the press, getting busted . . . ex-wives dragging them through court, scumbag detectives snooping around . . . What Sammy went through with his second ex made me glad I've never been hitched."

I digested that statement as we pulled up to his building. When we got inside, I took the package of books out of my backpack. "Here. I got something for you today."

Jack removed the brown paper wrapping. "You got me *Wise Blood*," he said, turning it over in his hands. "And what's this one?"

"*As I Lay Dying* by William Faulkner. It's about a poor Southern family with lots of kids. It has one of the best lines of all time: 'My mother is a fish.'"

Jack stared at me. "My *mother* is a fish?"

"It sounds strange, but when you come to it in the book, it's . . . mind-altering."

"I've had my mind altered before, but not by a book. So that should be a new experience. I appreciate this, Julia. You'll have to read me your favorite parts." Jack placed the books on the front table next to several piles of mail. He picked up an envelope, glanced at it and threw it down. "Mary Jo brought the post over today."

Arranged in neat stacks were invitations to parties, gallery openings, film premieres, museum first nights. "Boy, you really get invited to everything," I said.

Jack shrugged. "Most of it I toss out. I think Mary Jo's organizing a party at the Mudd Club next weekend. I want to take you shopping at some point, and get you a few more things to wear. Not that I don't like your outfits. This purple shirt's nice, even if it's a bit long on you." He fingered my sleeve.

"It's my favorite blouse from Alice's."

"Your wardrobe's kind of skimpy though. Wouldn't it be nice to have some things that aren't tatty?"

I was a little miffed at his comment; it was easy for someone with all his money to criticize my lack of stylish clothes. "I like shopping at thrift stores," I retorted. "I like the fact that someone else wore it first. It gives me a sense of . . . history, a connection with the past."

"You can have your historical stuff and some new things too. You seem so worried that you're going to owe me, or something. That you're not going to be 'independent.'"

"Already I.O.U. several nice dinners, and about a case of beer." I looked at the piles on the table. "Oh, what's this?" It was a catalog from a modeling agency; each page featured a full-length photo, eye and hair color, measurements, and ludicrous things like "Margot enjoys sunbathing and polo matches."

"The agencies send those," Jack said, flipping it shut. "Sammy likes to look at them."

"Hmm . . ." I thumbed it open. "They've left out the prices. Do they come with a nightly rate, or is it by the hour?"

"Put that thing up. I should tell Mary Jo to just ship them over to Sammy's place."

"Why are models always described as 'leggy'?" I asked. "Here's one, 'leggy blonde.'"

"Some of 'em are kinda leggy." Jack cupped my breasts from behind and kissed my neck.

"Isn't 'leggy' when a plant needs to be cut back?" I turned to face him; the length of him pressing into me felt so good. I ran my hands over his taut shoulders, nearly panting with lust. He felt for the buttons of my blouse as I unzipped his jeans, anticipation pricking my breasts and thighs. He tugged my clothes off and we kissed, his erection insistent against my belly, the sensation of his naked body overwhelming me.

"Let's continue this conversation later," Jack said. "Or not. I've been a good boy for three hours straight; that's my limit." He grabbed two pillows, threw them on the coffee table and lowered me onto them.

"Ahh, you feel so . . . inviting," he murmured in my ear. Our bodies began to collide and part in increasing rhythm. Suddenly Jack stopped and held me close, his heart thumping wildly against my chest. "Let's ease up for a minute," he said, pulling away. He lapped my nipples into hard pink buds, then ran his tongue along the curve of my breast, up to my armpit and across my collarbone, making my aureoles dimple.

"Mmm, your skin's so soft. Like tasting cream." He licked the outer edge of my other breast and slid his tongue beneath its weight, then took my avid nipple in his mouth. Craving him, I pulled him toward me.

"You're ready for more." Jack gave a languid stroke. "Happy to oblige. Wrap your legs around me, baby." He pushed my thighs higher and began moving slowly at first, holding himself back, tension mounting in his flexed arms. We gained momentum until we were breathing fast, careless of how we crashed together. I felt him tighten inside me.

"I'm going to come," he gasped.

I dug my heels into his back. "Come on," I said, and he drove into me with four pulsing beats. I gazed down at his dark tangle spread across my pale chest, blown away by the intensity of our coupling.

Jack rested for a while, and then pushed up from the table. He knelt and took my foot in his hand. "D'you know, it drove me mad when I saw you in that raggedy leather skirt," he said, nipping the inside of my calf. "I had fantasies of doing this." He slithered his tongue to tickle the crease of my knee.

"I like that skirt," I said, distracted by his lips roaming over my skin.

"So did I; at least it gave me a little glimpse of leg." He inched his mouth up my thigh. "Every time, I was hoping I'd get to see 'em. Then you'd come out in your jeans, and my hopes were dashed."

He edged toward my fold and gave a lingering lick, making me inhale sharply. Then he moved away, picked up my other ankle, and began tonguing a trail up my leg in infinitesimal increments. By the time he reached my cleft, my thighs were quivering. Without warning he slid his finger inside me, withdrew it and caressed my nipple, making it glisten. He sucked tender skin at my groin, and a finger glided in again. A moan escaped me.

"Are you feeling relaxed?" Jack's lips teased me as he spoke. I wound my hands in his hair and he switched to the other side. I shifted my hips, but he merely gave a few flicks of his tongue before he moved slightly to the left and lavished his attention there. He put another finger inside and rippled. I wet my dry lips.

"Please," I whispered.

"That's what I call asking nicely."

I was so utterly primed for his mouth that my hips jolted up to meet him. Jack put his hand under my rear, cupping me. He withdrew his fingers and slid his tongue inside me, moving in and out, then slowly drew it up the middle, making me cry out. He did it again, the sensation so agonizingly exquisite that I barely felt his pinkie entering my lower aperture. Doubly penetrated, his tongue whipping me into oblivion, my entire body lifted off the cushions when I came. I lay there floating, unconscious of anything but my humming senses, until Jack gathered me in his arms and carried me back to his bed.

When I finally came to, we were lying across the mattress, Jack's bony foot resting against my arches. I reached over and moved a wisp of bangs out of his face.

"I need a haircut, don't I," he said without opening his eyes.

"I didn't mean to wake you."

He smiled. "I was awake; I was just resting up a little. You're younger than me, you know."

"Not that much younger . . . seven years?"

"Try eight. I'm thirty-two. You sure you want to go out with an old man like me?"

"You're not old. If you had any more stamina, I'd be afraid of you. You have a twenty-year-old's physique with an adult mind."

"I've been accused of having it the other way around."

"Anyway, I don't think you need a haircut."

"No? Suzanne keeps wanting to get her hands on it. She used to work in a salon. Did you like how she did Mark's?"

"Not really. It looked like something crawled up there and died a slow, agonizing death."

Jack laughed. "I think he feels it makes an impression."

"*You* certainly make an impression wherever you go."

"What do you mean?" He rolled to his side and propped his head on his arm.

"People get so worked up when they see you. Like those women that glommed onto you at the gallery."

Jack shrugged. "Goes with the territory. It's not that they like you personally; they just think some of the gloss is going to reflect on them. I learned a long time ago to take it for what it is. They'd be into anybody with a band that made a name for itself."

"Oh, I think it's more than that. To be honest . . ." I hesitated.

"What?"

I decided to go ahead and ask; what could it hurt? "I don't understand why you're spending so much time with a book-worm. As opposed to those types in the catalog."

Jack looked at me, considering. "Well, for starters, you're very unusual, Julia. I haven't really been with anyone like you. I like it that you're into books. And the blues. Oddly enough, I even liked the fact that you really checked me out before you let me get next to you. You're kind of peculiar too, not being into the girly stuff so much. I never fit the mold, either."

"I wasn't fishing for a compliment. It just seems like you would be going out with a model or an heiress, or something."

"I get tired of being seen as just a big paycheck, or a photo op. Most models are more into the blow than the sex, if truth be told. They're blathering on about how great you are in bed, but meanwhile you can see their little minds ticking, wondering how soon they can ask you for another line." He saw me looking askance. "Which by the way, I'm taking a slight break from."

I assume he means the cocaine.

"Anyway, it's kind of refreshing to be with someone who reads more than *Vogue*. Plus you turn me on. A lot. That satisfy you?" he concluded with a smile.

"I guess. I mean, thank you."

Jack yawned and gave a catlike stretch, his underarm tufts a shade darker than his hair. "God, this week got away from me. We're on a deadline to finish cutting the tracks before L.A. What are you up to next week?"

Happiness flooded me, then I recalled Dot's visit. "My mother's coming up Thursday night through Saturday morning. A friend of hers drives a truck route to Jersey, and she's catching a ride with him. I'm kind of dreading it; she's a live wire."

"My mum's a pistol too. Fully loaded and cocked."

"Is your dad around?"

"He passed a couple of years ago. He was always pretty buttoned-up; I wish I'd gotten to know him better. I need to get back over to visit Mum, though," Jack added. "It's been several months."

"Does she ever see you perform?"

"A few times. It's not really her thing. My half-sister came to some of our concerts, before she got married to a stiff."

"Oh, I didn't know you had a sister."

"Yeah, after the divorce Mum remarried and had a baby. But I was so much older, we didn't connect much until we were grown. Sharon lives in Surrey, has two kids, married to an attorney. I see them several times a year, whenever I'm over there. Her old man always takes me aside and wants me to tell him wild stories about being on the road. As if I would." He gestured toward the bureau. "My nephew Oliver just turned six; he's a real kick in the pants. That's him in the picture there."

"I noticed that. He's adorable." I was glad to hear the boy wasn't his own child.

Jack beamed. "He runs his mum ragged, just like I did mine. He was bouncing around so much on Christmas Eve, I thought I'd never get him to sleep."

"I'll bet it's nice being there for Christmas." I pictured a lavish Victorian feast. "Does your mother fix a big dinner?"

"Oh yeah, she puts out a stonking great spread. My contribution is cooking breakfast the next morning after Oliver and Emma—she's four—have opened their presents. I get there a few days early and kind of go crazy buying them stuff." He smiled. "Sharon complains I go overboard, but I love watching them tearing into things. 'Uncle Jack, you got me a Sting-ray!'"

he said in a little-boy voice. "I would have bitten me arm off for a bike like that when I was a kid. Matter of fact," he added, tracing figure eights around my nipples, "You make me feel like a kid again."

He got up and left the room for a minute. "Here, put these on," he said, slipping the lavender heels on my feet. "Looks even better with you in the buff. Now . . ." He slid me toward the edge of the mattress, raised my legs high and put my ankles around his neck. "I'll show you just how much you turn me on," he said, lowering himself onto me.

I gasped.

"You all right?" he asked.

I put his finger in my mouth and bit it.

"I'll take that as a yes."

I stayed at Jack's all Saturday. He blew off going to the studio, telling Patrick he'd make up for it later. I'd never spent that much time lolling in bed. In fact, time seemed fluid with him. There wasn't a mealtime, or a bedtime; you ate when you got hungry, you slept when you got sleepy. In between lovemaking—which he seemed to have an insatiable appetite for—we lounged around listening to music, or I watched him play the guitar; occasionally having a read from one of the books I'd bought him, ordering in food when the fancy struck.

Once in a while I found myself talking to him—or doing other things with him—more or less normally, and then it would hit me that I was with Jack Kipling of the Floor. But then he'd crack a joke, or I'd say something to make him toss back his head and laugh, or we'd talk about our favorite blues artists, and I'd forget that he was a rock star and just enjoy being with him.

Around midnight, Jack put his head in his hand and gazed down at me. "I've always been jealous of women being able to come so many times in a row," he said, trailing his finger around my belly in lazy circles. "Then again, it's probably payback for childbirth," he continued in a philosophical tone.

I decided to ignore the mention of other delirious women. "I guess. This is kind of new to me."

"This . . .?"

"This whole, um, coming thing."

Jack gave me a sharp look. "You're not serious."

"I mean, I have, you know, by myself," I stammered.

"Of course. But never with a guy?"

I shook my head.

"They must not have known what they were doing. You're like a volcano."

"Nobody ever . . ."

Jack grinned. "I get it. You haven't been with a real man before."

"Obviously not."

"We musicians have a saying about that, but I can't repeat it because it's too dirty."

"What is it?"

"If you wanna get the honey, you gotta kiss the cunny."

I rolled my eyes. "That's just charming."

"I told you it was dirty. Now you've got my curiosity up," Jack said. "How many guys have you been with? If you don't mind my asking."

"Four," I told him truthfully. "Before you, I mean." I recalled the unsatisfactory gropings of the few college boys I'd known. Art had been much more worldly, but that didn't extend to doing what Jack did.

"Is that all?" He seemed astonished.

I pulled a pillow over my chest. "Not everyone sleeps around indiscriminately, you know."

"Now, don't get in a snit. It's just . . . you must have gone to school with a bunch of gormless fools."

"I never even had a date in high school. I was too studious for the guys in my town; they only went out with the flirts. Plus I wore these thick glasses that weren't exactly the height of seductiveness. I didn't get contacts until college."

Jack studied me. "That explains it."

"What?"

"You seem unconscious of your looks; you don't fuss over yourself the way some girls do. A lot of women sort of wallow in it."

"I guess I still see myself as a four-eyes. Anyway, that's my track record. And like I said, watching my mother around men turned me off the whole concept for a while."

"Well, I'm glad you got over that," Jack said with a smile. "Believe it or not, I wasn't Mr. Suave in school either. One thing about being in a band though, even the awful groups I played in as a kid; there were always some girls hanging around. What about at university?"

"I mostly studied."

"But you did have a few fellas. And the last one was that professor." He gazed at me through lowered lids.

"Yes, that was kind of hard to get over. Looking back, maybe I was just dazzled by him."

"Dazzled because . . ."

"I don't know, I was new to the city, and he had a lot of connections and had read everything ever written," I concluded awkwardly, thinking how odd it was that Art had called only a few days ago. "He had this slick apartment near the college. In fact, he didn't like my place much. The one time he stayed over, he wound up taking a cab home at two in the morning."

"I think your place is nice. Especially now that it's not a furnace. What about your boss? Vicky made some comment about Harold."

I could have killed her for that. "Harvey. He just makes these sleazy allusions to things. Like he'll mention that his marriage is stale, and then ask if I want to have drinks."

"Bastard. You should let me know if he bothers you." He ran his thumb up my bare hip. "You haven't asked me anything though. You seem very uninterested."

"I probably can guess." I definitely wasn't uninterested, especially with this Nicole lurking around. But I sensed that acting possessive or prying would be the quickest way to put him off.

"You might *think* you know all sorts of bad things about me," Jack said, raising his eyebrow. "But it's not quite as awful as it's made out to be."

"I hadn't given it a thought," I lied. "We didn't even know each other until a few weeks ago."

"So you're not the jealous type." He gave me a quizzical look.

"You can't go and un-sleep with people," I said.

Early Sunday afternoon I walked back to my apartment, feeling confused. I'd had an amazing time with Jack, and he'd seemed happy to be with me. Around noon, knowing that he was due at the studio, I told him I should go home and do some work. He suggested making breakfast, so I decided to stay a little longer. But as he fixed the eggs, he started acting distracted and distant. When I was loading the dishwasher his phone rang, stopped, and rang again. I heard him making muttered plans to meet someone at a fancy restaurant that night. Quickly I gathered my backpack, thanked him for the weekend and rushed out, puzzling over his sudden shift in mood.

I clumped up my stairs, wondering who he was seeing later on. *Is he bored with me already? He acted so into me this weekend, but maybe that was just his sex drive.* Perhaps it didn't matter to him who he did it with, as long as he had a warm body in his bed. Maybe my expiration date had already expired, and I just didn't know it yet. I felt so alive after being with him; so awakened. Like a lid had been lifted, and now I couldn't fit it back on again. How could I resume my normal life after being with Jack? I was falling, falling, with nothing to stop my downward plunge. I knew that when I landed, it would be with a really hard thump.

Chapter 13

BOTTLE IT UP AND GO

When Harvey waltzed in at ten-thirty, I handed him a stack of pink messages with the three from his wife on top. He shut his door, but his raised voice still came through. Ugh, today wasn't going to be too pleasant. He'd been extra irritable lately, but at least he was letting me take Friday off to deal with Dot.

In between obsessing about my work problems, I was mooning over Jack. Every time I thought about the past weekend, it was hard to concentrate on the task at hand. Who was this creature I turned into when I was in his bed? The lack of control was exhilarating, but also scary. And I'd lost sleep wondering who he went out with Sunday night.

I'd finally finished rewriting Isabel's chapters and had scheduled an appointment with her. I needed to get it ready as soon as possible, in light of Briar's pursuit of Pryce Rayner's memoir. After Harvey rushed out to his lunch date, I speed-walked over to the Chelsea.

"You sure weren't kidding when you said you had some suggestions," Isabel commented, leafing through the pages. "I don't think there's a single line left intact."

"The material is really strong; I'm just honing the language. I'd like to get it in a little better shape before I show it to my boss." I had hoped she wouldn't be annoyed that I'd done so much rewriting. "How soon will you have the next batch for me?"

"Maybe in a week or two. I'm having trouble remembering my teenage years."

I thought quickly. "Why not skip ahead and write about your TV career? Then you could go back and fill in the earlier parts."

"Oh, I'm definitely gearing up to write about the show. But I have to do it in order; I can't jump around. It's hard enough as it is." Absentmindedly she stroked Dinah.

"Whatever works for you," I said, giving up. "Would it help to tell me some stories about what went on?"

Isabel brightened. "That time of my life was so crazy. During casting calls I got involved with the director. I surprised him in his office with my pubic hair shaved in the shape of a question mark, and lo and behold, I got the part." She smiled, awaiting my reaction.

"That sounds like a stand-out scene. I could see *People* excerpting that section."

"Oh, I'm sure they'll all want it. Then my costar Richard and I were hot and heavy during the first season, until he caught me on the tripod with the assistant gaffer. It was Mario's idea; I didn't realize the whole thing would go crash-ing over and bring everyone running. It did get me on a couple of talk shows, though." She sighed. "Everything seems so tame now compared to back then." Handing me a folder, she added, "This batch brings me up to age twelve."

"I can't wait to read more." I consoled myself with the thought that if she ever did get around to writing about the sitcom, it sounded like something Harvey would enjoy.

I got home at eight and decided to go for a run. I needed air in my lungs, even if most of it was car exhaust; the only exercise I'd gotten this past weekend was on Jack's mattress. I was still recovering from the intensity of sex with him, complicated by his confusing brush-off Sunday morning.

The sun was a scarlet smear over the West Side Highway. I got into my pace and ate up the blocks on the way uptown. Passing a billboard for back-to-school supplies unearthed a long-buried memory. The teacher hadn't come into my ninth grade homeroom yet, and we were all waiting in our seats. A boy slid a folded square of paper onto my desk. It seemed like the whole class was watching me.

"Open it," he said with a smirk.

I didn't want to; I assumed it was some sort of eye-chart joke, since I'd been given a hard time about my thick glasses before. But with the others saying "Go on, open it," and the girls in nearby desks tittering, I quickly unfolded the paper. At first I didn't recognize the squishy sopping circle inside. The entire room convulsed with laughter.

"Your mom left that in my uncle's car last night!" the boy crowed.

I ran to the bathroom and hid in a stall until the bell rang. Even after all this time, the recollection made me cringe.

Pouring on more speed, I leaped over a puddle of urine pooled at the base of a lamppost and circled to head back downtown. Halfway there I came upon Pamela in a shiny pink evening gown, arguing with a guy in a suit who looked like he'd had a few too many. "How's it going?" I said. She winked at me as I sprinted by.

The phone rang at eleven when I was drying my hair. I was thrilled to hear Jack's voice, but I didn't want to seem too eager after he'd acted so weird and distant. "I went for a run, and now I'm reading Harvey's submissions," I replied. "I saw Our Lady of the Blue Sequins. Tonight she was even more glam in pink. She was having a fight with some guy; what a rough way to make a living." I turned off the droning air conditioner so I could hear better.

"There's some scuzzy characters hanging around over there. Crackheads and such, looking to score."

"I don't think they'd bother me. Did you make it to the studio today?"

"Yeah, I just got home. Sammy, Mark, and I were trying to get this one thing down. Why don't you come over?"

God, I really, *really* wanted to see him, but I knew it was a mistake to be available at the drop of a hat. Things could easily deteriorate into my showing up at his place for sex late at night; a convenience for whenever the mood struck. It was a drag to feel like I needed to play these games with him, but his going out with someone else made things tricky. Not to mention that my job was on the line. "I can't tonight. I have five proposals staring at me, saying 'Read me, read me.'"

"You can read some over here; I'll let you alone. For a little while. How much time do you spend working at night, anyway?"

"A couple of hours usually, and more on weekends. Lately I've been backsliding."

"My opinion, you haven't been on your back nearly enough," Jack said. "Okay, I can do that. I'll amuse myself with this evil bitch of a tune that's been torturing me for the past two months. I'll keep away from you until midnight."

I was tempted to jump up, throw some work clothes in my bag and race over there. I almost said yes, but then I remembered how awful I'd felt when he'd acted so remote on Sunday. It was a bad idea to come running whenever he called last-minute—it seemed like something Dot would do.

"Sorry, but I have to stay here and slog through these things. Maybe we can get together tomorrow."

"What's the big deal? Can't you read them later?" He sounded mad.

"Harvey wants to call the agents tomorrow. I can't let anything slip with Briar breathing down my neck. I really need this job."

"Is it dough you need? I'll have Mary Jo send you a check."

"It's not just the money. It's my career. Anyway, I'm not going to sponge off you."

"It wouldn't be sponging. I've got it to spare; it's no skin off my teeth. Why not let me help you out a little?"

"That's okay. It wouldn't help me when I have to face Harvey and tell him I didn't get the reading done."

"All right, be that way."

He clicked off, and immediately I had second thoughts. I hoped he wasn't now calling whoever he'd spent Sunday night with. I tried to decide if I should call him back. It would be fantastic to be with him, instead of lying here alone with these stupid manuscripts. I kicked a pile of pages aside. *What's wrong with me? I just turned down Jack Kipling—how dumb is that?* As I was vacillating, the phone rang.

"I really don't know if I can come over." If he asked me again, I'd be there in seconds flat.

"I believe I'll survive," Vicky said dryly. "But I would like to catch up with you on the phone."

I felt ridiculous. "I thought you were Jack."

"I figured. But my question to you is, aren't you worried he's going to take up with another woman who'll give him her undivided attention?"

"Harvey's expecting these reports by tomorrow; I can't let anything slide with Briar nipping at my heels. She's going after Pryce Rayner's book."

"Isn't he a little shopworn by now?"

"Harvey doesn't seem to think so." I lifted the hair off the back of my neck.

"Well, be that as it may, you need to listen to some good advice about your sex life for a change. When you're sixty, what are you going to remember: the times you got it on with Jack Kipling, or the times you stayed home editing *Navel-Gazing for Novices*?"

"If I race over to his apartment every time he has nothing better to do, he'll get bored with me. Anyway, he went out with someone else the other night, so this fling might be short-lived."

"At least he isn't trying to get over on other women while you're with him."

"What do you mean? Is that what Sammy does?" *Man, it's hot.* I clicked the AC back on, and it hummed to life.

"Oh, he's constantly checking out other girls. But then I'm not supposed to look at anyone else because he's a rock god, and I'm just a regular person. I think he's getting ready to scout some new talent, so I might make my move first. Better the dumper than the dumpee."

"Are you guys going to that party at the Mudd Club? Jack mentioned it, but I have no idea if he's taking me. He may be taking his Sunday squeeze."

"I think we're going. If I see her there with Jack, I'll bite her."

"Enough about my woes. Tell me about your latest publicity coup."

"I got up at four a.m. to escort Bobby Pavlocek to the *Morning Show* green room the other day," she said nonchalantly.

"He's the hockey player, right?"

"Yes, we've just come out with his memoir. He shags a new girl every five pages."

"Was he a jerk?"

"You could say that. He changed clothes right in front of me; stripped down to his bvds like I was part of the furniture. Then he yelled at me because I didn't have a tube of hair gel on me. As if I'm his personal groomer."

"And people say PR isn't glamorous."

Vicky snorted. "Good luck with Dot this weekend."

"I'll need it."

Chapter 14

BIG APPLE DREAMIN'

I was on edge all day at the thought of my mother's visit. At six I left the office and walked up to the 42nd Street terminal. Dot stepped off the bus, looking around with wide eyes. She had on a tight pink top that revealed her bosom crease, and white pants with polka-dotted bikini underwear showing through. Her hair had been subjected to yet another color job that left it a brassier blonde than ever.

"Hi Mom," I said, taking her bag. "How was your trip?" I didn't try to hug her; my mother wasn't touchy-feely, at least not with me.

"Oh, I had a great time with Darrell. He's a scream."

We walked over to the subway, Dot asking loudly "Is this safe?" as I led her into its overheated depths. "What is that *smell?*" she said, making people in the token line roll their eyes.

"Some kind of sewer leak." She got stuck in the turnstile and I helped her through. "Mom. Try not to stare." She'd been giving the hairy eyeball to a man who was mumbling and gesturing at the ceiling. The train roared into the station, and we pushed our way on. "Why do they let them write all over the walls?" she asked, looking at the graffiti. "You can't read a word of it."

When we got to my apartment, Dot glanced around, her nose wrinkling. "Geez, Julia, you're paying three hundred for this? It's teensy."

"I told you it was small. For the neighborhood, it was a steal."

"Not enough room in here to sling a cat." She plopped down on the couch.

"Want a rum and cola?" I asked, recalling what she'd been drinking at Christmas.

"Oh, I'm off that. Do you have any gin?"

I'd spent fifteen bucks on the rum. "I can get some."

"Don't bother, I'll make do with this tonight. What do you have planned? I thought we could go out dancing, since you like that so much."

I had no intention of taking my mother to a club. "I got up really early," I said, pouring her a hefty dose of liquor and topping it with an inch of soda. "Let's stay in and catch up, okay?"

"I swear, sometimes I think I'm younger than you are. Oh, have I told you what Erwin did the other day? I was only ten minutes late getting back from my lunch break, and he yelled at me in front of Marie. I told him what's what."

She jutted her chin in that familiar way, and suddenly I was back in high school, hearing her justification for telling off her boss at the KwikMart; her reasons for arguing with her best friend. I zoned out as she described her latest dust-up. "After that Marie's son's girlfriend came in; she's the one who had the baby, but it's been hard finding a sitter . . ." I listened to Marie's son's girlfriend's troubles for half an hour, then I offered to run out for a pizza.

We shared our meal on my overturned milk crate; I still regretted not getting that gold-leaf table. As I draped some sheets on the sofa—I'd bought an extra set on Canal Street, since I was letting her have the futon all to herself—I brought up the subject of Jack, without stating exactly who he was.

"You know how you kept saying I should try to meet someone? Well, I finally did. But I'm not at all sure where it's going."

"When did this happen?" she asked with a sniff. I could tell she was getting her back up that I hadn't mentioned it before.

"A little while ago. I didn't say anything because I didn't know if we were just friends, or what."

"But you're more than friends now?" She sat on the edge of the bed.

"Only for the past couple of weeks."

"When were you going to tell me? All this time I've been worried about you. It's hard enough being alone in a small town where you know everybody; I can't imagine being single in a place like this."

"I wanted to tell you in person."

"Is he cute?" she wanted to know.

"I think he is. He has kind of long hair."

"Is he a hippie of some sort?" she asked suspiciously.

"I wouldn't call Jack a hippie. Actually he's a musician."

"What does he do for a job? He's not mooching off you, is he? I know that type." She scratched a match and lit a smoke.

"Oh no, he supports himself. His job *is* being a musician."

"Does he do weddings and parties, that type of thing? He could probably make a pretty penny in New York City. There are a lot of rich people here," she said with rounded eyes.

"I don't think he's ever done a wedding. He does 'do' a number of parties," I added, smiling to myself. "Ready to turn in?"

"I guess. Try not to wake me if you get up at the crack of dawn. I like to get my beauty sleep."

I crept outside at six and ran south toward Battery Park. As a light fog misted my face, I had a vision of my mother in her faded bathrobe, arguing with my father as she stirred pancake batter in the kitchen of our old house. Surely they'd had some good times together, but I couldn't think of many. Mostly I recalled them sniping at each other about money or her job.

One of my best memories was when I was five, going with my parents to see a local band at the county fair. The air was thick with mid-July mugginess and the mouth-watering scents of funnel cakes and caramel apples, an undertone of cow-and-pig wafting over from the agricultural exhibits. Dad went to speak to the fiddler, a buddy from the factory, then came back and boosted me onto his shoulders to watch. My mother was regaling a group of her friends, her lipstick a vivid slash of red in the pasty-faced crowd.

There was a light smattering of applause when the musicians came onto the low platform. The fiddler made a joke about the ancient Chinese art of tu-ning as he corrected the pitch. Then he winked in my direction and spoke into the microphone: "I'm gonna start off with a Hank Williams tune, dedicated to Julia Nash, her Daddy's favorite girl in the whole world who's sitting right there on his shoulders." Several people turned to smile at me, but I only had eyes for my young, handsome father. I worshipped the ground he walked on.

In a sober mood, I picked up bagels and coffee on the way in, paying with the bills I'd tucked under my sneaker tongue. I read a manuscript while my mother snoozed, enjoying the solitude. Sharing the loft with Dot brought to mind what it would be like if I lost my job and had to move back home with her. I'd be subjected to endless questions about why I was fired, and I-told-you-so comments about the futility of trying to make it in New York. I could see myself sitting at Buck's with my mother a few years from now, trying to muster some interest in a guy on the next barstool who reminded me vaguely of a musician I once knew.

While Dot was in the shower, the phone rang.

"It's me," Jack said. "What are you doing tonight? I thought we'd get dinner. Unless you're still being a stubborn bitch."

God, I can't wait to see him!

Damn, I won't get to see him. "My mom got in yesterday."

"I forgot she was coming."

"Yes, she's here until tomorrow." I couldn't just ditch Dot. Unfortunately.

"So bring her along." He said it like a challenge.

I heard the shower cut off. "Oh no, I wouldn't—"

"Pick you up at seven. I'll see you then, unless something comes up."

"Okay, let me know if you change your mind."

"I'll let you know."

I hung up, wondering if he would call later to back out of it. I couldn't believe he'd suggest taking us both; how on earth would that go? I decided not to worry about it and just be glad I might get to see him tonight. When Dot emerged from the shower, I tried to compose my face so I didn't have a smile plastered on it.

As she buttered her bagel, my mother filled me in on all the goings-on in our little town, including the far-flung relatives of her three best friends. She seemed to forget that I didn't know the same people she did any more, or that I might not be fascinated by the details of Paulette's sister-in-law's divorce. She also asked a few more things about the guy I'd been seeing, such as how old he was. I told her she might meet him tonight, but I was still keeping Jack's identity to myself. I was reluctant to answer a bunch of questions about how I came to be dating someone famous, particularly if he wound up canceling.

"He's a little long in the tooth for you, isn't he?" Dot commented when I said he was thirty-two. "Has he been married a few times?"

"No, he's never been married."

"Humph. Must be something wrong with him if he's still single. You couldn't meet someone your own age?"

"He's the person I'm interested in." Contemplatively I stirred my coffee. "I'm just not sure how interested he is in me."

"*I* could be going out with someone thirty-two."

I decided not to take the bait. "Let's go for a walk. There are some places I want to show you." I planned to get her good and tired, so she'd be less tightly wound by dinnertime.

We left my apartment and rambled around SoHo, and then I showed her my former dorm at NYU. As we ate our sandwiches on a bench in Washington Square, she commented loudly on the rollerbladers, the guy with a python scarved around his neck, women holding hands, and other oddities to her way of thinking. "Let's head up Fifth," I said, brushing crumbs from my lap.

By five-thirty, all the sightseeing had taken some of the tar out of her. We'd walked to the Empire State Building and rode the elevator to the observation deck to admire the view; then we went to the 42nd Street Library to see the lions. On the way home we stopped by Macy's, which made the biggest impression of anywhere she'd been all day. "I've always wanted to go there," she said. "Joan and Paulette will be so jealous."

I let her shower first and fixed her up with a large gin and tonic while I got ready, having picked up the liquor on the way in. Instead of a beer I poured myself rum and drank it neat. I was so wired up to see Jack, I could hardly stand it. Selfishly I wished I could have him all to myself tonight.

At last we were all set. My mother wore a low-cut top and black pants that stretched tight across her rear. She'd put on a little weight over the years, but her figure was still good, and she had a pretty face under all the makeup.

At seven-thirty I heard Jack calling from the street. I ran to the window and told him we'd be right there, feeling tense about how this date with Dot would unfold. We went downstairs, my mother complaining about her aching bunions. Jack stood by the open car door, looking fantastic in my purple shirt from Alice's, which he'd confiscated.

I took a big breath. "Jack, this is my mother, Dorothea. Mom, meet Jack."

"Good to meet you, Dorothea," Jack said.

I saw her starting to put his appearance together with his name, his British accent, and the fact that he was a musician.

"Call me Dot," she said, staring at him.

"Let's get in the car," I said. "So we won't miss our reservation."

"Can you stay with me tonight?" Jack asked in a low voice as she was climbing in.

I was dying to be with him, but I wasn't sure how Dot would take it. "I think I can."

"Did you get your work done the other night? I hope it was worth what you gave up."

"What was that?"

"Me making you come until you begged for mercy."

Hopefully my mother wasn't overhearing this. I got in the middle, introduced Mom to Rick, and we took off. The heat of Jack's thigh snug against mine sent a ripple of lust surging through me.

"So Dot, I understand this is your first visit to the city," Jack said, leaning forward in the seat.

"That's right." She poked me with her elbow. "Is that Jack Kipling?" she whispered audibly.

"Yes."

"You're going out with Jack Kipling?"

"Yes," I said under my breath. "Mom, stop whispering, it's rude."

"I had to jump through hoops to get your daughter to go out with me," Jack said.

"I can't imagine why. She hasn't had a date in ages."

Jack cocked an eyebrow at me, biting back a smile. "What did you two do today? Did you see some of the sights?"

"She made me walk all the way up to the library and back," my mother said. "I thought I was going to die."

"You *walked* to 42nd Street and back? In this heat?"

"It wasn't that hot," I said. "We had lunch in Washington Square, and then I wanted to show her Fifth Avenue."

"Julia should've had enough sense to take taxis on a day like this," Jack said to Dot.

"Well, I survived," she replied. "And I got to see Macy's, which made it all worth it."

"I hear it's got quite a selection."

"You've never been? Oh Julia, you'll have to take him. I can't believe you live so close by and haven't seen it yet. That's just a shame."

The car stopped in front of Odeon, where we were hustled back to a banquette and given drinks. Dot polished off her gin in record time. The waiter immediately brought a refill, after which she picked up her menu and read each entrée out loud to us, along with the prices. "I'll have the chicken," she concluded. "Although I don't see how they can charge eighteen dollars."

"That's New York for you," Jack said. "For that price, it should come with a side of Moroccan. What do you have on the agenda for tomorrow?"

"I'd like to see the Statue of Liberty," Dot replied. "And Bloomingdale's." She got a fresh pack from her purse and shook out a cigarette. Jack reached into his shirt pocket and flicked his lighter for her.

"Those places are miles apart. I'll have Rick pick you up in the morning; I can take a cab to the studio."

"Oh, that would be great. My feet are killing me," Dot said. "Is that a… music studio you're going to?"

"Yes, we're working on a new album, trying to finish it up."

"I've always liked your songs. The earlier ones are better than your last few, though," she stated unapologetically. "But your hair looks better than before. You used to wear it much too long."

I stuck my tongue in my cheek to keep from laughing. Jack merely nodded and said, "I suppose a lot of people agree with you."

The waiter put our dishes on the table and brought fresh drinks all around. Dot stabbed out her cigarette in the bread plate and sawed into her chicken with gusto. She gestured at Jack with her knife. "Julia was keeping you a secret," she said, her words slurring a little. I hoped she wouldn't get too sloppy before the meal was over.

"She was? Hmm. She's a cool one, your daughter. Very closed-mouthed at times," he said, his eyes alight with humor.

"I would have come a lot sooner if I'd known." She forked up her mashed potatoes.

"You would?" Jack grinned. It occurred to me that he was enjoying this far too much.

"Oh, sure. I need to keep tabs on her. I'm not much older than you, you know," she added with complete lack of segue.

"I would have thought you and I were the same age, if you didn't have a grown daughter," Jack said flirtatiously.

"People do say I don't look a day over thirty-nine."

"I would have said thirty-five, tops."

Dot inclined toward him confidentially. "Julia's not getting any younger either. She's twenty-four."

"Jack knows how old I am," I interrupted.

"I'm starting to think she'll never get married," she continued.

"I think you should be concerned," Jack said, regarding me through his eyelashes. "She's no spring chicken."

"Can you not talk about me as if I'm not here?" I asked.

"Sorry, Julia. I didn't know it was such a sensitive topic," Jack said.

"It's not. You're the one who's no spring chicken."

"I thought I had a twenty-year-old's physique," he replied in an injured tone.

"You do look like you're in good shape," my mother said. "You just need a haircut."

"I was saying the same thing to Julia the other day. You caught a ride up here with someone; is he a beau?"

"I used to play the field, but Darrell's just a friend." Dot drew on her cigarette.

"How *is* the field in Pennsylvania?" Jack asked.

"Sometimes the pickings are slim," she admitted.

"I'll bet you don't find yourself without company very often."

"Lately I've hit a dry spell. The past couple of years, to be honest." Her expression slumped. "It's tough being alone at my age. At a certain point all the men want to go out with much younger women."

I glanced at Jack; he didn't seem to take this comment personally.

"It worries me to death, Julia being in such a big city all on her own. She thinks she can handle everything herself. I used to be that way too, before I got married. But life has a way of slapping you down. I don't want that to happen to her." She gave Jack a hard look. "And I don't want her to get hurt by anyone who doesn't realize how special she is."

I stared at my mother; never in a million years would I have expected this speech.

The waiter came by and I said, "Check, please," before Dot could order another drink. Seeing her rising unsteadily from the chair, Jack took her arm on the way out. I opened the car door so he could help her in, and he sat between us.

"So Dot, I might not see you tomorrow since I tend to rise late, and I have to be at the studio by one. But I'm glad I got the chance to meet you," Jack said.

"I'm glad you got to meet me, too," she muttered, her eyes at half-mast. She looked like she might pass out on his shoulder.

Jack held her elbow again so she wouldn't stumble going up my stairs. We entered the loft and I stood by the door.

"Mom. I'm staying at Jack's tonight. I'll probably be back before you wake up. Okay?" I hoped she wouldn't make a fuss about it.

Dot looked at us and shrugged. "All right, I guess you're a big girl."

We hurried downstairs and got in the car. Wordlessly we grabbed hold, kissing and feeling each other all the way to his place. We ripped off our clothes as soon as we got inside. Jack backed me up against the wall, bent his knees and impaled me. His strong hands cupped my behind, the force of his thrusts lifting my toes off the floor. Just as his entire body started to tense, he pulled away.

"Let's get in bed," he said in a husky voice, breathing hard. He led me back to his room. "I've put money in your meter, baby; now I'm gonna check your oil." He scooped me up and laid me on the sheets, pushed my thighs apart, and teased and licked until I writhed in pleasure. Immediately he glided into me again.

"I think you like this, Miss Nash," he murmured. In answer, I wrapped my legs around his waist to draw him in deeper. I felt his muscles gathering, but then he withdrew, moved down my body, and touched me with the tip of his tongue.

"That first time was all right, but I'm sure you can do better," he said. Syrupy and saturated, I didn't think I could—but he proved me wrong.

Once more Jack climbed onto me and parted me with his cock. His taut abdomen brushed me as he moved, creating exquisite aftershocks that made me want to hold completely still and relish the sensation. Just as I was sure he was letting go, he left me yet again and slid downward. This time I came so hard, I heard myself scream. Jack rammed into me, gave three molten strokes, and with a wild cry, finally erupted.

"God, Julia. You'll have to have your mother up more often," he commented as we lay there recovering.

"That was definitely . . . the climax of the evening," I said, trying to collect my wits. "Although the meal was delicious." It was hard to have a casual conversation with him after such an earth-moving experience. I turned toward him on the pillow. "I hope she didn't seem too awful."

"Not awful in the least. I understand she wasn't a great parent when you were younger, but she struck me as kind of lonesome."

"Part of the reason she's lonely is that she got a bad reputation. She broke up her marriage to my Dad by sleeping with her manager at the hardware store."

"Well, you never know what goes on between a couple. Two sides to every story."

"In this case, I think the fault was all hers. But anyway, thank you for being nice to her."

"It's always easier to get along when it's not your own. My Mum has her moments too. What time do you want Rick to pick you up, so you can see Bloomingdale's and the statue before she leaves?"

"I love how she lumps them together. I don't know, maybe seven?"

"I'll have him stop by. Oh, Suzanne told me to ask if you'd like to see her studio tomorrow afternoon. You said something about it the other night, so I gave her your number. She'd love to show her stuff to a new victim."

"That would be great." Having never been to an artist's studio, I was intrigued.

"Don't get your hopes up in terms of the artwork," Jack commented. "But at least you two could have a nice lunch, if she'll go for something other than tofu. I have to record some vocals and do an interview with Patrick, then we'll hit that party at the Mudd Club. If you aren't planning to stay in with your fucking homework."

I tried not to act too gleeful. "Sure, if it won't get in the way of your other plans. I have an idea; want to trade places with me, since you like my Mom so much? You can explore the perfume counters, and I'll fill in on guitar."

Jack smiled. "No such luck. What time's her bus?"

"Eleven o'clock. I'll get her there nice and early so she doesn't miss it."

I got up at five the next morning and walked back to my place. True to his word, Jack sent Rick over and we made it to both landmarks, much to Dot's delight. We got to the Port Authority terminal on time, and she told me goodbye with an unsolicited promise to return soon.

"I really liked Jack," she said. "His hair kind of grew on me."

I treated myself to a visual of my mother with a wild rock'n'roll 'do sprouting from her head. "He liked you too."

"You know, with the restaurant prices around here, Jack would probably appreciate you cooking for him once in a while. The way to a man's heart is through his stomach," she advised. "Maybe he'd like a cake."

"I'm not much of a cook." That was an understatement.

"Oh, it's simple. You just need an egg beater; I didn't see one in your drawers."

She'd probably rummaged through every nook and cranny while I was out. "All right, Mom. Have a good trip." With a sigh of relief, I put her on the bus and took the subway home.

Chapter 15

NITE KLUB

After unpacking my weekend reading, I put on Billie very low. I was editing a new nonfiction manuscript of Harvey's about the Korean War; something I didn't know much about, but had to trust that the author did. Just when I was ready for a break, Suzanne called and suggested we meet at her studio.

I walked across town to Avenue B, passing bleary-eyed people creeping out of decrepit buildings that appeared to be condemned. The entire East Village was basically one giant crack den, which meant you had to be on your toes even in the daytime. Picking my way around discarded syringes outside Tompkins Square, I reached Suzanne's place and took a creaky freight elevator to the top floor. The door opened into an airy loft with several big skylights. Suzanne looked the part in overalls spattered with paint, her red hair bandannaed out of her face.

"It's so nice of you to come." She gave a toothy smile and held her cigarette aside to kiss my cheek. "Let me show you what I've been working on." She gestured toward two unfinished pieces on easels.

"Those are very nice." She had daubed splotches of paint on the canvas and put feathers into the wet patches to dry. The effect was, as Jack had put it, like a parakeet had flown into a window and bled colors down the pane.

Suzanne smiled. "Thanks. I've been feeling kind of stuck lately." She dropped her cigarette and crushed it into the tarp. "I was thinking of adding another type of material; maybe glass beads?" She seemed to be asking my opinion.

"That might be interesting." I recalled the bird-watching guide I'd just finished proofing. "Or since you love birds so much, what about doing paintings of them? A lot of people are really into them."

"Hmm, that's an idea. I'll think about it." Suzanne put her hands on her hips and stared at the canvas. "To be honest, I'm getting a little bored with the artist thing. Maybe I should go back into fashion. I just feel . . ." She turned to me, a searching look in her eyes. ". . . like I need something of my own to do. Mark doesn't want kids yet, and I don't really either. But I need something to keep me occupied, other than organizing his life. You know?"

"I think it's good to do your own thing," I agreed. "Did you like being a designer?"

"Not that much, really. It was mostly Mark forcing his friends' wives and girlfriends to buy my dresses. Once they'd all bought a few, it kind of dried up." She lit another cigarette and blew smoke toward the skylights. "What I'd really like is to have my own hair salon, but he doesn't want me dealing with the public."

"Has Ariel been any help in getting into the art scene?"

"Not really. She's dragged me along to a few parties, but I always feel like they're laughing at me. I don't know why it has to be so difficult; I see ridiculous things selling like hotcakes. This Schnabel guy glues pieces of his dinner plates to canvas, and he's considered a genius. Let's get lunch," she said, her expression brightening. "There's a great macrobiotic place on First."

We hit the street and walked to a cubbyhole of a restaurant. A sullen waitress poured us green tea without speaking and put an ashtray in front of Suzanne, who lit another cig. "I usually get the brown rice and steamed vegetables," she said.

"I'll have that too." The waitress went behind a beaded curtain and started shouting at someone in the kitchen to wake up.

"I admire you for working so hard at your job," Suzanne said. "Aside from the painting, I haven't done much since I've been with Mark."

"How long have you been together?"

"Six years. We met when I was a stylist in a salon in London. I did his hair, and one thing led to another."

The waitress plunked down two steaming bowls.

"I feel so much better since I went macrobiotic. I'm very careful what I put into my body," Suzanne said, stubbing out her cigarette. "I'd like Mark to go all-natural, but so far no dice. He says Jack would give him too hard a time. They like to tweak each other, as you may have noticed."

"They do seem close." I took a bite of undercooked brown rice.

"They're like brothers, and Sammy takes everything up a notch. They egg each other on, which can be funny, but sometimes it gets tiresome." She put down her fork, having eaten only a few mouthfuls, and lit up again.

"Does Patrick hang out with them much?" I asked, since she hadn't mentioned him.

"Oh, Patrick is a special case altogether. He's been in his own world the past couple of years. The blow-me bubble, Jack calls it. But Jack doesn't let him get away with it. Mark and Sammy are intimidated by him, but Jack just lets it fly. Plus," Suzanne added, "they have their little four-way competition going."

"They compete musically?" I asked.

"Musically, socially, every way you can think of. Who has the best clothes. Who can hold the most liquor without getting squiffy. Arguing over who writes the best lyrics. Going after the same girl to see who wins. Once Mark and Sammy went out with a dancer on alternating nights for a month, before she broke it off with them both. That was before he met me," she clarified. "But I don't see why they need the one-upmanship. Actually," she leaned toward me, "I think fucking the same girl is the closest they can get to fucking each other, without really doing it." She winked.

Now that's a disturbing thought.

"I have another theory," she added in a low voice. "This one goes a bit deeper. From what Mark has said, none of them could get anywhere with women before they hit it big. Deep down, they still feel like those gawky guys who couldn't make it with a girl. So anyone who'd pursue them must not be worth it, right? Like any club that would want me, I don't want to join."

"I see what you mean," I said, spearing a tiny hooded mushroom.

"But if the girl has been with Patrick, then she really *must* be desirable because *he* wanted her, and he's one of the top rock stars in the world. So that makes it okay for Jack or Mark to want her. Or even Sammy, if he's feeling particularly lucky. And the same for Patrick; if a girl has been with Jack, then it validates him wanting her. Makes it even better in fact, because he's so jealous of Jack. Then he's one up on him."

"That's quite a theory you've worked out. I can see how it makes sense."

Suzanne shrugged. "You get to know a lot about human nature when you're doing hair."

I wondered if Jack had competed for a woman with Mark or Patrick in the past. If he had, obviously it could happen again. "Jack and I seem to be getting a little closer, but sometimes it feels like one step forward and two steps back."

"Jack can be a bit . . . elusive," Suzanne said enigmatically. "I should tell him to bring you to L.A. with us; it gets tiring being around Patrick's chippies. And you seem to be a steadying influence on Jack. Which hopefully will rub off on Mark." She smiled.

I'd love to go, but I don't exactly have an invitation. I thought about her "steadying" comment. "I'll bet it can be difficult being with a musician. Especially at their level."

"The star thing can get a little old. I'm not knocking the money or lifestyle; I'm definitely spoiled. But having to be on the alert all the time for other women prowling around—that wears me out." She frowned and signaled for the check. "And they're so wrapped up in their own world when they're making a new album, sometimes you feel like second fiddle. Or third or fourth."

"It sounds like it's smart to stay as independent as possible."

Suzanne sighed. "That's easier said than done. I'll be glad when this record is finished; they've been living and breathing it for months, and now they're getting ready for a couple of concerts they've decided to do while they're in L.A. You haven't been to see them rehearse yet, have you?"

"No, but I'd like to. I didn't know anyone outside the band could watch."

"I'll tell Jack to bring you along one night."

I got some money out of my bag, but Suzanne waved it away. "Oh no, my treat. We'll have to do this again soon," she said before we parted.

At six-thirty the phone rang and a twangy guitar chord resonated in the receiver. "Hello?" I said. Another chord, a little higher, then it dropped way down low and repeated for a few beats. "Could you tell what I was saying?" Jack came on the line.

"Um . . . you're almost done there?"

"I'm desiccated, I'm pixilated, I'm frustrated, I'm about to bust open, I'm so full of what I got to give you," Jack said in his black blues voice. "I'm gonna pass out if I don't get me some soon. I'ma boil your cabbage when I get home, baby."

"My cabbage can't wait," I said, laughing. "But I did get a lot done today. And I'm much more knowledgeable about the conflict in Korea."

"We have to work on your sex talk," Jack said in a normal tone. "Ko-rea just ain't doin' it for me."

"Sorry, but that's what I've been up to. Should I meet you at your place?"

"I'll see you there. You can assist me in the shower."

"Now I feel a lot better." Jack sat on the edge of the mattress and toweled off his hair. It stood up straight from his head, pointing in all directions.

"Hold on, I'll dry it for you." I went into the bathroom, where water was still trickling slowly down the drain. I picked up the sopping wet towels from the shower floor, wrung them out and hung them up, then got the blow drier. I plugged it in by the bed and stood in front of Jack, lifting strands of his damp mane and drying it piece by piece. He put his arms around me, eyes closed, his face resting against my bare chest.

"Mmm, you're putting me to sleep," he mumbled into my breast.

I wish we could just curl up together, stay in and skip the party. "Do you want to rest for a while? You must be tired." Five hours of playing the guitar, sandwiched between what we'd been doing, surely must have taken a toll.

"Nah, let's go to this thing; you've been stuck inside most of the day," Jack said. "I want to get out too. Thanks for the blow-job. I mean the blow-dry. Actually both," he added with a grin.

"You're welcome." He'd showed me a new technique in the shower that he definitely seemed to enjoy. "I guess we'd better get dressed if we're going."

"Why don't you pick something out for me to wear?"

"Okay," I said, going over to the closet. "If I don't come back in an hour, be sure to come find me."

"It's not that bad, is it?" Jack said, following me. "I just need to hang some of this shit up."

The tangle of clothing looked even worse than before. The laundry baskets were full to overflowing, surrounded by piles of shirts, pants, ladies' items . . . I spied the blonde wig laying on the shelf next to a top hat.

"I've got to let Carla in here to do the washing," Jack said. "She ruined a couple of my suede jackets throwing them in the machine, and ever since I've told her to just leave it."

"How about these?" I plucked a pair of pants from the floor. "With this shirt?" I indicated one of the few on a hanger.

"Good choice." The phone rang, stopped, and rang again. Jack went to rumble into the receiver. "Really, he won't go to back to sleep? All right, put him on."

I listened, curious about who it was.

"Hello Oliver," Jack said. "Your Mum tells me you got up in the middle of the night. You don't have a tummy ache, do you?"

For a minute he was silent. "I've had bad dreams too. They seem real, but they're not." He paused. "Sure, here goes. But promise me you'll go back to bed after this."

He waited for an answer, then crooned into the phone: "When Ollybear played, he played very hard; when Ollydog ate, he ate very much. When Ollyfish splashed, he splashed very big; when Ollycat bathed, he bathed very clean. When Ollyowl flew, he flew very high. When Ollymouse slept, he slept very soft . . ." He repeated the phrases several times, eventually drifting into a barely audible whisper.

"No trouble at all," he said in his regular voice. "Yeah, I'm going out with Julia tonight. Sure, she's wild for me," he added loudly, for my benefit. "Yeah, she's here now . . . I won't . . . I will. Okay, love ya."

Jack hung up and came into the bedroom, smiling. "Oliver had a bad dream and wouldn't go back to sleep 'til I sang him his bedtime number. I usually tuck him in when I'm there."

"Were you always into kids?" I asked.

"Nah, just lately. It was having my own nephew that did it. And Emma's getting to be fun too, now that she's bigger. She was more of a mama's girl before." Jack regarded me. "How about you, have you ever dealt with children much?"

I shook my head. "Never even babysat."

The phone rang again. "Yeah, we're ready. We'll see you there." He hung up. "That was Sammy. They're heading out now."

We went down to the car, and in a few minutes Rick stopped at the club on White Street. The photographers were out in force, and this time Jack had sunglasses for both of us. We started making our way through the phalanx of popping lights.

"Jack, Jack!"

"Jack, this way!"

We were almost to the door when a pudgy man stuck his camera in my face and blinded me with his flash. "Another new ladyfriend, Jack? I thought you preferred blondes."

Like a shot, Jack was on the guy. He pushed him into the wall. "Want me to rearrange your face, you cunt?"

The man exploded his flash in Jack's eyes. "Go on and hit me! I'll see you in court!"

Jack drew back his fist. "I'll kick seven shades of shit out of you!"

I snatched at his sleeve. "Jack! Let's go inside."

Jack glared at the man for a moment longer, then shoved him away hard. He took my arm and pulled me toward the entrance. Inside the music was so loud, the floor was shaking with the bass. *Has Jack brought his blondes to this club? Of course he has, since the photographers know his preferences.*

"Your party's on the fourth level," said a woman with a shaved head and studded collar.

We pushed through the churning mass of spiked and tattooed punks, Jack with his shades still on. Upstairs, the wall bore a mural by Keith Haring, an artist whose work I'd seen around the East Village. The crowd was less cutting-edge than the one below; slick-looking women in black leather—many of them blonde—lounged on couches, while others shouted over the noise. Several people made a beeline for Jack right away. He spoke to them and I nodded, but didn't catch their names. I was still vexed by the photographer's comment. It was starting to ruin my mood, so I forced myself to push the thoughts away.

A woman with a roundish figure and shoulder-length brown hair approached. "Julia, this is Mary Jo," Jack said, gesturing between us.

"Good to meet you," Mary Jo said, scrutinizing me with piercing hazel eyes. "Did you get your PR done this afternoon?" she asked Jack.

"Yeah, it went fine. Patrick did most of the talking."

"As usual," she observed. "Speaking of which, a new TV channel is starting on August first, called MTV or some such. They wanted to know if you guys would do an interview. No telling how big an audience they're going to get, so it might not be worth your time."

"Up to Patrick," Jack said. He asked what we wanted, then went to find the bar. Mary Jo looked at me. "Jack has mentioned you a few times. Maybe you and I could go out for a drink."

I had the distinct impression she wasn't too pleased with whatever he'd said. "How about Tuesday; six-thirty at Fanelli's?" She nodded. I wondered why she wanted to see me without Jack around. I hoped I'd pass the audition, but somehow I doubted it.

Jack sailed back to us pinching two plastic cups in each hand, Sammy and Vicky in tow. I embraced Vicky, happy to see a friendly face. Jack handed Mary Jo and me our drinks, belted down a whiskey, put his empty beneath the second cup and sipped it. Mary Jo left to talk to someone else.

"I like this music." Vicky twisted her hips to Bad Brains. "What do you think of it, Jack?"

Jack eyed her. "I figure we survived disco; we'll survive punk too."

"Let's go shake our tail feathers," Sammy said, and they went to where the dancing was.

"So here you two lovebirds are." Mark's hair was back to its normal color with only a few splotches of green on the ends, which made his beak of a nose even more pronounced. Suzanne's leopard-print dress accentuated her angular frame.

"That was fun today," she said to me. "Jack, you haven't invited Julia to the studio yet. She'd like to see you rehearse."

"She's so busy with her work, I doubt she'd have the time. Plus it's kind of boring."

"Oh, I'd love it," I said.

"Anybody want another drink? I'm going to get a chaser." He headed for the bar.

We were joined by Patrick, decked out in skintight chartreuse pants that looked like they'd been sprayed on, and a tangerine-colored top that set off his azure eyes. Patrick laughed at something Mark said, and then gazed in my direction.

"I see you have staying power," he commented, as if I was a burr stuck to Jack's britches. "I was reading an interesting book the other day on Nicholas and Alexandra. Is that the kind of thing your company publishes?"

"We do a little history, but it's mostly commercial stuff."

"Isn't that the way of the world. Did you finish your Proust?"

I was surprised he remembered. "I'm bogged down in the third volume. I just need an uninterrupted chunk of time to make a dent in it."

"What are you making a dent in?" Jack asked, appearing beside me with a foaming beer.

"Julia and I were talking about Proust," Patrick said, as if we'd been in a deep intellectual discussion.

"Only the fact that I haven't been reading much of it lately," I added.

"How d'you think the interview went?" Patrick asked.

"You dealt with 'em well. Like always," Jack said offhandedly.

Suddenly the music got even louder and Jack's distinctive guitar blasted into the crowd, which roared its approval. Yet the song was unfamiliar. Jack grinned at Patrick.

"It's the studio tape," Patrick said. "I thought we could see how it went over."

The tune was enticingly good; it made people immediately jump out onto the floor. Jack led me to where there was some space. He swayed his lean hips and sang along to the words, which of course no one else knew. I spotted Vicky dancing with someone else, and I wondered where Sammy was. Then I forgot everything and melded myself with the intoxicating rhythm. A guy with long blond ringlets and tight leather pants came up to Jack and put a hand on his shoulder.

"What?" Jack shouted over the music.

"I said, if she fucks like she dances, you're a lucky man." He gave me an oily leer.

Jack frowned. "That's for me to know." He turned his back on the guy, who shrugged and wandered off.

We continued moving to one great song after another until a slower number began. Jack came close and suddenly we were kissing and he was touching me, arousing me.

"Watching you dance turns me on," he spoke in my ear. "Like the first time I saw you. Want to go?"

"Yes," I breathed. He took my arm and we headed toward the exit. All at once he came to an abrupt standstill, staring at a slim, busty blonde in a midriff-skimming top who was gyrating frenetically around Patrick. Jack started to turn in another direction, but the woman spied him and bounded over to us. Jack stood in front of me, and with a sinking feeling I realized who she was.

"Having fun?" Nicole said, waving her cigarette. "Who's this you've got with you?"

"None of your concern," Jack said through his clenched jaw. "Let's go." He pulled me past the clots of people to the stairs. We hurried out to the street, where the photographers were still lying in wait. The bulbs popped again and again; I was so unnerved by having seen Nicole that I forgot to put on my sunglasses. At least from her jutting hipbones it was obvious she wasn't several months pregnant.

"I don't know who invited her, but I'm going to make it a point to find out," Jack said once we were in the car.

"She really seems to have it out for you." I wished I hadn't seen her; now that I knew what she looked like, I could envision him being with her. In fact, she was exactly the type of blonde I'd think someone like him would be with: tall, big-boobed, sort of slutty in an expensive way.

"What a night. I wanted to relax, and then she has to come along and fuck it up. Let's just forget about her."

Jack was pouring two mugs of coffee the next morning when the phone started ringing. "Didn't unplug the goddamn thing," he muttered, and grabbed it on the eighth ring. He listened for a minute, then I heard him snarl, "Mary Jo will send you one last check, and that's it. You've got to stop calling me." He pulled out a chair and sat with his head in his hands.

"I'll have to get Mary Jo to change my number," he said slowly. "I hate to do it, but she's not going to let up."

I was rattled by this renewed assault from Nicole. I wondered what he'd promised her when they were going out together. Something must have gone on between them for her to pursue him this way. An image of Dot scurrying after the guy in the pickup truck flitted across my mind.

"I'm going to head back to my place." I started toward the bedroom to get dressed. Frowning, Jack pushed back his chair.

"Were you two engaged?" I blurted out.

"Engaged? Why would you think that?" His voice had a rough edge to it.

"Just the way she's acting."

"I told you I only went out with her for a couple of months.

Very sporadically. My cock liked her for a while, but even that got old."

Is that what he'll be saying about me a few weeks from now? "I need to leave soon anyway. I have plans tonight."

Jack looked surprised, but that was too bad. He wasn't the only one who could go out with other people over the weekend.

Chapter 16

CROSS-EYED AND PAINLESS

The sky had just gone dark; I could hear music playing up on the roof. Vicky and I took the elevator to the top floor and climbed a short flight of steps. When she'd called me about this party in Brooklyn Heights—thrown by a friend who worked at Viking—I'd decided I should treat Jack to some of his own medicine. Maybe it would do him good to see that I wasn't hanging around hoping he'd want to spend all weekend with me.

Vicky adjusted her skirt, which had hiked up during the climb. The stars were beginning to sparkle, and up this high there was a slight breeze to relieve the oppressive heat. The crowd was an interesting mix of publishing people, artists, and punks; the partner of the Viking publicist was a videographer, and they had a lot of edgy friends. We found Kelly and Iris handing out miniature bottles of bubbles and little eggs of stretchy putty. Vicky gave them the bag of mooing cow cubes we'd picked up in Chinatown, as everyone had been told to contribute a favorite party favor. They were so cute, I'd kept a few for myself.

We caught up with the women and then went in search of beverages. I didn't recognize the music blasting out of the speakers, but Vicky said it was a group called Blue Angel whose vocalist, Cyndi, was fantastic. People were lying back on mattresses, smoking joints and gazing at the stars. Brando's *On the Waterfront* was being projected on one side of a brick wall; the other side showed one of Iris's video installations that interspersed women kissing with buildings being dynamited.

"Cool party," I commented.

"Yes, but why'd they hide the bar over there?" A shirtless guy was pouring drinks at a sticky table made of soldered-together television sets. As we waited, two pink-mohawked women shared lines of coke on a jagged piece of glass. We got our beers and went to the edge of the roof, abutted by a waist-high wall. The lights of lower Manhattan shimmered in the distance, the Towers' lids glowing like UFOs.

"Here's to being footloose for one night," Vicky said. "Just like old times. At least you're seeing somebody great, unlike me." She'd had a big fight with Sammy when she stumbled on him feeling up a girl at the Mudd Club.

"At least your job is going great, unlike mine. If romance *and* work ever click, I'll feel like I've won the lottery."

Vicky raised her eyebrow at something behind me; a couple of guys sharing a smoke. They came over and the first, wearing a scarlet Siouxsie and the Banshees tee-shirt, passed the joint to Vicky.

"How's it going?" he shouted over the booming music.

"It's starting to pick up." Vicky took a hit and held it out to me. I hesitated for a second; pot really wiped me out.

"Go ahead, it's homegrown on Neal's windowsill," the blond guy said. "I suppose you're from the publishing contingent."

"How did you know?" I inhaled and held the smoke in, trying to suppress a cough.

"You don't have any piercings or tattoos. That are visible." He had a really nice smile. "I'm Dave."

"I'm Julia; this is Vicky. How do you know Iris and Kelly?"

"I live in the building," Neal said. "I'm a med student. And part-time herbologist." He indicated the weed.

"How nice for your patients; natural anesthesia," Vicky said.

"I'm not allowed to share with them, but many of the staff partake. It helps with some of the student loans. Which I'll be paying off until I'm fifty."

"Are you of the medical persuasion too?" Vicky asked Dave.

"Lawyer. Neal will be hiring me when he leaves a roach clip in somebody's appendix."

"Hey, they make good sutures," Neal said. "Keeps the gore in check when we get a gunshot victim."

"Yeah, that tee-shirt of his used to be white," Dave commented as Neal lit another joint and passed it around. Feeling much more relaxed already, I decided to have one more toke, this time managing not to cough.

"Let's nab one of those comfortable-looking beds," Neal said. "I've just come off rotation; I've been on my feet for seventeen hours straight. Today we had the complete ER menu: several OD's, a teenager who gave birth in the admitting room, two working girls with STDs, a nice deep stab wound to the gluteus maximus, twins with double ear infections who screamed nonstop for three hours, and two crispy critters. They set themselves on fire with their crack pipes," he explained. "And another gay guy wasting away with that weird virus we've been seeing. So you'll have to excuse me if I'm incoherent."

We followed him to a mattress and sat with our backs against the low brick wall.

"Do you do litigation?" I asked Dave. I stifled a yawn; the pot was already making me feel out of it.

"No, I'm a boring corporate type. Not as interesting, but it pays well." He glanced at my legs stretched out beneath my leather skirt; I hoped the staples in the hem weren't too obvious. "What do you do, other than spend a lot of time at the gym?"

"I'm an assistant editor. I can't afford a gym; I run."

"Me too, I do the loop around the park. I'm on West Eighty-Third. The neighborhood's a little iffy but it's slowly gentrifying. How do you like publishing?"

Disconcerted by his close gray-blue gaze, I wondered if Jack was out on the town tonight. "It's okay. The goal is to be a full editor, but that takes a while."

"Kind of like making partner, I imagine." Dave smiled.

"Minus the big paycheck."

Beside me, Vicky and Neal were stretched out, murmuring to each other. "Do you want to dance?" I asked.

We went over to join the crush jumping around to the B-52s. My head was starting to swim. The effect of the movie projected drive-in-size, combined with the crashingly loud music, was surreal—or maybe it was just the pot. The constellations were chasing each other around in streaky loops. It hit me that living in New York had the same effect as stargazing; it made you feel tiny, inconsequential, and alone.

Dave touched my arm. "Want to go over there and get some air?"

I nodded. I should have eaten something before the party if I was going to be drinking, much less smoking. I sagged against the wall, trying to quell my dizziness. Suddenly his arms were around me and he was kissing me. I started to kiss him back, but then I pulled away. "I'm sorry, I'm seeing someone."

"That's all right; so am I."

"I'd better go home. I feel kind of faint. Can you tell Vicky I'm leaving?"

"Why don't you let me take you home?"

I just shook my head. Dave returned in a minute with my backpack. "I don't see them. I'll get you a cab." The elevator's sinking sensation made me feel like I was going to throw up. Dave hailed a taxi and handed me a twenty. "It's going to be an expensive ride," he said when I tried to give it back. "Here's my number. Call me sometime." He shut the door and I gave the driver my address, asking him to take the turns slowly.

When I unlocked my apartment, the phone was ringing. It stopped just as I reached it and I crawled into bed, grateful that I'd made it without losing my lunch. After a few minutes it began again. Woozily I crept over.

"Hello?" I croaked.

"You finally got home," Jack said. "How about if I stop by? I'm in the neighborhood." A car horn blared; he must be using a phone booth.

I look like something the cat dragged in. "I'm really beat."

"That's okay, I won't molest you. I'll just go to sleep."

"I can't make it out of bed again."

"Go straight to your window. I'm on your block now."

I went to peer out and saw Jack striding down the street. I tossed the sock and got back in bed. In a minute I heard his boots thunk on the floor, followed by a low moo.

"Who's Dave?" He was holding the strip of paper I'd dropped on the table along with the cow cubes.

"Some guy I met at a party with Vicky."

"Nice fella?"

"Yes.'"

"Smart? Good-looking?"

"Very."

Jack took the paper and went into the bathroom. I heard the toilet flush. "That takes care of him," he said.

I started to tell him he had no right, but I was too wasted to muster the energy. Jack stripped off his clothes and got in beside me, his erection poking my hip. He sniffed my hair. "I thought you didn't do too well with the maryjane."

"I don't. I almost threw up."

"Want some water?"

"I had some."

"Feeling better now?" He nuzzled my neck.

"Mmm ..."

His lips on me felt so good. I touched him, and he groaned. "You'd better not do that unless you want to be up for a while."

"I think you've awakened me."

Chapter 17

SLIPPERY PEOPLE

I tiptoed around my apartment getting ready, trying not to disturb Jack. He was still conked out face-down on the pillow as I put on my shoes. I took one last look; tangled hair spread across his shoulders, stubbly chin already needing a shave, silky black lashes brushing his cheekbones as he slept. His bare bottom had such a lovely peachlike curve that I was tempted to take a bite.

Walking uptown, I mused about the weekend. Dave was cute and witty; if I wasn't seeing Jack, he was exactly the type of guy I'd want to go out with. But Jack's irresistible pull drew me like a moth to a flame. I thought about his surprise visit to my apartment last night. Maybe the way to hold Mr. Kipling's attention was to keep him guessing; there was no doubt he'd lain in wait to see if I came home with someone. And he'd seemed to want me so burningly. Recalling the forceful way he took me caused a catch in my throat.

I was in such a daze for the next forty-eight hours, it took me twice as long to get anything done at work. Tuesday night I hoofed it down to Fanelli's feeling sweaty and disheveled, my jacket balled up in my backpack. I shrugged into it before I entered, hoping to convey a professional impression. Mary Jo was already seated on a stool, wearing a tailored pants suit. Hal brought my draft and we caught up for a minute.

"This is your local bar," Mary Jo observed.

"I'm right over on Broome," I said before recalling that she knew this already.

"Getting to be a pricey neighborhood." She arched her eyebrow.

I wondered what she was implying. "I have a pretty good deal on my rent right now. Hopefully my landlord won't raise it."

"So you work in publishing, Jack tells me."

Here comes the interrogation. "Yes, I'm an assistant."

"He described you as an editor," she said in a challenging tone.

"I'm an assistant editor, which means I have a tiny office," I added, not knowing why I felt the need to explain.

Mary Jo seemed to consider this. "Jack says you're different."

I started to ask "Different how?" but decided to just leave it alone. I took a sip of my beer and let the silence sit for a minute.

Mary Jo cleared her throat. "I haven't seen any money flowing your way yet, which certainly does set you apart in that respect. Just an air conditioner, which is probably mostly for Jack since he hates being hot."

So this was why she was here; she wanted to see what I was going to cost him. "I didn't ask him to buy me that air conditioner."

"So I understand." Her manner implied she only half-believed me.

"How long have you and Jack known each other?" I said, trying to turn the tables.

"Seven years." Her voice softened. "He was so kind when I went through my divorce; he let me cry on his couch many times."

"He seems to rely on you a lot. Not that I know him very well yet, but he mentions you often. We only met a few weeks ago."

"Yes, I remember when he first met you," she said with a wry expression. "He called me the next afternoon and went on and on about this beautiful girl who wouldn't let him walk her home: 'She's a cracking stunner, Mary Jo.'" She eyed me appraisingly. "That was a shrewd move on your part, not letting him come home with you right off the bat. Sharpened his appetite."

I bristled at her snide comment. "I had no intention of sharpening his appetite," I sputtered. "He tricked me into going out for a drink."

"I heard all about it."

I put some bills on the bar. "Good meeting you."

She grabbed my arm. "Hold on a minute. I'm very protective of Jack. He tends to be overly enthusiastic in these situations initially, and then later on it's difficult for him to extricate himself. Some of these ladies he's been with were quite the little mercenaries."

My spirits sank at hearing that he got unduly enthused at first; I'd suspected that might be true. "I can see why that would concern you," I said stiffly. "I can promise I won't ask him for anything."

Mary Jo frowned. "I don't want to give you the wrong impression; he does seem to really like you. He'd kill me if he thought I implied something else."

"I guess I'm in the pre-extrication phase."

"Forget I said that. You know about that whackjob Nicole, right?"

"I know she keeps calling. He was upset about having to change his number."

"She's been charging thousands of dollars' worth of clothes to him, lying about being preggers, threatening a paternity suit, and demanding more money on top of that. They only went out for a couple of months off and on, for Chrissake. She's no more pregnant than I am." Mary Jo looked at me. "So you can see why I'm in defensive mode. Jack's vulnerable right now. Please don't do anything to hurt him."

"*Me* hurt *him*?" I asked incredulously. "I would never do anything to hurt him."

"Well, Julia, you seem like a nice enough girl. I just hope appearances match reality." She stood and smoothed down her pants. "I imagine we'll be seeing each other again."

I bolted out of the bar. All the way home, I thought about what she'd said. Of course I was just a small eddy in an endless stream of his lovers; I'd be a fool if I didn't take the warning to heart. But it still hurt like hell to have the truth shoved in my face.

I tried to put the encounter out of mind by immersing myself in Isabel Reed's latest batch of pages. I had just settled in when the phone rang. A British voice spoke, but it wasn't the one I expected.

"I finally got past the madeleines last night," Patrick said. "Let's go out for dinner Thursday. We can talk about our favorite writer."

Is this a joke? "Hold on a second." Quickly I thought about how to deflect his sticky question. "Jack, are we free for dinner this Thursday?" I called out, then waited as if listening to a reply. "I think we could do it then. Where should we go?"

For a minute there was silence on the line. "All right, I get the picture," Patrick said. "Maybe another time." After he hung up, I recalled Suzanne's comments about their one-upmanship. I figured Patrick was just testing me, and would have told Jack if I'd said yes. I decided not to mention his prank to Jack.

Immediately the phone rang again.

"Remind me not to give you any more reefer."

"Where did you and Neal disappear to? I had to get a cab home by myself."

"He wanted to show me his potted plants," Vicky said. "Or should I say, his potted pot. Sammy and I just broke it off. I told him I didn't expect monogamy, but groping a girl right under my nose at the club was a bit much. He didn't get why it was a problem. Did you see that long-haired blond guy staring at you while you were dancing with Jack? Someone said he's a producer from a rival record label."

"He came over and made a dumb comment."

"Since you've been hooked up with Jack, you're really giving off sparks. That's always the way with me, too—the minute you're seeing somebody, a million other guys are interested. But when you're not with anyone and you could use a little attention, it dries completely up."

"I think you're onto something there. Too bad it's over with Sammy."

"Oh, I'm not obsessing about it, although I will miss the rock star ambiance. Tomorrow I'm having dinner with Kurt, the guy I met at the club."

Vicky never needed any down time in between. "Good for you," I said.

Two nights later I was pacing my floor. For the third time I checked to make sure the phone plug wasn't loose. I put on yet another album and applied a little more lip gloss, then did a fifteenth lap around the room. I sat in my windowsill and watched for the black car that should have pulled up an hour ago. Finally at eleven I washed off my makeup and got undressed. Jack had said he'd come by at eight when he left the studio, and we'd get dinner. But now I guess I'd officially been stood up. I got into bed and finally drifted off.

Around three, I heard a hoarse voice croaking my name. I looked out to see Jack swaying unsteadily below.

"Julia. Lemme in."

"Go home. You're drunk."

"Thass right! Lemme in."

A window on the second floor flew open. "Do you have to wake up the whole building?" someone screamed.

I guessed I had to let him up; Mr. Iaccone hated complaints from his tenants. Rather than braining Jack with the key—he looked far too stoned to catch it—I went down and opened the door. He followed me up, leaning heavily on the wall, and collapsed on my couch.

"I thought we were having dinner," I said, keeping my distance.

Jack squinted one eye. "Some people came by. We hit a few bars."

"You can sleep out here. I'll bring you a sheet."

"Don' need any sheet."

"Suit yourself."

He turned to his side, and I caught a whiff of a faint flowery scent that definitely was not eau de Jack. I got into bed fuming. Why did he come over? He could have just gone to his own place, especially if he'd been with someone else. I tossed and turned, unable to sleep, and left for work exhausted, leaving him passed out on my sofa.

"Did you ever hear from Jack?" my mother wanted to know.

"He showed up drunk last night after he stood me up for dinner. I let him in, but from the way he acted, I should have sent him home."

"Maybe you shouldn't have let him in. It doesn't do to be too available."

This, from her, was astounding advice. "Right, Mom. I imagine you've found that to be true in your dealings with men." Part of my annoyance was that I *had* been too available. I should have sent him away, even if he woke the whole building.

"Julia, that's not fair. Lately I've been much more particular."

I stopped myself from saying "About time." I had a sense that this recent selectivity was more on the male side than on hers. "Anyway, what have you been up to this week?"

"We finally finished inventorying, so I'm back on the register. Oh, and I finished that new Joyce Sutter book. Did I tell you about it? The one about the Civil War?"

"Lots of good battle scenes?" I teased.

"It's about this plantation owner's daughter who falls in love with a Union officer. She meets him when he's watering his horse at the spring, and they fall in love. Her father arrives just as they pass under the crossed muskets," she wound up.

"Sounds like a good one. Well, I'd better get some things done around here."

"Keep me posted on what happens with Jack."

What happened with Jack was that he called the next day and asked me over after work. After his standing me up, I was spoiling for a fight. When I reached his building, Jack was standing outside holding a paper cup.

"Moth?"

"Ladybug."

We watched as the little creature balanced on the lip, opened her elegantly dotted wings and flew away. Jack joked with Tom and Stan as we waited for the elevator. Upstairs, he wanted to get right into bed. For once, I put him off.

I took a deep breath. "Can I ask you something?"

"What?" He had a wary look on his face.

"I realize you're busy during the week. But that was really shitty of you not to call when you decided not to show. And it's also weird for me to spend so much time with you on the weekend, and then not hear from you for days on end."

"Weird how?" he said in a testy tone of voice.

I started to back down, but then decided to go for it.

"Normally if I'm seeing someone, we'll at least talk every few days."

"I'm not into being locked in a schedule," Jack said. "I'm not some English professor that gets off on grading papers. I've got a lot going on."

"Don't think I'm hanging by the phone, holding my breath. I have plenty to occupy me," I said, feeling my face scorch. "But you could take a minute to check in with me, instead of showing up drunk seven hours late."

"Okay. You nailed me," Jack said with a roll of his eye.

"And if we're going to get together on the weekend, I'd like to know a day or so beforehand. If not, I'll make other plans."

"Don't get in a strop about it. You got that point across, going to the party with Vicky. And meeting Dave."

"You go out on Sunday nights. Why should I stick around?"

A slow smile stole across his face. "You really like to bust my balls, don't you? The phone works both ways, last time I checked."

This wasn't exactly going how I wanted it to. He'd dodged the question, meanwhile putting the onus on me.

"When were you going to tell me Patrick called?" he asked abruptly.

"It wasn't a big deal," I said, thrown off-balance. "I forgot about it the second I hung up."

"He rang you while he was at the studio with me. All of a sudden he left the room for a few minutes. He came back laughing and told me what he'd done. He also told me what you said; that was good thinking on your part." Jack gave me a penetrating look. "So were you tempted to go out with him?"

"No. I'm seeing you."

"What if you weren't seeing me? Would you go out with him then?" He eyed me through his thick lashes.

"Patrick doesn't appeal to me. I'd rather be with you."

"Really?" He folded his arms. "Tell me why. Indulge me a little."

I thought about how much I was starting to care for him, but I wasn't about to confess that. "Well, you seem loyal to your friends," I said, with Sammy and Mary Jo in mind.

"Great. I sound like a fucking sheepdog."

"Okay; I think it's nice that you treat everyone the same. You talk to Tom and Stan the same way you did those posers at the Mudd Club."

"So you only like me because I'm not a snob?"

"You're the most phenomenal musician I've ever heard in my entire life. And that was my opinion before I ever met you."

Jack gave a broad smile. "Much better. Anything else?"

"I think I've flattered you sufficiently for one night."

"Fair enough. You feel like some dirty blues? I had Memphis Minnie on earlier." He got up and placed the needle on the vinyl. "'Baby, I'm your bumblebee, I got all the stinger you need,'" he sang, moving his hips sinuously. He grabbed my waist and gave me a kiss that made my head spin. "Let's us make some honey, baby. If you're over your snit."

"Honey," I said, pulling him toward me by the loops of his jeans.

Chapter 18

JUST LUST

Freeman Fyfe arrived from San Francisco to do interviews for his new novel and for his launch party the following week. Harvey had worked himself into a lather over the details, driving Rachel, our publicity director, crazy with his demands. Erin told me that Briar wanted to come, but for once Harvey had refused his little darling.

Isabel Reed had just messengered me the section on her teenage years. Although it was a mess, in my anxiety to move forward I gave a copy to Meredith.

She stopped by the next morning, and quickly I slid the *Post* under some papers. "I can see the potential," she said. "But that last chapter was practically incoherent."

"I know," I said ruefully. "That's why it's taking me so long. And she's writing at a snail's pace. I tried to get her to skip ahead to the sitcom era, but she won't."

"That would definitely be the section to show Harvey," Meredith said. "By the way, I heard Briar set up a meeting with Pryce Rayner and his manager. They're coming to the East Coast in a couple of weeks."

"I may as well give up!" I burst out.

She gave me a concerned look. "Don't give up yet. A meeting doesn't necessarily mean Pryce has a book in him."

After I'd been knocking for several minutes, a woman with red-rimmed eyes cracked Jack's door. The pungent fug of pot almost knocked me over.

What am I walking into? "Is Jack here?" I asked.

"Come on in." She moved aside, and I went past. A haze hung over the room; you could get high just by breathing. Two skeevy-looking dudes and another girl were sitting around the glass table, which was covered in a thin residue of powder. Jack was sprawled back in a chair, shirtless and barefoot in jeans ripped at one knee.

"*Now* it's a party," one of the guys said, eyeing me.

"Am I interrupting something?" I said to Jack.

"They were just leaving." He jerked his head toward the door.

The men got up grumbling and left with the girls trailing behind. Jack grabbed a Heineken and came over to me, hair disheveled, exceedingly sexy in his rumpled maleness.

"Here, it's beer o'clock." He handed me the bottle and relieved me of my backpack. All day I'd been looking forward to getting into bed with him; I really couldn't wait. I hoped he wasn't too high or stoned. Or that he hadn't already sated his appetite.

"Who were those people?" I asked, undoing my top button.

"Just some guys I know."

"Was your guitar ready?"

"Dan has to adjust the pickup. Hard day at the office, dah-ling?" he asked in a high-pitched, housewifey voice. "How many manuscripts did you bring with you? Any psycho-pop?" he asked, rummaging in my backpack. "What's this?" He held up a proposal.

"That's a therapist who's doing a book on why men won't commit. I'll read you some choice passages from it later," I said, grabbing the backpack and dumping it on a chair. I didn't want to discuss my homework; I only wanted him to ravish me.

Jack picked up a glass from the table and took a sip, slivers of ice swirling. "What do you feel like listening to?"

For once he wasn't in an amorous mood. I started to say something about the girls and the coke, but I didn't want to act like it bothered me. "I'd love to hear the tape of the new album. Those songs at the club were incredible."

"I'll have to bring home a copy. We still need to figure out the first single—what's the A side, and what's the B."

"The A side's the one you think will be the hit, isn't it?"

"Yeah. Although sometimes we're completely wrong, and it's the B side that takes off."

"How do you decide which songs to use?"

"Patrick and I argue for about three weeks, and then we flip a coin."

Jack put his hand on his lean hip, the line of dark hair below his navel suggesting black powder leading to a lit fuse. He looked so gorgeous standing there with his bare muscled chest and raw hipbones that I couldn't wait any longer. I came close and gave him a smoldering kiss as I undid his jeans. Dropping to my knees, I took him in my mouth, tasting the tang of liquid pearl at the tip. I took the drink from him and sipped it, capturing an icy fragment. Then I wrapped my cold tongue around his rigid cock, gliding up and down in the way he'd showed me he liked. I pressed the chilled glass against his backside and drew him in deeply, hearing his breathing become uneven.

"Julia." Jack pulled me up, taking the glass from my hand. "Come over here." He went to the couch and put the drink on the table as I followed him, shedding my clothes. He pushed me back on the cushion and captured both my wrists in a one-handed iron grip above my head.

"I'm not letting you up, you know." He looked at me, eyes glittering. "You started this." His long fingers searched in the glass for a piece of ice. He slid a cold shard down my breast, making me gasp as I watched my nipple harden into a rosy bullet. Jack put his warm mouth over it and tongued me roughly. Then he took the ice and ran it across my nipples again, making me squirm. I tried to free my hands from his grasp and started to speak.

"No talking," he said, putting the tiny remnant between my lips. "I think you've melted that one. Let's see what else needs cooling off." He got another sliver from the glass and traced a shivering track down my belly. "I can think of one place that's always nice and hot." Still holding my wrists tightly above my head, he slid the ice inside and began to stroke me.

"Bet I can get this one melted really quickly," he purred in my ear as I writhed under his touch. "Yep, it's gone already. Let's try a bigger piece." The shock of the cold combined with the light brush of his hand was unbelievably erotic; my hips rose to meet his fingers as they molded me into a scalding mound. I was verging on the brink when Jack suddenly stopped. He kissed my breasts and smiled down at me.

"All right, we've done the B side. Now let's flip you over and try the A." He pulled me up and tipped me over the arm of the couch so that my ass was angled high. "I think this one's going to be huge," he said as he dipped his cock inside. I began to moan as he reached around to caress me. "A really . . . big . . . hit." He thrust in all the way just as I climaxed, my cries lost in his guttural growl.

Jack crooked the phone in his shoulder and zipped his jeans as he ordered dinner. I was flaked out on the sofa, still catching my breath. *I guess there was something I hadn't done with him yet, after all. I wonder how many other variations he has in his repertoire.* The thought gave me the shivers.

Jack hung up and came over to me, grinning. "So where were we when you started to go down on me? I believe you were saying how much you liked the new album."

I laughed. "I don't know what got into me today."

"I think it was a piece of ice. And then after that, something really big and hot." Jack cocked his eyebrow at me.

"Ha, ha. I was saying how much I liked those songs we danced to. My favorites were always the hard-driving ones you sang, even when I was a teenager."

He thought for a moment. "So let's see, when you were seventeen, I was . . . twenty-five, right?"

"That's right."

"Huh. Barely legal. I'd like to see a picture of you back then. Tell Dot to send one, okay?"

"Do you have any old pictures around?"

"I have one box. Most of 'em's back at Mum's house."

"Could I see them?"

"Sure, if you're interested. Nothing too thrilling." He went to his room and returned carrying a battered cardboard box with masking tape around it. "I haven't opened this since my last move," he said, slitting the tape. Inside, there were stacks of photographs, black and white and color, decades old and more recent, in no particular order. Jack began passing them to me. I saw a young, freshly scrubbed Jack and Patrick buttoned up in stiff suits; Jack, hair below his shoulders, his arm around Sammy; a school portrait of Jack that resembled the picture of Oliver on his bureau. He handed me one of a handsome older woman in a Sixties-style hairdo, a twentyish Jack in psyche-delic threads kissing her cheek. "That's Mum," he said. "I have a more recent one of her somewhere."

"I can see the resemblance." He had her arched eyebrows and wide smile.

Jack considered a sullen photo of him and Mark with some men in suits. "Busted," he commented. "What a load of crap."

"Did you have to go to jail?"

"Yeah, just for a few days. The buggers were only after making an example of us."

He dug around in the box and gave me several shots of him onstage. "I liked that outfit," he said, indicating a rhinestone shirt. "I always wondered where that got to."

I selected a picture of him with an extremely thin blonde woman, both looking very stoned. "That's Caroline. I went out with her for a while in my mid-twenties."

"She looks like the model/heiress type."

"She was sort of an heiress; her father owned a huge shipping company. So she was rebelling against all that. We split up before I moved to New York."

"Why did you break up?"

"So you are interested in my past," Jack said wryly. "We broke up because she started acting like a ball and chain. I thought she was a free spirit, but she really just wanted to play house. Eventually she reverted to type and settled down with a diplomat. A real prig, from what I heard."

So that's his way of letting me know he isn't into anything long-term. All right—I've been warned.

I was quiet for a few minutes while we looked at more photos, Jack finding a recent one of his mother, some gray in her hair, and Sharon, a petite young woman holding an infant Emma. We came upon a shot of Oliver brandishing a toy truck, almost concealed by a mountain of wrapping paper.

"He's adorable. He looks so much like you," I said.

Jack beamed. "That's what everyone says. I took him to the zoo when he was three, and the papers went wild, thinking they'd finally found my love child. It drove the attorney up the wall. Ollie doesn't look a thing like him."

"You really don't care for Sharon's husband," I commented.

Jack scratched his chin. "He asked me once if I could get him some 'backstage action' when we had a gig in London. Like I'd do that to me own sister." He dumped the pictures in the box. "I think that's it for the blast from the past."

The buzzer rang for the delivery. Jack looked in the take-out bag and removed two eight-track tapes. "Everybody thinks they're a musician," he said, shaking his head.

While Jack was having a joint in bed before turning out the light, I decided to tweak him a little about Freeman, since he'd made such a point of saying he couldn't be tied down. "Did I tell you our big author's in town?" I asked with a faraway look in my eyes.

"Who's that?"

"Freeman Fyfe. He's a rather glamorous guy, for a writer. Kind of debonair."

"Sounds like you have a thing for him." Jack drew deeply on the joint, making the tip spark.

"I have to admit I thought he was attractive at first, but then I realized he's just a playboy. All the women at work think he's sexy. But I don't. Not really."

Jack blew a stream of smoke toward the ceiling. "Are you seeing him while he's in town?"

"We're having a party for him next Thursday at Pierre's. It's a really fancy event; I expect I'll wear that black dress of Vicky's."

"What time's the party? I might stop by and check it out."

This took me by surprise. "I don't have the details yet," I said, trying to backtrack. "There's going to be press there and everything. You might start a stampede."

"I know how to be cool," Jack said, stubbing the roach in the ashtray.

"They sent out the guest list ages ago. I'm pretty sure you have to have RSVP'd."

"I never RSVP."

Chapter 19

THE HARDER THEY COME

I was changing in the office bathroom for Freeman's fete, trying to shimmy into Vicky's form-fitting dress in the cramped confines of the stall. Jack hadn't mentioned the party again, and I was relieved he'd dropped it, imagining the flurry if he showed up.

I stuffed my pantyhose into my backpack and pulled out the garter belt and black stockings that I'd bought as a little treat for Jack, since I was planning to go over to his place afterwards. I had never worn one before, but imagined he'd seen a few in his day. I stepped into the garters and drew a stocking up my right leg. My knee bumped the toilet paper, which burst out of its socket and rolled under the door. No one was in the bathroom so I quickly scuttled out, holding up the hose with one hand while reaching for the roll. Just as I was standing up, Meredith walked in. I kept my grasp on the roll but not the stocking, which slithered down to my ankle.

"Getting dolled up for the party?" she asked with raised eyebrow.

Of all the timing. "I just knocked the paper loose," I said, retreating to the stall. After several attempts, I got the first stocking hitched in a way that would allow forward motion. Balancing on one foot, I leaned against the door and tried to wrestle the second one up my leg. It seemed to be several inches shorter than the other; I should have known better than to buy them at discount on Canal Street. Only by straining the belt could I get the elusive snap to reach the edge of the hose. The tampon box clanged loudly as I wheeled around trying to hook the one in back; I was circling myself like a dog chasing its tail.

"Those things are a bitch to get on, aren't they?" came Meredith's amused voice.

How utterly humiliating. "I ran out of pantyhose, and this was the only thing I had left in my drawer," I replied lamely.

"Let me know if you need help." It sounded like she was laughing.

At last I was fixed up, but with all the twisting and turning, I now had to pee. I pulled down my underpants, which came to an abrupt halt, trapped by the garters. Were you supposed to wear them *underneath*? Darn, I'd have to unhitch the things to get my panties down.

Now I really was in a rush. I decided to ditch the less complicated undergarment, realizing no one would ever know. I stowed the undies in my bag, got the garters sorted out again, and finally exited the bathroom. The day had turned freakishly cold due to a hurricane coming up the East Coast; I knew I'd be chilly in my strappy dress, but I'd just have to cope.

I caught a cab to Pierre's with Erin and Rachel, shivering with the draft up my skirt. We said hello to the coat-check girl behind her half-door partition—a last-minute afterthought, but one Harvey felt necessary since it was so frigid out—and started stacking books that Freeman would sign for anyone who bought a copy.

People began filing in and Freeman arrived, escorted by Harvey. Freeman spoke to a couple of reporters, was photographed with our sales director, and then came over to kiss me on the cheek. "I really appreciated your careful editing," he said courteously. "Your ideas about the ending rounded it out very nicely."

"Thank you. I can't wait to see the reviews." I so rarely got this kind of feedback; his compliment made my day.

Rachel led Freeman away to meet some bookstore owners, and Erin and I commented on how well the party was coming off. Suddenly her face took on a strange expression. "Is that . . .? It can't be." I turned in the direction she was staring and was astonished to see Jack entering the room, Sammy in tow. Jack looked absolutely dashing in a sleek black suit that I'd never seen before, his long hair a sensual counterpoint to the formal attire. He stopped and gazed around, then strode over to me. As he kissed me on the cheek, I caught a drift of whiskey.

"Where is this guy? I want to meet him," Jack said, oblivious to the swiveling heads.

"Jack, Sammy, this is my friend Erin. We work together."

Erin's eyes were glazed; she looked like she might pass out

"Nice to see you," she said faintly.

"Hello, Erin," Jack said.

"You want to meet Freeman?" I asked.

"Yes." Jack crossed his arms.

"Okay," I said with a smile. I led him and Sammy over, and touched Freeman's arm. He turned, his elegant white hair contrasting with his weathered face.

"I'm sorry to interrupt, but a friend of mine wanted to say hello."

Freeman took him in. "So nice to meet you, Jack; I adore your music. This darling girl was an enormous help with my novel."

For a moment Jack looked flabbergasted, then his mouth stretched into a broad smile. "Good to meet you," he said. "Julia has told me a lot about you. Here's our keyboardist, Sam."

Sammy stared at Freeman. "This is him?"

"I didn't know Freeman Fyfe was friends with Jack Kipling," someone said in a hushed voice.

"So you're in from San Francisco?" Jack asked.

"Yes, I've lived there for thirty years."

"It's a great town," Jack said. "Well, I know you're in demand tonight. Congrats on your new book."

"Thanks so much for coming," Freeman replied.

Jack turned to me. "You little bitch," he said, grinning. He took my hand and motioned for Sammy to follow.

"Where are we going?" I asked as Jack pulled me toward the door. He continued down the hall to the cloakroom, his grip firm on my wrist, Sammy trudging behind us. Jack fished out some bills and gave them to the coat-check girl. "Take the rest of the night off, sweetheart. We'll handle it from here."

She stared at the money in her palm. "Thanks!"

"Coatroom's closed," Jack said to Sammy. "Stay here and stand guard."

He opened the lower partition of the doorway, hustled me through, closed it, then shut the top half and locked the bolt.

"What are you doing?" I said.

Jack took off his suit jacket, tossed it over a chair and grabbed me, holding me tight. "'All the girls think he's so sexy,'" he said in his high-pitched Julia voice. "'Then I realized he was just a playboy'… That guy must be seventy if he's a day!"

"Were you a little jealous?" I asked, laughing.

"Was I jealous? What do you think? You're gonna pay for this." He swept a bunch of coats off the rack and dumped them onto the floor, the empty hangers jangling.

"Hey, those are people's things!"

"This looks comfortable." He seized a big mink and threw it onto the pile. "Now …" He spun me around and tackled me face-down onto the fur.

"Jack, we can't do this here!" I cried, my cheek against the plush mink.

"Want to make a bet?" He lifted the back of my dress. "What's this, garters? That looks so … My god, you've got no underwear on." I heard the sound of his zipper.

"I was going to surprise you at your place tonight," I gasped.

"I had no idea you were such a naughty girl," Jack said. "Now you're gonna pay for what you did." He slid his hand underneath and played me as he thrust from behind, eventually strumming sounds out of me that I'd never heard before.

We lay there on the coats, panting. I heard Sammy arguing with someone outside. "It's closed for now. Come back in twenty minutes."

Jack gave a wicked laugh and pushed up from the floor, rearranged himself and helped me off the mink, which looked a little worse for wear. He knelt and clasped one of my garters that had come unhooked, then pulled my dress down over my hips.

"How'd that feel?" he asked.

"Incredible. But I hope I still have a job after this." I tried to finger-comb my hair.

"Don't worry. Just wait here and get yourself together. I'll go out and be nice to all the old bags so they can talk about it to their friends. I'll give them lots of signage too," he said, making an autographing gesture. "You won't get in trouble." He unlocked the top partition and stuck his head out. "Sammy, we've got some coats that need hanging up in here."

When I made it back to the party, Jack was in the middle of the room with his arm around Freeman, being photographed. Then he sat at the table, autographing each book and handing it to Freeman to sign. We sold more copies than we ever had at a publication party in the history of the company.

The whole time, Harvey looked like he was about to choke on his martini olive.

"Maybe that yobbo will leave you alone now," Jack said as we rode to his place.

When we got inside, I opened my copy of Freeman's book and showed him my name in the acknowledgments. "It's my very first one."

"That's fantastic, Julia. You're going to be a top editor. He'll have to promote you now." He looked at me for a moment.

"We leave for the coast in a week and a half to do the mixing. We're doing those concerts while we're there too."

My heart sank; I had wondered when they were going.

"It'll be good to be onstage again," Jack added. "Everyone claims to hate L.A., but I always have a great time out there. All kinds of crazy situations come up when we do a show." He raised an eyebrow and grinned at me. I couldn't believe he'd be so blatant about what he was planning to do, but I wasn't about to give him the satisfaction of acting like it bugged me.

"That does sound like fun. I guess I'll set up some things for that week, too. There are a couple of people I've been meaning to get together with, but I've been so tied up lately." I sighed. "Sometimes I wish there were two Saturday nights a week."

Jack eyed me. "I thought you said you didn't go out that much on weekends."

I smiled. "Not unless there's something I really want to do. It'll be nice to have a little space though; I hate feeling like I'm in a rut. I'm sure you feel the same way."

"Yeah. You could say I like my space."

I dreaded seeing Harvey the next morning; I suspected he'd have some caustic comment about Jack, and he didn't disappoint. When I went to empty his outbox, he glowered at me, the skin around his cold little eyes puffy from all the drinking the night before. "How on earth do you know one of the Floors?" he asked. "I didn't picture you as a groupie type."

"We met through a mutual acquaintance. We're just friends."

"I see." He watched as I backed out of his office.

At lunchtime, Erin and Rachel crowded into my office, wanting to know how long I'd been seeing Jack. Again I played it down, saying that we were just acquaintances. They seemed to accept the explanation—and why not? It was more plausible than thinking a rock star would be romantically involved with a lowly publishing drudge.

When I went to give Meredith some flap copy, she gestured for me to shut her door. "So *that's* who you've been seeing. I'm so impressed; I love their music. Is he nice? He has such a wild reputation."

"I don't know about 'nice'. He's definitely one-of-a-kind. I'm trying not to get too carried away."

"Well, good for you. I heard Briar interrogating Erin about it this morning; she seemed to believe Erin had mistaken him for someone else. She kept saying, 'You think Julia is going out with *Jack Kipling*?'"

I had to laugh at that. "I keep asking myself the same question."

Chapter 20

TALK OF THE TOWN

)⊃⊂(

Twice I'd reminded Jack about watching the band rehearse. At first he told me he'd be too distracted with me there, but finally he said I could come. After work I swung by my apartment to change into jeans, and then walked up to Eighth Street. I heard the entwined jangle of guitar and bass as I followed the guard inside. Jack came out looking tired, his shirt wrinkled, hair standing up in back. "C'mon, you can sit with Mary Jo. I asked her along to keep you company."

My mood plunged at this; I didn't look forward to another run-in with his manager. We went into the studio, where several people were sitting on the sidelines. Mary Jo nodded as I took a folding chair next to her. Jack put his Gibson strap over his shoulder and held the pick in his mouth as he tuned the strings. Patrick, wearing a silk shirt that looked as if it had just been pressed, not a blonde hair out of place, was laughing with Sammy as he poured a glass of orange juice and vodka from the array of bottles on top of the keyboard. Mark sat at his drums, creating a whispery beat.

"How is it going?" I asked Mary Jo in a low voice, hoping to start on a friendly note.

"They bicker a lot, but it'll be unbelievable when they're onstage."

"So where were we when we got interrupted?" Patrick asked in a petulant tone, picking up his bass.

"You've been interrupting all day. We were at that bit in the middle of the five bars," Jack said. "We should do it as it was originally."

"Do it my way again," Patrick said. "Dropping back to the fade."

Jack made a face at Sammy, who grimaced and stubbed out his cigarette. Jack hit a few chords, Sammy fingered an octave, and they swung into one of the tunes I recognized from the Mudd Club tape. Mark came in on the backbeat as Patrick strummed his bass and belted out the lyrics. Seeing Patrick perform blew me away; the minute he opened his mouth, his presence took over the room. His voice was at once insinuating, insulting, arousing; one moment velvety, the next a snarl.

When he suddenly stopped singing, I realized I'd been holding my breath. Patrick stepped back from the mic and shook his head. "It's too fast. You've gotta slow it down."

"That's how we did it for the album," Jack replied.

They argued for a minute, then seemed to reach a compromise and ran it at a more moderate tempo. Patrick gyrated before the microphone; Jack paced, crouched on the floor, took a belt of whiskey, all the while teasing out a complex tangle of notes. Mark gazed at the ceiling as he played, Jack shut his eyes, and Sammy kept his glued to Patrick.

"Let's move on," Patrick said after the fifth repeat, his voice raspy. "Can someone bring me a tea with honey?"

"Lillian," Mary Jo said over her shoulder.

A girl sitting behind us jumped up to fetch it. Jack unplugged his guitar from the amp and batted at the strings, making a scratchy noise.

"I've got to rest. Why don't you do one of yours?" Patrick put down his bass and went to sprawl on a couch.

Jack approached the microphone, lean legs apart. He readied himself with a little hip shimmy, and I gripped the edge of my seat. He struck four razor-sharp chords and plunged into one of his hits from a few years ago.

Without Patrick haranguing them, Sammy and Mark were in their element. The keyboard and drums seemed to be in a race as the song escalated. Once or twice Jack looked in my direction, each time jolting a thrill through me. The acoustics of the room took effect again, but this time it was much more intimate. Jack's voice was in my ear, vibrating in my throat, deep within me. They pounded into the last verse, with a final resounding twang from Jack.

I clapped and yelled "Bravo!" Mary Jo frowned, as if I'd broken some cognoscenti rule of cool. Jack took a quick belt of Patrick's juice, and immediately they flew through the song twice more. Finally he lifted the strap over his shoulder, propped his guitar and snatched a towel off the stand. Vigorously mopping his face, he came over and sat in the empty chair next to me. "How was that?" he asked, putting his hand on my knee.

"Fantastic! I love that song."

"You said you liked the hard-driving ones." He angled back and stretched out his legs. "I was up last night going over the lyrics so I wouldn't screw it up."

"You sounded great," Mary Jo offered from her seat. "Better than ever."

Patrick ambled over. "It's . . . Julia, right? Hard to keep all of Jack's girls straight. Although you're certainly more memorable than some."

His gaze drifted to my chest as Jack scowled. Patrick turned to him and pursed his lips. "Why don't you set up a few sessions with my voice coach? That was rough around the edges."

"It isn't meant to be smooth," Jack retorted.

"It's gonna need a lot of work before it's road-tested," Patrick said disdainfully. "You done with your gabfest here?"

Jack glanced at him. "Just about." He leaned over, put his hands on my waist, and to my dismay gave me a deep, tongue-thrusting kiss. "Now I'm done."

Patrick stomped over to the mic, and Jack sauntered to his guitar. My face was flaming from the public display, but no one else seemed to have noticed it.

Mark said something and they all burst into laughter. By the time the session wrapped, Patrick had his hand on Jack's shoulder, speaking into his ear and making him grin, so it seemed their moods had been sorted out.

"That's it for the day. Don't forget to punch your time cards," Jack quipped as they hung up their instruments. I was melded to my chair, I'd been holding still for so long. Mary Jo introduced me to Lillian, her frightened-looking assistant. Jack came over and put his arm around me.

"Sammy and I are gonna take a quick shower, and then we'll bolt. Patrick said you reserved Caliban," he said to Mary Jo.

"I thought we deserved a treat after all the hard work," she replied.

"I'll be done in a sec. I brought a change of clothes." Jack pulled his drenched shirt away from his chest. The others cleared out and I sat alone, wishing I'd known about the dinner plans so I could have worn something nicer.

A few minutes later, two extravagantly dressed women came into the room. "Are they done already?" the first one asked. I could smell her perfume from six feet away.

"They just finished." I wondered who they were.

"Is Jack still around?" I looked at her more carefully; a statuesque blonde with luxurious hair, she had a studied pout below calculating green eyes.

"He's showering now." My mind raced. *Has she been coming to the studio all this time?* "Are you a friend of his?"

"Who wants to know?" she said in a haughty voice.

I stood and crossed my arms. "We're going out to dinner. Do you want me to give him a message?"

She smiled condescendingly. "I'll catch up with him later. Just tell him Trina came by. And he owes me one for the last time." They flounced out.

So that's why he didn't want me to come; she's been meeting him here! I snatched up my backpack as Sammy came in toweling his hair. "Jack's still prettifyin' so he can be beautiful."

"Who says my natural self isn't beautiful?" Jack walked over in clean jeans and shirt. "You accusing me of primping?"

"Far be it from me to accuse you of that," Sammy said. "Let's high-tail it over to this place. I'm gonna chew my own shoe leather if I don't get somethin' in me soon."

Jack looked at me. "What's up?"

"Some friends of yours stopped by," I said frostily. "Trina and another woman."

Jack met Sammy's eyes. "Want to wait for us in the car?" he said, and Sammy scooted out. "What did Trina say?"

"That you owe her one for the last time."

Jack drew a pick from his shirt pocket, glanced at it and put it back. "She's just someone I fooled around with a while ago."

That was all I needed to hear. I started for the exit, but Jack's hand stopped me.

"Hold on. She's come by a few times. We went to a bar when I was wired up and didn't want to go home."

"That's fine, Jack. Have fun at dinner." I knew I didn't have any claims on him, but neither did I have to stick around and have my nose rubbed in it. I headed for the door, but Jack caught my arm again.

"Wait a minute." He turned me to face him. "It was one of those nights you were tied up with your editing; I was a little ticked off."

"How long were you seeing her before? If it's not too inquisitive of me to ask."

Jack gave me a frustrated look. "Who knows? I didn't keep track. I was screwing around with a few of 'em."

"Well, screw you!"

"Suit yourself." He charged out the door.

I stood there for a minute, my chest heaving. I guessed that was it; *finito*. It was bad enough for him to show up at my place reeking of perfume; even worse to be confronted with the source of the reek in person. His true colors came out after all, just like I knew they would. Dejectedly I shoved through the door, then jumped back in surprise as Jack pushed away from the brick wall.

"I thought you weren't the jealous type," he said.

"I'm not jealous; just disgusted."

"At me? I'm not all that disgusting, am I?" He put his hands on my shoulders. "Listen, all she could talk about was some new shop on Rodeo Drive. Not nearly as interesting as Alice Underground." He smiled and gave my arm a squeeze. "C'mon baby, let's go to this blowout."

Either he was the smoothest liar on the planet, or he'd really only gone to a bar with her. I stood my ground for a few moments before lunging for Door Number Two. "I guess I'll come. If you can promise none of your other girlfriends will show up."

We went to the car and Jack pulled me in next to him. Sammy broke the seal on a whiskey bottle. "Jesus, it was hot in there. I was sweatin' like a whore in church," he said, obviously trying to lighten the atmosphere. "Felt good to change into something dry." He took a gulp and handed it to Jack.

"Yeah, I've dressed up, and Julia's dressed me down, so I'm somewhere in the middle." Jack swigged the liquor and passed it back to Sammy.

"At least you have someone to set you straight," Sammy said mournfully.

"Now don't start in," Jack said.

"Julia, Vicky's done took up with another man. I'm gonna have to strut mah jelly and get me a new gal."

"Watch out ladies, he's going on the pull." Jack rolled his eyes at me. "You should check out the talent in L.A.; plenty of loose women there."

"You need to hit a few bars out there with me, Jack. That's always a real leg-opener."

Jack laughed as I stared out the window. *Thanks a lot, Sammy. Just the kind of reassurance I needed.*

At the restaurant we were taken to a back room divided by a long table. Mark and Mary Jo arrived with Suzanne, whose teal blouse set off her red hair strikingly. "So you attended your first rehearsal," she said, smiling. "I hope they behaved themselves."

"We were on our best behavior," Jack said. "Some of us, that is."

Patrick entered the room with a brunette in a hot pink bustier that displayed bountiful tanned breasts. "Hullo, you lot. Didn't you order the Dom?" he asked Jack.

"I was waiting for you, since you always bitch about what I pick."

Patrick made a dissatisfied moue and told the waiter to bring four bottles.

"Let's tuck in; I'm beat," Mark sighed. He took a chair next to Suzanne, and Jack and I sat across from them.

"Carmen, you know everyone but Julia," Patrick said.

"It's Cara, silly," the woman giggled. To my surprise, she slid in next to Jack as Patrick sat on the other side of me. Sammy flopped down beside Cara; Mary Jo sat across from Patrick and immediately started going over concert details. Cara launched into a long, meandering story about how her luggage got left in Tahiti after a shoot, and how it took a week to get it back. Jack said "Uh-huh" at various intervals, but looked bored despite the golden cleavage on display. The waiters popped the corks and poured champagne all around.

I took a sip as Patrick turned to me. "The Roederer I served at my party was better than this."

I had hoped he'd just ignore me. "I think this is nice too."

"Easy to please, huh. But I guess I knew that already," he said, looking over at Jack. He took the menu the waiter handed him. "Jack, why don't you get the filet mignon; it's great here."

Jack picked up his menu, glanced at it and put it down. "Maybe I will."

No such entrée was listed. "Actually it's strip steak," I said in a low voice to Jack, who frowned in Patrick's direction.

"Jack's a big one for ordering things that aren't on the menu, and then we all have to wait while they scrounge around for it." Patrick smirked.

"At least I don't try to stick everyone else with the check," Jack said.

I asked the waiter for the halibut, and Jack said, "I'll have what she's having." Cara requested steamed asparagus, and then began describing her recent bikini shoot in Helsinki.

"The photographer did everything he could to get my nips to stand down, but they'd just pop back up," she warbled. "Even through two bandaids."

Jack grinned. "Julia has that problem sometimes too, don't you, darlin'?" He leaned toward me and muttered, "What a nit-wit."

More champagne flowed as the others debated the pros and cons of various hotels around the country, many of which they'd been kicked out of. It sounded like they'd be touring at some point next year; I wondered where I'd be then.

"So what do you do in your spare time?" Patrick asked, his gaze flitting around the table. "Do you have any interests, aside from books?"

I wish he'd just leave me alone. "I like paintings."

"Really, who d'you like?" Patrick turned toward me and let his glance fall below my neckline.

"I like Picasso. And Van Gogh."

"Oh, that's right, you're just out of school, aren't you? Did you take an art history course?"

I didn't reply, not wanting to give him fodder for a fresh put-down.

"I like Picasso's nudes." Patrick sidled closer. "Those big ones with the huge tits. I can really get into a pair of nice tits," he said, his hand suddenly sliding up my waist. I scooted away and tapped Jack, whose ear was still being bent by Cara, on the arm.

"Do you know where the bathroom is?"

"Straight over there." He indicated a door across the way. I crossed the room and entered a stall, dreading going back to sit next to Patrick. *Maybe I can get Jack to switch seats with me.* Someone came in; I hoped it wasn't Cara. I waited for a few minutes and went out to wash my hands, then stepped back in shock. Patrick was calmly scoring lines of cocaine on the countertop. He snorted one with a rolled-up dollar bill and extended it to me.

"Want a little toot before we fuck?" he said. "We'll have to make it fast."

I stood still for a second, unable to articulate an answer. "I won't be having either," I finally blurted out, brushing past him. As soon as I exited, the door opened behind me. I met Jack's eyes across the room, and then saw his expression change. I glanced over my shoulder to see Patrick following me, zipping up his pants, a broad smile on his face. Jack darted a furious look in our direction and bolted from his chair, fists clenched. After a moment's pause he stalked out. I hurried after him and breathlessly caught up with him outside.

"Jack! I hope you don't think I was doing anything in there with him."

"That didn't look too good from where I was sitting," he said through gritted teeth.

"Nothing happened! I was only using the bathroom. Just like you were only having a drink with Trina."

"So you're getting back at me for that? I didn't think you were the type to play dirty. Rick will take you home." He spoke to him through the open car window and charged off down the block. Reeling, I got in and Rick dropped me off at my apartment.

Slowly I undressed and got into bed. *My god, does he really think I'd blow Patrick in the bathroom?* For one thing, anyone could have walked in. And I'd never screw around with one of Jack's pals while I was seeing him. What kind of women had he been with to think I'd do something like that? It made it even worse that he'd lump me in with that sort.

The next morning I tried calling Jack to insist that he give me a chance to explain, and to demand an apology. But he was either there and not picking up, or he was out with Trina—or a Trina type.

Chapter 21

SHOULD I STAY OR SHOULD I GO

I sat in my open windowsill Sunday afternoon, listening to Patsy Cline. "I Fall to Pieces" came too close to what I was feeling, so I moved the needle to the next song. There was no telling who Jack had spent the weekend with, but I had an idea. Trina had probably been stroking his oversized ego—not to mention other parts of him—all weekend long.

I didn't get it; I was supposed to sit by while women came on to him, but his bandmate plays a stupid joke and Jack freaks out. The unfairness of it made me want to scream. *It isn't exactly a confidence-booster to have your lover mauled by gorgeous girls everywhere he goes. But now I guess he's my ex-lover.*

I watched the traffic lumbering up Broome, my tears dripping down like drops of rain. Falling to pieces didn't do it justice; my heart was cracking in two.

The phone rang, and I blew my nose so it wouldn't be obvious I'd been crying.

"Hi, it's Suzanne. Can you come over? Jack's at our place."

I tried to gather my thoughts. "I didn't do anything with Patrick. Doesn't he know I wouldn't do that?"

"I told him. Patrick's always trying to stir the pot. Can you come now? He wants to talk to you. We're on Commerce Street, the gray house with the raven over the door."

"I don't know, Suzanne," I said slowly. "He does these questionable things and expects me to believe him, but once the tables are turned, he flips out and doesn't even let me explain. It's such a double standard."

"I know what you mean," she said soothingly. "Patrick really knows how to push his buttons. Could you please come? I think he just needs to see you."

Anxious to see him but resenting having to make the first move, I threw on some clothes and walked up Sixth Avenue. I turned onto the narrow street of hundred-year-old wooden homes and found the one with the raven.

"He's in here," Suzanne said, letting me in. She led me to an olive-green sitting room lined with dusky paintings in flaking gilded frames. Jack was sprawled on a settee, whiskey bottles and ashtrays on the low antique table before him.

"I guess I deserved that," he said.

I put my hands on my hips. "I didn't do anything with Patrick. I don't even like him. Not only that; I don't even *know* him."

He gave me a long look. "I was using other women as a yardstick."

"Well, don't. What happened was—if you'd given me a chance to explain—I heard someone while I was in the stall. Patrick was doing lines of coke on the counter. Then he followed me out and played his little joke." I wasn't going to tell him what Patrick had said; that was too explosive.

"It was the look on his face that set me off. Like the cat that got the cream." Jack grimaced and took a long swallow from the bottle. "I thought you were getting back at me for Trina. I had to run outside to keep from punching our lead singer in the teeth, right before we do four shows back-to-back."

"Maybe you should have, instead of taking it out on me."

"Patrick knows that shit really sets me off. Next time he can sit next to his own date. Did you hear Cara telling me about her 'nips' standing up in Helsinki? Man, he can really pick 'em." Finally he smiled.

"That whole thing seemed like some sort of setup," I said.

"Could be. He doesn't like me to be happy with any one woman. As if it would take away from the band, or something. He once told me I wrote better songs when I was in the dumps."

"So you're supposed to be miserable?"

"I dunno, it's messed up. And once again I fucked up." Jack stood and slipped his hands under my blouse. "Let's go upstairs and forget about that toe-rag."

I pushed his hands away. "Your fingers are cold." I was dying for it though. Where did my self-control vanish to when I was with him?

Jack raised an eyebrow seductively. "I can think of a way to get them warm." He drew me close, his erection poled against me. Lightly he slid his palm over my ass. "Are you going to make me beg?"

"I might." I shut my eyes as he sucked on my earlobe. *Ahh, he's melting me.* I slid my fingers inside his shirt.

"Come on." Jack grabbed my hand and led me up the thickly carpeted stairs to a jewel box of a bedroom, the ceiling sloping to curtained dormer windows overlooking the street. A pre-Raphaelite portrait of a blushing pink nude hung over the ornate iron bed frame.

"Now there's a pair of nips," I said.

"Doesn't hold a candle to yours." He kissed me hungrily and pulled me onto the goosedown.

"Let me do something nice to you," Jack said, pushing down my jeans. "In fact, let's do it together." He unzipped himself and began exploring me with his tongue as I slid my lips over his eager cock. At first I only concentrated on what I was doing, but then the sensations he was arousing started to take over. He brought me to the edge, then retreated ever so slightly, leaving my entire body quivering. He did it once more, then again; just as I couldn't take it any longer, he let me come. As my cries abated, he plunged into my mouth and filled me with his pungent spume.

I lay there recuperating, rocked by the surge of my reaction. I got so lost in the things I did with him. All sense of who I was and how I was supposed to behave vanished like a wave dissolving into sand. Nothing seemed to matter beyond this moment in time: the two of us, tangled in a sea of sheets.

Jack switched positions and gave me a deep kiss, commingling his flavor with mine. "Man, I didn't know I was so salty," he said. "'69 was a very good vintage."

"God, Jack, you really knock me out." I trailed my fingers down his abdomen, twining them in the silky whorls at his groin.

"Remember when you told me I was the first person who'd ever made you come?"

I nodded.

"Is that true?" he asked me softly, his deep brown eyes pooling into mine.

"Yes."

"That made me feel really good. I know I made a joke about it, but I still think about that sometimes. It makes it even better, knowing that. Especially when you catch fire like just now."

"You make me feel amazing. Patrick doesn't interest me in the least."

"He'd better not. You shake my maracas too, baby. Make my eyelashes grow and my toes curl up."

I took a deep breath. "I'm glad to hear that. But it's hard to tell with you because every time we get close, you pull away from me. It's almost funny, it's so obvious. After we finally spent that first weekend together in July—which was amazing, at least to me—"

"It was to me, too. At last I got my hands on you."

"You sent me those gorgeous flowers, then you didn't call me for a week. You vanish for days, or you show up smelling like some other woman's perfume. But isn't the point of . . . all this . . . not to do that sort of thing?"

"What do you mean by 'all this'?" He gave me a dark look.

I wished I could take it back. "I just meant us seeing each other."

"Is that all we're doing, 'seeing' each other? I don't really have much of a sense of it, to be honest," Jack said, running his hand through his hair. "I admit I have a problem with getting close. I start to feel like the walls are closing in on me. It's not anything you're doing; you're the least clingy woman I've ever met." He raised his eyebrow. "Which annoys the hell out of me sometimes, come to think of it. But you like to keep it cool too, don't you, Julia? To keep yourself independent. Right?"

I felt incredibly nervous. Finally we were having this talk— *the* Talk. "You must know I like you a lot."

"You like me." Jack pinned me with his penetrating gaze.

"I'm starting to really care for you," I said slowly. "And that's scary, because I don't want to get hurt."

He gave a wan smile. "If it's scary to you, it's terrifying to me. Sometimes I wake up at night in a cold sweat."

Jack put his arms around me, making my heart thump wildly. "I caught myself telling Mum about you the other day," he said. "So now every time I call her, she asks about you."

He'd told his mom about me? That was music to my ears. "Well, Dot always wants to know what you're up to. Talk about annoying."

"So we're even, in terms of the nosy mothers." Jack started to say something, but then stopped. "I guess I should tell you—" He pressed his lips together. "Look, it isn't only about me poking you, if that's what you're wondering. Although I admit, that is just beautiful." He smiled. "Are we all squared away now?"

"I think so." I'd hoped he might use the "L" word, but I guessed that was just wishful thinking. "I don't want you to feel claustrophobic though."

"If I start acting weird, you can kick me in the arse." Jack looked at me and exhaled deeply. "Listen, come to L.A."

"To L.A.?" I couldn't believe my ears.

"Tell that fuckwad of a boss you're taking a long weekend. We'll be stuck in the studio for a few days before and after, but you can come for the concerts."

"I would love to. I'd absolutely love it!" I threw my arms around his neck and smooched his face. *Maybe he isn't going on the prowl out there, after all.*

Jack smiled through my kisses. "I figure you can't call yourself going out with a musician if you haven't seen me perform." He thought for a minute, and grinned. "Outside of bed, that is."

Chapter 22

DON'T GET ME WRONG

Halfway down the block, I could hear the Cramps emanating from Beirut's propped-open doors. I'd been to the hole-in-the-wall a few times with Vicky. We liked its funky atmospherics—and where else could you listen to the 4-skins and Stiff Little Fingers, back-to-back? The green-haired bartender nodded at me as I glanced up at the huge papier-mache deity dangling from the ceiling, arms outstretched as if blessing the heathens below. Usually the displays of East Village artwork were rotated every few weeks, but "god" had turned into a permanent fixture. I peered down the length of the shotgun joint and picked out Vicky's blond head. Taking the stool she'd been saving, I signaled for a beer.

"You lucky dog," she shouted over the jarring chords of "Strychnine". "Maybe I should have hung in there with Sammy after all. I can't believe you get to go to L.A."

"I can't either. Nor can I believe Harvey's letting me leave early on Friday to catch my flight. But of course he had to dump more editing on me. I'm now immersed in a guide to toilet-training toddlers."

"Well, I'm doing a tour for a self-actualization shrink. That's pretty similar to what you're working on, in terms of being a load of excrement." Vicky smiled and licked salt off the rim of her margarita.

"Who knew publishing was such a catch-all: pop psychology, military history, juice fasts, dog-training...not to mention the latest New Age fads that ooze out of Northern California," I added.

"But just think how well-informed you'll be if you ever have your own toddler."

"Reading this book is the best kind of birth control anyone could ask for."

As the jukebox blasted the Killjoys, a healthy-sized cockroach dropped onto the bar in front of us and scuttled off.

"That's the third one tonight," Vicky observed, glancing up. "I think 'god' is infested."

"Do me a favor; if one lands in my hair, get it out fast," I said with a shudder.

Vicky scoured the last drops of tequila with her tongue. "I'd better head home; I have an early meeting tomorrow. We're bidding on a top-secret book by that Jersey politician who was caught in bed with his aide. Although you didn't hear it from me."

"My lips are sealed," I said.

"At least until you get to L.A.," Vicky said with a smirk.

Although the next day was insanely busy, it seemed to crawl because I couldn't wait to see Jack; it was our last night together before he left for the West Coast. He'd be in the studio for three days, and then I'd arrive Friday evening and leave Monday morning. After that, they had a few more days of mixing before returning to New York.

I caught the express and zipped downtown. Tom pressed the button for the elevator and introduced me to a new doorman named Walter. I stepped into the loft, but didn't see Jack.

"Back here," he called to me from the bedroom. He was standing in a maelstrom of clothes, guitars, boots, belts, and scattered sheets of his itinerary, with two large suitcases open on the bed. The only things he'd put into them were several packages of guitar picks and some Zig-Zag rolling papers.

"Hi," I said, going over to kiss him. He hugged me distractedly.

"I planned to have all this done by now," he said, running his hand through his hair. "I got stuck on the phone going over some stuff with Mary Jo, then Mark called, and then Suzanne. Then a bean-counter from the record company, telling me how much studio time is costing by the millisecond, and wanting to know why we aren't done yet. Sammy stopped by to see which guitars I'm bringing ... then I smoked a couple of joints to calm down." He shrugged. "Maybe you could help me pull it together."

"Sure." He fell back on the mattress as I ticked off the days on my fingers. "You'll be there nine days, so maybe you need ten pairs of pants?"

"More." Jack sighed. "Anything I wear to the studio will be stiff with sweat by the time we get out of there."

I decided not to focus on the fact that he'd be going out every night. "Okay, so maybe twelve pairs of pants, twelve shirts—six dressy and six regular. Does that sound right?"

"Sounds good. The concert stuff's going in a separate shipment." He shut his eyes and rubbed his temples.

I picked through his things and found an adequate supply. "No underwear? Not even a couple pairs?"

"Nope."

"Let's see, socks . . . I rummaged through his drawer, crammed full of slogan tees sent by his droves of fans: Things Go Better with Coke, Funky Mon, Disco Sucks, Better Living Through Chemistry . . . "Hmm, what else?"

"See if you'll fit in there?" Jack said, opening his eyes.

I smiled. "I wish I could stow away with you; might get a little cramped by the time we flew over Iowa though. Do you want to bring this for the flight?" I held up his copy of *Wise Blood*.

"Ah," Jack said. "Good thought, but I wouldn't want to lose it." He sat up and looked at me for a minute. "Actually . . . I've never told anyone this. Not a soul. But reading is kind of difficult for me."

I sat down beside him.

"I had all the basics in school; I'm not an ignoramus or anything," he said. "I can manage larger type, single sentences at a time. Even a paragraph if it's written big. It's just . . . the words sort of smoosh together when I try to read anything with a lot of lines in it, like a book. Menus drive me bonkers because they're always printed so small."

I had never heard of anything like that, unless he was nearsighted. "Do you think you need contact lenses?"

"No, I've had me eyes checked out." He swiped his face tiredly. "Before we could afford lawyers, Patrick used to pass the contracts and I'd fake reading them, but I couldn't handle the fine print. Same with sheet music; the one time I tried to learn it, the notes got all blurry. School was pretty tough too. So you see, I'm not a serious reader, as you always say about your intellectual friends. You still like me?" he asked, his pupils so dilated that his eyes appeared black.

"You're a composer; you have more poetry in your little toe than any writer we publish. You're a Flannery O'Connor of music."

Jack smiled. "I figured I ought to tell you, in case you saw it as an insurmountable character flaw."

"Well, I'm not musical except for liking to listen to it. Does it bother you that I don't play an instrument?"

"Hey, you can play my trom-bone any time you like," he said, grabbing me.

After a while, Jack stirred and faced me on the pillow. "Are we all sorted out about the other night?"

"I am if you are."

"You're telling me the truth about Patrick, right?"

I couldn't believe he was still questioning it. "Do you think I'm the kind of person who has sex with a man in a bathroom?"

Jack contemplated this. "You've had sex with me in my bathroom." He grinned.

"It isn't funny."

"I know it's not. I told Patrick I'd break his fucking neck if he ever did anything like that again. He just acted like I couldn't take a joke."

"Some joke." I couldn't get over his supposed friend behaving so sleazily, but I still wasn't sure what the policy was on seeing other people. "What about you; all you did was have a drink with Trina?"

For a fleeting moment Jack got an odd look on his face, but then he smiled. "She tried putting her hand on my leg, but I told her I wasn't that type of guy. So I'll pick you up at the airport Friday," he changed gears. "The driver will meet you at luggage claim and bring you to me in the car."

"I can't wait to see you play." I took his brush from the bedside table to unsnarl a tangle. Out of habit I checked the bristles. Seeing a silvery glint, I lifted it up to the lamp. An ache started in my gut. "What is this?" I asked, extracting a long blonde strand.

"What is what?"

I held it up. "Blonde. Which is not your color. Or mine."

Jack plucked the hair from my hand and held it under the light. "No idea." He let it fall and went over to his dresser.

"Is it Trina's?" I asked, getting agitated.

"Why would you think that?" he said, rummaging in the drawer.

"So it just floated in the window?"

Jack turned to face me. "What's the big deal? Mary Jo was here yesterday afternoon; who knows, maybe she tried on the wig. Maybe it's Patrick's."

Unless his bandmate's hair grew abnormally fast, it definitely wasn't his. "How many people are usually over here?"

"Different guys come over to mess around on the guitars. And other people."

I thought of the coked-up gang from the other day. "And their girlfriends?"

"Whoever they bring along. What is this, fifty questions?" he asked with an edge in his voice.

I guessed the hair could have come from one of his friends' women, although I didn't see why they'd be in his bedroom. It sounded like there was a constant flow of people in and out. "I'm just trying to get a picture of what you do with your time."

"The needle moves from dull to exciting, depending on what's happening." He picked up my bag from the chair and dug around in it. "You got that editing pen? I'm gonna make sure no one gets near you while I'm gone," he said, uncapping the marker. "Now hold still . . ."

Before I could stop him, he started writing on my stomach.

"What are you doing?" I felt him draw a line to my breast, then another down my abdomen. I sat up to see what he'd done. "PROPERTY OF JACK KIPLING" was scrawled on my middle, with arrows pointing to my body parts. "I'll have to scrub that off when my lovers show up," I said.

"You'd better not," he growled. "Listen, I'm tired of having to holler up at you and have you throw that sock at me every time I come over. I'm not gonna be much of a musician if I'm blinded in one eye by a goddamn key. Make me a copy while I'm gone, all right?"

I could barely contain my bliss. "I'll think about it. Okay, my turn." I pushed him back on the pillow, uncapped the pen and considered for a minute. I started writing on his ridged abdomen, making him writhe. "Ooh, that tickles."

"Try to hold still." I finished composing my message.

Jack got up on his elbows to look. "I can't make it out upside down."

"I'll read it to you." I smiled. "DON'T FORGET TO TAKE YOUR SYPHILIS MEDICINE."

Chapter 23

SUGAR ON MY TONGUE

After fielding a bunch of routine inquiries, the ninth call of the workday came as a surprise. "I've waited a whole month," Art said. "Have you caught up enough with your editing to meet me for a cappuccino?"

Hearing his voice made my innards roil. Memories rushed in: walking through Washington Square with our arms twined around each other's waists, kissing in the back of cabs, holding hands across the table in an intimate Village café. Reading side by side in his bed.

"I'm still kind of busy," I said tentatively.

"Come on, you won't meet an old friend for a cup of coffee?"

It did seem churlish to say no. I had to admit, I was curious about what he'd been up to and what he'd have to say to me. "How about tomorrow at seven?"

"Great. I'll see you at Reggio's."

I hung up, my mind whirling, wondering why he wanted to see me again. Maybe it was a bad idea to stir up all those old feelings. But I guessed I could handle seeing Art, since I was now completely hooked on Jack.

One o'clock rolled around and I headed down to the Chelsea. The air was so sweltering, I could see wavy lines of heat rising from the sidewalk. I went into the lobby and asked the perspiring front desk guy to let Isabel know I was there. I started to wait for the elevator, but changed my mind when two derelict-looking men punched the button. I took the stairs and knocked at her door, the fluorescent light directly above buzzing angrily as if a hornet was trapped in its tubing. The door opened a crack, and a bright blue eye appeared above the chain.

"Good to see you, Julia. Was the chapter up to snuff?" Isabel asked as I sat on the sofa. Chess climbed into my lap and kneaded pinpricks in my flesh.

"I'm still working on it, but it's very compelling. The Cadillac commercial was memorable," I said, recalling the scene in the backseat with the ad agency's director.

"In those days, men could take advantage any old way they wanted. Has your boss seen any of it yet? I'm ready to have our deal nailed down."

"I'm going to show it to him when the sitcom section's ready." *I just hope to god Harvey will let me acquire it.*

Isabel smiled. "I have good news; my career is rising from the ashes. My agent called last night and said I got the part in the film."

"Isabel, that's fantastic! I'm so happy for you!" This also boded well for the book, since a big movie role would bring her into the public eye once again.

"Yes, I'm thrilled to be back in the game. And here's the next batch." She handed me a bunch of pages.

"I'll take it with me this weekend. I have a long flight to see some friends in L.A., so I'll have a lot of time to read." The way "L.A." tripped off my tongue felt sort of glamorous.

"I can't wait to hear what you think." She cocked a penciled eyebrow. "I hope you're doing something exciting out there. You never mention anything aside from work. Are you living with someone?"

"I've been seeing a guy this summer." I decided to open up a little, since she'd been so candid with me. "I'm crazy about him, but I'm not sure how he feels. He seems to be into me physically, but it's hard to tell about the rest."

"Well, I hope he's good to you." She scrutinized me for a minute. "And if he isn't, I'd think there would be a line of men waiting to treat you right. Take my word for it; you've got to use it while you have it."

"Thanks. I'll keep that in mind."

She walked me to the door. "Have fun out there. Don't do anything I wouldn't do. Which is leaving it wide open." She smiled. "Give me a hug." I was engulfed by a pillowy, patchouli-scented bosom before she let go.

Her pages tucked under my arm, I took the subway to the 42nd Street library and delved into several medical texts until I found an extremely informative entry.

At midnight I was barely hanging on to consciousness, nodding off as I clutched a handful of Isabel's manuscript. I started awake when I heard the ringer and stumbled over to pick it up.

"Sorry to call so late," Jack said.

"I was up," I lied. "How was the flight?"

"All right, except I can never sleep on planes, with the babies crying, and the pilot telling you what's the weather in Omaha, and the stewardesses asking if you want a drink every half hour. I never manage to turn them down," he said ruefully. "It's much better when we're on tour and have a private jet."

"You must be tired. In fact, you sound exhausted." I hoped he'd just stay in his room and hit the sack. Alone.

"I'm getting my second wind. I think we're all going out in a while." Ice cubes clinked as he took a sip of something.

"When do you have to be at the studio in the morning?"

"Depends on when everyone rouses themselves. Too bad you aren't here with me now. We could go for a dip in the pool, then I could bring you back up here and lick the chlorine off . . . Hang on." The phone clunked, and I heard him open a door and have a conversation with someone. He came back on the line. "They're waiting for me downstairs."

"Say hi to everybody for me."

The next day I rushed home before meeting Art. I changed clothes three times, ultimately deciding on a skirt and print blouse. The purple shirt from Alice's would have been nice, but it was lost somewhere in the tornado of Jack's closet.

By the time Art showed up at Reggio's, my stomach was churning. I took a deep breath and stood as he came toward me. He was just as good-looking as I remembered; clean-cut and sharp-featured, his sandy hair slightly longer than he'd worn it last year. He was dressed in professor casual: a tailored tweed jacket with suede elbow patches, a crisp button-down shirt and khakis.

Art put his hands on my shoulders and gave me a warm hug. "It's good to see you, Julia," he said in a low voice. I tried to calm down while the waitress took our orders. Art surveyed me with his slate-colored eyes.

"You look fantastic. Life must be agreeing with you," he said. "Is work going well?"

"I'm doing more editing now." I spoke over the pounding in my chest.

"That's great. I know how much you wanted that." He took a sip of his cappuccino. "I've been busy finishing my paper; it's coming out next spring. And I presented my Henry James article to the Boltleuss Society."

"Congratulations. I remember you researching that one." I dumped sugar in my coffee, wondering where all this was leading.

"Are you still making your way through Proust? I have a vivid memory of when you started the first volume," he said, gazing into my eyes.

I knew exactly what he was talking about. While Art was asleep one morning, I had pulled a copy from his book-shelf and began reading it next to him in bed. I had gotten so absorbed in the language that I kept going as he awoke and started kissing my breasts. Eventually I put it aside so we could make love.

"Yes." I paused to clear my head. "So you and Phoebe wound up ... not together."

Art frowned. "We tried for a while, but we've grown in two different directions. She wants to move out of the city and start a family. My career's ramping up, and I have no desire to leave New York." He sighed. "It's sad to realize you've spent eight years with someone, yet you really didn't know them well at all."

I felt like saying, "It's also sad when you tell somebody you love her, but then one week later you've changed your mind."

"And you've been seeing someone. Is he with a publishing house? Or is he an author?"

"He's not an author." I didn't want to elaborate.

"Well…I've thought about you so often, Julia. And I wanted to apologize for the way I broke things off. That was so unfair. I had to give my marriage one more shot; so much of my life was bound up in her. But I never should have gotten involved with you if there was a chance we'd get back together."

A lump rose in my throat. I had imagined this very moment so many times; Art saying he was sorry, and that he wanted me back. But now I was completely over him—wasn't I?

"That's all right. It's in the past," I said, my voice quavering.

"No, it's not all right. I'd like to try to make it up to you, if you'll let me. Are you really with this guy?"

"I … think so."

Art gave me a searching gaze. "You don't sound too sure."

"We haven't been together very long. I'm playing it by ear."

"Well, maybe there's hope for me, then. I just want to have another chance."

"Let's keep in touch," I said vaguely. I got up and rushed out of the café.

Further down the block, I passed an awning that Art and I had once ducked under during a downpour. We'd started kissing, and only stopped when the shop owner made us move on.

Seeing him had aroused so many long-buried painful feelings. I wasn't sure I wanted to get together again.

Chapter 24

BOOM BOOM

"Miss Nash?" The driver lifted my bag off the luggage carousel. I followed him to the LAX arrivals lot, where a long black limousine waited, motor running. Jack stepped out, looking dangerously seductive in an electric blue jacket and open-collared shirt. His face was tanned, making his dark eyes and hair even more striking.

"Hello," I said, feeling a little shy. He really did look like a famous rock star with his bronzed chest and California-style clothes. I was suddenly very aware of my wrinkled blouse and faded makeup.

"Come here." He drew me inside and pulled me onto his lap. "I have something I want to give you. Did you pack those garters like I told you to?" he asked as he untucked my skirt. I felt him stiffen beneath me. "Mmmm, you feel good," he hummed, sliding his lips down my neck, prickling my skin with goosebumps.

"The driver will see," I whispered, glancing at the partition.

"That's what the curtains are for." Jack reached over and yanked them shut.

I tried to adjust my disarranged clothes before we got out at the towering white hotel. A crowd of photographers set off their cameras as we sprinted into the entrance of Chateau Marmont. I had a fleeting impression of a plush red-carpeted lobby before we took the elevator to Jack's suite. An oleander-scented breeze drifted in from the open balcony, billowing the curtains.

I stood in the middle of the elegantly furnished room, taking it all in. "Wow, this is nice."

"Bedroom's even nicer." Jack grabbed me and boosted me up. I wrapped my legs around his waist and he carried me in, laid me on the bed and stripped off his clothes. God, he looked sexy, brown all over like he'd stepped right off a desert island. I reached for him as he tongued my nipples, the sensation so exquisite I arched my back to meet him.

"This is what I was thinking about all that long limo ride," he said, tugging off my skirt.

"Me, too," I gasped. I clung to him until he bucked and bucked, giving a long, drawn-out wail.

Jack slept deeply for a while, and I took the opportunity to observe him. His silky eyelashes looked very dark against his burnished skin, and his hair seemed even longer and thicker than when he'd left. From the small band of white on his rear, he'd obviously worn a skimpy swimsuit. His eyes fluttered open as I was trying to ease my numb arm from beneath him.

"Man, I was knackered. We were out 'til all hours last night."

Seeing the shadows under his eyes, I wondered what he'd been up to. "But now I'm getting re-energized."

Jack reached for me again, his lips caressing my nipples until they tingled. "Now I want to taste you," he said in a husky voice, lying back on the pillow. "Come sit on my face, baby."

I got up and spread my legs over him, holding onto the headboard as his tongue began to flicker on me. He slid one finger inside, then two. I gripped the bed more tightly, my breath coming in a ragged pant. A shuddering quake began in my thighs and rippled up my abdomen, heat washing over me in waves as uncontrollable cries tore from my throat. Tremors were still jolting through me when he put his hands on my hips, moved me down his body and thrust up into me. My hair fell into his face and his hands urged me on as I rode him faster and faster. He pulled me to his chest and we rolled so that he was on top, plumbing my depths. He gripped me tightly, coming long and hard like a racehorse thundering into homestretch.

We rested for a while, my entire body humming. I was so happy to be in his arms again. *This will be the most time I've ever spent with him*, I thought. *Hopefully this trip will bring us even closer than before.*

Jack stirred, interrupting my musings. "You just sang both verses and the chorus," he said with a grin. "I think you missed me."

"Maybe a tiny bit," I said, making a pinch with my fingers.

"Baby, you can't tell me that. You were shakin' hands with me johnson. 'Sooo nice to meet you, sir,'" he said in a falsetto.

I took a breath. "I did miss you, Jack. I couldn't wait to see you."

"Little Jack couldn't wait to see you too."

I sighed. "Is that the only thing you missed?"

Jack pretended to think about it. "I had no one to put lotion on the hard-to-reach bits at the pool."

Somehow I doubted that. "Looks like you got some sun." I traced the outline of darker skin encircling his hip.

"I brown up pretty good, don't I? It bugs the shit out of Patrick because he just burns. Were you grinding away at those manuscripts all week? I was picturing you curled up on your futon with your papers."

I flashed on my coffee date with Art. "Mostly," I said. "How's the mixing coming along?"

"We could spend two months trying to get it right. But doing it live should help it gel. Sometimes you have to play for an audience before you tease out what it needs." Jack propped himself on top of me. "Did I tease out what you needed?" he asked in a low voice, his warm brown eyes holding mine. "I can give you more of that, if you've recovered."

My stomach rumbled. "I'm going to take a rain check until after dinner. I've only had a bag of airplane peanuts."

"I'm being selfish. All I could think about was ravishing you, when I should have been feeding you."

"First things first."

"Let me call Suzanne; she's really glad you're here. And after dinner, I'm gonna make you come about four more times." He licked my earlobe, igniting a flare of lust in my loins.

We got dressed and descended to the lobby, where Sammy shambled over holding a half-empty bottle, his shirt buttoned off-kilter. He kissed me on the cheek, exhaling whiskey fumes. "I'm drinkin' to forget your cruel, heartless girlfriend."

Jack reached over to straighten his collar. "You're nicely irrigated. And spliffcated."

"Nah, I'm jober as a sudge," Sammy replied.

Mark and Suzanne stepped out of the elevator. Mark's hair was dyed a flaming orange, and he wore a canary-yellow jacket with no shirt underneath. Suzanne was in a low-cut white jumpsuit that emphasized her red hair and stick-thin frame. "Now at least it's two against three," she said with a smile.

Mark drew a pair of drumsticks from his back pocket and rat-a-tatted them lightly on Sammy's head. "That's a nice hollow sound."

"He's just jealous," Sammy said to me. "You know what they say when it's time for the band to go on: 'Will the musicians and the drummer please come to the stage.'"

I laughed as Mark touched my arm. "Do you know why the keyboard was invented? So the musicians would have a place to put their drinks."

"That line's old as the hills," Jack said.

"Do you know what it means when the guitar player's drooling out of both sides of his mouth?" Mark added. "That means the stage is level."

"Enough of that, let's go get some vittles," Sammy said. "Dealin' with those valley girls gave me an appetite."

"You can keep that bit of information to yourself," Suzanne said.

Jack rolled his eyes at her. "Don't even try to put a lid on it; it just encourages him. What's the plan?"

"We were going to go to Musso's but they're closed for a private party, so we're heading to The Ivy," Suzanne said. "Mary Jo booked it at the last minute."

"Tripendicular," Sammy said.

All of them put on sunglasses, and Jack handed me a pair. Outside, the horde of bulb-flashers had grown even larger; they must lay in wait to see who they could shoot. A flock of women in hot pants and high heels shrieked. Jack pulled me into the backseat of the limo as the others slammed the opposite door. The women ran over to the car; *thunk* went all the locks. With one accord they lifted their tops and smashed their bare breasts against the windows.

"Oh my god," I said in disbelief. "What are they *doing*?"

"Welcome to L.A.," Suzanne said, lighting a cigarette. "Home of the boob job."

The driver tried to edge the car away. Jack was sitting with his head back, shades still on; Sammy and Mark were laughing, enjoying the show. Finally the women peeled themselves off.

"That was really gross," I said. "What were they thinking?"

Suzanne blew smoke in Mark's direction. "I don't believe much of that goes on in their empty little heads."

As we rode to the restaurant, I marveled at the fact that I was in a limo in L.A. with three world-renowned rock stars. Seeing them out of the usual NYC surroundings made it even more unreal. I noticed that the buildings weren't nearly as tall as in Manhattan; I assumed because of earthquakes. We reached The Ivy, where a crowd of tourists and photographers loitered behind a white picket fence. The host ushered us through an arched doorway into a back room. Hungrily I focused on my meal while the others bantered.

When the men ordered more drinks, I went to hit the bathroom. As I was washing my hands, a woman with closely cropped hair sidled up next to me. "I see you're with Jack

Kipling," she said. "I hear he's outrageous in the sack. I'll pay five thousand for any good stories we can print." She showed me a card from a big national rag.

"I'm not interested." I returned to the table, trying to compose my face. I wondered what she'd heard about Jack's performance, and who she'd heard it from. I hoped this was just leavings from his previous visits to the city, but even so, it reminded me that I was one in a long, long line.

I awoke deep in the night, hearing faint cries below. Thinking someone might be hurt, I got up quietly and went onto the balcony. Looking down, I could barely make out three men and five women in the pool, all of them nude. A blonde head rose and dipped rhythmically above someone leaning back on his elbows. The man's face fell forward and I saw a bright flash of orange. Quickly I retreated inside, not wanting to think about who was doing what to who.

As the sun crept through the drawn curtains, I began working on Isabel's pages next to Jack, who was still comatose. I was dying for some coffee, but I didn't want to disturb him by calling for room service. Finally at eleven-thirty he snorted, rolled over and squinted at me.

"We've got to cure you of this habit of waking up so early." He grabbed his guitar and sat strumming as I went to order breakfast. "There's OJ in the fridge if you want it," he said.

I poked around between the beer and wine bottles. "What's this?" A sealed pitcher of brownish liquid sat on the top shelf.

Jack made a face. "Carrot juice. Patrick hired this astrologer-slash-dietician to do our charts the other day. Then she advised us on our eating habits." He grinned. "She got Patrick and Mark all hennaed up in tattoos, but of course they didn't want permanent stain, so she used dye that would come off. Then Patrick forgets and jumps in the pool… the whole damn thing turned this garish orange. The hotel manager about had a 'popleptic fit. It looked like somebody'd dumped a bucket of Tang in there," he concluded, laughing.

"Was she in your room?" I blurted out, thinking of the newspaper woman's comment about his prowess.

"Ah, I see a little green-eyed devil peeping over your shoulder." Jack laid down the guitar. "I seem to recall you saying 'I haven't given any of your old girlfriends a thought…You can't un-sleep with people…'"

"I was just curious," I said, wishing I hadn't asked.

"I've been a . . . pretty good boy this week. Maybe not so much with the stimulants, but I didn't have you here to stimulate me," he added. "In fact, I'm probably the only one who *didn't* fuck her."

I winced.

"Well, you asked. This one's definitely on the bizarre end of the spectrum, even for Patrick's ladies. It always amazes me how many nutters you run into out here," he said musingly. "I was talking to this guy at a party; his company's developing a phone you carry with you everywhere. Can you imagine that?" Jack looked aghast. "I just want to get *away* from my phone. Imagine *wanting* people to be able to get hold of you, wherever you are."

"You'd never be able to stop working. Harvey could reach me at lunch, dinner, all weekend."

Jack did a mock-shudder. "Ridiculous."

The waiter knocked and put our food on the balcony table. I glanced down at the pool; the only signs of last night's bacchanal were several scattered wineglasses.

"What's the plan for today?" Gratefully I took a sip of my coffee. I wanted to run over to Book Soup, a bookstore Erin had said was fantastic, but I knew there might not be enough time.

"I'm supposed to do some interviews with Patrick at noon. I'll come back here, give you some more of Jack's special sauce, and we'll hang out until it's time to go to the stadium. The first concert's at seven; second one's at ten. Same for tomorrow night."

I didn't point out that it was already quarter past twelve. Jack ate some toast, took a leisurely shower, strummed his guitar naked for a while, eventually put on a crumpled shirt and jeans and went to meet Patrick. I figured the reporters were used to being kept waiting.

There came a brisk rap on the door and Mary Jo stepped inside. She didn't look the least bit glad to see me.

"I heard you got in last night. Patrick wanted me to give these to Jack, so he can review the lyrics before they go onstage." She handed me an envelope. "I've reserved seats for us. And whatever dimbos Patrick brings along."

"I can't wait to see the show."

"Julia." Mary Jo paused as if deciding whether to say something. "I wanted to warn you about Jack."

My mood dipped.

"He likes you. Quite a bit. I'm sure you know that."

"I assume so. He invited me here."

"I would just watch yourself around him. I've seen him really get into someone, and then get distracted by something new. He even thought Nicole hung the moon for a while, before she showed her stripes. He's not a bad person, but he's very impulsive." She frowned. "It seems like every woman in town has been trying to get into his pants this week. I don't know that he's been entirely successful at fending them off."

She left, and I went to sit on the balcony, feeling numb. *Was Jack with someone else earlier this week? He seemed so glad to see me last night. But according to her, he can turn on a dime.* I gazed down at the pool, wondering if I should have come.

There was a thumping at the door; Jack must have forgotten his room key. Surprised the interview was already over, I went to open it and found three bedraggled teenaged girls, fists raised to knock again. They looked all of fifteen.

"Oh! We thought ... someone told us this was Jack Kipling's room."

My god, has he been fooling around with a bunch of teenagers? "Who are you?"

"We hitched down from Sacramento," the freckled one said.

"Do you know Jack?"

"Not personally. We just wanted to meet him."

That was a relief. I took a closer look at the girls; they seemed like they were about to keel over. The chubby dark-haired one was very pale, mascara streaked down her cheek. The third was propped against the wall, halter-top askew. "Could we sit down for a minute? We aren't feeling too great," she said.

"I guess for a minute." They trooped in behind me and flopped onto the couch. "What are your names?"

"I'm Tanya," freckles said. "This is Nell," indicating the chubby girl, "and Free. We're so wasted; we haven't had anything to eat since yesterday. Do you have any candy bars in your fridge?"

I didn't want them passing out on me. "Would you like some sandwiches?"

Eagerly they nodded, and I ordered room service as they whispered among themselves. "After you eat, I want you to call your parents and go home. I'll give you money for bus tickets." Jack had a big stash of cash in his luggage.

"We wanted to try to get into the concert," whined Free.

"It's sold out. What are you doing, hitchhiking all this way on the off-chance you'll meet him? For one thing, he's way too old for you."

"But we love him," Nell said tearily.

"You don't love him; you don't even know him. You should spend time with boys your own age. Something really bad could happen if you showed up at the wrong guy's hotel room."

The food came, and the girls fell on it as if they were starving. I rounded up the cash, making them promise to use it for bus tickets, which I doubted they'd do. I heard a key in the lock.

"What's this?" Jack stopped abruptly in the doorway.

"These girls hitched down here to meet you. I was just giving them some lunch."

Jack backed out into the hall and glared at me. "Are you out of your mind?"

"They're pathetic. They were about to collapse."

"I don't care. Get 'em out. I'll be in Sammy's room."

He went rapidly down the hall, and sheepishly the girls left. I phoned Jack to let him know they'd gone.

"Did they take any pictures?" he asked when he returned.

"No. They just sat on the couch and gobbled up the food."

Jack gave me a stern look. "That could have gotten me in a lot of hot water."

"Why?" I didn't see the problem.

"Underage girls in my room? You're kidding."

"But I was there."

"Julia. They could say you were helping me seduce them."

I stared at him. "That's disgusting."

"I'm just telling you. I have to be careful. A lawyer gets hold of one of them, and the next thing you know, you're in court."

"I assume you don't have firsthand knowledge of that kind of thing."

"You think I'd do that?"

"No ... but it was disturbing to see such young girls at your door. I promise I won't invite anyone else in. How was the interview?"

"All right." He opened a beer and gestured with the bottle. "You?"

"I'll get one later. Mary Jo dropped off these lyrics."

"Patrick always sends them over. You can imagine how helpful they've been to me in the past."

"Want me to read them to you?"

"Do you mind? I'm a bit rusty on some of the older ones."

"Actually I did a little research at the library," I said, unsure how he'd react. "On what you said about it being hard to read."

Jack looked at me expectantly.

"I think it might be dyslexia."

"I've heard of that. Does that mean I'm retarded?"

"Not at all. You just use the right side of your brain instead of the left. It makes it harder to read longer words or fine print," I said quickly.

"Weird." Jack frowned.

"A lot of scientists, inventors, and artists are dyslexic. Albert Einstein probably was."

"Einstein, huh. I always wondered if something was wrong with me. The teachers just stuck me in the slow classes," he said, shaking his head. "That's why playing the guitar was so great; it was something I could be the best at."

"It's a shame they didn't help you, especially when so many people with dyslexia are brilliant. It could be considered a sign of genius."

Jack's mouth twitched into a smile. "That's the first time I've been called that."

"There's no doubt you're a musical genius."

"Thank you. Is there any way to get over it?"

I recalled what I'd read. "I think there are tutors that teach people using a certain method."

"Maybe I'll have Mary Jo look into that."

We sat on the balcony as I read him the lyrics. I was fascinated to see the mix of their early stuff and brand new material, and quizzed Jack about how they decided which songs to play. Jack wasn't acting cagey or distant, as Mary Jo had suggested. Maybe she was hoping to create a rift between us to prevent me from running up big bills on his tab.

After a while Jack had had enough of the review. He stood up and stretched. "The concert gear's in the closet. Pick out something for me to wear tonight."

"Great, I get to dress you." I hopped up, went inside and unzipped the hanging wardrobe. A dozen sparkly tops took up one half, pants on the other. I pulled out a shirt that shimmered with red rhinestones. "What about this? You look so good in that color."

Jack slipped out of his clothes and into the shirt, his ass bare. "I might cause a sensation if I came out like this," he said, nudging me.

"You could do the first-ever X-rated rock concert. How about these pants?" I showed him a pair with vertical stripes.

"I like 'em, but I've worn them a million times. Maybe I'll just wear jeans." He removed the shirt, his chain catching on a button.

"I've been meaning to ask you where that necklace comes from." I assumed it was special, since he never took it off.

"When our first album came out, this big-shot critic said we were just a flash in the pan," Jack replied, fingering the lightning bolt. "Mum had this made for me. She told me, 'Ignore that wanker. You're going to be a flash of lightning across the music world.' I've worn it ever since; it's me good luck charm," he concluded in his adorable accent. "Let's get in the shower, I'm sweaty again. They interviewed us on Patrick's patio."

We went into the bathroom and I started stripping off my clothes. All at once, a memory came to me. "When I was a kid, I used to love Saturday nights," I said, unhooking my bra. "Dot took a job as a cocktail waitress, so Dad and I were home alone together. I'd get into my pajamas and he'd put me on a stool and wash my hair in the sink. It's one of the nicest memories I have of growing up."

"Why don't I wash your hair?" Jack offered.

"Oh, that's okay. I don't know why I thought of it."

"C'mon, it'll be relaxing." He wound a towel around his hips and left the room, returning with a bottle of champagne and two flutes. I wrapped a towel around my waist as he popped the cork.

"I guess we have to get you wet first." He motioned me over to the sink and ran a stream over my head. I sat in a chair facing the mirror, water dripping down my back, amused by how much he was getting into it. "The front desk sent up all this goop," he said, rummaging in a basket filled with various vials and soaps. I sipped my champagne as he poured a puddle of shampoo and massaged it into my hair.

"That's a lot of bubbles," I said, laughing.

"You want to get a good lather going." He looked at the suds foaming down my shoulders. "Maybe I did use a little too much."

"Is that bubble bath or shampoo?"

Jack squinted at the label. "Whoops. Oh well, we can start over in the shower. Wait a minute though." He regarded me in the mirror. "Let's see." He took two big batons of bubbles and shaped them in a bouffant. "Marilyn."

I stood and tried to strike a *Seven Year Itch* pose. "How's this?"

"Very nice with your bare tits."

"Now your turn. What do you remind me of . . ." I pushed him down in the chair, took handfuls of suds and shaped them into points on either side of his head. "Devil."

Jack looked in the mirror and grinned. "That fits. I've got one for you." He carefully dabbed at my nipples, then leaned back in his seat. "Stripper."

I took a scoop and modeled it on his forehead. "Unicorn."

"Bunny." He tried to shape tall ears on me, but they flopped. We giggled as I filled our glasses again.

"All right, I have one." I cupped my hands in the lather and fashioned it on his chin. "Santa."

"You can be Santa's helper," Jack said, reaching for me. "Santa needs some help with this." He tugged my towel off, yanked his open and pulled me onto his lap facing him.

"Ohh, you feel good," I whispered. "Ohhh..."

After we finally made it out of the shower, we lay in bed and passed the bottle of champagne between us.

"God, Julia. You really make my water boil."

"You do the same to me. Especially when you had those horns on your head."

"I'm sure you think I'm just a sex fiend," he said.

"The thought may have crossed my mind."

"Well, I do have a reputation to uphold. Hang on, I've got an idea."

Jack went to get the garters out of my bag, drew the stockings up my legs and expertly hooked them to the belt. He settled in between and lifted a thigh over each of his shoulders. "Now that's a beautiful view. Deserves a little special something." He pulled a garter back and released it, snapping it against my backside. I gave a sharp intake of breath.

"You like that? I'm going to do that again, but you won't know when it's coming." He cocked an eyebrow. "Kind of adds an element of suspense, if you know what I mean. Now hand me the bottle. Hold still, this might tickle a bit." He held me open and poured a small trickle. "Stop laughing, you're gonna make it spill. Lemme see how this tastes." He put his lips on me and slurped. "Mmm, nice . . . a top note of fruit with an undertone of funky," he said in a plummy voice. "Okay, stop wiggling. I'm gonna get down to business."

Chapter 25

FAME

By the time we got to the arena, I was groggy from all the sex and champagne. *He doesn't seem bored with me yet*, I thought defiantly of his manager's warning. We were directed down a long hall to a dressing room, where Jack put on the shimmery red shirt over his jeans. We emerged into a brightly lit room lined with mirrors, sundry people milling around, Mary Jo patrolling the flow. A hard-looking woman grasped Jack's arm. "There's a pile of toot in Patrick's dressing room. It's going fast."

Jack glanced at me. "Want some?"

I shook my head. If pot made me out of it, I could just imagine what coke would do.

"I'll pass," Jack said.

The woman gave him a skeptical look. "You're kidding. You never turn down blow."

"I'll nab some before we go on."

A thin man in a tight lavender tee-shirt motioned Jack over to the makeup chair. "Now I've got to get pretty," Jack said to me. "How's it going, Gary? This is my friend Julia."

"What incredible forget-me-not blues," Gary said to me. "I'm going to give your hair a little trim," he added to Jack, brandishing scissors.

"Needs it," Jack said. He shut his eyes as Gary clipped, then pinned curlers on top and sprayed liberally.

"I bet you didn't know you're really going out with a woman," Jack said to me as Gary dabbed on eye shadow and blush.

"All in the name of show biz," I said. "You do look luscious." His face had an exotic quality with the makeup, lending a trace of femininity that was extremely erotic.

"You still have to come out dancing with me sometime, Jack," Gary said flirtatiously as he undid the rollers.

"Sure, if it's not too much of a Crisco disco. Can I bring Julia, or is it guys only?"

"Oh, there are lots of ladies. I think you're all set now. With those eyelashes, he never needs mascara," he said to me.

Suzanne came into the room in a bright green jacket and capris, as dramatically made up as if she herself was going onstage.

"We need to take Julia shopping at some point," she said, smiling at me. I was wearing one of his silk shirts, which I'd thought looked nice except for being long.

"Yeah, good luck getting her to go." Jack got out of the chair. "Your turn," he said to me, and went to talk to Mark.

"Go on," Suzanne said, seeing me hesitate. "Let Gary do his magic. We can't let the guys outshine us."

"First time? Don't worry, I won't do anything that doesn't come off in the wash," Gary reassured me. As Suzanne watched, offering suggestions, Gary put large rollers in my hair and began dabbing on various creams and powders. When he was done, I felt like I had two pounds of paint dragging my face down. He spun the chair around so I could see in the mirror; a wild biker chick with high cheekbones and bee-stung lips stared back at me.

"Hey, I kind of like this look," Jack observed as Gary teased my hair. He examined me as they went to touch up Mark. "He's done you like a loose woman," Jack said with raised eyebrow. "We'll have to explore that concept later."

Just then Patrick made his entrance in a long velvet robe, a miniskirted model on each arm. The trio surrounded Jack.

"I brought one along for you," Patrick said with a grin. "Oh, I forgot she got in last night," he added, seeming only then to notice me.

I felt like sinking into the floor at his withering gaze. I would have to let these suggestive remarks by Patrick, Mary Jo, and women who seemed to know Jack from before, slide off me for now or the trip would be ruined. I'd have plenty of time to mull things over later.

The room cleared out as the booming drums of the opening act resounded. "We'd better take our seats," Mary Jo said.

Jack gave my waist a squeeze. "See you out there."

"I can't wait."

Suzanne, Mary Jo and I followed a guard down the hall. We passed the open door of a large dressing room. Patrick was lying on his back on the floor, eyes closed, as a woman pranced circles around him, ringing little bells on her fingers. "Deep cleansing breaths," she crooned.

"That's the astrologer Patrick hired to get his stars aligned," Mary Jo said as we continued down the corridor. "To the tune of three thousand dollars."

"That little eejit. Did you hear about their experience with the henna?" Suzanne asked me.

"Jack mentioned something about the pool turning orange."

We reached the arena, and a guard led us to the middle of the very first row as the funk band wound up. Everyone in the adjoining seats turned to stare at us, which was an uncomfortable sensation. Mary Jo plunked down beside Patrick's ladies. I took my place between her and Suzanne, feeling a slight sting as I sat. My rear was still tender from Jack's garter-snapping, but at the time the effect was outstanding. Suzanne spoke to a man with a notepad sitting behind her. "The music critic from the *L.A. Times*," she explained to me.

The opening act left and the stage went dark. "Are you ready for . . . Four to the Floor!" the announcer said, and the audience began to scream. Sammy and Mark came out, and the noise behind us avalanched. "You'll get used to it in a minute," Suzanne shouted. "I have earplugs if it bothers you." The spotlight caught a glitter of red; Jack walked on, followed by Patrick. The screams and shouts became a savage roar. Jack's guitar twanged, and the beam hit Patrick's face.

"Good to be back in L.A.," Patrick said, and the crowd went berserk.

The lights flared as Jack hit the opening notes. Patrick's bass entwined with Jack's guitar was so loud, I could feel the vibrations deep in my belly. Patrick sang and gyrated spellbindingly, but my eyes remained on Jack as he moved sinuously across the stage, nimble fingers eliciting ecstatic moans from his Telecaster. Sammy kept up a jangling keyboard, and Mark flogged his drums like a madman. The girls next to Mary Jo were bouncing in their seats, boobs flopping in their casings. An acrid joint, rapidly followed by another, made its way down our row. The men flew into a second number and then slowed it down with the third, when the spotlights went scarlet against the pitch-black stage. Another bluesy tune ensued, ending with Patrick lying in a fetal curl. Then he leaped up and Jack came forward.

The audience began to stomp and shout Jack's name. Chills prickled my entire body as he looked right at me and hit the four jagged chords. He belted out the song, his voice rasping on the higher notes. Watching him perform was the most electrifying experience of my entire life. When he finished, he hung his head briefly, acknowledging the mass adoration. Then Patrick came forward and they did several of their biggest hits, faces close together at the mic, Patrick occasionally mouthing lyrics to Jack between verses.

A large plastic cup was being handed down our row. I saw that the thin straw was sunk into a well of white powder. I gave it to Suzanne, who inhaled a big snort and passed it along. One of Patrick's girls popped something open under her nose and fell back in her seat, flaked out cold. Mary Jo calmly poured a splash of her soda down the woman's low-cut top, and she shuddered awake. Mary Jo's bored expression made it clear she'd seen it all before.

The rest of the concert flew by too quickly. People extinguished their lighters and filed out of the stadium. We went backstage to where the men, drenched in sweat, were stripping off their shirts and gulping cold beer. I hung back as Suzanne and Mary Jo approached them. Seeing Jack onstage was like watching a different person than the one I'd been spending time with; it made him seem larger than life, and again brought home to me that he really was this huge rock star. Who was I to be with someone like him?

A bunch of people burst in and flocked to the men. Several women approached Jack, eyeing him voraciously. Jack listened to them and nodded, then looked around and crossed the room bare-chested. "What are you doing over here?"

"Just taking it all in. That was amazing." I kissed his cheek, tasting salt. "It was the best concert I've ever seen. Your song was fantastic; it was such a thrill to see you play. I felt like I'd died and gone to heaven."

Jack smiled. "Glad you liked it. Let's go relax for a while before the next one."

We went to his dressing room, where he reclined on a couch and I massaged his shoulders. I couldn't believe they had to go back onstage in less than an hour.

"Room service!" Sammy cried, pushing a delivery cart down the hall toward Patrick's poolside bungalow. Perched on top were two busty blondes, giggling as the trolley tipped precariously. Jack held the door, and we followed them in. Patrick was holding court in the middle of the lavish suite. "I guess your room isn't the party room anymore," he said to Jack, eyeing me. "The good whiskey's hidden in back of the cabinet."

As Jack went to get our drinks, two dolled-up women in their thirties approached and fawned over Patrick. He managed to respond, yet look supremely bored at the same time.

"Mutton dressed as lamb," he commented when they left. "What did you think of the show?"

I decided to play nice. "I liked the way you switched the tempos around in the blues numbers. I'm so glad I'm getting to see you guys perform."

"Me too." He scrutinized me for a moment. "You don't look like such a demure little book editor tonight."

I blushed. "Gary did my makeup."

"Quite delicious." Patrick glanced at Jack as he handed me a beer. "Marissa's here; you should say hi to her. Remember when she stripped in the hotel elevator?"

Jack took a gulp of his whiskey. "I don't recall much of anything from that tour. Neither do you."

"Now that you're old and married, you can't recall."

"I'm no more married than you, last time I checked," Jack said with a bite in his voice. "Were you too cheap to order food? I'm starving."

"Out by the Jacuzzi. Have at it."

I followed Jack to the patio, where a cluster of smokers converged around a laden table. Suzanne rushed over to us, cigarette in hand. "I can't find Mark. Have you seen him?"

"Not lately," Jack said. She went to question Sammy, who was soaking in a bubbling hot tub with the now-topless blondes.

"I don't believe I've seen him since right after the show," I said to Jack. Mark had been laughing with a couple of young women in the dressing room while Suzanne hovered nearby.

Jack looked at me. "He's a big boy, he'll find his own way here. Let's get something to eat." We loaded up on food and sat in chairs by the foaming tub. I tried to avoid looking at the glistening breasts on display. Sammy raised his bottle to me. "We've banned the bra, baby!"

Suzanne circled by again. "I can't find Mark anywhere. Did he tell you where he was going?" She sounded frantic.

"He didn't say," Jack replied. "Why don't you hang here with us? I'm sure he'll show up. Maybe he's resting in your room."

"I've called four times; he's not picking up." She stalked off.

"Should we help her find him?" I asked, feeling sorry for her.

"No." Jack cut into his salad.

"But she's so worried."

"That's their deal. It doesn't pay to get involved." This seemed to be his final word on the subject.

A man started throwing shrimp to the women in the Jacuzzi, who caught the pink nuggets in their mouths. A few other girls stripped and jumped into the tub. People began dumping entire bowls of food into the water, creating a revolting soup. Sammy got out laughing as the women, draped in linguine and spattered with cocktail sauce, entreated him to come back in.

By three a.m. I was wiped out. I didn't want to curtail Jack's fun, so I told him I'd see him upstairs and left him joking and toking with Sammy and Patrick. I got into bed, but couldn't sleep. I wondered if Mark was with the girls from backstage. I tried to avoid thinking about what Jack might have done earlier this week, other than a lot of cocaine. I recalled my coffee date with Art, his slate-gray eyes taking me in.

Just as it was starting to get light outside, I heard Jack fumbling with the key. I got up to let him in and he fell back onto the bed. "Man, I'm hammered." I tugged off his clothes, which reeked of pot, and brought him a glass of water. A limp noodle was stuck in his chest hair.

"Is that from the Jacuzzi?" I asked, yanking it out.

"Ouch, you're pulling. Sammy dumped a bunch of it down my shirt." He smiled sleepily as I lay next to him. "You know at the end, when people get out their lighters for the encore? That always reminds me of fireflies. It's like the whole arena's full of them, all flickering just for me." His expression gave me a glimpse of the little boy he'd once been.

"That's a beautiful image."

"Yeah, it is." He sighed. "Julia, what's your biggest fear?" His eyes were inky pools in the dim room.

I wondered why he was asking. "I guess . . . the fear of turning out like my mother."

"She's entirely different from you."

"It's a kneejerk reaction. Whenever I start to do something that reminds me of her, I do the exact opposite. What's yours?"

Jack gazed up at the ceiling. "I'd have to say . . . I'm afraid I might not be able to have children."

I was startled by his admission. "Why?"

"It seems odd that all this time I've been sowing my oats, I never got a woman pregnant. Not that I wanted to have a baby with any of 'em. But at times I wasn't always so careful."

Ugh, I love hearing this. "And you're positive . . ."

"I never had a kid. It would have been made public, believe me."

"Well, maybe you were more careful than you realized. That doesn't mean you can't have a child."

Jack looked at me. "I hope you're right." He closed his eyes, and I thought he'd fallen asleep. "Do you ever think about trying to find your father?" he said after a few minutes.

"No. He left me behind with Dot, knowing what she was like. And he never called me or anything; he just vanished."

"You were a fourteen-year-old girl. That wouldn't have been easy for a single man to deal with. Especially if he was moving around."

"I haven't heard from him once in ten years. It makes me feel so . . . rejected." Even after all this time, the hurt was still piercingly fresh.

Jack turned to his side, our faces almost touching on the pillow. "I know what you mean. For years I thought my dad moved out because of me; I was kind of a handful. Nobody ever explained to me that adults can stop loving each other." He put his warm hands on my waist and pulled me closer. "I resented it like hell that other kids had their dads around at night, and I only saw mine every other weekend."

A dark strand fell into his eyes and I smoothed it back. "You never mention your stepfather. Did you get along with him?"

"It felt like he was taking my place in the house. For a while there, I just wanted to destroy things. I moved to London when Sharon was little, but he probably would have kicked me out if I hadn't gone on my own. At least I had some contact with my dad through those years; yours just got cut off."

"He must not have cared enough about me to keep in touch." I spoke over the lump in my throat.

"He might've had his reasons," Jack said, his face in half-shadow from the dawn light coming through a slit in the curtain. "Maybe he was afraid of your mum. You should try to locate him, before it's too late."

"I guess that's another big fear: if I found him, he wouldn't want me back in his life."

We slept in until early afternoon; even highly charged Jack seemed exhausted. The insistently ringing phone woke us up. I answered and told Mary Jo we'd get going, not bothering with any pleasantries. "That was short and not too sweet," Jack said after I hung up.

I sank back on the bed. "Mary Jo doesn't seem to like me much. She took it upon herself to inform me that you jump around a lot. From woman to woman."

Jack frowned. "She did? When was this?"

"Yesterday when she dropped off the lyrics."

"I don't jump around more than anyone else. Anyway, none of that is Mary Jo's business."

I saw an opening and decided to take it. "A lot of these girls seem to know you from before. This newspaper writer cornered me at the Ivy, wanting details."

Jack sat up and ran his hand through his hair. "It's been pretty crazy at times," he said. "But they weren't girlfriends; just women on the road. What do you want to ask me? Shoot."

"Well . . . I know people throw themselves at you. I guess obviously you've slept with a lot of them," I said carefully.

"There was never a reason not to. You know me; I need a lot of it. Sometimes it's just a mechanical type of release." He paused and looked at me. "There isn't all that much joy in it. Even a couple of years ago, I was barricading my room half the time to keep 'em out. Most of those backstage types aren't too appealing anyway."

"What about . . . that woman made the comment about you doing a lot of coke."

"Yeah, you know I do some blow. I've been cooling it a little at home, but on the road it makes things less dull. And it ramps us up for the show. It's not exactly an aphrodisiac, once you've scarfed a pile of it." He gazed at me wearily. "Is that it for the interrogation?"

"I haven't asked you much of anything before. I think it's only fair, since I'm spending so much time with you. Lately."

"I know you haven't asked me much. You like to play it close to the vest."

"You can blame that on my experience with Dot."

Jack considered me. "All right, now I want to say something to you. About your mother."

I glanced away. "I don't want to talk about her."

"You don't have to; just listen. Dot seems like she's trying to get her life together. If we were all judged by things in our past, none of us would make the grade." He gave me a pensive look. "I believe you have more sympathy for those hookers on the West Side than you do your own mum."

"That's because they seem so lost."

"So does Dot."

I snorted. "She ruined my life because she couldn't resist getting in the sack with her boss. I lost my dad because of her."

"It sounds like your parents were headed for a divorce, regardless. Everyone screws up sometimes; your mum messed up royally, and maybe to you, that's unforgiveable. But I do know you have to be able to forgive someone before you can trust them. So, Julia." He lifted my chin so I was looking him in the eyes. "You have to forgive me for all the stupid shit I've done in the past, so you can trust me going forward."

I got back to the empty room after having my first-ever massage with Suzanne. A message slipped under the door directed me to call room 696. I dialed, and Patrick picked up the phone. "Jack and I are running through some stuff. Do you want to meet us here and we'll head over together?"

"Can I speak to Jack?" I wanted to be sure this wasn't some dirty trick.

"Jack! Your old lady wants to talk to you."

"How'd your massage go?" He came on the line.

"It felt kind of weird. But she worked out some of the kinks."

"So you're not kinky anymore; too bad. Want to come down? We need to leave soon."

I hurriedly put on some makeup and went to Patrick's bungalow. A tall woman wearing a bikini answered my knock. "They're out by the pool," she said, and I stepped through the open French doors.

Jack and Patrick sat in ornate garden chairs bordered by hibiscus bushes, sheets of paper scattered around on the grass. Hovering near an open blossom, a honeybee was drunkenly lurching from flower to flower. As I watched, it landed, still humming, on the arm of Jack's seat. He held out his finger; the bee climbed onto it and proceeded to shake golden powder off its legs. Jack noticed me standing there. "They like me," he said. The vibration of his voice disturbed the bee, and it took flight.

"Did you catch a buzz?" Patrick said caustically. "Can we get this wrapped up? I need to get ready."

Jack reached out and dragged a chair over, the iron legs scraping divots in the lawn. "Let's see what Julia thinks. She has a good ear."

Patrick scratched some notes on a pad and narrowed his eyes. "All right, we'll go to third-party negotiation. What do you think we should open with, 'Storm Front' or 'Higher'? Or keep it the way it was last night?" He tapped his pencil on the notepad.

I held back, not wanting to insert myself in their argument, particularly since Patrick was in such a pissy mood. Jack swirled the cubes in his glass. "Spit it out; we're not getting anywhere. He won't listen to you anyway."

"The guy from the *L.A. Times* told Suzanne he's coming back again tonight, so it might make sense to do the set in a different order," I said. "I'd vote for 'So Good' to start off, then "Storm Front,' and move 'Higher' to the end. That way it won't seem like a rerun."

"I see you two discussed this before you came down," Patrick snapped.

"No, we didn't. I don't need Jack to monitor my opinions." I didn't care who he was; I was tired of his condescending remarks.

"Oh, right, 'coz you're so independent-minded. But it doesn't bother you to be part of the entourage, does it?" Patrick smiled at me disdainfully.

"I'm only here because Jack invited me. I'm not part of your entourage."

Jack was laughing into his drink.

"That's true. You left before the party really got going last night. You missed a lot of the fun," Patrick said insinuatingly.

"Jack's so good at doing two things at once. Or should I say, two girls. But I'm sure you already know that."

I bolted out of my seat. "I don't like extra baggage in my bed. Unlike some of these imbeciles you surround yourself with."

I marched out to the hallway. The door slammed as I pressed the elevator button, and Jack came toward me, grinning. "About time you set him straight."

Hair and makeup perfected, the men were waiting to go on in the echoing corridor behind the stage. Jack patted his shirt pocket beneath his guitar. "Damn."

"What is it?" I asked.

"Left my extra picks in the dressing room."

"I'll get them." I spoke at the same time Mary Jo said, "I'll go."

We looked at each other. I smiled, but she didn't. "Should we draw straws?" I joked.

Mary Jo gave me a venomous glare, turned on her heel and scurried down the corridor. It suddenly hit me that her warning me off Jack might not be out of concern for my well-being. I had a feeling his manager had a little crush on him—or maybe a really big one.

"We'd better go sit down," Suzanne said. She took my arm and we made it to our seats just in time.

The songs came in an order completely different from what either Jack or Patrick had discussed by the pool, but it worked like an elixir on the audience, which seemed even more hyped than the night before. The whole house was rocking as they finished their sixth big number. Patrick bowed and looked over at Jack, who took his guitar off his shoulder and walked over to Sammy. Jack handed Sammy the guitar, and the crowd started rumbling in confusion. Jack sauntered back to the drums and took Mark's seat, to a collective gasp. Patrick gave his bass to Mark and sat at the keyboard. They swung into one of their simpler early hits, but were almost drowned out by the hysterical reaction. I glanced over my shoulder; the *L.A. Times* guy's jaw had dropped. "I've never seen anything like this, ever!" he shouted. The men made it through the tune without stumbling and pounded into the finale. Grinning amidst the roaring acclaim, they traded instruments, resumed their usual places and plunged into the next song.

"That was amazing! Did you know they had that planned?" I shouted into Suzanne's ear.

"I had no idea. They must've practiced it in secret," she replied.

After a while, Patrick went offstage as Jack brought out a stool and tuned his acoustic guitar.

"Hey, Julia," he said, looking directly at me. The hair stood up on my arms as everyone in the surrounding rows craned to see who I was. Jack began strumming and eased into a song I'd never heard before. Its melody was mournful and haunting: *Sick of crawlin' round filthy dives, what I want's right by my side. But I ain't out to pasture yet; still wanna be rode hard and put up wet.*

When he finished, I sat stunned as the crowd screamed his name. Jack smiled at me, Patrick ran out and grabbed the mic, and the rest of the show went at fever pitch. Mary Jo never showed up to claim her seat.

"I'm gonna make an ice run," Mark said. We were relaxing in

his and Suzanne's suite after a long, rowdy post-concert dinner in the Villa's restaurant.

"I'll come with you," Suzanne said, jumping up. She was smoking her hundredth cigarette and looked haggard from chasing him around all night.

"Let me know what time we're hitting the studio tomorrow," Jack said.

I hugged Suzanne and told the guys goodbye. Jack and I returned to our room and went out on the balcony to gaze at the starry night sky, the pool an aquamarine opal glowing in its dark setting.

Jack wrapped his arms around me. "Too bad you can't stay longer."

I was elated that he felt that way, but unfortunately my plane ticket was for tomorrow morning. "I'd love to. I would if I could."

He thought for a minute. "'I Would If I Could.' Now there's a title for a song."

"That new one you sang tonight was so beautiful. I felt like . . . you were singing it to me."

Jack's eyes shone in the reflection from the glittering pool. "That's what's bothering me. I *was* singing it to you."

Chapter 26

HIGHLIFE

The office was a whirlwind when I returned on Tuesday. Newly tanned from a long weekend in Martha's Vineyard, Harvey charged back in a cantankerous frame of mind. He dove into "working the phones"; if I heard him say "When I was at Esiness" once, I must have heard it a million times. His stack of submissions grew in a sloughing pile. Like Sisyphus, no sooner did I reject three, than another ten arrived in the mail. On top of that, he gave me two of Briar's manuscripts for a "backup read." I tried to find out what was happening with her celebrity project, but neither Erin nor Meredith had heard an update. At least Isabel finally had made progress and gave me a juicy chunk about her television career. I was determined to skimp on sleep until I got it rewritten.

Jack and I had only had one rushed conversation on the phone since I left. I'd tried calling him, but he hadn't picked up. I didn't get the sense he was spending much time in his room, but

I knew they were on a deadline with the mixing. After the long weekend, missing him was like a constant itch that I couldn't scratch. I was counting the minutes until I saw him again.

Adding to my turmoil was a call from Art. He said he was preparing lecture notes for his fall classes and wanted my take on the material, but I was pretty sure that was just an excuse. Before we hung up, he invited me to a symphony at Lincoln Center. I declined, but felt a slight tug when I did.

"Please tell me you don't have plans tonight."

I wondered what Vicky had in mind. "I don't."

"Good. Can you help me out with Lucinda Matlock's party? Our other publicist went home sick." Lucinda was a bestselling women's novelist with a rabid following; previously Vicky had described her as "high-maintenance".

"Emily's taking the agent, and I'm supposed to pick up Lucinda at her hotel and deliver her to her rich friend's penthouse on Fifth," Vicky continued. "Then I have to work the door, make sure Lucinda schmoozes the reviewers, and get her to sign a book for every single guest. I could really use another warm body."

"That sounds like fun. The most exciting thing I've done at work lately is make Harvey's lunch reservations."

"When it's all over, you can tell me how much fun it was. I'll stop by your office at six. The theme is Chinese since the book's set in Shanghai, so I'll bring you an outfit."

Vicky showed up with an Asian-style dress, borrowed from one of her Garment District friends. I slipped into it in the bathroom and we rode the elevator down in our shantung silks. A long black limousine was waiting on the curb.

"You're kidding, we're going in a stretch?" I said. The driver opened the back door and we slid inside.

"Only the best for Lucinda. She complained the last time I picked her up in a town car." Vicky cracked a window.

"Pluttner Press must be raking it in. Harvey gets annoyed if the editors take cabs."

"Lucinda's the reason we didn't have layoffs like everyone else. Her last novel stayed at number one for twelve weeks, so I really can't blow this."

The driver pulled a sharp U-turn. A van laid on its horn, and our guy gave the international signal for "Fuck off."

"We'll pick her up at the Plaza and then head to the party," Vicky said as we zoomed up Park Avenue. "So tell me more about L.A. How are things with the long, lean love machine?"

"I had an amazing time with Jack, and the concerts were incredible," I said. "Jack even sang a song about finding what he'd been looking for—then of course the last verse was about not being ready to settle down. When I left, he was saying he wished I could stay longer. Although he hasn't picked up the phone in three days."

The limo stopped for a column of taxis being sluggishly digested into 42nd Street. A man with a dripping squeegee approached, but the driver waved him off.

"They're probably working nonstop to finish the album," Vicky said. "Sammy once mentioned that the record company was freaking out. Speaking of work, I had some good news: I booked my first author on the *Early Morning Show*. As a reward Emily upped my expense account."

"Congratulations! That's really great, Vick; I'm so happy for you. I just got something from my boss too."

"From Harvey?" She rolled her eyes. "What, gonorrhea?"

"He's dumping the work that his star assistant doesn't feel like doing on me."

"What a putz. When are you going to show him Isabel's manuscript?"

"As soon as I get this section ready. So far she's had two ménages and fellated three film agents, so it should be right up his alley."

The limo stopped in front of the Plaza. "There's Lucinda. I lied and told her the party started at six-thirty so she'd be on time," Vicky said. The driver opened the door for an impeccably groomed woman in her forties, dark hair coiffed and expertly made up.

"I can't wait to see the book," Lucinda said to Vicky as she tucked in her scarlet mandarin dress. "That box you said you sent never arrived."

"I would have messengered some to your room if I'd known," Vicky said. "I was rereading it last night. I loved the way you described the couples switching partners in the car. Oh, Lucinda, this is my friend Julia."

"Do you have any hand lotion? This city smog wreaks havoc on my skin," Lucinda said impatiently, ignoring the introduction.

Vicky dug around in her purse and produced a vial. Lucinda briskly rubbed some in, then took a can of hairspray from her own bag and spewed an asphyxiating cloud.

"How do I look?" she asked, patting her stiffening helmet.

"Gorgeous," Vicky choked out.

The mansions across from Central Park glowed softly with inner light. We entered the Fifth Avenue building and whooshed soundlessly to the top floor. The apartment glittered in candlelight, opulent vases of red tulips a brilliant burst of color against the all-white decor. A wide expanse of windows overlooked the Metropolitan Museum and the lush emerald-green park.

An elegant man in his fifties embraced Lucinda. Emily arrived with the agent, and they swooped over to surround the author. A short, curly-haired woman came up to us. "Hi Vicky. I see you got her here in one piece."

"She was bitching that she hadn't seen the book yet, but I shipped a box straight from the warehouse," Vicky said.

"Don't worry about it. She'll see it tonight."

"Sarah, this is my friend Julia Nash who's helping me with the signing. Julia, meet Sarah Wittner, Lucinda's editor."

"So you're Harvey's assistant. You have my sympathies." Sarah smiled. "I worked with him briefly at one point."

"I'm hoping my stint will be brief," I said, smiling back at her. "Although fetching his coffee is a thrill. It's nice to know there's life beyond."

"We should have a drink sometime, compare horror stories. Uh-oh, she's spotted me. I'd better go kiss up." Sarah rushed off to exclaim over Lucinda's outfit.

Waiters in black tie navigated the rapidly filling room, and we snagged some eggrolls and fortune cookies. "I didn't have any lunch," Vicky said after wolfing down three wontons. "Do I have scallions stuck in my teeth?"

"Just a little soy sauce on your chin. This party must have cost a mint; one of those floral arrangements would keep me in groceries for a month."

"Her friend made a killing in the stock market, pre-oil crisis.

Okay, I see two reviewers I have to introduce to Lucinda. In a minute we'll set up her autographing table."

Vicky went to corral the critics. Hoping for a good omen about my future, I cracked open my cookie: "You will be hungry again in one hour."

Sarah dinged her glass and made an elegant speech about Lucinda's new novel. As Emily began her own tribute, I fantasized about someday having bestselling authors of my own, mingling with the hoi polloi at lavish parties and making witty toasts. Vicky interrupted my daydream. "Can you help me unpack the books?" I followed her to a marble table, and she handed me a box-cutter. "Once she starts signing, just try to keep the line flowing," she said as we ripped into the cardboard.

Lucinda approached, and with a flourish, Vicky handed her the first copy. "Congratulations; doesn't it look great?"

Lucinda glanced at the cover, then flipped it over to the full-bleed photo on back. "This isn't the right picture!" she shrieked. "This makes me look ancient!"

Vicky examined the image. "Your hair looks perfect, and that blouse goes so well with your eyes."

"But my expression! This is the worst headshot of all. I can't believe they screwed it up!" Lucinda wailed. "Tell you what— I'm just going to rip the back covers off." She made a motion as if to do so, eyeing Vicky as she did. Emily and Sarah began to hurry over from the far end of the room.

"I know exactly how you feel," Vicky said calmly. "Go ahead and tear it up."

I was startled that she'd suggest this. Lucinda stared at her. "You think I should?"

"Sure, if you're not happy with it. There's no excuse for a mix-up like that."

Lucinda reached for the first copy.

"I do feel badly for all these reviewers who've come to see you. I'll make an announcement that due to publisher's error, they won't get an autographed copy tonight. I suppose they'll have to wait for Desdemona Bricknell; she's in town next week," Vicky added, naming another bestselling novelist.

Lucinda's eyes grew wide. "Oh no, I wouldn't want you to do that. I hate to disappoint the press. I guess it's not that bad," she said, scrutinizing the jacket. "I just wish they'd used the one I told them to."

"All right, if you're sure you want to go ahead with it. I can imagine how upsetting this must be."

"It is, but I'll have to manage," Lucinda said with an air of hardship.

"Everything all right here?" Emily asked breathlessly.

"Everything's under control," Vicky said. "Let's get started." She gave me a nod, opened the book to the title page, and placed it before Lucinda. I sent the first person over, and we kept the line moving until the last guest left clutching their copy.

"Oh. My. God," Vicky said, peeling off her shoes. We had dropped Lucinda at the Plaza, and were sprawled back in the limo as it headed downtown. "You certainly got to see our bestselling author in top form."

"I really thought she was going to tear up the books. Very impressive, the way you handled her."

"I find it helps to think of them as small children, then they're not quite so irritating. But Lucinda really knows how to push my buttons."

"Well, that was an adventure," I said.

Vicky grinned at me. "Confucius say: 'Next time, make sure author see headshot before party.'"

Chapter 27

STRANGER IN THE HOUSE

Jack didn't get in touch with me until the day after he got home; he said he'd been too wasted to call the previous afternoon. I raced out of the office as soon as I could and made it to his place by six. He looked completely wiped out, deep shadows under his eyes. I put my arms around his neck and kissed his cheek.

"How did the rest of the mixing go? I called a few times, but you weren't in your room," I said.

"Pretty intense. We hit a lot of parties afterwards." He rubbed his face tiredly.

"Do you want to rest? You look exhausted."

"I may lie down for a bit."

I followed him to his room, disappointed that we wouldn't get to make love, but excited to be with him. The covers were rumpled; obviously he'd been asleep earlier. He flopped down on the bed and I snuggled next to him, stroking his back as he drifted off. *Actually this is a good thing*, I thought to myself. *We can just relax with each other now; it doesn't always have to be about sex.*

I woke once in the night, listening to his breathing on the pillow next to me. I moved closer so we were spooning, my cheek against his warm back, my arms wrapped around his waist. In the morning he was still asleep when I had to leave, so I found a takeout menu, wrote a sweet little note and left it on his kitchen table, along with the set of keys I'd had made for him. Walking uptown to the office, I felt so happy. It seemed like we'd turned a corner; we had become a real couple.

When I handed Meredith a jacket mechanical, she told me she'd liked the rewritten chapters on Isabel's TV career. My confidence boosted, I finally got up the nerve to give it to Harvey.

"Well, you've been quite the eager beaver," he commented. "But I still say her career's washed up. Who cares about Isabel Reed anymore?"

"She just landed a role in a new movie that sounds promising. And her story's really compelling. She had a tough childhood and clawed her way up all on her own."

"I'll take a look, but I wouldn't get your hopes up. Pryce Rayner, on the other hand, had some very interesting things to say in the meeting he took with Briar. She's looking into getting him hooked up with a ghostwriter. I have a feeling it's going to happen very soon." Harvey narrowed his piggy little eyes at me. "Of course you and I could discuss your project over dinner one night. If you aren't all tied up with your rocker buddy." He smiled, and my spirit shriveled. "By the way, how do you handle his friends—two at a time, or all four at once?"

"None of the above." I thrust the pages at him and left.

That afternoon we had a fire drill in the office building and afterwards maintenance couldn't get the alarm to shut off, so we all had to leave. I considered stopping by my apartment, but decided instead to go to Jack's place and surprise him. I spoke to Tom, who said he'd just come on his shift and didn't know if Jack was home. I stepped into the loft, anticipating his arms around me, but the place seemed empty.

"Jack?" I called out. I heard a rustling in the back. I dropped my bag on the couch next to his guitar and walked toward the bedroom. The door was cracked a tiny bit. I went in smiling, expecting him to be waiting for me.

There was someone in the bed. Pale blonde hair flared over the pillow. Big tanned breasts flopped as she rolled to her side and propped her head on her hand.

"Jack'll be back in a minute. He went to get me some cigarettes," Trina said. "Did you need something?"

I stood there in shock as the meaning of it sank through my skin. Backing out of the room, I turned and ran to the door. *I have to get out of here before he comes back!* was all I could think. I got into the elevator and dry-heaved. The door opened, and blindly I stumbled through the lobby and into the too-bright street. *If I can just make it home, I can hide away and never come out.*

Once I got in, I fell into bed, my whole body shaking. The image of Trina's naked torso was seared onto my brain. *The bastard was screwing around with her, after all! That's why he didn't want to have sex when he got back.* Then suddenly it hit me: *The blonde hair in his brush was hers. He's been seeing her all along.* Everything he'd ever said to me—all of that bullshit about trust—was a lie.

Hours passed. I paced the room, sobbing, and collapsed on the couch. Then I got up to walk the floor again. Jack must have come home by now, and Trina would have told him what happened. The fact that he didn't call meant he knew there was no use trying to talk his way out of it. God, what a gullible idiot I'd been! But at last I'd learned my lesson—the one I should have learned before. At least I could thank Jack for that: he'd taught me that I should never trust any man again.

Nobody wants you, the voice in my head taunted me. *Not even your own father.* I spent a horrible, harrowing night, crying until my ribs were sore.

Chapter 28

LOVE BITES

Four days later, I was reliving the scene in my mind for the millionth time when the phone rang.

"Julia, it's me. Listen, I really didn't—"

"Fuck you!" He thought he could call me after all this time and casually talk his way out of it? "You think I'm so naïve I'll believe anything, don't you! But I'm not like Suzanne, clinging to you for dear life. I have my own life—I don't need you!"

"I know you do. Let me explain!"

Hot tears ran down my face. "You think you're god's gift to women, don't you, Jack? I always knew you were lying about Trina, and all those other groupies like Nicole." Suddenly, viciously, I wanted to hurt him as much as he'd hurt me. "They're more your type anyway—dopey bimbos with tits for brains. So they don't present too much of a challenge, right? Get what you came for and go? Well, at least I got something out of all this."

His voice was steely. "Oh, what was that?"

"I went out to some nice places on your dime, and I finally got to see L.A. Even if I was bored with the level of conversation most of the time, at least the sex was decent."

For a minute there was silence. "I guess that's all I needed to know."

"Fuck you!" I screamed, but he'd already hung up the phone.

The next few weeks were pure misery. I kept thinking about Jack; what he was doing, who he might be with aside from Trina. I'd wake up in the morning expecting to feel his arm around my waist, his light rumble on the pillow next to mine. I missed the way his intense gaze softened when he looked at me. His wicked offbeat humor that made me laugh. I longed for his touch so badly that it was a tangible ache pulsing beneath the surface of my skin.

What an idiot, to trust a guy like that. Why would you think he'd stay away from girls like Trina? All that time, I had believed we were getting closer. I had even let myself think he was falling in love with me. I'd gotten caught in the very trap I'd tried so hard to avoid.

One morning on my way to work, I passed a taxi stopped at a corner. One of the Floor's songs was pouring through its open window. I listened until the light changed, Jack's voice fading away as the cab moved on. Feeling like I'd been kicked in the chest, I almost walked back home. I must have looked distraught, because even Harvey softened his usual curt manner. Several people asked me what was wrong, but I kept it to myself. My instinct had been not to tell anyone I was romantically involved with Jack, and it turned out to be right. That way,

I only had to tell Vicky and Meredith that we'd broken up.

Vicky tried to cheer me up over drinks. "Look, you've had an experience not many women get. You went out with a British rock idol! Try to go with that and move on. Just because he turned out to be a prick doesn't mean you aren't great." She finished her vodka and waved the waiter over for the check.

In my defense, I did try to think of it that way—but it did no good. I didn't care that Jack was a superstar; I just missed the man I'd stupidly, hopelessly fallen in love with.

Three weeks after I'd given Isabel's chapters to Harvey, he called me in to discuss them. His dour expression made bile rise in my throat. "I know you're champing at the bit to acquire something, but this didn't grab me at all," he said. "You have to wade through so much drivel about her childhood before she gets to Hollywood. Then it picks up somewhat, but these B-list celebs are a dime a dozen. I published a bunch of them at Esiness, and not one netted more than fifteen thousand copies."

All my hard work, all my visits to Isabel—my chances of getting promoted—were circling the drain. Frantically I tried to come up with a rebuttal. "I think women readers will respond to her mother's abandonment. And so many people were fans of her show. You don't think they'd want to read this?" I ended weakly.

"I'm just not seeing it. Tell you what, have Briar take a look. She's great at scoping out what the public wants, in terms of celebrities."

Slowly I returned to my desk. There was no way Briar would support my project, particularly since she was still waiting to hear if Pryce Rayner wanted to sign on the dotted line. Apparently he'd been awol for the past couple of weeks.

"How'd it go?" Meredith came into my office.

"He hated it. But he threw me a bone, saying I could let Briar weigh in since she's the expert on all things celebrity."

Meredith scowled. "He's so full of shit."

My jaw dropped; I'd never heard her curse.

"Here's what we're going to do," she said. "Make some copies, and I'll give them to Charlie and Kate. She at least owes you for all the reading you've done for her. If they like it, they can help you defend it at the next meeting. If not, they can just zip their lips. Don't bother giving it to Briar; she'll just shoot it down."

I went to the copy machine, feeling like this was a waste of perfectly good paper.

Art had been calling me, and eventually I decided to have dinner with him. Since I'd been picking up my phone on the weekends, he'd figured out that I was single again. I wasn't sure it was a good idea, but told myself it might help to take my mind off of things. He looked handsome in a blue button-down shirt under a navy dinner jacket, his sandy hair cropped short from a recent haircut.

"It's great to see you," Art said. As he pulled out a chair for me, I recalled his charming old-school manners. His gray eyes regarded me as I ordered sake along with a Japanese beer to calm my jumpy nerves. "You've been working hard lately."

I took a sip of the hot sake, letting it scald my throat. "I've had some catching up to do. How are your classes going?"

"They're great. I'm doing the survey of American Lit, and my usual Faulkner seminar."

"People used to rave about your seminar. I would have taken it if I'd gone for a Ph.D." His courses were considered among the best in the department; it didn't hurt that he was younger and cuter than most of the other professors.

"Do you ever think of going back?" Art asked as our sushi came.

"To school? Not really. Right now I'm focused on trying to get promoted."

"I'm sure you can do anything you set your mind to. You always underestimate how smart you are. And how beautiful." His gaze took me in. "But you look like you've lost weight. Are you doing all right?"

"I'm okay." My eyes misted. I pushed my plate away and belted back my sake.

"Hey. Let's get out of here." He signaled to the waitress and we stepped into the cool September night. I shivered in my jean jacket; I needed to make a trip to Alice's soon and find a winter coat.

"Come over for a brandy?" When I didn't answer right away, he took my arm and drew me along Thompson Street. Stepping into his immaculate, smoke-free apartment after a year's absence was strange, as if I were going back in time to my bright-eyed younger self. As Art went to pour the drinks, I scanned the titles on his built-in bookcases, all neatly ordered by subject. Suddenly I flashed on the piles of 45s spilling off Jack's shelves; the overflowing ashtrays; his chaotic closet. I saw Jack standing in his kitchen, naked but for a frilly apron;

Jack shirtless, eyes closed, strumming his guitar. As Art came toward me holding out a snifter, I blinked to rid myself of the image.

"Have a seat," he said, indicating the leather couch. Instead I perched on a chair. "It's been a while, hasn't it? Did you see I tiled the kitchen wall?"

"It's really nice." Like everything else in his apartment, his kitchen looked like it could be in a home décor magazine.

"Thanks. I've been teaching myself to make a few dishes. I get tired of eating out all the time."

"I should learn to cook too," I replied thickly, the brandy numbing my tongue.

"You don't look very comfortable over there." He patted the spot next to him.

I sat on the sofa, and he moved closer. "You aren't seeing that guy anymore, are you? The editor."

"We're taking a break. Actually he wasn't in publishing."

Art looked surprised. "What's his line of work then?"

I gazed into the honey-colored liquor in my snifter. "He's a musician," I said quietly.

"Oh. What orchestra is he with?"

"Not classical. Rock."

"Where does he play, those clubs on MacDougal?"

I shrugged.

Art frowned. "I can't see you with someone like that. Did he read much?"

"He was very smart. And a brilliant composer." I tipped my glass and drained the remaining brandy.

"Well, I'm composing a paper. Does that count?" Art asked with a smile.

I tried to smile back, but I was too sad. "I'd better go." Unsteadily I stood up.

"Let me get you a cab. I don't think you should walk home."

We took the elevator to the street. Art gazed into my eyes. "It's good to see you, Julia. Can I call you again?"

I wasn't sure how to answer. Art put his hands on my shoulders. Before I knew it, he'd pulled me to him and was kissing me. I'd forgotten how nice it felt to be in his arms; his crisp clean scent of spicy cologne. "Why don't you come back up?" he asked, holding me close.

"N-not tonight," I stammered.

Art hailed a cab for me. "I'll talk to you soon," he said before shutting the door.

The phone rang as I was gulping my second glass of water, trying to dissipate the effects of the sake. Dot had been calling more often since Jack and I broke up, saying she was worried about me. Tonight she regaled me with her friend Paulette's middle son's girlfriend troubles, and then asked where I'd been earlier. "You're seeing that professor again? I thought he got back with his wife."

"They're getting divorced. Anyway, it wasn't really a date; we were just catching up."

"I imagine it was a date in his mind. Most men don't take you out to dinner just to be friends."

"Things have changed since you were dating, Mom."

"Who says I'm not dating?"

"Are you?" Maybe it would be good if she were seeing someone; she'd seemed awfully solitary lately.

"Not at the moment. But I could be."

I sighed. "I realize that. Anyway, I'm not sure what's going to happen with Art."

"You're really through with Jack? I liked him a lot."

"I know. You've told me that about six times." And every time she said it, I felt even worse.

"Maybe that woman in his apartment was just a one-time thing. People do make mistakes, you know."

"I don't think that qualifies as a 'mistake'. Anyway, he hasn't even called me again. He's probably forgotten all about me by now."

Chapter 29

THE BED'S TOO BIG WITHOUT YOU

I had planned to go to a movie with Erin, but I was so depressed I took a rain check. I put on Billie and stared at the pigeon convention on the rooftop across the street. Maybe Dot had been right; maybe I shouldn't have come to New York, after all. Both my love life and my career seemed to have gone up in smoke. Midway through "Am I Blue?" the phone rang.

"Julia, how are you? It's Suzanne."

With mixed emotions, I managed to say hello.

"Jack doesn't know I'm calling you." My spirits sank; for a second I'd hoped that he'd asked her to get in touch with me. "I just got back from visiting my Mum in England. I wanted to tell you about the thing with Trina; what a cockup. But it wasn't what you think."

"How could it not have been?" I asked, hurt that she'd try to sweep it under the rug. "She was in his *bed*."

"Just listen to what happened. She used an old picture of her with Jack to convince the new doorman to let her up. She probably bribed him too. Anyway, he's been fired. Jack had no idea she was there; he was over Sammy's place. When he got home, she wouldn't leave and he had to call the cops. It's all on record, if you don't believe me."

I could hardly take it in—Jack hadn't been sleeping with Trina after all? "But why did he wait four days to call me?"

"I know. He was being a sod. Then when he finally did call, of course you were furious. He's been running around like a wild man lately, out until five in the morning, dragging Sammy and Mark from bar to bar, party to party. It's like he's having his last meal on death row."

Tears brimmed my eyes. For a second I felt much better, but then I thought about his waiting so long to call me. Letting me believe the worst all that time was unbelievably hurtful. And then when he did call, I'd implied I never really cared about him. Now he was off on a binge of partying, which meant he was getting hit on every time he turned around.

"We had a pretty big fight on the phone. I said some awful things. But he deserved it."

"I told him he needs to get down on his knees to you and apologize. Look, I know Jack pretty well. He cares more about you than anyone else he's been with, ever since I've known him. And that covers quite a lot of girls," she added matter-of-factly. "If he loses you, he's going to wind up regretting it. You're the best thing that's happened to him in a long time.

You really seem to love him for who he is, not what he can do for you. That's why he's being so skittish; he knows he needs to make a commitment to you, but he's terrified to do it."

"If that's true, then why he hasn't gotten in touch with me?"

"Why don't you call him? I'll bet deep down he's hoping you will."

"*Me* call *him*? Shouldn't it be the other way around?"

Suzanne sighed. "You know these guys and their pride. He mentioned that you said talking to him bored you. And you were only using him to take you places."

"I was really upset. I didn't mean it."

"I told him that. I'll try to get him to call you. The two of you have to work this out."

On the way back from my run the next morning, I came upon a messenger standing on the curb, gazing up at my building. I took the box upstairs, peeled off my sweaty clothes and tore it open. The first thing I saw was Jack's face staring at me from the cover of his new album. He looked rakishly handsome in a torn shirt and frayed jeans, his arm around Sammy's shoulder, Patrick and Mark pointing at something outside of the frame.

Behind the record was another thin cover. Carefully I eased off the brown paper wrapping. It was a vintage Hank Williams album, protected by a sheet of opaque vellum. On the lower right hand corner Hank had inscribed his name. A piece of notepaper fell to my lap. I could barely read Jack's slashing scrawl: "I began looking for this in July. Also wanted you to have a copy of our new one."

I ran to the phone; this was the perfect excuse to call him. Maybe there was hope for us, after all. But although I dialed his number again and again over the following week, he never picked up. Apparently he was sleeping somewhere else.

Several days later I was supposed to go with Art to his department's annual cocktail party. I had been seeing more of him lately; he'd been so sweet to me, asking me how I was doing without prying into what had happened. And from the way he looked at me, it seemed that he really did care for me. I'd told him I wasn't ready for a romantic relationship yet, but it would be so easy to slip back into it. We had so much in common; knowing the same people from the Lit program, loving the same books.

This was the first time I'd been in the English lounge since I'd graduated. I was anxious about appearing with Art, but everyone was welcoming.

"You remember Julia," Art said to Phil, his best friend and racquetball partner.

"Nice to see you again." Phil shook my hand. "I hope we'll be seeing a lot more of you in the future. Did you hear Chuck's giving Farley tenure?" he asked Art.

"Only because Farley covered his Dimensions of Diaspora course for the metacriticism conference."

"I'm going to check out the hors d'oeuvres," I said. As a student I'd been in awe of the professors' scholarly talk, but now it seemed a little removed from reality.

After the party, Art and I walked to his apartment in the brisk late October wind. He poured brandies and we settled in on the sofa. "I hope that wasn't too boring for you," he said.

"Oh no, it was great to see everyone." I sipped my drink, feeling the pressure of his thigh against mine. His hair was growing out some; I liked the way it curled around his ears.

"What were you doing the other day at work? You seemed in a big rush to get off the phone," Art said.

"Harvey needed a bunch of letters done right away."

"You must be really fast; I still hunt and peck. I need to brush up on my typing so I can get my paper in to the journal."

I pictured the pile of work on my desk, then I reminded myself of how nice he'd been to me. The least I could do was help him with his paper. "I can type it for you."

"I wouldn't impose on you like that. I know you're really busy."

But I felt like I should. "Give me a chunk of it to take home tonight."

Art put down his drink. "I was hoping you wouldn't want to go home." He wrapped his arms around me and pulled me close. His lips met mine slowly at first, and then became more demanding. We slid back and he lay on top of me. I was getting caught up in his caresses, my defenses crumbling. It felt good to be held and touched; I'd missed Jack's hands so badly.

Jack's hands . . . I sat up and buttoned my blouse.

"I'm sorry. I'm just not ready for this yet."

Art followed me as I went to get my coat. "I don't understand, Julia. It was so good before. Don't you want to be close?"

"I'm not really sure what I want right now. Let me have your paper."

Art got it from his desk and gave me one more lingering kiss before putting me into a cab. On the way home I gazed out the window, my breath fogging the pane. On every corner it seemed there was a couple laughing, holding hands, oblivious to the rest of the world. I wondered who Jack was with tonight.

Chapter 30

SCARY MONSTERS
(AND SUPER CREEPS)

When I dropped off an author photo in publicity, Erin invited me along with some friends to watch the Halloween parade in the Village. That night we waited behind the barricades as a group of majorettes with hairy legs started things off. Virginal Princess Dianas passed by, decked out in lavish wedding gowns.

"I bet that doesn't last a year," Erin commented on the royal union.

"It'll take at least that long for Di to get the thank-you notes posted," I said.

Jesus and the apostles followed, discoing to music from a boom-box and tossing communion wafers to cheering onlookers. A Ziggy Stardust in a bright red mullet and silver bodysuit went by on stilts; several other Bowie incarnations flitted past, blowing kisses. I looked beyond Cleopatra's float to see what was coming next—and pulled back in dismay. Patrick and Jack were walking down the street, calmly waving at the crowd.

As they got closer, I realized that of course it was only an extremely good costume. Patrick's double was tarted up in a glittery tank top and platform heels, his feathered blond hair a convincing imitation of the real thing. "Jack" wore an astonishingly true-to-life black wig pointing in all directions, his eyes mascaraed darkly. The two passed a fake foot-long joint back and forth as they paraded.

Jack looked in my direction and winked. Erin glanced at me. "Are you okay? You're pale as a ghost."

"I think I need to get home. I must be coming down with something."

When I got in, I put on the Floor's new album, lifting the needle to play Jack's song over and over, absorbing his voice. After the fifth repeat, I debated myself as I stared at the phone. Finally I picked it up and dialed.

"Yeah." There was a lot of noise in the background; people shouting over blaring music.

"Hi, it's Julia." I froze. What did I want to say?

"I'll call you right back," Jack said.

I hung up, wondering who was at his place; it sounded like a big party. The phone rang. "Here I am. How have you been?" He must have moved to his bedroom.

"I was . . . I went to see the Halloween parade."

A woman's voice sounded in the background. "Jaaack, come on!"

Jack shouted something and slammed the door. Muted music pounded through the walls. "Now I can talk."

"It sounds like you're busy." This was a lousy idea; I didn't want to force myself on him.

"I'm not busy. What are you up to?" Someone was banging on his door. Jack held the phone away and yelled, "Hang on!"

"I'll let you get back to your guests." I regretted giving in to the impulse since obviously he had someone with him.

"These aren't my guests. It's a bunch of idiots Patrick invited over."

"I was just calling to say hello."

"Fine. Up to you." The receiver clicked, and I passed a restless night flipping my pillow, trying to find a dry place to park my head.

The phone rang bright and early at seven-thirty. Wondering who'd be calling at that hour, I crept over to get it.

"Did you go for your run yet?"

I tried to collect my thoughts. "What are you doing up?"

"Never went to sleep. I kicked them all out, and Patrick and I stayed up working on some songs. He just left. Meet me for coffee, okay? I'm gonna have the Irish flu if I don't get some caffeine."

My heart hammering, I raced around getting ready, trying to look less like the living dead. *Has he missed me at all? I wonder what he'll have to say. Can we get past that stupid incident with Trina and make up—or has he already moved on?*

When I entered the café, breathless from hurrying and a bad case of nerves, Jack was sitting in the corner with his back to the entrance. His creased leather jacket looked like it had been slept in.

"Julia." He smiled at me, sooty shadows under his eyes. "I thought you might not show." He ran a hand through his hair, which was longer than I'd ever seen it. "I ordered coffee for you. Milk, one sugar, right?"

"Yes," I said, my mouth dry. I took a sip of the scalding mug. "How have you been?" I tried for a breezy tone.

"I'm not sleeping much, but this has been awfully good for the songwriting. Patrick loves the stuff I'm cranking out." He gave a wry smile, creating those handsome parentheses around his mouth. I didn't know if he was implying he wasn't sleeping because he missed me, or because he'd been out partying.

"I've seen ads for the new album everywhere. Congratulations."

"Reception's good so far. Mary Jo's been reading the reviews to me. And she's found me a tutor."

"How is that going?" It was awful to make small talk with him, as if we were only acquaintances.

"It's hard, but I need to do it. So why did you call me?" He gave me his chocolate gaze.

"I just wanted . . . to thank you for those albums you sent. That was so nice of you."

He nodded. "Glad you liked them. What have you been up to?"

I thought of how he hadn't been in his apartment for days on end; the woman calling his name last night. I didn't want him to think I'd been pathetically sitting by the phone all this time. "Actually I've been seeing Art again. He and his wife didn't stay together after all. It's been nice to reconnect."

Jack scowled. "I bet you're having deep intellectual talks about all sorts of things." He dumped the container of sugar packets onto the table, ripped one open and poured it into his mug. "Unlike the ones I've been having lately."

"What do you mean?"

"Oh, the champagne on the Concorde was flat. Or the nail on their pinkie finger got torn right before a big shoot, and what a disaster that was. Or how they had to fuck three different guys and then they didn't even get the part, but at least the flake was excellent."

"Well, it's your choice who you spend time with."

Jack began carefully restacking the sugar packets. "And I guess your choice is some dusty old English professor."

His comment made me bristle. "At least he isn't jumping into hot tubs with naked bimbos. Or an old girlfriend turns up in his bed, and he doesn't bother to let the person he's with—" I couldn't finish for the lump in my throat.

Jack looked at me for a minute. "You're right. I'm just a raunchy, tasteless rock musician." He frowned, and then pulled a piece of crumpled paper from his shirt pocket. "My tutor gave me a list of books I'm supposed to get." He unfolded it and smoothed it out on his knee. "She recommended this place, Books of Wonder. Want to come?"

"Sure, I'll come with you."

It was strange to be in the car with Jack again. It brought back vivid memories of our fevered kisses the first night we got together; our steamy makeout after we left Dot at my place.

"Let me see your list," I said, determined to treat this outing lightly. He handed it to me as we entered the shop. "All the Beverly Clearys are great. There's this hilarious scene where Henry and his dog Ribsy try to capture a giant salmon."

Jack gave me an intent gaze. "I do believe we have similar tastes in books; I still think about those people in *Wise Blood*.

Although I'm a little below that level right now." He smiled. "Actually, this list is for once I make some more headway. I still get tripped up on the longer words. Like 'Heffalump.'"

A clerk came over to greet us. "What ages are your kids?" she asked as I handed her the list. She had stared at Jack when we first came in, but her manner didn't give anything away.

"They're for a friend," I said.

Jack and I browsed some lavishly illustrated fairytales while she stacked his purchases on the counter. "Oliver would love this," he said, opening a Grimm's. I stood close to see the page, but any thoughts about it were driven away by his nearness. Instead of the brilliant bookplate of Rapunzel letting down her locks, I gazed at the fine dark hairs on Jack's wrist. He chose several volumes for Oliver and Emma, and we left with two big shopping bags.

"I imagine you need to get back home," he said as Rick pulled out.

"I guess." I hoped he'd invite himself over. I didn't want to ask, since he might have plans with someone else for the afternoon. It was hard to sit so close and not touch him; it brought back in torturous detail how good his body used to feel.

"Thanks for coming along," Jack said. "I have to do this parallel thing where someone reads with me, and then I do it alone. Somehow I can't see doing it with Mary Jo. She can be a little impatient, you know. Although I dearly love that woman."

"That sounds like a good exercise."

"Maybe you could help me with it sometime, if your professor wouldn't have a problem with that."

"It wouldn't be a problem. He knows you and I aren't seeing each other anymore." I thought Jack might pick up on that so we could discuss it, but he just looked out the window for a few minutes.

As we pulled onto Broome, Jack draped his arm around my shoulder. "In a way, it's nice just being friends." He regarded me with his warm brown eyes. "Kind of takes the tension out of it, if you know what I mean." His face was close to mine, the heat of him searing my skin. "It's good to see you, Julia," he said in a low voice. I waited, holding still, tipping my face slightly toward his. He leaned in and kissed me on the cheek.

"I'm going to take you up on your offer of help with the reading," he called to me as I got out of the car.

So he sees us as just friends now. If possible, I felt even worse than before.

Chapter 31

MAKING FLIPPY FLOPPY

—⟫⟪—

"Time for the meeting, Julia," Meredith said. Surreptitiously I folded the *Times* over the *Post;* I'd been absorbed in a fascinating tidbit on Page Six. I followed her into the conference room, where everyone was already seated.

"All right, any additions to the death list?" Harvey began. "We've got Bette, Marlene, and Katherine, but we need a few more." He'd brought from Esiness a running list of actresses who might be expected to pop off at any moment. A hack writer was waiting in the wings, ready to cough up a quick biography within weeks of their demise.

"Liz isn't looking too hale and hearty, but she hasn't even hit fifty yet," Charlie said.

"This isn't for the D-list, but I might have an in with Ruby Carr," Briar piped up. "I got to know her agent when the magazine did a piece on her Broadway show."

Harvey beamed. "That's fantastic, Briar. Why don't you set up a meeting with her? The rest of you need to put on your thinking caps and see who you can come up with. Charlie, anything good?"

"I have something I'm excited about: The Fireman's Diet," Charlie enthused. "These guys in one station in Queens have lost fifteen pounds apiece in two weeks."

"Isn't that kind of bridge-and-tunnel?" Briar asked.

"Too down-market. Don't waste any time on it," Harvey said as Charlie scowled. "Kate?"

"I've got a novel about four women who meet at Woodstock, and how the concert affects the rest of their lives. I'm on the fence about it; maybe Julia could take a look," Kate said.

"Sure," I replied. Anxiously I wondered if she'd read Isabel's manuscript. I'd asked her about it a few days ago, but she hadn't gotten to it yet.

"To be continued," Harvey said. "Edgar, anything new in the fascinating world of crafts? Sea glass collections, bottle caps?"

"I'm considering a book on quilt making," Edgar said in a dignified tone. "I'll get back to you about it."

"I'll be on tenterhooks. Anyone else?"

I clenched my icy hands in my lap. "I wanted to bring up Isabel Reed again. I know you didn't love it, but I wanted to get some other opinions. Did anyone else have a chance to read it?"

I held my breath during the pause. Meredith removed her half-rims. "She writes so poignantly about growing up without her mother. And any fan of the show would be fascinated by the peek behind the scenes. That moment with her costar in the dressing room is priceless."

"But does anyone care about Isabel Reed these days?" Harvey asked.

Briar sat forward in her seat. "No one I knew ever watched her show. *I* certainly didn't. That whole singing teacher gimmick was just a lot of hype."

"No, it wasn't," Charlie countered. "She has a real cult following. You can still catch reruns if you stay up late."

"She's been getting some nice press about this new big-budget film," I added.

Kate tucked her hair behind her ears. "I think it's great. She was a huge role model for young women, and they're just now hitting book-buying age."

I could have kissed her feet.

Harvey frowned. "We cranked out a lot of these things at Esiness. They're a drain on the publicity department, and in the end most of them don't earn out."

"I disagree," Kate said. "This one's special."

"If we positioned it right, we could have a real sleeper on our hands," I said, gaining steam. "And I don't think we'd have to pay that much for it."

Edgar nodded. "You'd be absolutely insane not to grab this. She has a huge following among gay men."

"I still think Rayner's memoir would be a much bigger draw," Harvey said. "In fact, let's go ahead and pass on Isabel, in lieu of Pryce."

Briar gave me a triumphant look.

I cleared my throat. "Interesting you should say that. I was just reading in the . . . in the newspaper that he's been checked into rehab in Orange County. Apparently he ran a bunch of red lights, crashed his car, and punched a cop after a police chase. It sounds like he's in for a pretty long stay."

My heart pounded as everyone looked at Harvey.

"Well. That certainly puts a new spin on it," he said, glancing around the room. "His book was supposed to be all about his big spiritual conversion. Okay, Julia. Run some numbers after the meeting and see if you can come up with an offer that works."

Hooray! I felt like doing a victory lap around the conference table.

Harvey left, and the others came over to congratulate me. Briar rushed out, looking like she'd sucked a lemon.

I raced over to the Chelsea to make the offer in person.

"I was really hoping for a little more," Isabel said slowly. My mood took a nose-dive. "But," she smiled, "I guess I can make it up in royalties. Yes. I accept."

I gave her a big hug, inhaling a hit of patchouli. "I'll get the contracts drawn up right away. And our publicity director wants to set up a meeting as soon as possible."

"I'm absolutely thrilled. I couldn't have done it without all your hard work," she said graciously.

"I really appreciate that, Isabel."

"Are you all right? You've seemed down lately." She regarded me with her keen blue gaze. "Did something happen with that guy?"

"We broke up." It felt even worse to say it out loud.

"I'm sorry to hear that. Sounds like a bad one."

I sighed. "It's been pretty awful. I thought he'd been with another woman, then it turned out he hadn't, but I said some terrible things. I saw him a few weeks ago, but he hasn't called me since."

Isabel patted my hand. "Well, he's crazy if he's letting a girl like you go. Take some advice from someone who's been around the block a few times: either get him back or find another guy who'll appreciate what you have to offer. Grab hold while you're still young and beautiful. It all goes so fast." She glanced at the beaming portrait over the mantel. "Sometimes I lie in bed at night and look at pictures of myself when I was your age. What I wouldn't do for just one day of having it all back, especially if I knew what I know now. I'd be unstoppable." She smiled. "And that's the end of the lecture."

"Here's your paper. I'm pretty sure I made all the corrections," I said, handing Art the manila envelope. I wanted to drop it off before we went with a group of his friends to see a Philip Glass opera. I'd stayed extra late at the office for the past two weeks to retype the eighty-page annotated document, which struck me as dry and heavily footnoted. But I reminded myself that this was almost a requirement of academic writing.

"I'm totally in your debt," Art said as he uncorked a bottle of wine. "I just saw the *Times* review of Fyfe's novel. Congratulations; that's a real coup."

"Yes, everyone was pleased. And his new one's even better. I'm about two-thirds of the way through it now."

"It's great that you get to edit your house's big author. They must have a lot of confidence in you." He got two glasses out of his neatly stacked cabinet.

"It's probably more about divvying up the work load."

"Maybe after this, they'll give you something you can really sink your teeth into." He noticed my frown. "You know what I mean, Julia. Freeman Fyfe isn't exactly an intellectual giant. I need to reconnect with some of my publishing confreres. Maybe Farrar, Straus has an opening; their list would be more your cup of tea."

"I appreciate it, but you don't have to manage my career."

"Well, I'm eternally grateful to you for retyping my paper. I can think of one way to show my gratitude."

He took my wrists and drew my arms around him. Warm and tender, his kisses were so easy to fall into. I sighed when he stopped and went to get our coats. I really needed to get past this longing for Jack and move on. Art was smart, good-looking, and interesting; anyone would consider him a catch. There was no logical reason for me not to get involved with him again.

"Do you ever hear from Jack at all?" Dot asked me over the phone the next morning.

"Not since I saw him for coffee a while ago. We aren't getting back together," I said morosely. I'd left Art and his friends at a bar after the concert and took the subway home alone. I hadn't been in the mood for socializing.

"Well, guess what? I'm coming there to cheer you up."

"Up here?"

"I'm taking the bus to Philadelphia next weekend, then straight to New York."

"But that's an awfully long trip. Are you sure?"

"I've already bought my tickets. You sound so out of sorts lately. And I want to meet this professor."

"I don't know, Mom. Art's pretty busy," I said uneasily. I couldn't imagine what the two of them would have to talk about.

"Busier than Jack? I'm sure he can make time to meet your mother," she replied in a confident tone.

The next morning Harvey summoned me to his office. "Have a seat."

I perched on a chair in front of his desk, wondering what I'd done now. Harvey cleared his throat. "Briar is leaving the company. She's decided to go back to school."

I tried to assume a nonchalant expression, but inside I was euphoric.

"I'm going to have to reassign the things I'd given her to handle. Are you up for taking on some more? I know your plate's pretty full as it is."

"I'm always up for work." I knew I didn't have a choice.

Harvey surveyed me with his icy blue eyes. "That's true. I was wrong to think a pretty young woman like you would have more frivolous interests. But you're very serious about this job, aren't you? No one else is staying until seven o'clock every night."

I folded my arms. "I couldn't be more serious about it."

"Well. Given the sudden staffing gap and the fact that you've brought in Isabel's book, I'm going to promote you to associate editor. If you can start pulling in some submissions. You'll have to really get out there and lunch the agents."

I almost had to ask him to repeat himself. "That's great! I mean, thank you. I'll do my best."

"I'm giving you a three-thousand-dollar raise, and you can have a small expense account. More of both when you start acquiring. You'll have to continue doing the things you do for me," he added. "I don't have the budget to hire a new assistant."

"I can definitely do that." I stood up to go.

"Julia." Harvey cleared his throat. "Congratulations. You deserve it."

I stopped in his doorway. "Thank you, Harvey. I think I do deserve it."

I ran to find Meredith. "I hear your friend Briar has decided to go back to school for photojournalism," she said.

"Good riddance, isn't it? Guess what, I'm getting promoted!"

Meredith gave me a warm hug. "I may have had something to do with that. I told Harvey he'd better promote you, or else another house would snatch you up once word got out that you'd landed Isabel. I keep reading about this new film she's starring in; it sounds like it's going to make a splash."

"Thank you so much!"

"It's purely selfish; no one else gets their jacket copy in on time. I also told him," Meredith said, lowering her voice, "that if he doesn't stop making inappropriate suggestions to the young women in this company, I'll call his wife and tell her what's going on."

"I hope he won't get back at you for that. What did he say?"

"He just glared at me, but I think he got the message. I was talking to Vicky's colleague Sarah Wittner the other day. She mentioned that Harvey's father-in-law footed the bill for their fancy apartment. We thought that might give me a little leverage."

"You're the best." I hugged her again, and then ran to my office to call Vicky. For once, her line wasn't busy.

"You won't believe this: Briar quit, and Harvey just promoted me!" I exclaimed.

Vicky gave a whoop. "That's fantastic! Finally things are looking up for you, Julia. We're going out tonight to celebrate—I won't take no for an answer."

I smiled. "I wouldn't dream of saying no."

Chapter 32

THREE LITTLE BIRDS

)⊃⊂(

"I want you to come to my opening this Friday. There's a party at our place afterwards," Suzanne said the next morning once we'd caught up for a few minutes. "After all, it's the bird paintings that got the gallery owner's attention. If you hadn't suggested them, I'd still be trying to bluff my way into a group show."

"I'm so glad you're getting to do this." I was genuinely happy for her; at last her efforts had paid off.

"Jack's going to be there, so you'll need something fantastic to wear. I know what— let's go shopping. Mark owes me one."

My stomach flipped at the thought of seeing Jack again. "Does he ever say anything about me?"

Suzanne was quiet for a minute. "He did mention that you're back with the guy you were seeing before. Is that true?"

I wanted to downplay it, knowing what I said could get back to Jack. "I've been seeing him some. Not all that much, really."

"Well, I don't know. Maybe Jack isn't ready to be with any one person yet. To tell the truth, he's with a different girl every night." My heart sank at hearing this. "But let's hope for the best," she added. "Maybe seeing you again will break the evil spell."

That Friday night I walked to the gallery on Spring Street, wobbling in my lavender heels on the uneven cobblestones. It felt good to have on the new things I'd bought with Suzanne; the periwinkle blouse brought out the blue of my eyes, and complemented the minty tones of the short striped skirt. I just hoped Jack would notice me in the midst of all the other girls swarming around.

Outside the gallery, several photographers milled about smoking on the sidewalk. I peered into the plate-glass window. There was already a crowd clutching plastic glasses of wine, admiring Suzanne's large, splashy paintings. Perched on stands were live exotic birds that she'd rented from Bird Jungle in the Village. The toucans, mynahs, and cockatoos were used to being cageless, since that was how the pet shop displayed them.

Taking a deep breath I stepped into the high-ceilinged room, where a dazzling blue macaw glared at me from his golden perch. I spied Patrick in a long brocaded coat, enveloped in a throng of admirers. Suzanne was surrounded, so I walked over to gaze at her rendition of a parrot. The artist's sense of color was startling, and her love for the creatures shone through in every brushstroke.

A man with long blond ringlets, sporting a shiny white tux, was making his way over to me. With an inner cringe I realized it was the guy from the Mudd Club who'd made the comment when I was dancing with Jack.

"Well, hello," he said. "I'm Chip. I'm with Kappa; we give the Floor's record label a run for their money. And you're Julia, right?"

"Yes. Hello." I didn't smile, not wanting to encourage him.

"You seem like you could use a drink. Why don't I snag us something?"

I said okay, just to get him to leave.

"You look stunning!" Suzanne extricated herself from her friends and threw her arms around me. "Maybe this will wake the bugger up," she added in a low voice.

"Thank you. These paintings are absolutely brilliant; you've really found your calling."

Suzanne seemed pleased. "That means a lot to me, coming from you."

Mark joined us and gave me a hug. "Hullo, hullo. Haven't seen you around lately." He glanced at me sheepishly.

"Thanks for my new outfit. Suzanne took me shopping."

"Thank *you* for suggesting the birds. Three of 'em's got red dots already, so I'd say it's a blindin' success."

Mark moved away as Patrick strutted over. "Look who's here. I guess you didn't have much staying power, after all. But don't feel bad; Jack doesn't focus on anything for very long."

There was a commotion at the door, bulbs igniting. Jack walked into the room with the thinnest woman I'd ever seen. She was as tall as he was, and drop-dead glamorous in a slinky silver and gold halter dress that clung to her protruding hipbones, her dark hair piled dramatically high. I watched as they approached Suzanne to give their congratulations. Mark said something to Jack, and he looked over in my direction. He came toward me, skirting laughing groups of people, ignoring the stir he created. His hair was windblown over a torn leather jacket; he looked like he'd been up five nights running. My heart pummeled my ribcage as he approached.

"Well, if it isn't the prodigal," Patrick said.

Jack didn't take his eyes off of me. "Go talk to Clio. She's dying to meet you."

Patrick smiled sardonically and left. Jack reached out and lifted a strand of hair off my shoulder.

"I was right," he said.

"About what?"

He dropped his hand. "That little beauty mark's on the left side."

I flushed, remembering the heat of his lips on that particular spot.

"And you've got on a new frock." He looked me up and down.

"Suzanne took me shopping."

"Verrry fetching." He glanced around the room and ran his hand through his hair.

"Listen, Julia." His brow furrowed. "Have you missed me?"

I looked down at the toes of my shoes. "Yes," I whispered.

Another pair of heels aligned themselves with Jack's boots. "What are you doing over here?" Clio wrapped her long jeweled fingers around his arm, French-manicured ovals pressing in. "I'm ready for a drink."

"Can I get you something?" Jack asked me.

I surveyed Clio's sinuous body in her soigné dress. Next to her, I felt like a twelve-year-old trying on her mother's clothes. "No thanks."

"I'm on it." Chip inserted himself between us and handed me a glass of wine. "How are you, Jack? Hey, those last couple of tracks on the new album could have used a bit more testosterone." He put his free hand on my lower back, practically on my butt. I tried to edge away, but he pulled me closer as Jack scowled. "I hope you aren't losing your touch."

"Odd you'd say that. Your boss just called Patrick and offered twenty mil for our next one. We were going to consider it, but if that's what your label really thinks …" Jack shrugged as Chip went a few shades paler than his tux.

Turning on his boot heel, Jack accompanied Clio to the bar. She said something and he laughed, tossing his head. Watching them together made me nauseous. While Chip brayed at a guy he knew, I slipped away to take in more of the artwork. After a few minutes I found Suzanne and congratulated her.

"Aren't you staying? I thought you were coming to the party at our place."

"I think I'm going to go."

Suzanne looked disappointed. "I wish you'd stay longer, but I understand. I'll call you. We'll have lunch soon."

Chip came up behind me. "I've got two more parties to hit. Why don't you come along?"

"I'm going home. I'm not feeling too well." I couldn't stand another minute around him, or watching Jack flirt with his arm candy.

"We'll have some toot on the way over; that'll perk you up."

"No thanks, I've got to go." Quickly I went out and flagged a taxi. As I was telling the driver my address, the door opened. Chip flung himself in beside me just before the cab accelerated.

"You're not getting away that easy," he said. "Have some of this and I'll take you somewhere you'll like." He took a creased credit card from his pocket and tapped a tube against it. White powder spilled out in a practiced thin line.

I couldn't believe he thought he could just hijack my cab. "I don't want any! I need to get home."

Chip hoovered up the line. "Now that you've fucked Jack Kipling, you think you're too good for anyone else?" he sneered. "Lots of us have had his discards. Don't worry, I'll make sure you have a good time."

"I'm not interested. Can you stop the car?" I said to the driver.

The cabbie pulled over. "Problem, lady?"

"I'm getting out here."

"Keep moving. I'll give you a fifty," Chip said.

I opened the door and jumped out. The taxi sped off and I stumbled home, repelled by Chip's pushiness and feeling utterly discouraged. Tonight had been one big mistake after another. Instead of shooting the breeze with Jack, I should have told him I didn't mean those things I'd said. And I should have slapped Chip's hand off my butt. It was horribly frustrating that we hadn't managed to say one meaningful thing that would help us reconnect. But when I pictured the woman in silver, I realized it was too late.

Chapter 33

RECONSIDER, BABY

)━━⊏━━(

"I'm glad I finally get to lay eyes on this Art fellow," my mother said. Her bus had been delayed, so I'd sat in the dingy Port Authority station for two hours, fending off solicitations from the hordes of pitiful homeless.

Now we were in the warmth of a snug tea shop on Sullivan, awaiting Art's arrival. For some odd reason she'd been insistent that I arrange this get-together. After fifteen minutes he stepped inside, a cashmere scarf tucked into the front of his charcoal coat. He took off his gloves to shake hands with Dot.

"It's good to meet you," Art said. "I hear you're just up for a quick visit."

"I have to leave tomorrow. Erwin wouldn't give me Monday off." Dot gave a disapproving sniff.

"Did Julia tell me you work at a hardware store?" he asked politely.

"Plumbing supply: 'You name it, we drain it.' Erwin always says, 'We fix leaks so you can take one.'"

Art looked puzzled for a second, then he chuckled. "I understand you're really good at what you do. Erwin should value you more highly. Let's order; unfortunately I have to wade through twenty compositions today." He signaled the waitress and asked for loose-leaf oolong, and I requested green tea.

"I'm a Lipton gal. Do you have any of that?" Dot asked hopefully.

The waitress smirked and said she'd try to dig around in back for some. "If not, I'll have what she's having," Dot said. She turned to Art. "So you teach at the college. Do you have to read all the time, like Julia?"

"I reread everything I assign so it's fresh. And of course I keep up with the scholarly articles. There was a very good piece on solipsism in Joyce's *Portrait* that I'll have to show you," he said to me.

"Joyce who?" Dot asked.

"Joyce is the last name. James Joyce."

"Oh. I thought you might mean Joyce Sutter," Dot said, citing her favorite novelist. She took a sip of green tea, made a face and dumped in some milk.

"I'm not familiar with her work. Is she good?" Art dipped his silver tea ball.

"Oh, she's fantastic. All her books take place somewhere different. This last one was in northern Scotland. The ending had the earl, whose wife died during childbirth, falling in love with the wench that was in charge of his linens. For a while you thought he was going to go for the rich lady from the estate next door, but it turned out she was a real two-timer and was seeing this duke on the side." She looked at Art expectantly.

"That . . . sounds like quite the storyline," he managed to say. "What do you two have planned for the rest of the day?"

"Mom needs to do some Christmas shopping at Macy's, so we're heading there next."

"I love Macy's," Dot said. "My friend Paulette wants to take the bus with me next time I visit Julia and go there. She wanted to come this trip, but she's saving up to have her teeth fixed."

Art smiled uncomfortably and glanced at his watch. "I'm afraid I'd better be going." He pushed back his chair. "It was so nice to meet you. Don't rush on my account," he said to Dot, who had no intention of it. As he opened the door, cold air billowed into the cozy shop.

"He sure was in a hurry," Dot commented.

"He has to get his final grades in for the semester." I was annoyed with her for making me set up this ridiculous meeting.

"Are you planning on marrying him?" she asked, widening her eyes.

"I'm not planning on marrying anyone. Not everything has to be a romance, unlike those novels you're always reading."

"Usually there is romance, if you're going out with a person," Dot observed.

After traipsing Macy's various floors for three hours, watching my mother pick up, exclaim over, and then replace all the things she couldn't afford, we left with a small box of candles and a soap caddy. We ate takeout on my couch while she described her ups and downs with Erwin and people from Buck's. As always, she seemed to forget that I didn't know them, and therefore might have only a passing interest in these stories. Finally she seemed to collect herself. "I guess I do ramble on a bit. It's nice to have someone to talk to at night; I'm used to eating alone with the TV on."

"Why don't you go out with Joan or Paulette sometime?"

"Oh, their husbands expect dinner on the table." She folded her arms. "I know you don't want to hear this, but I liked Jack much better than Art."

"I realize that, Mom."

"Art could go back to his wife at any time. Technically he's still married, you know," she said primly.

This was annoying, coming from her. "I didn't think you of all people would have a problem with an extramarital affair."

My mother narrowed her eyes. "What's that supposed to mean?"

I tried to back-pedal. "Never mind."

"No." She sat up straight. "I want to know. What did you mean by that?"

"You were still married when you started messing around with that guy from the hardware store."

She turned to face me, eye shadow bleeding into the wrinkles at the corners of her eyes. "I didn't start seeing him until your father left me."

After all this time, I resented her lying about it. "Come on, Mom. I know you were."

She looked like I'd slapped her. "Your father accused me of that, but it wasn't true. I flirted a little with Wayne, but it was harmless." A shadow crossed her face. "Your dad was very possessive, you know. He accused me of having affairs, but it was all in his mind."

I had the strangest sensation, like a fuse had blown. Like the top of my head had been forcibly unscrewed and things were flying out of it. I licked my dry lips. "Then why did he leave?"

Dot sighed. "He never wanted me to work, but I was going crazy at home and we needed the money. He couldn't stand me being around men on the job. I was a flirt; just silly joking to pass the time. But he would accuse me of all kinds of things. Then he got fixated on Wayne; he was convinced we were sleeping together. I think it was just an excuse to get out of our marriage."

"But this changes everything. Why didn't you ever tell me this?" My mind was racing. My mother hadn't had an affair? More importantly, she'd never cleared it up for me. How could she let me keep thinking terribly of her, the way I had for years?

She shook her head. "You always saw things in black and white, Julia. You needed to think one of us was to blame, and it wasn't going to be your dad. You idolized him. And then once he left, I did start seeing Wayne, so I knew you wouldn't believe me."

I sat there, stunned. I'd foolishly thought there was only one person at fault in their divorce. I'd always believed my dad was the wronged one; I'd put him on a pedestal like a saint. But he'd left my mother for no reason—just because he was possessive and delusional? All this time my opinion of her had been polluted by that one unfair belief—no, *delusion* of my own.

What my father did was ... oh my god, it was what I'd done to Jack. I never let him explain anything without assuming I already knew the answers. I hadn't even let him explain when he called about Trina—albeit four days after the fact.

Something caught deep in my chest. I'd never fully put my trust in him. And that was because I'd always expected Jack to cheat; it was what I'd known about relationships since I was young. I'd assumed it was just a matter of when.

In the midst of my trance, a hand touched my knee. "I know I messed up after your dad left," Dot continued. "I was so scared and lonely. I drank too much and slept around; I know that was hard on you. I was such a wreck, I wasn't thinking straight half the time. And I was desperate to get married again—which of course didn't happen," she added bitterly.

I blinked away tears, feeling ashamed of myself. "Mom, I need to apologize. All this time I blamed you. I've said some awful things."

"I deserved a lot of it. Here, don't cry." She reached out her arms, and I dove into her embrace.

"Julia, listen to me," she said, dabbing at her eyes. "I think you're making a mistake about Jack. I know you said all these women come after him, and that one was in his bed. But you should give him another chance."

I studied my hands. "He doesn't seem interested anymore. The last time I saw him, I got my hopes up but then nothing happened. Anyway, I'm sure he has a new girlfriend by now."

"Not necessarily," Dot said.

Chapter 34

WHITE RABBIT

First thing the next morning, I told Art that I didn't want to keep seeing each other. There was no point; I wasn't going to fall back in love with him, and I didn't want to string him along. We were supposed to get together later after Dot left, but I took the coward's way out and called him on the phone.

"Why?" he asked, sounding hurt. "I thought we were getting along so well."

"I only want to be friends. I'm sorry, but it's not going to turn into more than that."

"You're running back to that musician, aren't you?"

"I'm just not ready to get into a relationship right now. Thank you for everything, Art. I really am sorry. Goodbye."

From the futon, Dot gave me a thumbs-up. I found the Port Authority's number in my address book so she could check the bus schedule, and got into the shower as she was drying her hair. When I emerged, she was hanging up the phone.

"The bus is on time," she said gaily. "I'd better get a move on." Quickly she applied a bit of makeup and stuffed clothes into her bag. Before we went downstairs, she put her hands on my arms and looked me in the eyes. "I love you. I realize I don't tell you that very often. But I hope you know it."

"I love you too, Mom." Feeling emotional, I kissed her cheek.

When we got outside, a black car was waiting at the curb. "Did you call a limo service?" I asked Dot, confused.

The back door opened and Jack emerged holding a slim book. His tangled mane looked like it hadn't been combed in a week; his face had a midnight shadow, and there were dark smudges under his eyes. He was the best-looking thing I had ever seen in my life.

"Fancy meeting you here," Dot said, putting a hand on her hip. Jack came over and gave her a big hug. He tossed her bag into the backseat and opened the door in front. "Rick is giving me a ride to the bus," she said to me. "I'll talk to you tomorrow." She blew me a kiss, and they took off.

Jack looked at me curiously. "Your Mum called. She said you wanted to see me."

"Yes," I said slowly. "She was right; I do. Want to come up?"

"Absolutely." He followed me upstairs and ambled over to the blues crate. "Ah, good. I see you still have my albums."

"I'd never part with them." I couldn't stop staring at him; he seemed like something I'd conjured up. "What's that book?"

"It's what I've been reading." Jack sat on the couch.

I sat next to him, feeling myself start to tremble. Jack held up the cover; it was a beautiful edition of *Alice in Wonderland*. "I never knew what a trippy imagination Lewis Carroll had;

'a grin without a cat . . .' Here's where I left off." He opened to a page marked with a Zig Zag paper and held the book between us.

"A-hem. 'When the procession came opposite to Alice, they all stopped and looked at her, and the Queen said sev . . . erely, Who is this? She said it to the Knave of Hearts'—" He glanced at me. "Back then, that's what they called the Jack; a knave. Fitting, isn't it?" He smiled, and my emotions lurched. "So . . . where was I?"

A fat wet drop splatted onto the page. Jack turned toward me as I tried to stave off more tears. "Julia. You're crying, and I haven't even gotten to the sad part yet." He put the book aside. "The part where Jack does something really stupid. He's so terrified of his feelings for his woman, he doesn't call her right away to straighten out a bad misunderstanding. Then she goes back to her old lover, and his heart gets ripped into shreds."

I looked into his eyes, which mirrored the pain in mine.

"Forgive me," he whispered. I wrapped my arms around his neck and brushed my lips over his. We kissed again and again, my famished mouth drinking him in. Rising from the couch, I drew him back through the loft to my bed. With shaking fingers I undid the buttons of his shirt as his lips touched my neck, igniting me, his breath coming in jagged gasps. I ran my hands over his chest, feeling his nipples harden, and reached for his straining zipper.

"God, Julia," he groaned. I tore off my clothes and we tumbled into bed, feverishly touching each other. I pushed him back on the pillow and lowered myself onto him.

Jack inhaled sharply. "Let's go slow or I'll . . ."

"I want you to." I tightened my thighs.

"Ahh . . ." Jack shut his eyes, gripped my legs and held me still for a moment. I began cascading up and down, the trajectory setting off a waterfall of sparks within. He grabbed me by the hips to slow me down but I kept going, feeling him rocketing inside me. Gritting his teeth, he began to seethe and then his moan became a roar as he got impossibly hard, right before he flared.

"Are you sure you want me back?" Jack asked as we lay there together. "I've been acting like an ass. I almost took up some really bad habits again."

"I'm sure." I gazed into his depthless dark eyes and decided to take the plunge. "Jack . . . I love you."

He sat up. "You do?"

"I love you with all my heart and soul. I felt like I'd withered up and died, these past weeks."

"Well, that's good, because I realized something while we were apart." He paused, and I held my breath. "I love you, too."

He . . . loves me! My emotions soared to a dizzying height as Jack gave me a soulful kiss that made my belly flutter. I never wanted to kiss anyone else again.

He lay back and studied me. "Are you definitely through with Art? Your Mum said you broke up with him."

"Yes. I want you to know something: I never slept with him."

"Really?" Jack's face split into a huge smile.

"I had no desire to. I just kept missing you."

"That makes me so happy, baby. I can't tell you what I was imagining." He gave me a guilty look. "Listen, I didn't bring anyone into my bed while we were apart. I couldn't work up enough interest. I may have . . ." He pressed his lips together. "I'm going to tell the truth, so you can decide if you really want me back. I let a couple of them blow me. Just because it was the path of least resistance."

Nasty images filled my head. Jack put his arms around me.

"I'm sorry, sweetheart. After you said you were back with your professor, I figured why not. It wasn't that I went after it; I just didn't stop it from happening. Mostly I just got trashed every night."

That didn't make me feel any better. I knew he'd been screwing around, but it was awful to hear the details. I thought of the woman in the silver dress. "What about Clio? She seemed to think she owned you."

"I didn't fuck that bag of bones. Her publicist set up those dates through Mary Jo. Every time I'd look at her, I'd see your eyes." He gazed at me. "You've ruined me for other women. Whenever I was out with one, I'd find myself comparing them to you. They'd make a dumb comment, and I'd think about what you would have said. Or I'd crack a joke and it would go right over their heads. It got to be . . ." He shook his head. "You've really gotten under my skin. Which is where I want you."

I flashed on the blonde in his bed. "Why didn't you call me right away after I found Trina at your place? I was so devastated."

Jack looked up at the ceiling and exhaled. "Tom told me you'd run out of the lobby, but he didn't know why. I went upstairs and found her there. When I told her to get out, she started screaming and throwing things. I had to get a couple guitars away from her before she smashed them up. Then I called the cops and they wrestled her out."

He paused to swipe a hand over his face. "I was going to go right over to see you, but they made me come to the station to get a restraining order. They kept me there half the night, then I stopped by Sammy's to use his phone to call Carla. I wanted the mess cleaned up before I came home. All these people were at Sammy's. I was so strung out; I had some weed to relax, and then some blow." He sighed. "They were heading out to a party, so I figured I'd go for a while and then call you. Before I knew it, it was the next day, and then the next . . . it turned into this four-day blitz. By the time I got back to my place, you were ticked off, and rightly so. I knew I'd totally fucked up, but I couldn't figure out how to fix it."

"I'm sorry about those awful things I said. I didn't mean any of it. I was so hurt, I wanted to strike back. I always loved talking to you, Jack. I loved every minute I was with you."

Jack wove his fingers through mine. "Once I calmed down, I realized you didn't mean it. I knew you weren't using me; you wouldn't even let me take you shopping! The whole thing was idiotic. I just got it into my head that it was too late. And then when you said you were seeing that professor, I *knew* it was too late. All because I went out and partied to avoid dealing with the situation."

"You can't ever do that to me again. Are you sure you want to get back together?"

"I'm more than sure. If you'll have me. Being apart has been the worst." He traced the curve of my cheek with his thumb. "So . . . about us. I want you to come live with me."

I could hardly take it in. "Really?"

"Yes. Pack up a month's worth of stuff, and after that, bring over some more. No more of this back and forth, in and out."

He thought for a second and grinned. "Correction: we're gonna have a lot of the in and out. But no more sleeping alone. All right?"

I was more than all right; I was on cloud nine. "That sounds great to me. As long as I can do a little work at night." I smiled.

"I'll let you do some of that. After I bang you senseless. I have sooo much lovin' stored up from all this time without you." He kissed his way down to my breasts. "God, I missed this. I missed *you*. Off with my head if I ever do anything like that again."

Chapter 35

'DEED I DO

On the way home from work, I stopped by Books of Wonder to buy more Beverly Cleary novels. I planned on putting them under the huge Christmas tree we'd set up near the glass-topped table, since Jack was enjoying *Henry Huggins* so much. I was no good at trimming packages, so I'd had the shop do it for me. They did look pretty in their purple and blue paper, next to the praying mantis farm I'd already had wrapped for him. After I placed them under the spruce, I received a gift of my own.

"I see you got some more cards," I said. Every day he got reams of them—many from women who were obviously former lovers. At night I made a little bonfire out of those particular ones in his fireplace. "Who's this with the cute kid?" A caramel-skinned woman and an adorable tow-headed girl smiled at the camera.

Jack looked over my shoulder. "That's Carla and her daughter Lottchen. Her husband's German."

I looked more closely at the girl's long blonde locks. "Does she ever come over when Carla's cleaning?"

"Once in a while, when school lets out early. I've run into her several times; she's a pip. She loves dancing to our tunes, so I usually put on a record before I clear out."

I spun around and gave him a passionate kiss. He slipped his hands under my blouse. "I was gonna let you relax some before I jumped you, but . . . what is it?"

I was grinning like a fool. "I think I've figured out where that hair in your brush came from."

Jack looked puzzled for a moment, then nodded. "Yeah, could be. She's very proud of her hair; always twirling it and playing with her ribbons." He smiled. "I never thought it was Mary Jo. Somehow I couldn't see her trying on that wig and striking a sexy pose in my mirror."

I laughed at the image.

"Although any time you feel the urge to do that," he added, "I'd be happy to watch."

Later that night, I put the final touches on Isabel's manuscript as Jack took a little nap beside me in bed. I was pleased with the work I'd done, and Meredith was convinced it would be a bestseller. I stacked the pages on the bedside table, right next to my marbled notebook. Jack stirred and squinted at me as I snapped the rubber band.

"Finally finished with that thing?" he asked.

"No thanks to you."

"You told me you were ready to take a break."

"A fifteen-minute break. That was two hours."

Jack propped his head on his hand. "If you wanted a fifteen-minute man, you've got the wrong guy," he said, gazing at me through his eyelashes.

"That's for sure. But you are the right guy."

"Good. Listen, I spoke to Mary Jo today. The record company told her we're making shitloads of money from the new album; they're really chuffed about it. I want to take you somewhere nice and tropical over Christmas. After we go to England. Maybe Dot can join us for the first couple of days."

I smiled at the thought of Mom telling Erwin to shove it. "She'd be over the moon."

"Least we can do; after all, she got us back together. And you have the whole week off since you're an associate editor now?"

"That's right." He'd been very proud of my new title, and insisted on having business cards printed for me since Harvey said it wasn't in the budget.

"I'm gonna get you a very skimpy bikini to wear on the island. We'll have a private beach, so I'll expect you to go topless most of the time. And when we're not rolling around getting sandy, you can read your Proust and I'll tackle more Henry and Beezus. But I want one week with no manuscripts, all right?"

I gazed at his hair sticking up in a wild tangle, stubble peppering his face, lightning bolt askew. "I promise I'll only read for pleasure. If you don't watch out, you'll turn me into a hedonist."

"Whatever that is." Jack pulled up my tee-shirt. "Take this thing off. Thinking about that bikini has got me all fired up again."

ACKNOWLEDGMENTS

I began writing this novel in 2009, on the thirtieth anniversary of my arrival in New York City. I wanted to describe what it was like in the years 1979-1981, when Manhattan was still rough along the edges. When SoHo was still the domain of artists and galleries, and the occasional local bar or cafe. And when nightclubs like the Palladium, the Roxy, Danceteria, and the Mudd Club attracted a huge mix of people from many different strata of society.

Back then, you could go out dancing and run into just about anyone: actors, politicians, rock musicians. Celebrities weren't surrounded by bodyguards; the assumption was that if you were allowed into a club, you were cool. No one was going to harass anybody; after all, this was *downtown*. And there were no cell phones back then. People didn't walk around with a camera in their pockets 24/7—so if you were famous, you didn't have to worry about being photographed every time you turned around. That made for a much more open atmosphere, where regular people rubbed shoulders with the glitterati as everyone cut loose on the dance floor.

I also wanted to write about book publishing before the advent of e-readers and computers, when we were all lugging home 400-page manuscripts every night. As with the music biz, the changes have been seismic. Unfortunately the salaries are pretty much the same, especially for assistants (when you account for inflation). I really did find those lavender shoes on the street, and I wore them until they fell apart.

A number of people have been extremely generous with their time and advice as I revised this novel over the past five years (even a long-time editor needs an editor for her own work). In 2010, my good friend Peternelle Van Arsdale did a thorough and thoughtful edit, and helped me figure out what needed trimming from my first draft. In 2012, Benee Knauer provided good suggestions for my third draft. In 2013, I received judicious notes from my friends and publishing comrades Cynthia Cannell, Jennifer Levesque, Kiki Koroshetz, and Nina Shield. The amazing Kirsten Neuhaus provided fantastic editorial advice and huge support. Jessica Hatch gave it a final polish, not to mention invaluable help with social media. Thanks to Allison Winn Scotch for her generous advice, and to wonderful Nicole Dweck for her encouragement and guidance.

The tremendously talented Laura Klynstra did a brilliant job with the book cover and interior design. Kassiah Faul of Creative B Design Studio created an amazing website for me, and Amy Bruno of bookjunkiepromotions put together a great virtual book tour.

Thanks to Bob Miller, Wendy Lefkon, Mary Ellen O'Neill, Will Schwalbe, and Gretchen Young, all of whom have been incredibly supportive of me in my publishing career. A huge shout-out to Jane Rosenman for thirty-four years of good advice, love and friendship.

Back in the day, weekend nights found me out dancing with my good friend Janet. Thanks for all the great memories.

Molte grazie to the ladies of the Hallelujah Dinner Club: Aleaze Hodgens, Dana Lester, Sue Nicoletti, and Marcia Schenk; extra gratitude for HDC founder Hilary Osborn

Malecki, a dear friend whom I always know I can count on. Also thanks to Amy Turza, a great friend for life.

I have an amazing family: Mom, Dad, Emily, Kevin, Jessica, Will, Eric, Mark, Sheri, Eric, Emma, and Nikki. I love you to the ends of the earth.

Finally, thanks to my children for putting up with their mom constantly editing other people's books, and then working on my own novel early mornings, late nights, and weekends. A huge thank-you to Peter for reading eight zillion versions of this novel and patiently, thoughtfully commenting on each draft, each paragraph, each word. Three words for you: Up, up, up.

ABOUT THE AUTHOR

Leslie Wells left her small Southern town in 1979 for graduate school in New York City. After receiving her Master's in English Lit, she got her first job in book publishing. She has edited forty-eight *New York Times* bestsellers in her over thirty-year career, including thirteen number one *New York Times* bestsellers. Leslie has worked with numerous internationally known authors, musicians, actors, actresses, and television and radio personalities, athletes, and coaches. She lives on Long Island, New York.

Visit Leslie at www.lesliewellsbooks.com for bonus scenes and more

If you enjoyed *Come Dancing*, I would so appreciate it if you'd post a review. Thank you so much!

Leslie